Critical Accl

M000201513

"A quick reading, entertaining story. [G]reat companion on a hot day sunning at Waikiki . . ." *Waterman's Library*

"Hughes's pastiche of hard-boiled noir and the zen goofiness of surfing bliss is effortless and entertaining." *Honolulu Star-Bulletin*

"[E]motional, almost spiritual connection to the sun-soaked, wave-washed Hawaiian Islands." *Wish You Were Here: Travelers Real and Imagined*

Critical Acclaim for *Kula*

"Zips right along . . . pacing is first-rate . . . dialogue is snappy . . . strikes a nice balance between the Hawaii of today and the film noir memes of yesterday." *Honolulu Star-Advertiser*

"A must-read for dog lovers, surfers-at-heart, and mystery fans alike." *Island Dog*

"Fun way to pass time on a summer beach day." *Waterman's Library*

Praise for Surfing Detective Mystery Series

"Hughes has captured the semi-hardboiled vernacular of the classic gumshoe novel, and given us an authentic Hawai'i, believable surfing scenes, good pidgin, and realistic local characters." *Ka Palapala Po'okela Excellence in Literature Award*

Surfing Detective Double Feature Vol. 1

KULA

MURDER ON MOLOKA'I

two mysteries in one volume

Other Surfing Detective books
by Chip Hughes

WIPEOUT! & HANGING TEN IN PARIS

MURDER AT VOLCANO HOUSE

HANGING TEN IN PARIS TRILOGY

S L A T E   R I D G E   P R E S S

P.O Box 1886
Kailua, HI 96734
slateridgepress@hawaii.rr.com

ISBN: 0982944489
ISBN-13: 9780982944486

Murder on Moloka'i © Chip Hughes 2004

Kula © Chip Hughes 2011

SURFING DETECTIVE

CONFIDENTIAL INVESTIGATIONS : ALL ISLANDS

MURDER ON MOLOKA'I

A Surfing Detective Mystery

CHIP HUGHES

SLATE RIDGE PRESS

For Stu Hilt,

Honolulu P.I.

ACKNOWLEDGEMENTS

Many thanks to my wife, Charlene Avallone, for her inspiration and editorial instinct, and to my mother, Kathryn Cooley Hughes, and to Stu Hilt for generously sharing his forty years' experience as a Honolulu P.I.

Specialist editors who assisted include Ku'ualoha Ho'omanawanui and Puhi Adams, Hawaiian language and culture; Rodney Morales, pidgin dialect; Scott Burlington, Hawaiian spellings and place names; Steve and Donna Curry, surfing scenes; Peter Read Smith, Big Island topography; Dr. Max B. Smith, mule behavior; Karen Roeller and Dr. Bani H. Win, medical examiner's procedures, Dr. Randy Baselt, blood work.

Thanks to Lorna Hershinow, Laurie Tomchak, and my Mānoa writing group: LaRene Despain, John Griffin, Linda Walters-Page, Sue Cowing, and Felix Smith. And to Buddy Bess, Bennett Hymer, Roger Jellinek, Eden-Lee Murray, and Ian MacMillan for their help; and to virtuoso with piano and pen, Les Peetz.

Special thanks to John Michener at Mediaspring for the Surfing Detective website, and to Island Heritage CEO Dale Madden and Art Director Scott Kaneshiro for the series logo and cover art.

Finally, a big *mahalo* to my invaluable editor Kirsten Whatley.

'A 'ole kānā wai ma kēia wahi.

In this place there is no law.

one

"Mr. Cooke?" The throaty voice came through my office door in deep, honeyed tones that told me this was a woman I wanted to meet.

"Be right there." I slipped on some holey Levi's over my wet skin and groped in vain for a T-shirt, cursing myself for having gone surfing so close to a client appointment.

I opened the door to a tall, slim woman in her mid-twenties with chestnut hair and eyes the cool blue-grey of a glacier. Tommy Woo, my attorney, who had referred her, was right. I was "damn glad" this woman had come to see me, even if all I could remember was that she lived in Boston.

"Mr. Cooke . . . ?" She asked again in those rich tones, her brow furrowing as her eyes fell on the crescent of pink welts on my chest. *Tiger shark. Laniākea.*

She turned away.

I wrapped my damp beach towel around my shoulders. "Sorry, I . . . lost my shirt."

"I'm looking for Mr. Cooke, the private detective." She tried again.

"You are Miss . . . ?"

"Ridgely. Adrienne Ridgely."

I gestured to the Naugahyde chair by my desk and she sat. Her fruity perfume soon replaced the sharp odors wafting up from Maunakea Street below.

"I'm Mr. Cooke. Call me Kai."

She surveyed my soaked board shorts atop an expanding puddle of sea water on the dusty linoleum and then said without much conviction, "Mr. Woo told me you are the best detective in Honolulu."

"That was generous of him." I glanced down at my towel. "The reason I'm dressed this way is . . ."

She cut me off. "Nothing but the best for Sara. That's what I told Mr. Woo."

"And Sara is . . . ?"

"My sister."

"Why don't you tell me about her." I pulled a yellow legal pad from the jumble on my desk and found a pen.

"We were very close." Adrienne blinked her cool grey eyes and I wondered if she were about to cry. "Sara was the best sister I could ever have."

I jotted on the legal pad.

"She was always good to Mother and Father when they were alive. And she was good to me. She left me everything."

"She must have been a fine person."

"Sara was an attorney, you know." Adrienne said this as if I *should* know. "And a gifted teacher. And then there were her causes. She gave unselfishly to those causes."

"What happened to your sister?"

From a Louis Vuitton handbag of soft calf's leather she pulled a tissue. "Sara was only thirty-two."

"When she died?"

"Yes, in that horrible way." She worked the tissue with her fingers. "She fell off a cliff . . ."

I jotted on my pad.

"From a mule," she said.

"On Moloka'i?" Her story was beginning to sound familiar.

"Yes, they said it was an accident. But from the beginning I had my doubts."

"I remember now. I read a tribute to your sister in the *Advertiser* a while back."

Sara Ridgely-Parke had had a freak accident on Moloka'i. Ascending the switchback trail above the former leper colony at Kalaupapa, her mule had stumbled and catapulted her down the face of a thousand-foot cliff. She had been killed instantly. The newspaper had called the Harvard-trained attorney an "ecofeminist" committed to preserving the *'āina,* as Hawaiians call the land. I had seen her once in action at a rally to save a pristine surfing spot called Coconut Beach from a proposed strip mall. The fiery, strawberry-haired woman had galvanized me—and the crowd.

"Sara Ridgely-Parke." I jotted her name on my yellow pad. "So you want me to investigate the mule tour company?"

"No." Her voice lowered. "I have no intention of suing the tour company."

"Then why did Tommy send you?"

"I'm not here about money. I want justice."

I nodded, unsure how to reply.

"Sara was the first person ever to die on the Moloka'i mule tour. But she was no novice. We used to ride horses together in Brookline."

"Her experience with horses probably didn't matter,' I said. "There's nothing to riding a mule. You just sit there and the animal does the rest."

"Sara wouldn't fall from a mule," she insisted. "Anyway, I'm told those surefooted animals rarely stumble."

"Didn't the newspaper say the mule broke its leg?"

"I don't believe it." Adrienne fixed her teary eyes on me. "My sister was murdered."

"Murdered? By who?" I was starting to think she had an overactive imagination.

"Her ex-husband. J. Gregory Parke."

"Why would her ex want to kill her?"

"Sara received half of their home in the divorce." She daubed away a tear. "It's an oceanfront estate in Kāhala. Worth a fortune. Greg wouldn't part with the place, so he had to pay her off."

"How much did she get?"

"After lawyers' fees, about four million."

"Parke had that kind of cash?"

She shrugged. "He's a developer."

"Your environmentalist sister married a developer? That's hard to imagine."

"I never understood what she saw in him. We didn't always have such different taste in men."

"So you think Parke was so angry after forking out all that money that he killed your sister?"

"Yes." Her lower lip quivered.

"Do you have any evidence?" I was sympathetic, but still skeptical.

"Greg abused her during their marriage. It all came out in the hearing. And after the divorce he wouldn't leave her alone. I think he finally just boiled over."

"Wait a minute." I stopped writing on my pad. "Your sister fell from a mule on Moloka'i. How could Parke have been responsible?"

"I don't know." She crushed her damp tissue into a little ball. "I just know he was."

"Was Parke on Moloka'i when the accident happened?"

"That's why I'm hiring you. To find out."

"I'll have to fly to Moloka'i. My regular hourly rate, plus three hundred a day for neighbor island travel."

"Cost doesn't matter. I'm doing this for Sara."

"O.K. I'll start with the tour company, then check out the accident scene and interview witnesses. After that I can give you a better idea if you have a case. For the initial investigation I'll need a two thousand dollar retainer."

She didn't even blink, just pulled out her checkbook. Her tears were gone now. "Will my Boston check be all right?"

"Sure. Where are you staying?"

"The Halekūlani."

"Can I give you a lift back to Waikīkī?"

Her blue-grey eyes took on a touch of frost. "My cab is waiting in the alley behind the flower shop." She was referring to Fujiyama's Flower Leis, on the ground floor below my office.

"I'll call you as soon as I have anything to report," I said, reaching for my wallet. "And here's my card."

She glanced at the sand-toned card that said "Surfing Detective" and "Confidential Investigations—All Islands." Above these words was a full-color longboard rider with toes on the nose: back gracefully arched, knees bent slightly, arms outstretched like wings, turquoise wave curling over board and surfer alike. A thing of beauty.

Unfortunately, my card failed to make much of an impression on her. Her expression didn't change.

"You might be surprised by the crank calls I get." I tried to lighten the moment. "Just the other day this wacko phones for Jack Lord. 'Book 'em, Danno!' the guy says, delusional from watching reruns of 'Hawaii Five-O,' I guess."

"Interesting." Adrienne rose and edged toward the door.

"And then a few weeks back," I continued, on a roll now, "some woman with a breathy voice whispers into my phone, *'Thomas Magnum?'* Before I can break the news that her heartthrob Tom Selleck left the islands, she hangs up. Crazy, huh?"

"Call me if you need more money." Adrienne abruptly stepped from my office. I watched her silky dress sway like an undulating wave as she glided down the stairs.

A moment later I gazed down onto Maunakea Street and saw a taxi pull in front of the flower shop. Adrienne climbed in and glanced up at me with those cool eyes.

Suddenly I felt a rare chill in the tropic air.

two

Later that day I flew to Moloka'i. It was Wednesday and turbulent for early October. Squeezed into a propeller-driven Twin-Otter airplane, slightly larger than my car, I had my first leisure to think about the bizarre events that had sent me on this impromptu jaunt.

So far there were only questions and none of them added up to what I'd call a case. Instead, there was a death by falling from a mule, which could be nothing more than an accident. But the victim's sister was crying murder. And she had pointed the finger at Sara's ex-husband–J. Gregory Parke. This seemed unlikely. Unless media accounts of the accident had been totally wrong.

Was I bound for Moloka'i on a fool's errand? Maybe. But at least I was getting paid.

I tried to get comfortable in my tiny seat and opened up the afternoon *Star-Bulletin.* On the front page of the business section was an artist's sketch of a proposed Moloka'i resort called Kalaupapa Cliffs. Brainchild of Umbro Zia, a shadowy Indonesian developer, and the islands' largest private landholder, Chancellor Trust, Kalaupapa Cliffs promised to loom grand and blindingly white. It resembled an art deco Taj Mahal with marble spas and meandering pools and hundreds of ocean-view suites—another luxury palace for the super rich.

Evidently, a technicality concerning the building site was holding up construction. Its fate awaited a vote of the Land Zoning Board. Considering the clout of the Chancellor Trust, the outcome was hardly in doubt.

The Twin-Otter rattled along, barely above the Honolulu skyline. The Aloha Tower drifted by, then the ivory crescent of Waikīkī Beach. Longboards floated below on the turquoise sea like pastel toothpicks. Outrigger canoes etched frothy trails through the rolling surf.

Soon we left Oʻahu behind and below us lay wind-whipped Kaʻiwi Channel—the twenty-five miles of whitecaps between Oʻahu and Molokaʻi. The tiny plane bumped along as if plowing through the choppy swells beneath us. Between jolts I folded my newspaper and took out some clippings I had gathered on the subject of my dubious case.

The obituary photo showed Sara Ridgely-Parke to be the striking, youthful woman I remembered so vividly from the rally. Her eyes had the same flinty quality as Adrienne's, though with an emerald tint.

A Harvard-trained attorney who taught environmental law at the University of Hawaiʻi, Sara had crusaded for affordable housing and "green" stewardship of the islands. Her greatest victory had been the Save Coconut Beach initiative, in which she and other activists saved the pristine windward surfing spot from development.

From the news coverage at the time, I remembered that developers and conservative politicians alike despised Sara's "ecofeminist" views. Being both an environmentalist and a feminist put her at the very radical end of the spectrum in their eyes. The article went on with lavish praise from Professor Rush McWhorter, Sara's law school adversary and legal counsel for the Chancellor Trust. "A tragic loss to the people of Hawai'i," his quote read, which seemed at odds with the public rancor between the two during her life.

Another jolt of turbulence shook the Twin-Otter. I set down the obituary and picked up a wedding clipping.

After her Coconut Beach victory, Sara had become the darling of local environmentalists. Yet she then married developer J. Gregory Parke, a bald blimp of a man twenty years her senior, and lived with him in the ritziest neighborhood in the Hawaiian Islands.

What an odd couple! Their contentious divorce seemed predictable given their strange conflict of interests. I tucked the clips back into my briefcase and peered down at the inky whitecaps below. Sara's short and admirable life had had its contradictions, as I suppose all lives do. But could these contradictions have any bearing on the fatal stumble of a mule?

It was a stretch to think so. A long stretch.

Our first sighting of Moloka'i revealed the West End's pristine Pāpōhaku Beach, a three-mile ribbon of frothing surf and golden sand. One of the longest, most stunning beaches in the islands, it's remote and often deserted. I saw not one surfer, swimmer, or sunbather.

This dramatic beach, and most of Molokaʻi, has escaped the urban sprawl so prevalent on the other islands because residents here, primarily Hawaiian, have rallied repeatedly against unwanted development. Though jobs have been scarce since Molokaʻi's pineapple plantations closed, forcing more and more *kamaʻāina* to scramble for a living, few long-time residents see Waikīkī-style resorts on their unspoiled island as the answer.

The Twin-Otter angled and crossed over the island's arid West End. From previous visits, I recognized the rugged terrain. Sloping plateaus painted the west in cocoa brown and rust red; sheer sea cliffs in the east soared in moss green. The thirty-eight-mile island pointed east like an index finger with one small irregularity—a bump on the north side where the middle knuckle would be. This knuckle was my ultimate destination: Kalaupapa. The once-infamous leper colony, now a national park, sat on a small peninsula beneath the world's tallest sea cliffs. It was from these cliffs that Sara Ridgely-Parke had plunged.

In Honolulu, I had obtained the medical examiner's report on Sara's autopsy. It offered little new information. I had also phoned the mule tour company and learned there was a log of all riders, including the four others in Sara's party. A guide named Johnny Kaluna had agreed to walk me down the cliff trail to the site of the accident, then on to Kalaupapa. I arranged to meet him at seven thirty the next morning.

The Twin-Otter began its bumpy descent as we passed over red dirt fields, inhabited by stunted *kiawe* and grazing cattle. Only one thread-thin highway, devoid of cars, gave evidence of civilization. A few other rusty side roads branched off from the highway. But I saw no vehicles there either.

Once in my rented car, I turned east onto a two-lane blacktop that wandered over terrain as red and rugged as I had seen from the air. With a blood-orange sun sinking behind me, I headed toward my motel in Kaunakakai and continued wrestling with the case.

I tried to imagine a disgruntled ex-husband wanting to kill his former wife, a wealthy developer who felt cheated out of more money than I could make in a lifetime. But J. Gregory Parke had far more to lose than money if he got caught as a murderer. And surely he could not hope to get away with murder when he and Sara were so in the public eye. Unless he could make murder look like an accident.

But how could even a millionaire arrange for a mule to break its leg halfway up the Kalaupapa trail?

I suspected Adrienne Ridgely was grasping at straws. She was grieving the loss of her sister and needed to do something to make herself feel that justice had been served. It was unlikely that the facts I had would add up to murder, but I planned to work hard to earn her retainer. I would follow every lead until either the trail turned cold or her money ran out. Then it dawned on me. With Adrienne's sizable inheritance, her money would never run out.

On the way to my motel, I drove through Moloka'i's commercial hub, Kaunakakai–three short blocks of ramshackle shops with tin roofs and hitching posts for horses and mules. The familiar signs rolled by: Kanemitsu Bakery ("Home of Moloka'i sweet bread"), Friendly Isle Market, Moloka'i Fish and Dive, Sun Whole Foods.

An old yellow dog with a hoary white muzzle ambled in front of my car. I braked. Though I should have expected him.

This ghost-like retriever has been hanging out by the pumps at Kalama's service station for years. His slow gait takes him across the main street each day, to the lawn of the public library, where he curls up in the shade for a snooze. The fact that this old yellow dog has survived so long says volumes about Kaunakakai.

One block *makai,* on the ocean side of town, I checked into my "deluxe" oceanfront cottage, more expensive than the 'Ukulele Inn's other rooms because it was farthest from the notoriously lively Banyan Tree Bar. But my digs were still rustic–a shack really, without TV or phone, but with a beachside *lānai* just wide enough for two plastic lawn chairs.

At sunset I sat in one of these chairs and peered across the mango-tinted water at the humpbacked island of Lāna'i. Farther in the amber distance lay Maui, whose twin peaks resembled the sea-kissed breasts of a reclining goddess.

As night fell, I decided to investigate the sweet strains of Hawaiian music coming from the Banyan Tree Bar. A three-piece band was crowded onto the tiny stage, strumming and singing my favorite song about Moloka'i:

> *Take me back . . . take me back . . .*
> *Back to da kine.*
> *All over, mo' bettah,*
> *Moloka'i. I will return.* [1]

I stepped up to the bar and ordered a beer. The bartender, a Hawaiian guy about my age, mid-thirties, turned out to be a

---

[1] Song lyrics from "Moloka'i Slide" written by Larry Helm and first recorded in 1997 by Ehukai.

surfer. We hit it off right away. As he pulled the tap, then slid a frothy mug across the bar, we began "talking story" above the sweet sounds coming from the band.

I'm not Hawaiian, but I can talk like one local when the situation calls for it. I was *hānaied*, or adopted, when I was eight by the Kealoha *'ohana*, a Hawaiian family related to me through my aunt's marriage. Because of that, most Hawaiians I meet don't consider me *haole*, but just another guy who loves the beauty of the *'āina* and the surf as much as they do.

The bartender and I talked about Moloka'i's uncrowded breaks and the effects of commercialization on surfing. From my wallet I reached for a ten, setting it on the bar under my two-dollar mug. My newfound friend glanced at the green bill.

"Heard anyt'ing 'bout dat *haole* lady," I asked off-handedly, "who wen' fall off da Kalaupapa cliff one mont' ago?"

"She one lawyer or somet'ing?" he replied.

"Dat's her."

"Nah," the bartender said. "At first ev'rybody talk—'good-looking *wahine*'—and dat kine stuffs, but aftah da accident I nevah hear nut'ing."

"Da Hawai'i Tourism Board like hush 'um up? Bad fo' business, eh?"

"Dunno, brah. Maybe dey t'ink so."

I stood up to go, leaving my ten on the bar.

"T'anks, eh?" the bartender again eyed the bill.

"No mention." I started for my room. "Maybe see you laytah."

The Hawaiian music faded as I walked across the grass lawn. This conversation had cost me a few bucks and yielded little of immediate value. But that wasn't the point. If ever

I needed information on anyone at the ʻUkulele Inn, or anywhere on Molokaʻi, I felt sure I could count on my new *bruddah*.

Later that evening, I climbed into bed and reviewed the medical examiner's report again. Cut and dried. Sara had the fractures and internal injuries anyone might receive from a long fall. No sign of foul play. No traces of drugs or medications.

I needed more to go on. Maybe tomorrow's mule ride would reveal something I was overlooking, something to give me reason to believe that Adrienne Ridgely was not deluding herself. I listened to the faint sounds of the Hawaiian band as I switched off the light.

three

"Errr-Errr-Eroooo! Errr-Eroooooo!"

A rooster strutting the grounds of the 'Ukulele Inn jolted me awake the next morning before dawn.

I slipped on some makeshift hiking clothes and drove into Kaunakakai. At Kanemitsu Bakery I ate some Moloka'i French toast and ordered a take-out coffee before heading for the cliffs of Kalaupapa.

The narrow highway hugged the arid shoreline, then climbed north through miles of open land. The rugged desert-like plateau of the West End soon transformed into upland mountains and emerald forests. The air grew cool. The higher the curving road climbed, the lusher the canopy of green.

At the highway's summit, my windshield clouded with mist. I cranked on the wipers, but the mist kept obscuring the glass like steam on a shower door.

Across from the ridge overlooking the former leper colony, I spotted the mule pack station. Guided Mule Tours read the sign. The Western-style lettering above the red clapboards and a rusty tin roof looked right out of a cowboy movie. An empty corral choked with grass suggested no mules had been there for a while.

I pulled up in front of the barn and went in search of the guide I was supposed to meet. Inside was a small office with not much more than a water cooler, Coke machine, and display of T-shirts for sale that said: "I'd Rather Be Riding a Mule on Moloka'i." Beyond the office was a tack room and stable containing wooden feeding troughs, rubbed smooth and shiny by the mules' muzzles. But no animals.

"Johnny Kaluna?" My voice echoed off the clapboards.

My watch said seven thirty. The time of our appointment. Maybe he operated on Hawaiian time–that leisurely island pace that pays little attention to the hands of a clock? Then I heard the approach of a rattling vehicle. An old Jeep pickup appeared on the ridge, bed piled high with yellow bales of hay.

A wiry *hapa*-Hawaiian in a black felt cowboy hat climbed down from the truck. His mustache was flecked with silver and his face tanned reddish-brown like *koa*. The fine lines around his eyes and deep creases of his smile suggested he was more than sixty. His jeans were worn white at the thighs– not fashionably faded, but really worn. A pair of scuffed and muddied boots and a red *palaka,* or checkered Western shirt, rounded out his rugged appearance.

This man was a *paniolo*–a Hawaiian cowboy.

We stood in the mist and introduced ourselves. The guide's deeply tanned face wore an expression of dignity, softened somewhat by his easy smile.

"Call me Kaluna, eh?" He spoke in pidgin, extending his right hand. "Eve'body does."

"Kaluna, where da mules?" I replied in kind and shook his hand by hooking thumbs, island style.

"West Moloka'i Ranch, waiting fo' lawyers to draw up new papahs."

"What papahs?" I studied the *paniolo's* lively brown eyes.

"New liability waiver for customahs to sign. Eva since da accident we suspend da tour." The guide eyed me warily. "Kai, you one lawyer?"

"Private investigator." I handed him my card.

"Detective, eh?" He eyed the full-color wave rider. "And surfah too?"

I nodded. "No worry, my client no like sue da tour company."

"Hū!" Kaluna let out a big breath. "Not much work while da stable shut down, except driving to da ranch and feeding da mules."

"Kaluna, you like tell me 'bout da accident?"

The mule guide's smile faded. "Was worst day of my life." He paused to reflect, his expression turning more somber. "Da *wahine,* Sara, she wen' fall 'bout one t'ousand feet down da *pali*. Was one doctor in da party, but he no could do nut'ing—fo' da *wahine* or fo' Coco."

"Who Coco?"

"Da mule, bruddah." Kaluna's brown eyes glistened. "Good mule. Not like Coco fo' stumble. I bury him wit' one backhoe by da trailhead. You see da grave when we hike down."

"You bury da mule yourself?" I wondered at such trouble and expense for a pack animal.

"Was my favorite." The guide spoke slowly, holding back emotion. "I had one tour helicopter hoist 'em up da trail."

Kaluna motioned me toward the barn. "Ovah hea. I get you da doctor's name and da oddahs."

We walked into the office. From a drawer behind the counter Kaluna pulled a guest book of black leatherette with silver trim. He opened to Wednesday, September 6.

"Dis' da day. Slow day. Was only four riders besides da *wahine*, Sara. All come separate. One was da doctor. And two more *kāne* and anoddah *wahine*."

"Three men and one woman?"

He nodded.

"O.K. if I take picture of da four names?"

"Whatevahs." He handed me the dusty black book. The doctor, Benjamin Goto, lived in Honolulu. The second man, Milton Yu, gave an address on the Hāmākua Coast of the Big Island. The third, Emery Archibald, listed only "Island Fantasy Holidays, Glendale, CA." And the woman, Heather Linborg, lived on Maui. With the 35-millimeter camera I always carry along on cases, an old but dependable Olympus, I photographed the relevant pages of the book.

"What you remembah 'bout da four people?" I asked.

"Was one mont' ago," Kaluna replied. "Usually forget after dat long, but da accident, you know, stay *pa'a* in my mind."

"No can blame you, bruddah." I encouraged him.

"Da oddah *wahine*, Heather—*hū!*—was one nice-looking *pua*. Young flower, yeah? Blonde kine." He winked. "If only I one handsome young *kāne* again!"

"Da blonde *wahine* wen' talk with Sara?"

"Nah, Heather wen' talk mo' wit' da local *Pākē* guy, Milton Yu."

"How 'bout dis Archibald? He wen' talk with Sara or act funny kine around her?"

"He talk wit' her. But no diff'rent from anybody else. Jus', you know, talk story kine."

"And da doctor?"

"Same t'ing. Dat doctor was *momona*. Fat, plenny fat. I give him my biggest mule, *Ikaika*. Means strong, you know."

"Did da doctor help Sara when she wen' fall?"

"No use," the mule guide continued. "Da *pali* too steep. No can reach her."

I pulled out the photo Adrienne had given me of Parke and showed it to Kaluna. "Evah see dis guy?"

Kaluna's brown eyes squinted. He twitched his silvery mustache. "'*Ae,* I seen him."

"You have?" I tried not to show my surprise.

"On da mule ride to Kalaupapa—one, maybe two days befo' da accident."

"Can prove dat?"

"By da guest book." He turned the dusty book back one page to the day before Sara's fatal ride. Sure enough, on the list was "J. G. Parke." Could Adrienne be right after all?

"You remembah anyt'ing 'bout Parke?"

"Not much. Was quiet. He nevah take no interest in da tour."

I put away the photo, still trying to cover my surprise. "O.K. We hike down da trail now to see where da *wahine* fall?"

He nodded and took out a cash box. "You wanna pay now or laytah?"

"Now is fine." From my wallet I handed him some bills.

"I no like ask, but no paying customahs since da accident."

"Nah, no worry."

We trekked on foot toward the cliffs. Although I was still unsure what I was hoping to find, Kaluna's registry with Parke's name in it had made me hyper-alert.

To reach the trailhead, we hiked through some ironwoods, then down a curving path sprinkled with mule droppings and rotting guava, whose pink meat lured clouds of fruit flies. The air was ripe. All along the path were warning signs: *Kapu:* Unauthorized Persons Keep Out.

The mist that had fogged my windshield suddenly descended, as we approached the trailhead. Wind whistled through a stand of ironwoods at the cliff's edge. On the precipice overlooking Kalaupapa stood a crude wooden cross inscribed, "Coco."

"Carve dat myself . . ." Kaluna said softly.

"Coco' one special mule." I consoled the *paniolo* as I glanced down toward the peninsula below—a steep fall indeed, and one from which not even a veteran horse rider could expect to survive.

four

The Kaluapapa trail began like a stroll in the park, wide and gently sloping. But soon the path narrowed, descending over rain-slick boulders, potholes dug by mule hoofs, and red mud.

At the first opportunity, I peeked over the *pali* and gazed down again nearly two thousand feet to Kalaupapa. Wild seas from the north pounded its craggy shore. Wind-whipped mists drove slantwise across the salt-bitten land, gathering like gauze against the towering sea cliffs. Their rocky faces rose like prison walls from the boiling surf.

Awesome beauty. Stark desolation. Fierce, unforgiving nature. No wonder this forbidding peninsula had once been called a living tomb. No wonder I suddenly felt bleak again about my long shot case.

We passed a gate posted with a more severe warning than the first *Kapu* signs: Hawai'i Law Forbids Entry Beyond This Point Without Written Permission.

Kaluna explained that access to the colony had been strictly controlled before sulfone drugs rendered leprosy, known today as Hansen's disease, non-contagious. The *pali* trail first opened in 1889, the year the colony's most celebrated savior, Father Damien, died. For many years after, the three miles and twenty-six switchbacks were traversed mostly by pack mules ferrying supplies to the victims below. The savvy mules could pick their own way down the sixteen-hundred-foot cliff without a human guide, and likewise return. So it was nothing for mules in modern times to carry tourists safely on thousands of trips. That is, until Sara Ridgely-Parke's fall.

Why had Sara come here? Was her trip connected in some way to her ecological passion, or her desire to evade her ex-husband's constant hounding? Did she perhaps feel affinity for the sufferers of Kalaupapa—victims of rape and sodomy and murder, not to mention starvation?

'A'ole kānā wai ma kēia wahi had been the cry of leprosy victims. "In this place there is no law."

The first official switchback in the trail—marked by a big red "1"—brought a cool, shady corner canopied by trees. No slippery rocks. No outrageous drop. Not even a view. Therefore, not likely the turn where Sara had fallen.

Before reaching the second switchback we passed yet another warning: Stop! Go Back Unless You Have Written Permit. We hiked on.

The red numeral announcing switchback three brought a dramatic view of Kalaupapa, and a difficult section of trail. Kaluna picked up the pace. I kept my eyes glued to my feet.

Halfway down the *pali,* at switchback thirteen, we heard the first faint rumblings of surf. Beyond this hairpin turn, boulders lay in the trail above a sheer drop. Kaluna stopped suddenly and glanced up.

"Wish I had da money Chancellor Trust gonna make on dat development." He pointed to a ridge towering over us.

"Development?" I said. "But dis national park land, yeah?"

"'Ae, jus' to da *pali,* but Chancellor own da conservation lan' beyond dat." Kaluna scratched his silver-flecked mustache. "Dey own da lan' and da politicians too!"

"What Chancellor going to build up there?"

"'Kalaupapa Cliffs'–hotel, condos, spas. All dat kine stuffs."

"Now I remembah." I linked the development to yesterday's *Star-Bulletin.*

"When da last leprosy patient pass on, Kalaupapa be one busy kine national park. Da tourist flock hea . . ." Kaluna paused. "Chancellor make plenny *kālā*–plenny money."

"Good fo' your business? More mule riders?"

"Maybe, but I no like condos up on da cliff."

I nodded in agreement.

"Anyway, jus' 'round da next bend where da *wahine* fall."

We turned a sharp left at switchback fifteen and gazed down the pocked, boulder-strewn track–a treacherous-looking patch. The wicked combination of jagged boulders and pitched steps was apparently the best the trailblazers who chiseled this rocky path could do. My knees involuntarily trembled as I listened to the waves lapping the shore a thousand feet below. We could see the beach clearly now:

milk-chocolate sand, ultramarine swells, sparkling white foam. No guard rails obstructed the view.

If a four-hoofed animal were prone to stumble anywhere on the trail, this would be the place. Kaluna must have read my mind.

"Da *wahine* ride Coco up da trail toward da bend." He pointed to the red "15." "I take da lead and she ride near da back." Kaluna paused. "Den hear Coco bray and da *wahine* scream. Dat's all. I no can see her fall."

"You spot her down below? Or hear more screams?"

"Nah." Kaluna shook his head, a tortured look on his face. "No can do nut'ing. I call to her. Da oddahs do too. But no use."

"What happen' den?"

"Since no can do nut'ing, I took da oddahs to da top and call da police. They wen' send one helicopter. Meantime, I take my rifle back down to Coco. He still lying dere on da path, peaceful kine. Look at me wit' big brown eyes and I say, 'You been one good mule, Coco.' Den I do what I gotta do."

"Sorry, bruddah."

"T'anks. Den da helicopter pick da *wahine* off da *pali,* fly her to O'ahu. But too late."

"About dis Parke guy." I tried to make a connection. "He 'round here da day of da accident?"

"I no remembah seeing him." The mule guide shrugged.

I took some photos, then searched around the site for evidence but found nothing. During the month since Sara's death the trail had been washed by rains, blown by gusty trade winds, and scorched by the sun. The winds alone would have carried away anything not bolted down.

If Parke was behind Sara's fall, he had left no evidence here. But that probably wasn't going to change my client's mind. Adrienne seemed hell-bent on her murder theory and might never stop believing it—unless my investigation proved otherwise.

five

Just before switchback sixteen, a sharp jackknife turn, I noticed a flat-topped boulder beside the trail. On top of it stood a makeshift shrine of religious figurines–Madonna, baby Jesus, turbaned wise men–encircled by a dried *maile lei* and rosary beads. A wilted red rose lay beside this somber, huddled group. And a fresh rose lay next to it. The roses struck me as odd amidst these rugged surroundings.

Had some adoring admirer fondly remembered Sara Ridgely-Parke on this remote stretch of trail? Someone who was feeling pain at her loss? Red roses, I imagined, were not that easy to come by in this remote part of Moloka'i. Who cared that much for Sara?

As we passed, Kaluna quickly crossed himself, making me wonder how long the shrine had been here. Before I could ask, the old *paniolo* abruptly launched into a homespun speech about Kalaupapa, sounding like he'd given it hundreds of times before.

The peninsula, he began in a tour guide voice, was first settled by Hawaiians in about 1000 AD. The small spit of land had been a fishing and agricultural village until 1868, when King Kamehameha V sent the first boatload of leprosy patients to be quarantined there.

Leprosy at the time was misunderstood and greatly feared, much as AIDS is today. Boat captains tossed helpless victims overboard to swim ashore. Those who drowned were the lucky ones. Those who didn't had to fend for themselves on the isolated peninsula. Their average survival rate was about two years.

Kaluna explained that there was little to support patients here: no dependable food supply, shelter, clothing, or medicine. Helpers called *kōkua* were permitted at first, but soon forbidden. Victims remained utterly alone, without family or friends. Kalaupapa became known as "the place where one is buried alive." No wonder people dreaded being diagnosed and sent here.

I wasn't surprised that Father Damien, now a candidate for sainthood, was not uniformly appreciated during his life, especially by the State Board of Health. He took under his care seven to eight hundred leprosy patients, whose number eventually grew to as many as thirteen hundred. Now, Kaluna said, only about fifty residents remained—of their own free will—and most were growing old. He said they stayed for various reasons, some from their attachment to the only home they have ever known.

At nine that morning we finally reached sea level. The quiet village of Kalaupapa lay another quarter mile to the east. The path to the village wove above the deserted beach we had seen from the cliffs, a gorgeous, wide beach lined with stately ironwoods whose needles padded the trail. No

one swam. No one surfed. No one beach walked. It seemed
a shame. As we drew nearer, we saw the expected warning:
Stop! Entry Pass Violators Subject to Citation.

In the village, a young woman in a park service uniform
introduced herself as our official guide. Haunani offered us a
tour in her Jeep, and I began to wonder what I was looking
for here as we passed Kalaupapa's simple amenities: a one-
pump gas station, a small general store, a souvenir shop in a
converted Buddhist temple, a carpenter's shop, a government
motor pool, an invitation-only guest house dubbed the
"Kalaupapa Sheraton," a pier for the biannual barges that
ferried heavy supplies, three churches, and seven thousand
graves. Mostly unmarked.

If Kaunakakai was a slow town, Kalaupapa was frozen
in time. I watched as a half dozen axis deer roamed the
village like pets, grazing on cottage lawns. The cottages
looked empty, but Haunani explained that residents seldom
showed themselves among strangers. There was a deafening
silence to Kalaupapa. The only sound beyond the surf was the
whispering fronds of lonely palms.

Haunani said she remembered Sara's striking appearance
from her visit to the colony. And when I showed our guide
the photo of Parke, she recognized him as well. After a full
month she still recalled his grim, determined face, so unlike
other visitors' expressions of curiosity and wonder. What had
Parke had on his mind?

The return hike up the *pali* to "topside" Moloka'i took
about an hour and a quarter. We didn't push. Kaluna let me
lead. I'm fairly sure I slowed him down. But he patiently

stayed behind me, step for step. Despite my conditioning from surfing, my chest heaved and my heart drummed. Sweat stung my eyes. My thighs burned. At least the steady climb allowed me to comb the trail again for clues to Sara's mysterious death. But no clues did I find.

We finally reached the top at half past eleven. As I drove back to the 'Ukulele Inn, I reluctantly admitted to myself that Adrienne's hunch about Parke might have some basis in fact. His mere presence at Kalaupapa near the time of Sara's death seemed more than a coincidence. I itched to interview Parke immediately upon return to Honolulu. But those were my emotions talking, not my head. I knew the best course would be to gather information about him first, since he might not consent to see me more than once, if at all.

I collected my things from the beach cottage and checked out at quarter to one—nearly an hour late, but still in time to catch my flight. Before long another Twin-Otter was winging me back to O'ahu. I was too preoccupied with questions about the case to pay much attention to the bumpy ride.

My trip to Moloka'i had served more to increase the mystery surrounding Sara's death rather than to solve it.

six

The flower *lei* shop beneath my office is the perfect buffer between me and the pungent aromas of Chinatown below. And it offers my clients a degree of anonymity. They can linger among the perfumy *lei*, then slip unnoticed up the orange shag stairs. Even if detected, they can pretend to be patronizing one of the four other tenants of Mrs. Fujiyama's building, a decaying pre-war specimen ornamented with two-headed dragons, serpents, wild boars, and Chinese characters in red.

Inside the flower shop today, Mrs. Fujiyama was ringing up a customer with a ginger *lei*. The ginger's sweet, pungent odor raised the hair on the back of my neck.

"Good morning, Mrs. Fujiyama." I said as the customer departed.

Mrs. Fujiyama peered up at me knowingly over her half-glasses. "Ah, Mr. Cooke. One pretty young lady come see you. Bought tuberose and orchid *lei*."

"Adrienne?"

"Upstairs now. Very pretty!"

"Thanks for the tip." I smiled.

"Nice young lady for Mr. Cooke." Mrs. Fujiyama bowed graciously.

I climbed the stairs to the musty second floor and peered down the hallway toward the surfer airbrushed on my office door. Adrienne Ridgely stood by him statuesquely, clutching a *lei*. She looked transformed. The tropic sun had deepened the color in her cheeks and highlighted the reds and golds in her chestnut hair.

As I approached, Adrienne stretched her arms toward me and placed the *lei* around my neck. Her perfume, mixed with the intoxicating odor of the tuberose, drew me nearer. We touched. She abruptly stepped back. The blush heightened in her cheeks.

"Ah, what a surprise," I said, searching for more intelligent words. "Why the *lei*?"

"For taking my case." She quickly regained her composure. "My sister is finally going to get the justice she deserves."

"I'm not sure we have a case yet," I admitted. "Although I did discover something on Moloka'i yesterday."

I unlocked the two dead bolts and swung open the thick mahogany door. The tuberose *lei* instantly revived the stale air in my office. I opened my window and couldn't help but notice how gracefully Adrienne slid into my client chair. She glanced atop my filing cabinet at the tarnished trophy teetering there–Classic Longboard–Mākaha–Third Place– then turned her cool gaze back to me.

"So the big news is," I started, "your former brother-in-law rode to Kalaupapa the day before Sara died."

"He *did?*" Adrienne's eyes widened. She seemed even more surprised than I had been.

"The guide doesn't remember seeing Parke on the day of the accident, but said he acted preoccupied when he took the tour the previous day. His mind was apparently elsewhere."

"I know where it was," Adrienne said almost to herself, her expressive brow working again.

"It's going to take more than his mule ride to build a case against him," I said, trying to give her a sense of the magnitude of evidence needed to convict a man of murder. "We have a long way to go. But, fortunately, there were four witnesses besides the guide, Kaluna. I plan to interview each in person before confronting Parke. Their testimonies may give us more leverage against him."

"When will you start?" She looked at me hopefully.

"Today," I said. "The first witness is a doctor named Benjamin Goto who practices here in Honolulu. I lined up an interview for eleven o'clock. It should require little time and expense."

"Whatever it takes."

"Interviewing the other three may be more challenging. One lives on Maui, another on the rural Hāmākua Coast of the Big Island, and the last in a Los Angeles suburb. If you want to cut costs, I can try phone interviews, though I don't think they're nearly as effective."

"No," Adrienne agreed. "Interview each in person."

"Your retainer should still cover the trip to Maui. But I'll need another two thousand for travel to the Big Island and Los Angeles."

"Why don't I just write you a check now?" Adrienne reached into her calfskin purse. She was determined.

I took the crisp Boston check and tucked it into my top desk drawer. "I'll call you after the interview with Dr. Goto then."

Adrienne rose. The highlights in her hair caught the sunlight filtering through my window. "If anyone can undercover my sister's murder, I trust it's you."

"Thanks for the vote of confidence," I said, the intoxicating scent of the tuberose mixed with her fruity perfume starting to make me dizzy. "And for the *lei*."

She nodded and turned to go. I took the opportunity to escort her down the orange shag stairs. Mrs. Fujiyama smiled when she saw us together.

Outside the flower shop, Adrienne climbed into her waiting cab. The yellow sedan swept down Maunakea, past the lurid neon signs that glow day and night on Hotel Street.

seven

Before my meeting with Dr. Goto, I made some telephone inquiries about him. Benjamin Goto had practiced medicine on Kapiʻolani Boulevard for twelve years, I learned. His license was in good standing and only one minor complaint had been filed against him by a patient. Goto's field was infectious diseases. He had earned his medical degree in the Virgin Islands and spent one undergraduate year at the University of Hawaiʻi, where, before her untimely death, Sara had taught in the law school.

On my way to Dr. Goto's office, my Impala growled along Kapiʻolani, turning a few heads. I bought the teal blue ʻ69 Chevy with only fifty-two-thousand original miles. Its big V-8 engine was what hooked me, but equally important, the backseat was removable, so my longboard could slide right in.

The doctor's office was in a mirrored tower at 1555 Kapiʻolani near Ala Moana Shopping Center. Its lobby glinted with enough marble to sink the proverbial battleship. I rode the elevator to the eighteenth floor. A few minutes before eleven, I found a door with a polished brass plate: Benjamin Goto, M.D.

The posh waiting room contained the usual ferns, seascapes, and recent issues of *People, Good Housekeeping, Sports Illustrated, Honolulu,* and *Hawaii Business News.* A receptionist with a professional smile asked me to take a seat. Twenty minutes later–not bad for the medical profession–she sent me in.

Dr. Goto didn't appear at all like the rugged outdoor type, as I had expected, but was a paunchy and affable man, probably in his forties. His ample jowls and rounded belly reminded me of a contented Buddha. He greeted me with smiling dark eyes.

"Please be seated, Mr. Cooke." The doctor made a sweeping gesture with great formality.

"Call me Kai." I wanted to put us on more friendly terms.

"Ben Goto." He offered me his hand and we shook.

The doctor moved behind his spacious teak desk and directed me toward a matching chair. His medical degrees and certificates hung on the wall, along with a photo of Caesar's Palace in Las Vegas–a slimmer Dr. Goto standing proudly before the glittering casino with a black-suited man in dark glasses.

"That's a handsome picture of you." I pointed to the Vegas photo.

Dr. Goto grinned. "Ah, yes, my salad days," he quipped. "Shakespeare, don't you know?"

I wondered why the younger Goto would be in Nevada with a character dressed like a mafioso.

"Thank you for seeing me on such short notice, Dr. Goto. My client appreciates your willingness to talk about Sara Ridgely-Parke's death."

"Such a pity." The doctor rocked back, his belly protruding from his white coat. He spoke in precise, proper English. "She seemed a remarkably intelligent woman."

"Apparently she was."

"I regret that I could not render medical treatment, but she was simply inaccessible."

"The mule guide confirms that. Neither he nor the police fault you."

"Still, it was most vexing." He frowned. "I could do nothing, don't you see. Absolutely nothing."

"May I ask where you were when Sara fell?"

"Certainly . . ." Dr. Goto paused to gather his thoughts. "I rode at the front of the party, immediately behind the guide. Ms. Ridgely-Parke rode near the back."

"Did you see her fall?"

"I am afraid not. Though her scream was chilling enough."

"You saw nothing?"

"The accident happened quite quickly, Mr. Cooke. By the time I turned around, it was over."

"Was there any warning, any indication of something wrong before she fell?"

"Not that I recall. It was a tricky section of trail—steep and rocky—but other sections had also been rough."

"Did you know the victim before that day on Moloka'i?"

"I had heard of her, of course. During the Save Coconut Beach initiative one could hardly pick up a newspaper or turn on the television without seeing her youthful face."

"Did you have any particular opinion about her? Or about her political activities?"

"I admired her. That's why it is such a pity to lose her. Legions of people mouth pieties about protecting the environment, but how many willingly endanger themselves to further the cause?"

"If you don't mind me asking, why did you go to Kalaupapa?"

"I don't mind at all." Dr. Goto smiled with Buddha-like serenity. "I am a specialist in infectious diseases. Kalaupapa offers a rare opportunity to study Hansen's disease patients. They could come to my Honolulu office, of course. But I wanted to see them first in their own habitat."

"Had you been to Kalaupapa before?"

"Actually, no." He gazed at me placidly. "But I had always desired to go."

"Why didn't you before?"

"One thing leads to another. Time goes by." He managed two clichés in one breath.

"Did you study any patients at Kalaupapa?" I asked.

"This first time I merely toured the colony. When I return again I will make arrangements to meet with several patients."

"When will that be?" I couldn't help wondering, given his vague excuse for putting off a first trip.

"Next month, if I can manage," Goto said.

"One final question." I studied his dark eyes. "Was there anything to suggest to you that Sara's death was not an accident?"

"Not an accident?" Dr. Goto shook his head slowly in apparent disbelief. "How could it be anything else?"

"I'm not sure, doctor. That's why I'm asking you."

"Highly unlikely, unless someone stepped up behind her and . . ."

"Yes, go on."

"But if that were so, how would one account for the mule's broken leg?"

"Good question." I handed him the photo of Parke. "Have you ever seen this man?"

He glanced at the snapshot. "I do not believe so."

"You didn't see him on Moloka‘i the day of Sara's death?"

Dr. Goto peered at the photograph again. He turned it so the fluorescent lights would illuminate the snapshot from different angles. Finally he shrugged his sloping shoulders. "No, I did not see him on Moloka‘i." He returned the photo.

"Here's my card." I handed it to him. "If you remember anything more about the incident, would you please call me?"

"I will be delighted to help in any way."

I rose and thanked him. "You go much to Las Vegas?" I gestured again to the Caesar's Palace photo on his wall.

"Las Vegas is a fool's paradise," he pontificated. "I avoid it like the plague."

"You'll hang onto more of your money that way." I winked, noting two more clichés.

He smiled his amiable smile as I walked out.

eight

Later that afternoon I called Adrienne to report on the interview with Dr. Goto. I told her that if I had read the doctor right, he honestly didn't know Parke. I was still skeptical, though, about his reasons for taking so long to visit a place so important to his work.

Why would a well-paid physician delay for a dozen years an inexpensive neighbor-island trip? Also suspect was his means of transportation. If Goto were initiating a new research project, wouldn't he have flown to the tiny airstrip that serves Kalaupapa's medical staff, rather than squander time riding a mule like a leisurely tourist?

These things might have nothing to do with the case, but they struck me as odd. Nonetheless, Goto lacked plausible means of murdering Sara and, to all appearances, he lacked a motive as well.

I then called the next two witnesses: Heather Linborg, a masseuse employed by the Wailea Princess Resort on Maui, and Milton Yu, who grew orchids on the Hāmākua Coast of the Big Island. Fortunately, both agreed to see me on short notice. Unfortunately, the two appointments could be arranged only on the same day, Saturday, and just a few hours apart.

By the time I returned to my apartment, I was ready to surf. My answering machine was blinking, but could wait. I changed quickly into my board shorts.

Surfing relieves the stresses of my detective work and even helps me solve cases. Sherlock Holmes had his pipe–I have my surfboard. Floating on the glassy sea, scanning the blue horizon for the perfect wave, sometimes I drift into a kind of trance. From there I can disentangle the most intricate web.

When my wave finally rolls in, instinct takes over. In one motion I swing the board around, stroke, and rise. Slip-sliding down the thundering cascade, perched on a thin slice of balsa and foam, I find a precarious balance.

That's what surfing and my job are all about: balance.

I grabbed my keys and was heading out the door when my conscience nagged me. *The answering machine.* I stepped back in, one hand still on the handle, and pressed Play.

"Hi there," said the coy, sexy voice. "How's my surfer boy?"

My girlfriend, Niki, calling from California.

"I've got some bad news . . ." She made a little pouting sound. "My flight schedule the next few weeks is murder. Afraid I can't come and see you, baby. I really want to, but I can't. I'm so sorry."

Niki was a Los Angeles-based flight attendant who popped into Honolulu once or twice a month. She was a true California girl: blunt-cut blonde, twenty-seven, and ever ready for fun. Her photo in a string bikini and beaming a heartbreaking smile sits on my nightstand. My cousin Matthew had once called Niki a "fox"—he meant, I assumed, "good looking," rather than "cunning" and "sly," but he didn't say which.

Niki had requested a home base change, from Los Angeles to Honolulu, so we could spend more time together. Until then, she continued to fly between the West Coast and Denver and Indianapolis. Our relationship was intense but sporadic, like a night of fireworks followed by a month of rain.

I felt sorrier than she did—for myself anyway. I wandered into the kitchenette to warm up some Chinese leftovers, and carried them to my *lānai*. On the forty-fifth floor of the Waikīkī Edgewater, you can see for miles. "Edgewater" is a misnomer, since this tower sits nearly a half mile inland from the beach—unless you count the polluted Ala Wai Canal, which the building does indeed border.

My place resembles a Waikīkī hotel room, with kitchenette and bath at one end and *lānai* at the other. All that's missing to round out the hotel effect are those tiny complimentary bottles of shampoo, aftershave, and mouthwash. I haven't always lived in Waikīkī. I came here only about a year ago from a cottage in the lush Nuʻuanu Valley, just off the Pali Highway. The landlord wouldn't renew my lease—too many broken windows, he had said. And bullet holes in the clapboards. I tried to tell him the damage wasn't my fault, exactly. The friends of a scam artist I had helped to convict decided to get even. Their shots had missed me, but riddled the cottage.

After the landlord booted me I decided to seek the anonymity and round-the-clock security of a Waikīkī condo.

Equally compelling were close proximity to O'ahu's most consistent breaks and easy access for Niki. Her airline provided free transportation between the airport and Waikīkī, dropping her a half block from my building. Since Niki's visits were typically brief—less than twenty-four hours—my new location meant more time together. That is, when she was in town, which was becoming less often.

Picking at the lukewarm lemon chicken with my chopsticks, I opened Friday's *Advertiser* to the surf forecast, which promised two-to-four-foot waves on the south shore. That was all the motivation I needed. On my way out the door, I picked up the phone and, against my better judgment, called Niki back.

Her phone rang and rang. Then a sleepy-sounding man with a gruff voice answered, saying that I had the wrong number. I could have sworn I dialed correctly.

I phoned her again. This time I got Niki's answering machine. I told her I missed her and asked when I would see her again.

After hanging up I had a sinking feeling. Niki was indeed a fox—maybe both kinds. I imagined love-hungry corporation men aboard her flights to Denver and Indianapolis, drooling over my California girl.

I didn't often think about what Niki did when we were apart. I didn't let myself. Now I began to wonder.

Within minutes I was paddling my surfboard to my favorite spot in Waikīkī called Populars, a quarter mile offshore of the Sheraton. I navigated the crowded shore break. In Waikīkī, local surfers have to compete for waves with tourists swimming and cavorting on various watercraft. But farther offshore the crowd thins.

I paddled by the crowd toward the long, hollow, fast-breaking rights of Pops. Out here the water is a deep green and the swells come sweeping in. I rode the chest-high waves until it was almost too dark to see, reinvigorating my travel-numbed body and reviving my dampened spirits.

But the surfing brought no new insights into my case. The one revelation of my Moloka'i trip–J. Gregory Parke's appearance at Kalaupapa the day before Sara's death–had yet to be explained. Even if I accepted Adrienne's questionable premise that he had killed Sara, the tougher question still remained: How could he have done it?

When Sara's mule had stumbled, catapulting her down the *pali* to her death, Parke was not among her fellow riders. Could he have enlisted one or more of them to push, trip, or spook the mule in Kaluna's presence? Dr. Goto was an unlikely accomplice, even if his motives for going to Kaluapapa were questionable. The other three witnesses remained to been seen.

nine

Early Saturday morning I flew to Maui. At Kahului Airport I picked up a car and headed south to the sun-splashed resorts of Wailea. Heather Linborg was to meet me at the Wailea Princess at ten o'clock.

Several cases have brought me to Maui before, the most memorable a still-unsolved cane field murder. Actually, it wasn't the investigation that I recalled, but the evening that I wandered into one of Lahaina's jumping oceanfront bars. Two gorgeous flight attendants were sitting at the bar sipping Mai Tais in the sunset, one with a blonde pageboy and quick, wandering eyes.

I don't exactly remember how Niki and I connected. We drank some Mai Tais. Her friend obligingly disappeared. The next thing I knew I woke up staring at the ceiling fan in Niki's hotel room, my body tingling with love's afterglow. She lay naked beside me, dewy and laughing like I had just told a fantastic joke.

"You're *fun!*" She gave me an open-mouthed kiss that seemed to last forever, then breathlessly whispered into my ear: "What was your name?"

That's how we got started—and never looked back. Though that trip to Maui had failed to turn up a cane field murderer, I did uncover one 'ono wahine.

Today, however, there was no time for carousing in the Front Street bars. I hoped my interview with Heather Linborg wouldn't leave as many loose ends as the last one with Dr. Goto had. She said she would be waiting in the Royal Spa, where she worked, near the pool. When I arrived at the immense resort, I realized I should have gotten better directions.

Sprawling over forty acres, the Wailea Princess was one of those magnificent, world-class resorts with every conceivable luxury. A soaring marble foyer, misted by murmuring waterfalls, commanded a breathtaking view of the stunning grounds and white sand beach beyond. The pool was more of a series of pools, meandering through a dazzling tropical landscape with vibrant orchids, anthuriums, proteas, and birds of paradise that put Mrs. Fujiyama's wares to shame. As our appointment neared and the Maui sun blazed overhead, I decided to ask the advice of a groundskeeper who pointed me to the Royal Spa.

I stepped inside the cool marble palace. State-of-the-art saunas, green papaya and tropical enzyme baths, and ocean-view massage rooms dazzled the eye. Patrons roamed the marble aisles in fluffy terry robes. I approached an attendant, a pumped-up bodybuilder who could have stepped off the cover of *Muscle* magazine, and asked for Heather Linborg.

"Heather's sunning." He pointed with an athletic pose to one of the rapids in the swimming pool. His torso glistened. "Look for the gold bikini."

Around the pool I saw several women in bikinis sunning, but only one glinted like a newly minted coin. It was a brilliant, mirror-like suit designed for show, rather than for swimming. This woman had plenty to show: the breasts of a porn star, barely contained by her string bikini, and long, silky-looking legs.

"Heather Linborg?" I asked hopefully.

She put down her paperback book, *The Bridges of Madison County.*

"This is such a good book. I've been crying all the way through," she said in a shrill little voice that set me on edge. I noticed a small birthmark on her face resembling a dark heart–the only visible flaw to her otherwise calendar-girl looks.

I handed her my card. She glanced at it and raised her two perfectly penciled eyebrows. "You're a *surfing* detective?"

I nodded and sat on the edge of the lounge chair next to hers. "I just have some routine questions. Your recollections about the accident could be helpful."

"It was awful," Heather replied, instantly transported to that day. "I wish I'd never taken that mule ride."

"Do you mind my asking why you visited Kalaupapa?"

"I wanted to see the leper colony before it gets overrun by tourists." Heather crossed her tanned-to-perfection legs.

"And you're afraid it will be overrun soon?"

"Isn't that what's happening on all the islands?"

"This place isn't exactly the outback." I gestured to the Royal Spa, which was crawling with terry-clad patrons.

"I also do freelance jobs," she said, then frowned, as if she'd revealed a trade secret.

"About the accident, could you describe to me what happened?"

"I'm probably not the best one to ask. I rode up front near the guide. Sara was behind me. I didn't see her fall."

"What did you see?"

"Well, she screamed, so I turned. I saw the mule collapsed on the trail. One of its legs was apparently broken."

"Kaluna, the guide, was pretty shook up about that mule," I said. "Coco was his favorite."

"You know, the mule didn't seem to suffer. It just lay there with a calm look in its eyes."

"Had you met Sara before the mule tour?"

"I'd heard of her, of course. But I'd never met her before."

"What was your opinion of her?"

"I liked her. She was real and personable and very bright."

I pulled out the photo of Parke. "Have you ever seen this man?"

Heather winced. Then she composed herself. "No, I've never seen him." I noticed a drip of perspiration trickling down her forehead.

"Never? Not at Kalaupapa? Not anywhere?"

"No . . ." She wiped her brow. "I never saw him at Kalaupapa or anywhere else."

I tried to mask my disbelief with a faint smile. *Check for connections between Parke and Linborg,* I entered into my mental notebook.

She abruptly handed me the photo. "Got to run. Massage appointment in five minutes."

Heather rose, clutching *The Bridges of Madison County.* I watched the dancing glint of her gold bikini in the Maui sun as she walked away.

ten

Why had Heather Linborg lied? She obviously knew Parke. But in what capacity, I wanted to know.

People are like waves, I thought as my Hilo-bound plane rumbled over Kahului Bay. On the surface they may sparkle and gleam, but what really matters lies below. The most glassy tube can be the most dangerous. Under its luminous green barrel may hide a jagged reef—one heartbeat beneath the rushing foam.

Whether surfing or working a case, I've learned to keep my eyes open. Otherwise, I'd be a dead surfer by now. And a dead detective.

Below the climbing jet, the fabled Hāna Highway twisted and curved along the coastline. Inland, emerald canyons of bamboo, breadfruit, and flowering 'ōhi'a were pierced by silver waterfalls. As we glided over this craggy coast with majestic Haleakalā towering in the distance, I wondered if Heather had served Parke as a masseuse. And had she given him a mere rubdown? Or something more personal? That she knew him at all seemed ominous.

Soon the Big Island came into view. As the jet descended down the Hāmākua Coast, I saw lime green *kukui* and the fire orange flowers of African tulip dotting the landscape in brilliant contrast. Above these flamboyant trees rose Mauna Kea, Hawai'i's tallest mountain, cloud shrouded and dominating.

By one o'clock I had picked up my second rental car of the day and was driving north on Bayfront Highway. Milton Yu, the orchid grower, lived thirty miles north of Hilo, *mauka* of the old plantation town of Pa'auilo. I would make our two o'clock appointment in good time.

My hasty background check on Yu had turned up his former occupation as a computer consultant, and his arrest for possession of marijuana. Apparently, the quantity of *pakalōlō* had been small or the evidence circumstantial, because the case was promptly dropped and just as promptly Yu left O'ahu for the Big Island. He was either very lucky or very well connected.

Pa'auilo turned out to be a sleepy village whose decaying sugar mill, like others on this depressed coast, stood abandoned. Following Yu's directions, I turned onto a narrow paved road, climbing past rotting plantation houses and a small farm or two. As the road rose higher through fallow cane fields, the air cooled and brought fog. In a few miles, the pavement ended and the path turned red. My car kept climbing.

Beneath mist-shrouded Mauna Kea, on a plateau surrounded by jungle, sat Yu's redwood cottage. The soaring A-frame and encircling *lānai* suggested money—on a clear day, it would command an incredible view of the Hāmākua

Coast. Behind the cottage stood a huge greenhouse. And beyond that, acres of jungle and rain forest.

As I pulled into the gravel drive, a local Chinese man in faded jeans, a Grateful Dead sweatshirt, and rubber slippers emerged from the cottage. He was slim and looked to be in his early forties. His raven hair, prematurely grey, hung in a ponytail.

"Milton?" I stepped from my car into the cool mountain air and shook his hand.

Up close, Yu's shy, dark eyes had a deer-in-the-headlights look and were riddled with tiny red veins. I noticed his sweatshirt smelled faintly of smoke—though not tobacco and not wood.

Yu motioned me to follow him to his *lānai*, which was lined with a variety of colorful orchids—lavender, cream, yellow, deep purple. We sat in his two rattan chairs. The vista took in miles of sloping fields blanketed by fog. After some preliminaries in pidgin about his retirement from the computer business, I turned our discussion to the case.

"Milton, why you like go to Kalaupapa?"

"Da rare plants," Yu replied in a voice as shy as his eyes. "Kalaupapa get some you nevah see on da Big Island."

"Fo' real? You wen' find rare kine dere?"

"Some." Yu averted his eyes. "But on da tour dere's nevah time fo' collecting, yeah?" He glanced at his watch.

"On da ride up da *pali*, you wen' see Sara fall?"

"No, was behind me. Heard one loud scream, brah— *really* loud—den rustle in da bushes down below . . ." He paused. "Den nut'ing. The *haole* guy wen' ride behind her saw da whole t'ing."

"Archibald, da travel agent?"

"From da mainland, I t'ink."

"What Archibald do aftah da accident?"

"He stare ovah da cliff. He nevah do nut'ing. Jus' stare."

"You t'ink he involved?"

"In da accident?"Yu's eyes suddenly looked confused.

"Maybe he wen' push her or somet'ing li' dat?"

"Why ask me? I no can see nut'ing."

"But you wen' talk wit' her during da ride, eh?"

"Yeah, we wen' talk. Shoots, she one foxy babe–an' *akamai*."

"Akamai how?"

"Smart, you know. Like one professor or somet'ing. She say she give one lecture, brah, dat night."

"Lecture? She say where?"

"In Kaunakakai. At one health food store."

"I hearing dis right? She say she goin' talk at one health food store?"

He nodded and looked again at his watch.

"What she wen' talk about?"

"I dunno." He shrugged, warping the smile of the late, grey-bearded Grateful Dead bandleader. "Maybe she one vegetarian or somet'ing."

I pulled out the photo of J. Gregory Parke. "Evah see dis guy?"

Yu glanced at the photo and nodded. "Used to come into da computah store. He rich. He buy computahs like dey bin toys."

"You see dis guy Parke at Kalaupapa when Sara fall?"

"Nah."Yu rose abruptly.

"Thanks, eh?" Before he disappeared, I added, "Befo' I go, you like show me da kine rare orchid?"

A cloud crossed Yu's face, making him appear reluctant rather than proud to display his gems. He led me slowly into the redwood cottage. The rancid, musty odor of *pakalōlō*—literally "numbing tobacco"—filled the main room. Only about a half dozen orchids stood near his *makai* windows.

Yu ambled from one rare flower to another, softly uttering their Latin names. He then mumbled something about his business and pointed to an elaborate office with numerous electronic gadgets—a fax, photocopier, two computers, several phones with caller ID units, a cb radio, and a police scanner that crackled with distant voices. It seemed like far more equipment than a former computer consultant needed and certainly more than that of a fledgling orchid grower.

I handed Yu my card and asked him to call me collect if he remembered anything else about Sara's death, though I doubted he would. His phone rang. He answered it as I found my own way out, snooping as discreetly as I could.

Parked behind the cottage was a new Range Rover—black on black—a luxury four-wheel-drive dream wagon for the outback. I peeked inside at the leather seats, cell phone, scanner, and radar detector. Pretty high-tech for an orchid guru.

By three I was driving back toward Hilo. Milton Yu had given me something new to go on: Sara's lecture at the health food store in Kaunakakai. My background check on her had turned up no prior speeches or articles about either health food or vegetarianism. What would have been her subject?

I believed Yu was telling the truth about Sara, but not about his own occupation. His possible connection to the islands' drug underworld would require some further investigation.

Back in Hilo I made a call to the health food store, but the manager there told me that Sara had only alluded to the topic of her speech as "a matter of concern to all Moloka'i residents." Her reputation, if not celebrity, must have been enough to draw a crowd.

I then checked into Uncle Willy's Hilo Bay, and drank a beer in front of the evening news. The lead story was about a Honolulu man who had disappeared while fishing from a rock ledge at Bamboo Ridge, near the Hālona Blowhole on the southeastern tip of O'ahu. The twenty-three-year-old law student, Baron Taniguchi, still hadn't been found. Sipping my beer, I wondered if Taniguchi had ever taken a course from Sara Ridgely-Parke.

eleven

At sunset on Sunday evening I met Adrienne for drinks at the Halekūlani. More than a few rungs above Uncle Willy's, my client's hotel was the ritziest on Waikīkī Beach. I was surprised she had agreed to cocktails at this violet hour, but she sounded anxious to hear the details of my recent interviews. We had planned to meet early, since the next morning I would fly to Los Angeles to interview the last witness, Emery Archibald. Only he had been in a position to observe Sara's fall. Would Archibald shed light on what was beginning to seem a very suspicious accident?

Adrienne arrived wearing a baby blue dress that deepened the color of her eyes. I followed her subtly alluring scent to a table under the spreading boughs of the century-old *kiawe* tree that reigns over the Halekūlani's outdoor *lānai*. Named "House Without a Key," after the Charlie Chan mystery, this seemed an appropriate place to discuss our potential murder case. As the cocktail waitress brought us Maui chips and took our order, we heard the sweet sound of a slack-key guitar tune coming from the *lānai's* small stage, backlighted by red-gold arcs of the setting sun.

"So tell me," Adrienne said while we waited for our drinks, "do you have enough evidence to indict Greg Parke for the murder?"

"We have a ways to go before we can indict anybody, Adrienne. Parke included."

"I told you, no one would want to kill my sister more than her ex-husband."

"We'll see. I have an interview Tuesday in L.A. with the travel agent who rode behind Sara when she fell. If anyone can provide us more clues, it'll be him."

"How many witnesses besides the mule guide recognized Greg's photo?"

"Two. One admitted knowing him, the other didn't."

"One lied?"

I nodded. "The one who admitted knowing Parke is Milton Yu. He used to sell computers in Honolulu. Now he grows orchids on the Big Island, but that's just a cover for *pakalōlō*. Yu may be deep into the drug trade, or just a small supplier."

"What could he have to do with Sara's death?"

"Maybe nothing. Maybe everything."

"And the witness who lied?"

"Heather Linborg, a Maui masseuse. She winced when she saw Parke's photo. It would be interesting to find out why."

The waitress appeared with two Chi Chis, tall goblets frothing like milkshakes. They even tasted like milkshakes, with a coconut and pineapple sweetness that masked double shots of vodka. I raised my glass to Adrienne, stifling the impulse to make a toast, since this was hardly a date. Our glasses clinked.

"Let's look at what we have so far." I took a swallow of the icy drink and set my glass down. "If Parke had your sister murdered, who would he have hired to do it? And how would he have gotten the mule to cooperate?"

"What about the mule guide?"

"Kaluna's a *paniolo*. I don't think he'd harm a mule to kill anybody."

"And the doctor?"

"Dr. Goto didn't look like the type to handle mules. He told me he'd always wanted to do medical research at Kalaupapa, yet put off his first visit a dozen years. That makes me wonder. Though I doubt he conspired with Parke."

"Why not?" Adrienne sipped her Chi Chi.

"Goto doesn't know Parke. I could tell by his response to the photo."

"That leaves the Californian. Archibald has got to be the one."

"We can't write off the others just yet. Yu and Linborg both know Parke, and both are hiding something. Which reminds me, Yu said Sara planned to give a lecture at a health food store in Kaunakakai that same night. Any idea what that would have been about?"

"Sara gave public lectures all the time," Adrienne replied coolly. "She didn't bother to tell me the subject of each one." Adrienne turned her chilly gaze to the dying sunset, as if she was searching for something.

That was an unexpected response to what I thought was an innocuous question. I watched Adrienne's frozen expression, but it didn't change. I swallowed the last of my Chi Chi and ordered two more when the waitress passed by. Then I remembered a burning question I had neglected to ask Adrienne on our first meeting.

"When did you last speak with Sara?"

Adrienne kept looking into the twilight, as she sipped the last of her drink. "I can't recall."

"A few days? A month?"

She gazed down into her empty glass, then spoke in an uncharacteristically quiet voice. "Five years."

"Five years?" I stared at her. "You told me you and your sister were 'very close.'"

"We *were* close. But Sara was strong willed and so am I. Before she moved to Hawai'i we had a disagreement."

"So you never came to the islands to see her?"

"No."

"She never came to Boston to see you?"

Adrienne shook her head.

"And you never wrote or talked on the phone?"

"No."

This wasn't making any sense. "But you inherited her entire estate–four million dollars?"

Adrienne glanced up at the approaching cocktail waitress and smiled wryly, as if relieved for the interruption. The waitress gathered our spent drinks, set down fresh napkins, then placed frothing new goblets on them.

Adrienne waited for the waitress to leave. "Things happen between sisters that a man wouldn't understand."

She looked out again toward the darkening ocean, her lips set in a tight line. I decided not to press her further on what seemed to be a sensitive issue. The time would come.

As we reached the bottom of our second drinks, the moon was rising over Diamond Head. The singer crooned "Blue Hawai'i," his voice as gentle as the soothing tropical breeze: *"Come with me when the moon is on the sea . . ."*

Despite my objections, Adrienne put the Chi Chis on her hotel tab. When we stood I felt a bit wobbly. I wondered where her idea of the evening ended.

"Walk on the beach?" I suggested. "The moonlight is magic on the water."

She looked hesitant a first, then seemed to make an instant decision. "That'd be perfect."

I let her lead us to the shore, where she took her heels off and stepped onto the sand. A few off-balance strides put us at the ocean's edge. I steadied her by putting my hands around her slender waist.

Being that close to her, touching her, breathing in her perfumed scent made me almost dizzy. I wanted this woman. I had from the start. She looked at me with those eyes that kept turning from steel grey to baby blue.

By the time we returned to the Halekūlani we were strolling arm in arm like lovers. In the elevator she pressed "12," the doors closed, and we kissed. Before the doors opened again, we had abandoned ourselves to our Chi Chi-inflamed passions.

Down the hall, Adrienne hung a Do Not Disturb sign on the door of her oceanfront suite. I opened the *lānai* doors and let in the moonlight. She slipped off her dress and lay on the bed in the moon's buttery glow. As I unbuttoned my aloha shirt, Adrienne's eyes opened wide. The welts on my chest. I started to explain—but she stopped me. With a whisper-soft touch she drew me down on her.

twelve

Before leaving Adrienne's suite by the waning moonlight, my head still spinning, I had somehow managed to ask her to phone the University of Hawai'i Law School about Baron Taniguchi, the missing fisherman. Could he have been one of Sara's former students? Adrienne had agreed to call while I was in Los Angeles.

Five hours later, I was dragging myself aboard a crowded DC-10. Booking a last-minute fare had landed me in the cramped middle section of the coach cabin. I desperately needed sleep, but every time I tried to snooze, another passenger crawled over me to stretch or use the lavatory. Every time, I awoke with an aching head.

The airliner touched down in Los Angeles just as the setting sun tinted the hazy gray sky. I couldn't help thinking of Niki as we taxied to the terminal. I decided to call her that night from my hotel.

In the darkening twilight I picked up a car and crawled through Monday rush-hour traffic toward the suburb of

Glendale. I checked in at the Red Lion Hotel, about a half mile from Archibald's travel agency, Island Fantasy Holidays. Archibald had agreed to see me the next morning at nine. Still spent from my late night and long flight, I ordered dinner in my room. Then I slipped between the crisp king-sized sheets, all too reminiscent of Adrienne's moonlit bed at the Halekūlani.

I reached for the nightstand phone and started to dial Niki's number. I put the receiver back in its holder. Why not just drop by tomorrow on my way back to the airport? Maybe I'd discover the truth about what she'd been doing when we were apart. Hopefully she wouldn't have flown off to Denver or Indianapolis.

I fell asleep, reminiscing of those first few nights Niki and I spent together.

Tuesday morning I pulled up to Island Fantasy Holidays, which, according to a mauve marquee, specialized in Hawai'i vacations. The agency occupied one of several units in an upscale strip mall along Glenoaks Boulevard. The outer office smelled of new carpet and paint, which were both in soft pastels and illuminated by indirect lighting. New Age music wafted through speakers in the ceiling. The agency looked prosperous.

A twenty-something blonde, reminding me too much of Niki, directed me to an inner office, its wall lined with brass plaques. As I entered, a slim, elegant man in pinstripes rose behind his desk. His maroon ascot and tortoiseshell glasses gave him a dapper, almost flamboyant look. His full head of wavy copper hair had greyed handsomely at the temples. He was probably pushing fifty, but looked younger. Reaching for his offered hand, I whiffed the spicy aroma of his aftershave.

"Mr. Archibald, thank you for seeing me."

"Call me Emery." He winked. "Emery Archibald, the third. Grandfather started this travel business a half century ago. I'm his namesake."

"You've kept the business in your family a long time. You must be proud."

"We are." With an aristocratic flourish of fingers, Archibald straightened his tortoiseshell glasses. His gold wedding band gleamed. "I hope you didn't fly all the way from Honolulu just for this interview."

"Don't worry," I reassured him. "I have other business in Los Angeles."

"I'm relieved, since I can't tell you anything about the accident that I didn't already tell the police."

"Then I hope you don't mind going over the same territory again, for my client's peace of mind."

"Not at all." Archibald ran his fingers through his copper hair.

"May I ask you first why you were on Moloka'i the day of the accident?"

"Certainly." Archibald again straightened his glasses. "Let me give you some background. A few years ago, I changed the name of our agency from 'Archibald's' to 'Island Fantasy Holidays.' The original name sounded a bit old fashioned; besides, Hawaiian vacations had become our bread and butter."

"From those awards on your wall, it appears you've been very successful." I gestured to the armada of plaques from the Hawai'i Tourism Board, United Airlines, Hertz, Hilton, Sheraton, and a dozen others. Next to those hung a photo of him with a cozy group whom I guessed to be his wife and children.

"Hawai'i has been good to us, though the future looks cloudy."

"Why's that?"

"The airlines have cut our commissions." Archibald began toying with a maroon fountain pen. "It's tough. Very tough. Some smaller agencies have already gone under."

"But you're hanging on?"

"We book vacation packages–hotels, rental cars, tours– whole trips in tickets and coupons. That's what saves us. That's what took me to Moloka'i."

"I don't quite understand."

"To keep abreast of island tours available to our clients, I actually take them myself. I can sell a tour better if I've been on it first . . ." He leaned back in his leather chair. "Moloka'i is on the verge of a tourism boom. What's happening on Lāni'i is nothing compared to what you'll see soon on Moloka'i. More hotels, more resorts, more daily flights."

"Why do you believe tourism will boom?"

"Simple. Once Kalaupapa becomes a fully operational national park and that new Chancellor Trust resort goes in on the cliffs above it, the sky's the limit."

"So you took the tour in hopes of developing new business for your agency?"

"Precisely."

"Did you go alone, or did your family join you?" I nodded toward the portrait on his wall.

"The two boys had a swim meet here." Archibald again preened his copper hair. "Martha stayed home with them and our daughter. I went alone."

"About the accident . . ."

"Terrible. She was a lovely woman."

"You knew Sara Ridgely-Parke?"

"Oh, no—that is, not before this trip. We just got to chatting and she had these marvelous ideas about 'ecotourism'—you know, packages that stimulate nature lovers to travel, which of course would boost our business."

"Ecotourism was apparently a favorite theme of hers."

"She seemed to be a brilliant woman. Brilliant. That makes her passing all the more tragic."

"During the mule ride when Sara fell, where were you riding in relation to her?"

"I rode behind her by about ten feet. The mule stumbled, I heard her scream, and the poor woman hurtled over the cliff."

"Just like that?"

"Everyone was shocked. There seemed no reason for it to happen. Least of all to her, the only one of us who had experience riding, except of course for the guide."

"Before the mule collapsed, did it do anything out of the ordinary?"

"Well, let me think." Archibald rocked back in his chair. "It passed some gas."

"Farted?"

Archibald cracked a smile.

"Ah, did anyone feed it anything or behave suspiciously around it?"

Archibald shook his head. "We were with the animals all the time, except during the bus tour of Kalaupapa. Then the mules were tethered together under some trees."

"Did all five riders take the bus tour?"

He nodded. "Only the skinner stayed behind with his animals."

I pulled out the photo of Parke and set it on his desk. "Recognize this man?"

Archibald puzzled over the image. "Should I recognize him?"

"Not necessarily."

"I'm drawing a blank." He returned it, his expression suggesting he was telling the truth.

As I put the photo away, a muscular adolescent ambled in wearing a canary yellow tank top that said, "Gold's Gym." His biceps bulged, as if he had just pumped them up. On one muscular arm a bloody dagger was tattooed. *A rebellious son?*

"Stephan here is my assistant." Archibald handed his boyish helper some airline tickets. The two exchanged glances. A current of energy seemed to flow between them. I couldn't imagine what it might mean.

After Stephan departed I gave Archibald my card and asked him to call if he remembered anything more about the accident. Except for his fussy appearance and odd interchange with the boy, I found little reason to suspect the travel agent of anything. Nor had he provided me with much new information.

Had I flown all the way to Los Angeles to learn only that the victim's mount had passed gas? A five-hour flight for a mule fart?

By ten that morning I had checked out of the Red Lion and was heading back toward the L.A. airport. My flight to Honolulu didn't depart until two, so I had plenty of time to visit Niki.

A few mile's drive north of the airport on Pacific Coast Highway brought Marina Del Rey, a pleasure-boat harbor where sun-loving pilots and flight attendants reside. Niki lived in a condo called La Casa Nova, a pink stucco complex surrounded by a wrought iron fence. Since I wanted to surprise her, I didn't use the intercom to clear the security gate, but waited for someone to come along with a key.

The lushly landscaped Casa Nova consisted of several wings built around a heart-shaped swimming pool. Niki's apartment was 309-F. I hoofed up to the third floor of the F wing, then flew past a dozen apartments. My breathing was fast by the time I reached 309.

I knocked and listened with growing anticipation as I heard oddly heavy, lumbering footsteps inside. My smile tightened on my face as the door swung open.

My smile fell.

Standing before me was not Niki, but a middle-aged airline pilot who looked as if he had just crash-landed. His pilot's uniform was wrinkled, his ruddy face shadowed by mostly grey whiskers, and his eyes bloodshot.

"Who are you?" I asked.

"Captain Jacoby," he said in a gravelly voice. "Who the hell are *you?*"

I glanced inside the dark and disordered apartment, feeling suddenly short of breath. "Where's Niki?"

"Flying to Denver." He looked me up and down. "Why do you want to know?"

"Niki is . . ." I hesitated. "She's an old friend."

The pilot folded his arms across his chest. He seemed annoyed at having to deal with me at all during his catnap. I imagined it was his voice that greeted me when I had called Niki's number from Hawai'i. I wondered what stories she'd been making up to tell him.

"I was in the area and thought I'd see if Niki . . . still lived here." Then I added in a more conciliatory tone, "Have you two been together long?"

"A year or so." His face was registering suspicion. "So who should I say stopped by?"

A year? I could tell I'd lost this battle before it had even started. "Oh, it's been so long, she probably wouldn't even remember me."

I turned to leave and could feel the pilot's eyes on my back as I walked dejectedly down the hall.

thirteen

On my long flight back across the Pacific, I knew I shouldn't feel sorry for myself. I had no one to blame for Niki's fooling me but my own blind eye. I'd told her I didn't want to know what she did when I wasn't around. I guess she'd taken my request seriously.

Later in my studio, I mechanically went through my evening ritual of reading Honolulu's two daily papers. A back-page story in the *Star-Bulletin* caught my eye: "Missing Fisherman's Tackle Found."

In the trunk of an abandoned unregistered car near Makapuʻu Point—miles from where law student Baron Taniguchi disappeared—his tackle had been recovered. Investigators originally attributed the accident to heavy surf. But now that his tackle had turned up, foul play was a possibility.

The article said Taniguchi was an experienced fisherman who had fished the rugged coastline since boyhood. Number two in his class, he had been serving as an intern for the Good

Government Hotline, a sounding board for public service complaints and a hotline for confidential tips on suspected government corruption. The Hotline had been established by a small group of reformed-minded state legislators after a *New York Times* article exposed a too cozy relationship between some island politicians and land developers.

I called Adrienne immediately. She wasn't in. I left a message on the Halekūlani's voice mail: "I'll be in my office by one tomorrow. Come by if you can and bring anything you've found on Baron Taniguchi."

The next morning I drove around the windward side of the island to Waimānalo, a proud Hawaiian town of humble plantation cottages and oceanfront estates. It was the closest civilization to Makapuʻu Point, where Taniguchi's tackle had been found.

"Nalo-town," as locals call it, has a bizarre attraction— among its rustic dwellings is an evergreen-ringed polo field, complete with grandstands and a white picket fence suitable for an English lord. The incongruity between these two worlds has always struck me as odd. But contrasts of old and new, kamaʻāina and foreign immigrants are commonplace in the islands.

The politics of the polo field, however, was not what brought me today to Waimānalo. Where there is polo, there are ponies. And where there are ponies, there are large-animal veterinarians.

I tracked down Dr. Otto Frenz, who, according to the State Animal Quarantine Station, was the island's foremost authority on horses and mules. I met with Dr. Frenz in the paddock of a horse stable just outside of town. The native of Austria was robust and ruddy cheeked, with a barrel chest and frosty blue Santa Claus eyes.

I described the accident on Moloka'i, which the doctor recalled, and asked him how it might have happened.

"Das mule ist much like das horse." He spoke with a thick German accent. "Ven he ist spooked or, how do you say . . . ill, he vill stumble."

"This mule was neither, according to the guide and four witnesses."

"*Ach!* No symptoms?"

"None." I thought for a moment. "Though one witness said it passed gas."

"Hmmm . . ." The doctor scratched his chin. "Ven did das mule last eat?"

"In Kalaupapa village before the ascent, I think."

"Maybe digestion?" Dr. Frenz asked, as if talking to himself.

"Could that be all?"

"Vat about drugs? Das mule vas medicated?"

"Not according to the guide."

"Hmmm." The doctor again stroked his chin. "Very interesting. I vill check das veterinary journal and vill call you."

I thanked Dr. Frenz and handed him my card.

"Der 'Surfing Detective'!" He squinted at the card, then launched into a lengthy story about once meeting Tom Selleck when he was shooting a horseback-riding scene for an episode of *Magnum P.I.* The animated story went on and on.

"Der *Magnum* ist goot guy," the doctor concluded. I replied that many people had told me the same and then slipped away.

Driving back toward town, I turned off at the Hālona Blowhole and parked among tourists watching the natural sea spout shoot like Old Faithful into the air. About a hundred yards to the west of the Blowhole lay Bamboo Ridge, a narrow slab of hardened lava perched over heaving seas where fisherman traditionally cast their bamboo poles. Baron Taniguchi had hiked to this treacherous ledge the day of his disappearance. A novice angler could easily be swept away here, but Taniguchi was no novice. He knew this coastline. And from what I knew about cliff fishing, you don't leave your tackle at the top—the climb back up for more hooks or sinkers or leaders is too steep.

Taniguchi's gear had been found at Makapuʻu Point, two miles away, which didn't make sense. Driving back to town along these surf-battered cliffs, I considered what possible connection might have existed between Taniguchi and Sara Ridgely-Parke.

Waiting to meet Adrienne in my office that afternoon, I wondered how our one night together would affect our working relationship. Adrienne arrived and from the way she swept her eyes nonchalantly over my ramshackle office, I saw she wanted to pretend nothing had happened. She was avoiding looking at me directly, and the few times she did, all I saw on her face was a cool, New England reserve. Apparently she had drawn a crisp line between business and pleasure.

"Did you see this morning's paper?" she asked, pulling out a copy of today's *Advertiser.*

I hadn't.

"*Pakalōlō* King Held Without Bail." Under this headline was a photo of ponytailed Milton Yu in handcuffs, still wearing his musty Grateful Dead sweatshirt. Yu had been charged with masterminding a multimillion dollar underground trade in cannabis.

While Yu's arrest for drug trafficking didn't necessarily make him a more likely murder suspect, his connection to organized crime got me thinking. Could Sara's activism in Hawai'i have threatened this Big Island *pakalōlō* grower or his comrades? Seemed like another long shot. This case was spawning them like cane spiders.

Then a dark cloud crossed my mind. If Milton Yu believed I had turned him in, there would soon be—if not already—a price on my head. Some "mokes," big, local thugs, might be gunning for me right now. Not a pretty thought. It gave me chicken skin.

"Yu admitted to knowing Greg," Adrienne said. "There's got to be some link to Sara's death. Maybe Greg's mixed up in drug dealing. Maybe that's where some of his money comes from."

"Doubtful. Why would a developer like J. Gregory Parke, who's made millions in construction, dabble in a risky venture like trafficking dope?"

"Still, he could be involved with Yu."

"I'll see what I can find out from Parke himself when I interview him tomorrow."

Adrienne tensed.

"By the way," I said, wondering at her sudden edginess, "what did you learn at the U.H. Law School about Baron Taniguchi? Did he take any classes from Sara?"

"The school refused to tell me anything." She relaxed back in her seat. "We can order his transcript, but only with his permission."

"Catch-22."

"And what if Taniguchi did take classes from my sister? What's the point?"

"It's just a hunch. Sometimes a hunch leads nowhere. Sometimes it cracks a case wide open."

Our eyes met and I noticed a hint of baby blue in the slate hue of Adrienne's gaze. I made a bold move.

"How about dinner tonight? We can even eat this time."

A faint smile showed through her composure.

"Tonight I'm meeting one of Sara's law school colleagues, Rush McWhorter."

"McWhorter? Wasn't he your sister's adversary, and counsel for the Chancellor Trust?"

"Actually, Rush respected Sara. He knew her quite well. That's why I'm having dinner with him—to see if he can give us any more clues."

"Well, let me know how it goes."

"I'm sure it will go fine." Adrienne rose. "By the way, when you see Greg Parke tomorrow, don't take seriously anything he says about me."

She turned and strode coolly from my office, leaving me wondering about her parting words. *What could Parke possibly have on Adrienne?*

fourteen

On the brief jaunt from my apartment to Parke's Kāhala estate the next day, I passed some of the most expensive real estate in America. Kāhala Avenue stretches for over a mile between Diamond Head and the Wai'alae Country Club, and is graced by waterfront estates, each with its guest houses, servants' quarters, pool and spa, tennis courts, and secluded beach. Few properties in Kāhala, even on the back streets, sell below one million.

In Sara's campaign for affordable housing, she had argued that the continued climb in property values would soon reduce the islands' population to two classes—the rich and those who clean their toilets. Yet, ironically, during her marriage to Parke, Sara herself had called this ritzy neighborhood home.

Parke had made his millions erecting high-rise condominiums and office towers. He had poured his profits into Hawai'i real estate before Japanese investment more than doubled values in the mid-eighties, then he sat back and watched his fortune multiply. I still found it odd that

Sara, noted environmentalist and champion of affordable housing, should marry a man so opposed to her causes. Another case of *Sleeping with the Enemy?* What could attract two people so apparently unlike?

Parke's oceanfront estate couldn't be seen from the street. His mansion lay behind copper gates etched with dolphins frolicking in cobalt blue surf, deep within a forest of Manila palms. I announced myself on the intercom, and one of the handsome gates opened automatically. In front of the white-columned pseudo-colonial home was a cream Rolls Royce convertible whose plate said, "JGP 3." *If a Rolls is his third car, what does Parke drive as cars one and two?*

Beyond the mansion's fluted columns, *koa* double doors graced with more cavorting dolphins slowly opened. A short, bald, pink-skinned man waved me in. Soon I discovered this was not a servant, but Parke himself. He was round as a meatball in wrinkled Bermudas and a golf shirt that was stretched over his humpty-dumpty gut and stained with something bright orange like taco sauce. He stood only about five feet in his bare feet, and from the leather-like creases in his pink face and the grey sideburns beneath his shiny dome, he appeared to be easily twenty years older than his deceased ex-wife.

Parke led me through an enormous living room, carpeted in plush Berber wool, and bigger than my flat and office combined. Then we stepped down into a sunken bar that opened onto a steaming spa and, beyond that, the blue Pacific.

"What can I get you to drink?" Parke stepped behind the rose-hued granite bar, his pink scalp reflecting the afternoon sun through a skylight.

"Make it club soda," I said. "My clients unfortunately don't pay me to drink on the job."

"I'll have the same. With a splash of Scotch." Parke eyed the Scotch bottle furtively, as if it were his secret lover.

He loaded two crystal cocktail glasses with ice cubes, then poured fizzing club soda to the brim in mine, and half full in his. He filled remainder of his glass with Chivas Regal. I watched as the aromatic gold Scotch turned a shade paler in the bubbling water. I took my plain club soda from him and we toasted.

Despite Parke's sloppy appearance, he had shrewd, intelligent eyes and a magnetism I found strangely attractive. Rich, self-made men often strike me this way. But beneath his aura, I detected one of those hidden things I'm prone to discover in people and waves. I just couldn't fathom what.

After we exchanged a few pleasantries, Parke clinked his Scotch glass on the granite bar. "Now what can I tell you about my former wife?"

I decided to jump right in. "It puzzles me, Mr. Parke, that two people so different should marry." I watched his expression for change. "I mean, Sara being anti-development and you a developer."

"We weren't as different as you might think," he replied without a pause or blink. "Although we first met as adversaries at a hearing on Coconut Beach. I spoke on behalf of a friend of mine who proposed to develop a parcel across from the beach. Sara represented the Save Coconut Beach coalition, who opposed my friend."

"And Sara won?"

"Of course she won. And it's a damn good thing, because Sara wasn't a good loser." He made a grunting sound that was either a tight laugh or a groan. "Don't let those glowing sentiments you read about her fool you. Sara was tough. She could get down and dirty."

"Did you admire her for that?" I sipped my club soda.

"As I said, we were more alike than you might imagine. We both played to win." Parke eyed his Scotch, its color lightening as the ice cubes melted. "I found that out the hard way in divorce court. Sara tried to take my home. *This* home." He gestured to the sunken bar and mammoth living room, then outside to the sun-splashed spa. "She didn't invest a dime in it—not one damn dime—and she tried to take it all. Square that with her liberal causes!" He gulped half his Chivas in a swallow.

"How did the court settle it?"

"The judge was a woman and she was crooked." Parke wiped his Scotch-glazed lips with his hand. "Sara had no legitimate claim to any of my assets, yet that damn judge awarded her half of my home."

"That must have added up to a sizable piece of change."

"Then what does Sara do with the money? She buys a half acre of oceanfront at Lanikai, all the while claiming to be a champion of affordable housing!"

"Sounds like a contradiction." I tried to keep him going.

"Sara was full of contradictions." Parke poured more Scotch into his half-empty glass, again giving it a golden glow. "Publicly she criticized developers like me. Privately she adored our perks and privileges."

"That's not just sour grapes, is it?"

"Sour grapes!" Parke's face turned a brighter pink. "I listened in court to all those lies about me while keeping my mouth shut to save Sara's reputation."

"From what?"

"Sara cheated."

"She was unfaithful?"

"There were many men." Parke raised both fleshy hands in a gesture of philosophical resignation. "But I'll tell you only one: McWhorter."

"Rush McWhorter? Her colleague at the law school?"

Parke nodded and sipped his Scotch, his anger seeming to have passed. I made a mental note to talk with Rush McWhorter sooner rather than later, then shifted gears.

"Mr. Parke, why did you travel to Moloka'i the day before your ex-wife's death?"

Parke slammed down his glass on the bar, nearly shattering it. "How did you know?"

"You were identified by several people."

Parke looked into his Chivas, then peered at me with watery, searching eyes. "Sara was bad to me in court, but I just couldn't get over her."

Suddenly I realized the "hidden thing" I had detected in Parke: The wealthy developer was a painfully lonely man. He pined for his ex-wife.

"I wanted to see Sara." Parke cleared his throat. "I had called her a few days before to invite her to dinner. She declined, saying she was going on the Moloka'i mule ride the next day. So I flew over there. But she didn't show—she had given me the wrong date. Maybe on purpose. Maybe by mistake." Parked looked dejected as if it had all just happened to him.

"Does the name Milton Yu sound familiar?" I shifted gears quickly again, not wanting him to lose momentum.

"Too bad about Yu. He should have stuck with computers. *Pakalōlō* did him in."

"And Heather Linborg? She's a Maui masseuse who seems to know you."

"Yes, I've met Heather, but she could have nothing to do with Sara's death. And by the way, is Sara's sister paying you to dredge up this garbage?"

"Sorry, I can't say."

"You don't need to. If anyone was capable of harming Sara it was Adrienne. She stole Sara's fiancé back in Boston and Sara never forgave her."

"Then why did Sara leave her everything?"

"Adrienne was Sara's only family. But after we divorced, Sara had said she planned to change her will, giving it all to her environmental causes instead. She procrastinated. And now she's dead. How Adrienne found out about the will, I don't know. But there's her motive."

"Why would Adrienne hire me to uncover a murder she herself committed?" I tried to let on that I bought Parke's theory, hoping he'd give me more.

"To point suspicion at me." Parke thumped his fat index finger repeatedly into his chest.

"But she hadn't even seen Sara for years."

"If you believe anything Adrienne Ridgely says, you can't be much of a detective."

fifteen

"Greg Parke is a pathological liar." Adrienne bristled. "I told you not to believe anything he said about me."

"Is he wrong?" I aimed my Impala up the Pali Highway the next morning, heading for Sara's beach house in Lanikai. "Did your falling out with Sara have anything to do with a man in Boston?

"We had a disagreement. You knew that before you interviewed Greg."

"Was the disagreement over Sara's fiancé?"

"I can't listen to Greg's lies about me," she fumed. "You can believe him, or you can believe me."

We cleared the Pali tunnels and began weaving down to the windward side.

"To do the job you hired me for, Adrienne, there are some things I need to know." I glanced at her face, which was set in a rigid expression. "Parke claims Sara was about to change her will before she died, to cut you out completely. What about it?"

Adrienne was silent for a minute. "No, I didn't know. I suppose Greg thinks Sara's money should have gone back to him?"

"No, he says she planned to donate it to her causes."

Adrienne shifted in her seat. "So was your whole conversation centered on me, or did you find out anything about Greg?"

Was she being evasive or straightforward? I decided to give her the benefit of the doubt.

"Parke admitted knowing both Heather Linborg and Milton Yu. And he confessed to going to Kalaupapa to find Sara. He says he was still in love with her, though he claims she cheated on him."

"Sara cheated?"

"Parke even gave me a name."

"Who?"

"The man you just had dinner with. Rush McWhorter."

Adrienne turned from me and gazed silently at pale Kailua Bay.

When we reached Lanikai, I pulled into a gravel drive at the quiet, cul-de-sac end of the beach. Sara had spent a sizable chunk of her divorce settlement on two adjacent oceanfront lots shaded by coconut palms. Combined, they contained only one small cottage, which most new owners in her shoes would have torn down and replaced with a massive castle covering every available inch of land. I credited Sara for trying to retain the property's natural beauty.

The cottage itself was rustic and charming: shake roof, stone fireplace, hardwood floors, two cozy bedrooms, a *koa*-paneled study overlooking the twin Mokulua Islands, and a small kitchen—the total opposite of her ex-husband's Kāhala mansion.

I'd suggested we come here in search of more clues about Sara's talk at the health food store, or her connections to any of the witnesses. We focused first on Sara's study. Adrienne sorted through papers in Sara's rolltop desk. I worked my way through her filing drawers. Just as I started on the second drawer, Adrienne waved a torn sheet of yellow legal paper. "Look at this!"

"What is it?"

"An itinerary."

Written in Sara's hand, the itinerary listed her activities on Moloka'i that fateful day. The notes revealed she had planned to tour Kalaupapa, then to speak that night in Kaunakakai, at Sun Whole Foods as Yu had told me. The title of the Sara's talk was to be "Stop Kalaupapa Cliffs!"

"It's our lucky day," Adrienne said.

"If we can find a copy of her speech," I said. "Or did she write down her speeches?

"I have no idea.

We searched every drawer and stack of papers, but found nothing. As the morning grew on, we decided to switch tactics and visit the U.H. Law School, where Sara taught— and where she likely had a computer we could search. My curiosity was piqued by Parke's allegations of infidelity by his former wife, so I had already arranged to interview Rush McWhorter there at noon.

As we drove onto the Mānoa Valley campus, I recalled a retired professor telling me about a time when these grounds were once as pristine and garden-like as the misted valley that provides its spectacular backdrop. Another victim of overdevelopment, the university was now choked with mismatched buildings: plantation-era cottages with buzzing air conditioners, cement-slab shoe boxes from the 1950s, stark, avant-garde towers circa 1960s, and an art deco student center in mauve and hunter green. As my eye glanced from one façade to another, diverse architectural styles clashed.

In the sparse lower campus, on the edge of a defunct quarry, stood the bunker-like complex of the law school. Inside we easily found the door we were looking for: "Sara Ridgely-Parke, Assoc. Prof." A month after her death, the office still bore Sara's name.

"They're waiting for me to clear it out," Adrienne said, unlocking the door and pushing it open.

The office had one sealed window overlooking Waikīkī and that musty smell that accumulated paper always takes on in the Islands' damp air. I imagined Sara glancing from her office window at the ragged skyline of concrete, steel, and glass—the symbol of paved-over paradise—and renewing her resolve to fight overdevelopment. I couldn't fully buy Parke's description of Sara being so like him that she embraced the luxuries that development brought. Her life's work spoke too loudly for itself.

Scanning her office, I saw creative clutter everywhere: open files and law books, papers hastily arranged on the floor, colored sticky notes tacked up like Christmas cards, newspaper articles taped to the walls. One article discussed the re-interment at Kalaupapa of Blessed Father Damien's right hand, considered a holy relic. The most prominent clipping, titled "Chancellor Trust Plans 'Kalaupapa Cliffs' Resort," echoed the sketch I had first seen on the airplane on my way to Moloka'i.

We searched for a hard copy of Sara's speech without success, but we did find two class rosters that included the name of missing fisherman, Baron Taniguchi. Adrienne agreed to keep hunting for the speech while I met with McWhorter at the other end of the hall.

Russell T. McWhorter taught real estate law and was well-connected with both developers and politicians in a state where the two went hand-in-hand. Since government approvals were required to get any construction project off the ground, a developer would often share his or her spoils with key politicians. An investment group would then be formed called a *hui,* a partnership with all the influential players, even sometimes underworld types who funneled in ill-gotten dollars. Whenever an approval was required, the project would slide through slick as grease.

The door opened to a rod-straight man in his thirties with a well-rehearsed smile and darting eyes of drab olive. His pale blonde hair was cropped fashionably close, nearly shaved at the temples like a marine cut. McWhorter was rough-hewn handsome and wore the silk aloha shirt of a downtown banker.

He gestured woodenly toward a visitor's chair. Despite a No Smoking sign posted in the hall outside his door, on McWhorter's desk sat a pack of Marlboro Lights and an ashtray full of butts. I handed him my card as he positioned himself behind his wide desk. His stiffness and tight smile didn't make me feel very welcome.

He glanced at my card. "Quite a gimmick. That 'Surfing Detective' bit. You must get some interesting cases."

"True." I wondered if he was mocking me.

"Do you actually surf?" he asked in a voice thinner than his rugged "Marlboro Man" image suggested.

"When time allows."

"A dangerous sport." McWhorter smirked. "So you came to talk about Sara?" He wasted few words.

"Yes, I'm investigating the professor's death on Moloka'i."

"Adrienne mentioned it." McWhorter reached for his pack of Marlboros. "Want one?" He flashed the flip-top box.

"No, thanks."

"Sara's passing was a shock to everyone here." He pulled out a cigarette, then flicked his lighter. A tongue of yellow flame licked out. "I'm not surprised Adrienne hired you to investigate the accident, given her emotional state." He took a long drag, then exhaled a grey cloud. "But I seriously doubt her theory that Sara's fall was somehow arranged."

"I'm just doing my job." I said.

He took another drag from his smoke. "Sara was truly an exceptional woman and a top-notch attorney. We'd all like to bring her back."

"Your reflections on her career might benefit the investigation. First, do you know this missing law student, Baron Taniguchi?"

"Taniguchi?" McWhorter blew another grey plume. "Why?"

"Curiosity. His disappearance has been so much in the news."

"Baron took one class from me." McWhorter flicked his cigarette ash. "He did well. That's all I remember about him."

"Real estate law is your specialty?" I knew the answer, but wanted to keep him talking.

McWhorter nodded as he puffed on his cigarette, the air in his office becoming thick. "I also advise the Chancellor Trust on real estate matters."

"Representing the trust must have put you at odds with Sara."

"I admired Sara even though, politically speaking, we were on opposite sides of the fence. She opposed developing the islands, and took her opposition to extremes."

"What extremes?"

"Once on ABC's 'Nightline' she called Waikīkī a 'high-rise horror.' The tourism board did backflips!" McWhorter puffed. "'No building taller than a coconut palm.' That was Sara's slogan. She'd have us all living on the beach in little grass shacks."

"Interesting idea."

"Pure nostalgia. No sane person in Hawai'i today believes we can go back to that . . ."

The more McWhorter talked, the more I wondered how Sara could have found him at all attractive. Despite his rugged good looks and practiced smile, rigidity seemed to fix his character, from his stiff posture to his abrupt dismissal of those who held opinions different than his own.

"Development means jobs," McWhorter continued. "Sara forgot working people when she married Gregory Parke and moved to Kāhala."

What a smoke screen. McWhorter struck me as someone who couldn't care less about the average Joe or Jane.

"Does it seem strange to you that Sara married Parke?"

"Sara lost her senses for a while." McWhorter tapped off another glowing ash. "But at least she recovered and divorced him."

"Because she was in love with you?" I went out on a limb.

McWhorter's eyes widened. "What kind of question is that?"

"Just something I heard." I kept my gaze level.

"From whom?" The attorney peered at me through the haze. "Was it Adrienne?"

"No, not Adrienne."

"I'm surprised." He blew another cloud and frowned. "She knows me better than she'll probably admit."

His remark jarred me, but I tried not to show it. "How much better?"

"She's your client." He put on a tight smile again. "Why don't you ask her?"

sixteen

I marched back into Sara's office, steaming. "Tell me everything about you and Rush McWhorter," I said to Adrienne, trying to hold back my anger.

"Rush and me?" Adrienne tried to act incredulous. "What do you mean?"

"You know him better than you've said, according to McWhorter."

"Not this again." Her steely eyes pierced me like daggers.

"Not what again?"

"You're believing somebody else's word more than mine."

"Only when you don't tell me everything. Only when you leave out huge chunks about Sara or yourself, which seems to be happening often."

"All right, I knew Rush before."

"For how long?"

Adrienne glanced away. "About six years."

Now it was my turn to be incredulous. "You knew him even before your sister came to Hawai'i?"

"Sara was engaged to Rush in Boston."

"So he's the man you stole from Sara?"

"I didn't steal anyone," she said. "After Rush and Sara became engaged, he took an interest in me. I tried not to encourage him."

"Nonetheless, it nixed Sara's wedding plans."

"Their marriage wasn't meant to be. But after Rush left Sara, she wouldn't speak to me. It was horrible. Eventually I broke off with Rush."

"Then McWhorter suddenly wanted your sister again?"

"Yes, that's why he came to Hawai'i. Rush applied for a teaching job at the law school and was hired, but Sara would hardly speak to him after what happened in Boston."

"That's when she married Parke?"

"Rush hounded her with proposals. I think she married Greg, in part, to discourage Rush."

I couldn't believe she had been concealing this potentially major point of relevance. "Why didn't you tell me this before?"

"I didn't feel the need to reveal my personal life. Sara is our focus here."

"If Parke would kill your sister over jealously of McWhorter, then our focus just expanded. Have you ever considered suspecting McWhorter himself? Maybe jealously could have led him to revenge, too?"

"Inconceivable. Rush was mad about Sara. Always has been. Now if we can stop the interrogation for a moment, I have something to show you." Adrienne pulled a yellow legal pad from the bottom drawer of Sara's desk. "It was hidden in this tablet."

"You found the speech?"

Adrienne handed me the yellow pad. Sara had slipped each white page of her speech between as many yellow leaves in the legal pad, making the typescript virtually disappear.

"She must have thought someone was snooping on her," Adrienne said.

I liberated the first typed page from the pad. What Adrienne had found was probably a late or final draft, since the copy was clean and the speech appeared to be fully developed. In the upper left-hand corner Sara had typed the place and date: Sun Whole Foods, Kaunakakai. Wed., September 6. The day she died.

Adrienne moved closer to me and began to read:

Stop Kalaupapa Cliffs!

It's a pleasure to see so many old friends here tonight from the coalition against Chancellor Trust's proposed Kalaupapa Cliffs resort. You deserve heartfelt thanks for your grit and your perseverance. Already you have succeeded in mobilizing grassroots opposition. And by now you know what you are up against. I'm here this evening to offer you encouragement in your battle. But more important, I bring ammunition to help you win . . .

"That sounds like Sara," Adrienne said. "Always a fighter."

Few people realize what it's like to face off against a billion-dollar trust. Their fleet of lawyers can file endless injunctions, restraining orders, and suits against you; their friends at all levels of government – from the governor's office to the legislature to the courts – can put roadblocks at your every turn; their massive publicity and disinformation engines can smear and malign you. In sum, this Goliath has enormous power to intimidate and impede you through all these channels and more.

The single largest private landholder in Hawai'i, the Chancellor Trust owns, by some estimates, as much as 10 percent of the islands – more than the U.S. Government! The consequences of the Trust's real estate dominance have been devastating for most citizens. By hoarding immense tracts of land, the Trust – called by one economist a 'land oligopoly' – increases the already high cost of housing, pinching strapped island families. At the same time, its five trustees pay themselves annual salaries approaching a million dollars – each!

"Those salaries are notorious," I interrupted. "And the Trust calls itself a 'nonprofit' organization!"

Adrienne continued:

The Hawaiian people, whom the Trust was charged by the will of Marie Kaleilani Chancellor to aid, have too often fallen victim to its ambitions. You may recall an incident that happened in a peaceful valley in East O'ahu. To clear these remote and pristine acres for an immense housing track which would generate millions in profits, Chancellor Trust evicted several impoverished Hawaiian homesteaders in a confrontation so bitter it nearly ended in a shoot-out. The Hawaiians were driven from the land and some arrested. In their place the Trust constructed dozens of look-alike tract houses that those Hawaiians could not afford to buy, while enriching the Trust and forever altering the character of the once-tranquil valley.

Sara's speech made me recall my own silent support for those Hawaiian homesteaders. It had been a different era back then–before the rise of the Hawaiian sovereignty movement. The media had portrayed the embattled families as unfortunate impediments to progress, even as dangerous radicals. As Adrienne read on, I became curious as to Sara's promised "ammunition" against the Trust.

Chancellor Trust has now set its sights on Kalaupapa and the wishes of the Hawaiian people apparently matter little to the trustees. How large is the proposed "Kalaupapa Cliffs"? Kaunakakai, the biggest town on your island, could easily fit inside it. Or, to compare it to a familiar fixture on O'ahu, massive Ala Moana Shopping Center would fill little more than half of the site, leaving room for another medium-sized mall.

But why would Chancellor Trust invest so much of its own money in the sleepy island of Moloka'i? Why build a resort on a windswept, rainy cliff, when sunny beaches can be had on this and other islands?

The answer is simple: Blessed Father Damien will likely attain sainthood soon. His sanctification coupled with the adoption of Kalaupapa by the U.S. Park Service – and the certainty that the peninsula will become a full-fledged national park when the last remaining leprosy patients pass on – can mean only one thing: Tourism with a capital "T." Visitors from around the world, with religious pilgrims in the vanguard, will make this historic spot as populous as Lourdes.

There's only one hitch. The project cannot go forward unless the state Land Zoning Board re-designates the land from "conservation" to "urban." In the current political climate, with heightened environmental awareness and sensitivity to Hawaiian history and culture, such a re-designation, you might assume, would be unthinkable. Indeed, your coalition survey found that 94 percent of Moloka'i residents oppose the project.

The trustees have anticipated public pressure on the Land Zoning Board to deny the trust's request, and they have concocted a secret plan to overcome it. This secret plan has been uncovered by a courageous volunteer, who revealed it to me at his peril. Although he must remain anonymous for his own safety, we have him to thank for this potent weapon against the trust . . .

The tie-in with Baron Taniguchi was now more than a hunch. He must have received tips on the Good Government Hotline, then passed them on, against protocol, to his esteemed mentor at the law school. For this plucky act, the avid fisherman had probably wound up as fish food.

To win approval for its project over stiff, broad-based opposition, the trust has formed a clandestine *hui* consisting of several state legislators, the spouse of a Land Zoning Board member, a development firm partially owned by the lieutenant governor, the leader of a hotel workers union, a legendary Hawaiian pop singer, and even reputed underworld figures who will funnel illegally obtained moneys into the project. This *hui* includes the most influential, wealthy, and powerful players in the islands, as well as Indonesian developer, Umbro Zia.

Zia's name kept popping up. I had once seen a rare photo of him in *Hawai'i Business News*. The reclusive billionaire had been spotted in his trademark white suit and pale lavender button-down shirt, a young Asian beauty at his side. Zia had acquired his fortune through hit-and-run developments, mostly sprawling shopping malls, in locales in which he never lived, some say never set foot in. Before the last brick or tile was cemented into place, Zia would be off to his next project, and to the next after that. He was thus a fitting centerpiece of the Chancellor Trust *hui*

Since Land Zoning Board members are politically appointed and frequently beholden to politicians and their powerful friends, they are very susceptible to the kind of influential *hui* that Zia and the trust have assembled. Unless we act now to expose them, on Friday, October 20, when the Land Zoning Board makes its final recommendation on "Kalaupapa Cliffs," the outcome is inevitable.

That was exactly one week from today. Adrienne continued by reading the long list of names involved in the *hui*—a virtual "who's who" of Hawai'i. I wasn't surprised to hear Rush McWhorter's name, although Adrienne seemed to be, as she winced as her rollcall came to him. But I was floored when I heard the name of one of my very own *hānai* relatives–Uncle Manny, known to most as the famous Hawaiian pop singer Manny Lee. Never had I found myself so personally entwined with a client's case.

Not one of Sara's fellow mule riders made the list. Though if the *hui* was behind Sara's death, they most likely wouldn't send one of their own to do the dirty work. Rather, an unknown operative would be dispatched. So that didn't rule out the four witnesses. That Parke's name was also missing didn't mean he wasn't involved. As a big-time developer, he certainly had ties to the major players. And since Parke had shown me all the marks of a bitter, spurned ex-husband, a crime of passion still could not be ruled out.

At the conclusion of the speech, Sara revealed that she and her unnamed source had received death threats. Adrienne's eyes were beginning to tear as she handed the speech to me. Now there was no doubt. For the first time since Adrienne had stepped into my office with her bizarre murder theory, I was convinced we had a case.

seventeen

I suggested dinner that night at a Thai Restaurant in Waikīkī, and Adrienne agreed. She seemed to have dropped the cool act she was putting on after our night at the Halekūlani. But we kept the conversation on business. And, for better or worse, there were no Chi Chis on the menu here.

After dinner, Adrienne insisted on walking back to the Halekūlani, a half mile distance, alone. I sensed that this was her way of signaling the evening was over.

"Let me drive you. You shouldn't be walking alone at night." By now I had poked around enough in this case to know that whoever had killed Sara might be on to me—*and* Adrienne.

"Really, Kai! I'm accustomed to taking care of myself."

"Then give me a call when you get back to your hotel. O.K.?" I wrote my home phone number on the back of my business card and gave it to her.

She nodded grudgingly and turned with a wave of her hand.

When I got back to my apartment a while later, my phone message light was blinking. I pressed Play.

"Naughty surfer boy. Why haven't you called me?" Niki.

I almost tossed her photo off my *lānai*, a forty-five-story plunge to the sidewalk below. Suddenly I had a better idea. Removing Niki's picture from the nightstand, I pried open the retaining clips behind the frame, took off the cardboard backing, then slipped in Sara's speech, which had been folded in my shirt pocket. I replaced the backing and wiped the frame and glass. For the time being, Niki would provide a safe hiding place for my only hard evidence.

In bed that night above the murmur of the *Late Show*, I pondered the case. I began thinking more about one of the names on Sara's infamous list—Rush McWhorter. The two apparently had known a long, complex, and vexed relationship. How had it all played out? McWhorter's failed romance and his work for Chancellor Trust must have put him at constant loggerheads with the "ecofeminist" he once—and perhaps still—loved. Did Rush keep his distance or continue to pursue her? Did he become a more aggressive adversary? If so, he would have been in a perfect position to snoop on his colleague, considering the proximity of their offices and the fact that their computers were hooked to the same university mainframe.

Her computer. I decided to have another look at Sara's office in the morning. I switched off the television and tried to sleep. But something was bothering me.

Adrienne had not called.

I sat up and switched on the light. Dialing her number, I tried to estimate how long the walk would take. The phone kept ringing. She might not necessarily be back yet, and she'd probably think I was neurotic if I left a message. As she reminded me, she could take care of herself. I hung up the phone and tried to get some sleep.

The next morning I returned to the Mānoa campus and Sara's office. A key Adrienne had provided me opened the outside door of the office building, as well as Sara's own office. A quick look inside told me something wasn't right. Papers, files, notebooks, journals, pens, pencils–everything– lay essentially where they had been the day before, but the relationships among things looked different. Someone had been here. I checked the door for evidence of a break-in. No marks on the sill or the lock, though janitors' passkeys were easy enough to come by.

I wondered what had been taken. The most important document, Sara's speech, was safely tucked away in my apartment. And, of the suspects, only Milton Yu let on that he knew anything about it. A break-in seemed ill-timed–more than a month after Sara's death. What would be the point?

I turned on Sara's computer and scanned her many files, coming up with virtually nothing. Had the break-in artists cleared all incriminating files from her hard drive? I thought a minute. If there were any pertinent documents left, they were probably hiding in her email account since it would be more difficult to crack. Fortunately, I had learned how to circumvent the university's log-on and password requirements from an appreciative client who also happened to be a university computer science major.

Once in Sara's account, the computer flashed a message: "You Have New Mail." There were seventy-four new messages. About fifty appeared to be junk email and several were departmental memos addressed to all law faculty. A few looked personal. I noted one in particular dated the day before Sara died from baron@hotline.org, whom I assumed was Baron Taniguchi.

Sara,

Another threat came in today on the Hotline, this one aimed at you and me both. Be careful. I've never taken threats seriously before, but these *hui* guys sound serious.

I hope your Moloka'i mule ride pays off. What a clever way to let the folks at Kalaupapa know what Chancellor Trust is up to. Please give my regards to the folks at Sun Whole Foods. I'm sure your speech will galvanize the coalition.

The pressure of this trust business is getting to me. Only one way to handle it – night fishing at Bamboo Ridge!

Have a safe trip to Moloka'i.

Aloha,
Baron

I double-clicked on her Saved Messages folder, but before I could open any my solitude was disturbed.

Tap. Tap. Tap, A heavy hand rapped on the door. "Campus Secur-ah-tee," intoned a husky pidgin voice.

I rose from the desk and unlocked the door. A meaty local man in a khaki uniform peered in. He looked more like a heavy-weight wrestler than a security guard. I noticed his uniform displayed no official badges or patches.

"Wassup?" I asked in my best pidgin.

"Dis' professor Ridgely-Parke's office." He eyed me suspiciously. "What you doing hea?"

"Da Professor *go hala,*" I replied. "She's dead."

"Know dat awready," said the man. "What you doing hea?"

"Work fo' da professor's family." I reached into my wallet and handed him my card.

He studied the surfer logo, then put the card in his shirt pocket. "O.K., brah." He turned and walked away.

Closing Sara's office door, I had second thoughts about giving the man my card. But it was too late now.

Turning back to Sara's saved messages, I found several more emails from Taniguchi in which he revealed the names of the *hui* members that Sara was going to expose to the public in her speech. If the *hui* had hacked into Taniguchi's e-mails, they would have known everything–including Baron's and Sara's whereabouts to arrange for their elimination.

These emails made it clear that Sara owed Taniguchi a great debt. He was the unsung hero of the coalition against Kalaupapa Cliffs. But now with Sara dead and the law student missing, only two people remained alive who knew of the undelivered speech and the identities of every *hui* member.

Adrienne and me.

eighteen

I found a floppy disk in Sara's desk and copied all the emails from Taniguchi. I then shut down Sara's computer and left her office, locking the door behind me. I had the eerie feeling of being watched. At the end of the darkened hall, the security guard in khakis stood eyeing me.

Chicken skin. He got my adrenaline pumping, as I quickly exited the front doors.

I steered my Impala down Beretania toward Maunakea Street. After less than a mile, a smoke grey Dodge van suddenly appeared in my rearview mirror. It kept behind me for several miles–about ten car lengths back. By the time I turned onto Maunakea, the van was gone.

I pulled up to my office building and found Mrs. Fujiyama doing a brisk business inside the flower shop on this Saturday morning. The color and scent of freshly strung *lei* filled the bustling shop–orange *'ilima,* pale yellow plumeria, lavender crown flowers, fire red *lehua,* green *maile* leaves, pink rosebuds. Their sweet aroma compensated in some way for this foul business I'd gotten involved in.

I wove around several customers, nodded to Chastity, the *lei* girl, and hurried up the stairs. Only one other office tenant was in today, Madame Zenobia, the psychic. Behind her psychedelic bead curtain flickered a single candle. Incense wafted into the hallway as a musty haze. Perched on a throne-like wicker chair amidst the smoke, Madame whispered tremulously in her bejeweled turban. A shriveled woman with blue hair sat across from her, glued to every word.

"I see a messenger bearing bad tidings," the medium told her client. "For the rest of this day, do not answer your door. Do not pick up your phone. Respond to no one. With vigilance, the danger will pass."

The blue-haired woman nodded slowly, entranced.

I reached the familiar surfer on my office door, the thick mahogany and twin dead bolts so reassuring. Inside, on my desk, sat the same stack of invoices and bills that should have been filed last week, or the week before. It didn't take long to save on my computer's hard drive the vital files from Sara's office.

As I was ejecting her floppy disk, my phone rang. I let it ring twice, then three times. For some reason I hesitated. Was I thinking of Madame Zenobia's warning? I let it ring a fourth time. Just before my answering machine kicked in, I lifted the receiver.

"You are the 'Surfing Detective,' yes?" asked a Middle Eastern male voice.

"I'm Kai Cooke." *Another crank call?*

"Mr. Cooke, I am Dr. Majerian, emergency room surgeon at Halekōkua Medical Center. You would kindly assist us, please, in locating the next of kin of a mainland accident victim?"

"Actually, I'm kind of busy with a case right now, but I can give you the name of another investigator."

"You, Mr. Cooke, I called first," the doctor continued, "because in her purse the victim had your business card. Last evening she was struck by a hit-and-run driver in Waikīkī."

"Waikīkī?"

"Correct, Sir."

"Not Adrienne?"

"Yes, her Massachusetts driver's license says 'Adrienne M. Ridgely.'"

No words would come.

"Mr. Cooke? . . . Hello?"

I bolted out the door.

My Impala ripped along King Street at double the speed limit, through three yellow lights and one red. I squealed left against another red light at Punahou Street, then sped *mauka* up the hill toward the slopes of Tantalus. Just before the H-1 overpass, I screeched to the curb in front of Halekōkua Medical Center.

I ran to the emergency room and asked the first green smock I saw where I could find Adrienne. The orderly sent me to the ER admissions desk, where a receptionist sat behind a computer. She typed in Adrienne's name and gazed at the screen.

"ICU," she said. "Ms. Ridgely came out of surgery early this morning."

"ICU?" I asked, breathless from my run.

"Intensive care. Her surgeon was Dr. Majerian."

"Could you please page the doctor? Tell him it's Kai Cooke. He's expecting me."

I stood huffing by the desk with my arms folded while she paged. "Dr. Majerian, call ER reception . . ."

A few minutes that felt like hours passed. Then the phone rang. The receptionist answered in whispered tones I couldn't hear.

A minute later, a slight man with coffee-colored skin stepped off the elevator across the lobby and walked to the ER desk. His eyes were ebony and moist.

"How is Adrienne?" I asked.

He spoke softly: "Come, please, with me."

We rode the elevator up to the second floor. "On Lewers Street the police found her, yes, at about ten last night in Waikīkī," the doctor said. "From her purse was taken apparently nothing. Puzzling, no?"

"It was hit-and-run?"

Dr. Majerian nodded. He still hadn't told me Adrienne's condition. Now I was reluctant to ask.

We walked down a wide hallway ending at a pair of large double doors marked, Intensive Care–Medical Personnel Only. Dr. Majerian pushed through the doors into a big bay with several alcoves, each one holding a patient on a gurney surrounded by an awesome assemblage of high-tech medical machines. Nurses scurried from alcove to alcove. Patients were attached to the equipment through various tubes and lines and straps, like spacewalkers tethered to a mother ship. All looked utterly helpless. Ashen white, dependent for their existence on IV drips, oxygen hoses, tracheal tubes, and electronic hookups to measure heartbeat, pulse, blood pressure, body temperature.

It was a sobering sight. *No wonder the hospital doesn't let visitors in here.* I couldn't imagine Adrienne looking so defenseless.

"Please, this way . . ." Dr. Majerian walked on and I followed.

We approached a gurney holding another ashen creature. The same array of tubes connected this frail patient to the many machines, including a tracheal tube. She couldn't even breathe on her own. As Dr. Majerian scanned a clipboard at the foot of the gurney, I beheld the now-helpless woman from Boston who less than a week ago had made passionate love to me.

Gone was the color in her cheeks. Her skin looked not just pale, but paper white. She lay motionless except for the slow rise and fall of her chest. Those vivid grey-blue eyes now lay behind pale, closed lids. Her luxuriant chestnut hair appeared straw-like and was bloodied. She wore a plain smock, also blood splattered.

"She is in critical condition," the doctor said.

"What did she break?"

"Broken bones are not the problem, Mr. Cooke. The severe concussion, rather."

"Is she in a coma?"

"Later we will know. At present, she is still traumatized."

I watched Adrienne for any sign of life–the rustle of a limb, the blink of an eye, a sigh, a cough–anything.

"Mr. Cooke, sir," the doctor said. "Please, would you provide us with some information about her?"

"I'll tell you what I know."

I related to him the story of Adrienne coming into my office the week before and hiring me to investigate her sister's death on Moloka'i. I told him that both of Adrienne's parents were deceased, as well as her only sister, whose demise I was investigating. I frankly didn't know who he could contact in Boston. And while I did know one person who might tell us–

McWhorter—I wasn't about to give his name to the doctor until I could be sure he wasn't responsible for this.

Dr. Majerian jotted a few things on his clipboard. Before he was finished, I swore I saw Adrienne move—a slight flutter of a finger. But I must have been dreaming.

"Did anyone see the car that hit her?" I asked.

"I do not believe so. The police, they may have more information on the accident."

This was no accident. I approached the gurney on which Adrienne lay and touched her cold hand.

"I'll be back for you," I whispered into her unhearing ear.

nineteen

During the two-mile trip from the hospital back to Maunakea Street, I again saw the van that had been tailing me the day before. When I turned *makai* onto Maunakea, the van turned, too. I swung into my garage and watched the van slowly pass and pull to the curb. I kept my eyes on the van for several minutes, then walked the back route to my office, using the side door on Beretania Street.

The monitor of my PC still glowed. I shut it down, then peeked out the window onto Maunakea Street. The van was gone.

My phone rang. This time I heeded Madame Zenobia's warning and didn't pick up. After four rings the answering machine answered.

"Mister Cooke, dis ist Docktor Otto Frenz. I haf found somet'ing about das mule vich may interest you. Only one case I find in der journals vhere das mule stumble ven not spooked or ill."

Dr. Frenz paused. I heard the sound of shuffling papers.

"Ya, here." He paused again, then apparently read from a journal.

"Ven mule ist sedated, if large dosage ist indicated, he mus' be allowt sufficient recovery time bevore valking again, since he may be drowsy und not sure of foot. Drugs, Mr. Cooke," Dr. Frenz concluded. "Das ist best I can do. *AufWiedersehen.*"

He hung up.

I played Dr. Frenz's message again, recalling Kaluna's comment about his fallen mule: Even though Coco's leg was broken, he had lain peacefully. Heather Linborg observed the same. The veterinarian provided an explanation for both why the animal had stumbled and why it did not suffer.

But how could Coco have been drugged under Kaluna's watchful eye? No *paniolo* would let his animal be so abused. There had to be more clues—on the trail, in Kaluapapa town. It looked like I would be paying another visit to Moloka'i.

Sunday morning I visited Adrienne again at the medical center. She had been moved from intensive care to a hospital room—a positive sign.

In place of her tracheal tube, an oxygen line now led to her nose from a spigot on the wall marked O_2. Adrienne looked much as she had the day before: eyes closed, hair lusterless and drawn back, skin paper white. She had not shown any sign of consciousness since her accident. I sat beside her for nearly an hour, watching the barely perceptible movement of her breath.

At about nine I left the silent Adrienne and headed back to my office with a growing sense of urgency. In some strange way, I felt Adrienne's recovery depended somehow on my solving her sister's murder. I checked the rearview mirror. No van. Since Adrienne's accident, I could feel the *hui* hovering everywhere.

Fujiyama's is closed on Sundays, but when I walked up to the building, one of the front doors on Maunakea was open. *Strange.* I saw Mrs. Fujiyama inside, head in her display cases, her half glasses riding low on her nose. She gazed up when I walked in.

"There's some bad people in this world, Mr. Cooke."

"Surprised to see you here on Sunday, Mrs. Fujiyama. What's wrong?"

"The police just left. Last night robbers broke in."

"What did they take?"

"Nothing," she said. "They took nothing."

"Are you sure?" I didn't like the sound of this.

She nodded. "Better check your office," she added. "The police said the robbers went upstairs, too."

I ran up the orange shag stairs, trying to reassure myself that my two dead bolts and solid mahogany door could keep out any intruder. The flimsy, hollow-core doors of the other four tenants were closed and locked. *No break-ins there.*

With relief, I saw that my own door was also closed tight. I put my key into the top lock, which opened with the usual click. But the second made a different sound.

The door swung open to an office in shambles. My file folders and their reams of client records lay scattered on the floor as if hit by a hurricane. My computer was gone, its unattached power line and printer cable resembling torn umbilical cords. And my tarnished longboard trophy had taken a dive, head first, into the wastebasket.

The *hui* was giving me a wake-up call. They had killed Sara. They had disappeared Baron Taniguchi. They had run down Adrienne. Now they were sending a message that they could do the same to me. How had they managed to break into my office without busting down the door, then trash the place and not get caught? I grudgingly gave credit to their techniques, then wondered if they had done the same to my apartment.

I closed up my ransacked office and drove to the Waikīkī Edgewater. Packing into an already-crowded elevator, I pushed PH. The ride to the penthouses seemed to take forever, the elevator stopping six or seven times on the forty-five floor climb. Finally, the doors opened to the familiar floor and I hurried down the hall.

My door appeared to be locked just as I had left it. The turning of my key produced no unusual sound.

Inside everything looked in place. I rushed straight to the nightstand and grabbed my photo of Niki, still beaming a heartbreaking smile in her string bikini. I inspected the photo, the glass, the frame, and the cardboard backing. From the thickness of the backing I could tell all was well.

Relieved, I immediately called Johnny Kaluna, who picked up on the first ring. Since the mule guide's tour business was still suspended, he had time on his hands and agreed to hike again with me down the Kalaupapa trail. I told him I was in a hurry. We settled on the next morning, Monday, at nine.

After I made reservations for my impromptu Moloka'i trip, I called the Halekōkua. No change in Adrienne's condition. I walked out on the lānai and leaned on the railing. The mid-afternoon sun was reflecting in brilliant patches off the distant ocean. I might as well go back to the office and deal with the mess there, since I couldn't bear the thought of coming home from Moloka'i to ankle-deep files.

But I knew it wasn't my files the *hui* had been after. It was my computer. All of Baron Taniguchi's transferred email files, incriminating *hui* members, were now lost.

twenty

After a bouncy but uneventful flight later that afternoon to Moloka'i, I picked up another rental car at the tiny airport and drove to Kaunakakai. On the edge of town I saw that white-muzzled retriever snoozing at Kalama's Service Station, then I passed Sun Whole Foods where Sara was to have delivered her speech.

I arrived at the 'Ukulele Inn at sunset. At the front desk, a Hawaiian woman in a tent-sized *mu'umu'u* checked me in.

"Room 21d," she said. "Sign da book, please?" She opened a spiral-bound register on the counter. It contained guests' names for each day of year.

I signed, then asked in pidgin: "O.K. I can look an' see if any my frien's stay here?"

"When your frien's come?"

"Septembah—I t'ink maybe foah, five, maybe six."

"*Huli* da page." She made a page-turning gesture.

I turned the log back to "September 4," two days before Sara's death. I scanned the register. Among perhaps thirty autographs, I could decipher none of my suspects' names.

"You fine 'em yet?"

"Looking." Toward the bottom of the page, I squinted to read a tightly scrawled name: "J. G. Parke."

I tried to conceal my glee. "Maybe try da next page, too." Among the many names on the page dated September 5, was "H. Linborg" in a swooping, feminine hand.

"Find your frien'?"

"No can find." I attempted to keep a straight face. "Try one more page."

I turned to September 6, the day of Sara's fall. Three dozen names appeared, but no suspects, unless they had used aliases.

"Shoots. No luck."

"Maybe dey stay anoddah hotel?" she suggested.

"Where you t'ink?"

"Try Moloka'i Beach Hotel. Ask for my frien' in reservations, Mele."

"T'anks, eh?"

Within minutes, my rented car was flying two miles up shore to the Moloka'i Beach Hotel. I wandered among its Polynesian thatched cottages, soon coming upon an open-air lobby flanked by two towering *koa* statues–*ki'i* or tiki– apparently of local gods.

The reservationist I had been instructed to see, Mele, showed me the guest register for September 3 through 7. I scanned the pages for suspects Goto, Yu, Archibald, and McWhorter. Only Archibald's name appeared, on September 4 in a beachfront cottage. Listed in the same room with Archibald was another guest named Stevens.

The travel agent had lied, claiming to have journeyed to Moloka'i alone. I suppose if the *hui* had wanted a remote hit man with little obvious local connection, Archibald or this Stevens could have been their man—or woman. I asked if the receptionist could tell me more about the mysterious traveling companion. Was Stevens also a travel agent? Did the two check in together? Did they take meals together?

Mele didn't know. But she told me to come back on Sunday to talk to someone who might, a chambermaid named Raine who cleaned the seaside cottages.

After grilled *mahimahi* that evening at the 'Ukulele Inn, I stopped by the Banyan Tree. The same local surfer was tending bar as before.

"Hey, Kai, wassup?" he said.

I ordered a beer and put another ten on the bar. "Keep da change."

"T'anks, eh." He set a frothing mug in front of me and picked up the bill.

We talked story about surfing for a while, then I steered our conversation toward the case.

"Eh, brah, you remembah dis' guy?" I showed him the photo of Parke. "Was here 'bout one mont' ago. One *haole* guy, mid-fifties."

The bartender studied the photo. "Ho, how can I forget! I wen' see him sitting wit' one *ono wahine*."

"You remembah what da *wahine* look like?"

He smiled wistfully. "Was blon'. I t'ink she one masseuse, or somet'ing. *Lomilomi* kine."

"Was named Heather?"

"Maybe. Dey wen' meet in da bar and lef' togeddah. Dat's her style. I seen her operate hea befoah."

"She one hooker?"

The bartender shrugged his shoulders. "I dunno. Maybe. I no ask."

"Why you t'ink she work hea on Moloka'i? Brah, t'ink she no get plenny business on Maui?"

"Maybe she no like nobody fin' out."

"Like her boss?" I thought out loud. "Or maybe she get one boyfriend?"

"I dunno, brah. Whatevahs."

"T'anks, eh." I clasped his hand. "If you t'ink of anyt'ing else, try call me, 'kay?" I handed him my card.

Back in my room I mulled over our conversation. Heather was indeed in "the business." And as I assumed all along, she too had lied. She did know Parke. Intimately. Maybe she needed the money. Or maybe she was working for somebody else . . . A pimp. A crime syndicate. The *hui* itself.

I climbed into bed. The Spartan accommodations—no TV, no radio, no clock—hardly mattered this time. Morning was on my mind. Tomorrow I had a murder to solve.

twenty-one

"Errr-Errr-Erroooo!"

The ruby red rooster that struts the grounds at the 'Ukulele Inn crowed like clockwork before six the next morning.

I turned over in my bed, too groggy to rise. Last night the bar band had played Jimmy Buffet tunes until past midnight—evidently my room wasn't far enough away to block the sound. Then some rowdy and tone-deaf merrymakers in a nearby room had sung "Margaritaville" off-key for who knows how long. I would have had a rough night anyway. My thoughts kept returning to the Halekōkua Medical Center. Adrienne was in a coma and I felt responsible.

On the way to my meeting with Kaluna, I stopped at Kanemitsu Bakery, where I sipped Kona coffee and turned over details of the case. None of my theories were going to matter much without hard evidence. With a loaf of freshly-baked Moloka'i bread in hand, I headed up the two-lane highway to the cliffs of Kalaupapa.

A few miles from the summit, mist clouded my windshield, then cleared as the sun emerged. I passed the countless acres of conservation land Chancellor Trust proposed to plow under, where *kukui* and ironwood trees waved in the cool morning trade winds. The Land Zoning Board was expected to approve the project on Friday—just four days away.

I pulled up to the mule stable a few minutes early. The corral, as before, lay empty. Inside the barn the wooden feeding troughs still held no feed. Saddles, blankets, harnesses, bits—all the riding gear—hung as before, awaiting the animals' return. The barn was ghostly quiet, except for a hen pecking by the troughs where once seeds and morsels of food had been.

In what mood had Sara waited here before her fateful ride? Was she on guard, alarmed by the death threats against her? Or was she at ease, having escaped, if briefly, to the more pristine Hawai'i she was fighting to preserve?

I wandered outside to the corral, just as Kaluna's Jeep rattled into view. He hopped out in his signature black felt cowboy hat and worn denims, then ambled toward me in the elegantly bowlegged walk of a *paniolo.*

He extended his hand. "Kai, *aloha mai.*"

"I brought you one small *makana.*"From my car I fetched the gift—warm bread from Kanemitsu Bakery.

"Oh *mahalo.*" He breathed in the fresh-baked aroma. "We no get dis' kine bread up hea."

"I pay fo' da hike today, like da last time."

"*Mahalo,* Kai." Kaluna smiled. "Your client still not satisfy 'bout da accident?"

"My client in da hospital. Was run down I t'ink by da same *hui* dat kill da *wahine*."

"Nobody kill da *wahine*," Kaluna shook his head. "Coco wen' stumble."

"But Kaluna, you say yourself it no like Coco fo' stumble. You say, 'Coco one good mule.'"

"'Ae, real good."

"Well den, somebody wen' mess wit' Coco."

"Nobody mess wit' Coco," Kaluna protested. "Nobody go neah da mules but me and da customahs. And I dere wit' Coco da whole time."

"Da whole time? You sure?"

"All da time 'cept when da customahs take da walking tour down dere in Kalaupapa . . ." Kaluna paused. "Den Coco tether wit' da oddah mules and I talk story wit' some friens'."

"One vet in Waimānalo t'ink Coco drugged."

"Coco drug'?" Kaluna's leathery face contorted. "'A'ole! Nevah!"

"Maybe one customah give Coco drugs when you wen' talk story."

The mule guide ripped off his cowboy hat and grimaced again. "One customah drug Coco?"

"Is jus' one t'eory, but if we fin' evidence, your company get plenny *kālā*–plenny money."

"How?" The *paniolo* restored his hat.

"Ask your lawyers. Dey sue da guilty party fo' cause da accident and fo' damage your business. Da court award millions in case like dis."

"Millions?" Kaluna's brown eyes widened.

I pulled out my wallet. "I pay now fo' da hike."

Kaluna waved me off. "We fine dat drug evidence, Kai, an' you no owe me nut'ing."

We crossed the highway and walked down the winding red dirt road that led to the Kalaupapa trail. On my previous trip, this panoramic view of the tiny colony and leaf-shaped peninsula had been shrouded in mist. Today, under the bright October sun, every detail was sharply etched like a picture postcard. The waves washing the chocolate beach below were brilliant turquoise. The whipped cream foam looked good enough to eat. Above on the ridge a gentle breeze whispered in the ironwoods, carrying a fresh evergreen scent that stirred my senses.

I recalled the fabled motto of Kalaupapa: *'A'ole kānā wai ma kēia wahi*–"In this place there is no law." The saying was old, dating back to the nineteenth century, but its meaning had carried forward with a new twist. I glanced toward the eighty acres that Chancellor Trust, allied with a "who's who" of Hawai'i leaders, was poised to desecrate. Who would have dreamt that the lawless of today would be our own public officials sworn to uphold the law?

Before we started down the trail, Kaluna stopped at the grave of his fallen mule, marked by that pine cross with the crudely carved "Coco." Kaluna gazed at the cross. The red earth beneath it, once mounded high on the immense plot, already looked sunken like a little valley.

"If da mule nevah cause da accident," Kaluna said, pausing at the grave, then fixing his glistening brown eyes me, "I like clear Coco's name. Let's *hele!*"

We hiked through the first few canopied switchbacks, nearly every turn bringing breathtaking views of the wave-pounded peninsula. In the open stretches, the sweltering sun beat down, but to our great advantage: No rain-slick boulders or gooey red mud to challenge our footing today.

About halfway down the trail we began to hear the quiet wash of surf. At the red "15" marker, beneath the site of proposed Kalaupapa Cliffs resort, we made a sharp left to the rocky path from which Sara had fallen. I glanced down and involuntarily took a deep breath, envisioning Sara's slight body being thrown from her mule, lunging over the edge, clutching the air in a futile attempt to regain a hold on life before gravity dashed it from her on the rocks below.

I glanced back at the pockmarked trail. In the last month, mist and rain had washed the boulders and red earth. The searing sun had baked the crusty soil. I searched the accident site as before but, not surprisingly, came up empty.

Before turning at "16," we paused again at the flat-topped boulder with the makeshift shrine–Madonna, baby Jesus, wise men, *maile lei,* and rosary beads. The huddled, tiny figurines looked both sorrowful and jubilant. Despair and hope–two opposite emotions–portrayed in the same poignant scene. I noticed that atop the boulder the two red roses we had seen before were gone. In their place lay a fresh new rose, crimson and fragrant. Someone had recently–very recently–tended this shrine. I looked at Kaluna, who crossed himself as we passed. Then his eyes met mine.

"Fo' Coco and da *wahine.*" He walked on.

The trail seesawed down through the remaining switchbacks, the village of Kalaupapa growing under my gaze–from a grid of tiny specks to visible outlines of frame houses and gardens. Every so often I spotted a glinting object–a bottle cap, a plastic spoon, a piece of rusty pipe that recalled earlier days when mules ferried Kalaupapa's basic supplies. Around each object I scoured the trail with a falcon-like, circular search pattern, combing every inch of accessible ground on and off the trail. Nothing. In some places where the cliff dropped off too steeply, my search covered the narrow footpath alone. Still nothing.

Kaluna and I marched silently, scanning the trail as we covered the remaining few hundred feet. At the last switchback before Kalaupapa, the *paniolo* broke the silence.

"Eh, Kai, try look ovah deah. You see dat t'ing?" He pointed to a faint gleam about five strides off the trail. "What dat?"

I followed his finger, squatting to get a better look. The dully glimmering object lay on rocky soil under thick dwarf *kiawe,* so dense we would have to crawl on our bellies to fetch it.

I squinted to bring the subject into focus. "Look like one plastic bag reflecting da sun."

"I go take one closah look." Kaluna stepped off the trail.

"Might only be *'ōpala*–trash." I got down on my hands and knees. "But we no can afford to pass up nut'ing."

Kaluna stopped me. "I go."

"What fo'? Have to slither like one gecko under dat brush."

"*'A'ole pilikia*–no problem. I do it for Coco."

Kaluna crouched down and crawled. His black felt cowboy hat flopped off under the first low *kiawe* branch. He kept crawling until he was out of sight except for his well-worn boot soles. I remembered I had brought my camera and snapped a few pictures, in case this led to the discovery of evidence we might use.

Suddenly a long, slithering insect darted toward Kaluna's hand like an undulating snake. It had countless tiny feet moving in waves. Kaluna let out a whoop.

"You O.K.?" I called.

"Centipede! Da buggah is on me!"

I knew too well the centipede's painful and poisonous bite, which can send even a strong man like Kaluna to the hospital. When I crouched down to check on the guide, the many-legged insect was weaving its way across the trail.

"Dat was one close one!" Kaluna shouted back through the *kiawe* boughs. "Da centipede ran ovah my hand, but he nevah sting."

"Come out of dere before you get hurt, bruddah."

"Jus' anoddah few feet to da kine—plastic bag or whatevah." He edged toward the elusive gleam. I heard him groan as he apparently stretched out his hand. "Got da bag!"

"Plastic bag?" I asked. "What's in it?"

"Hū!" Kaluna slid out from under the brush with a weathered Ziploc bag containing three spent syringes. Though mist and rain had fallen throughout this last month, inside that sealed bag the syringes remained dry as bone.

I dared to hope for usable fingerprints.

twenty-two

Kaluna and I continued down the trail to Kalaupapa and searched the village for more clues. Fruitlessly. Later we hiked back up with our only potential evidence: three spent syringes.

At the trailhead we stopped to quench our thirst and catch our breath. I told Kaluna I needed another favor.

"Now what I goin' ask may sound *lōlō*—crazy, you know—but I gotta ask." I peered into the mule guide's eyes.

"Jus' ask."

"We gotta exhume Coco."

"Do what fo' Coco?" His brow furrowed.

"Dig 'em up," I said. "You can get one backhoe from da Moloka'i Ranch, eh?"

"'Ae. But goin' take a while fo' put da backhoe on da trailer and haul 'em hea."

"How long?"

"Two, t'ree hours."

"Den how long fo' dig up da grave?"

"T'irty minutes," he said. "Counting da shovel work, too. But no mattah." He grinned. "I put 'em in hea', I can dig 'em out."

"Jus' one more t'ing. You got one veterinarian?"

Kaluna nodded. "Dr. Wyllie."

"Call Dr. Wyllie." I checked my watch. "Almost noon now. Ask 'em if he like come hea' at . . ."

"Not *he*," Kaluna interrupted. "Dr. Wyllie one *wahine*."

"O.K.—ask her if she can come at t'ree."

"What reason I goin' give?"

"Blood test fo' Coco." With my forefinger I made a needle-like gesture poking his arm. "We gonna send da blood to one mainland lab fo' drug check."

Kaluna dashed up the winding red road to the phone in the mule stable. I followed, then hopped into my rented car and raced back to Kaunakakai.

Drugs and drug paraphernalia pointed first to the doctor, obviously. But while Benjamin Goto had the means, he seemed to have less motive than the other suspects. This, coupled with the fact that just about anyone can possess syringes and illegal drugs, kept my attention focused on the others.

Did Milton Yu trade in harder drugs than *pakalōlō*? Did Heather Linborg dabble in dope? Did the wealthy Parke partake with her? And might Emery Archibald's proclivity for drugs be revealed through the identity of his secret companion? Trying to picture the stiff Rush McWhorter shooting up strained my imagination, but he might well have worked behind the scenes. No matter, I would cast my net wide to catch the guilty—be it one or all.

I was still mentally casting that net when I pulled up to the Moloka'i Beach Hotel. I made a quick call to check on Adrienne—still no change—then approached the front desk. My request to see the housemaid Mele had suggested I interview was greeted with a scowl. The new receptionist on duty seemed to instantly dislike me.

"Raine will not see you," she said, hands defiantly on hips.

Was it my sweat-glazed face or my rank T-shirt and board shorts?

"There must be some mistake," I tried to explain. "You see, last night Mele said . . ."

The scowling lady interrupted. "Don't play games. I know who you are."

"I'm Kai Cooke." I handed her my card. "I've never met Raine."

She glanced at the card. "You're not baby Kanoe's father?"

"I'm a private detective."

She eyed me up and down. "You don't look like a private detective."

"I've just come from Kalaupapa. I'm working on a case that Raine could help solve. Now, would you please call her?"

"She's cleaning the beachfront cottages." The receptionist pointed. "Over there."

Among the dozen or so beachside cottages, I found one with the door opened to a housekeeping cart. I knocked, then walked in. An attractive local woman with raven hair was snugging a fitted sheet over a queen-sized bed.

"Raine?"

She glanced up warily. Her forehead shone with beads of perspiration.

"Mele suggested I talk with you about a case I'm working on." I gave her my card. "I'm a private detective."

Raine handed back the card without looking at it. "If Moku sent you about custody of Kanoe, you can forget it."

"I have no client named Moku," I assured her. "In fact, I rarely work on Moloka'i. I'm only here to investigate the death of a Honolulu woman on the Kalaupapa cliffs."

"Oh, da mule accident?" Raine's expression changed, and so did her speech. "Why you nevah say so?"

"Maybe you like help me wit' da case?" I replied in kind, heartened at a possible breakthrough.

"Last night Mele wen' show me in da hotel registah da name Archibald. He wen' stay in one oceanfront cottage wit' anoddah man guy name Stevens. Dey come Septembah t'ird and stay t'rough da seventh. You can remembah dem?"

"Was more than one mont' ago," Raine said. "Plenny guest come since den."

"Maybe dese two guest particulah. Maybe call attention to demselves?" I tried to jog her memory.

"What dis Archibald look like?"

"Slender *haole*. 'Bout forty. He wear fancy kine glasses–tortoiseshell–and dress elegant. Pinstripe suit. Scarf. Dat kine stuffs."

"Hmmm . . ." Raine was thinking.

"Oh, almost forget. He wear one spicy masculine cologne."

"I t'ink I remembah da man you call Archibald."

"What you remembah?"

"I t'ink he and da oddah guy–dat Stevens–dey *māhū*."

"Māhū?" I wondered if she had the wrong pair. "Da two men gay?"

"Two *men?"* Raine raised her raven brows. "One was only boy."

"Stevens was one boy?"

"Nineteen, twenty, max. Big muscles, you know. Liked fo' show them off. And da tattoo of one knife on his arm. How I forget dat?"

Stephan's bloody dagger. Suddenly it came to me. Stevens was Archibald's young assistant. I recalled Archibald's nervousness around the boy in my presence.

"Archibald and da boy wen' take drugs?" I tried to make a connection to the three syringes.

"I dunno," Raine said. "I nevah see dat kine in da room."

"Dey act funny kine," I said, "like maybe under da influence?"

Raine shook her head. "Dat's all I can remembah."

"Thanks, eh? You've been a big help."

I wished I could have thanked Raine with cash—to help with her baby—but if she were deposed to testify, the first thing the defense attorney would ask was if she had been given anything in exchange for her testimony. A potentially valuable witness might be erased. I could over-tip a bartender with impunity, but slipping a few bills to a chamber maid in a hotel where I was not a guest was another matter.

I said goodbye to Raine, wondering why Archibald's young friend hadn't taken the mule tour that day. Upon reflection, the answer seemed clear. For his business' sake, Archibald probably wouldn't want to have been seen with the boy.

Driving back toward Kalaupapa, I tried to sort things out. Archibald had come to Moloka'i, at least in part, to enjoy his muscular young assistant. So what did it mean? Was Archibald merely a middle-aged family man who sought an exotic getaway with his paramour? Or was he, and perhaps Stephan, connected to the *hui?* Since Archibald's travel business depended on Hawai'i tourism, he had some slim motive of his own to silence the woman bent on derailing Kalaupapa Cliffs. Maybe the *hui* had something on him, or he owed them a favor.

Archibald could not be ruled out. I stomped the accelerator and darted toward the cliffs of Kalaupapa.

twenty-three

When I returned to the trailhead, Kaluna had already dug a big hole. He sat up high at the controls of a dull orange backhoe, its long, thundering claw tearing away at the grave. Red earth surrounded the deepening pit.

Next to the grave stood a wispy woman with delicate features and angel-fine hair. She was young–fresh from veterinary school, I imagined–and looked more like a violinist than a large-animal vet.

When Kaluna saw me, he shut off the earthmoving machine and climbed down. I introduced myself to Dr. Wyllie, who extended her doll-sized hand, saying "Hello" in a surprisingly strong voice. Kaluna carried his shovel to the open grave and began spading gingerly around the edges.

"Mr. Cooke, you would like blood drawn from the dead mule?" she asked.

I nodded. "I'll be sending the blood to a California lab for analysis."

"And how long has the animal been buried?"

"One mont'," Kaluna said from Coco's grave, pitching out a shovel of red earth.

Dr. Wyllie frowned. "In this hot, humid weather, the mule may be decomposing by now. I'll be lucky to find a single vein."

"We need a blood sample to prove the mule was drugged." I showed her the three syringes in the sealed plastic bag.

"These are 3-cc syringes," she explained, "used more often on humans than large animals."

"Whoever did this probably wasn't a vet."

Dr. Wyllie's frown deepened. "I'll see what I can do." The slight doctor walked toward the backhoe, its orange claw now resting on mounds of red earth surrounding the open grave.

Down in the pit with the dead mule, Kaluna tossed up one last shovel of damp soil. Hands covering his nose from the stench, the *paniolo's* eyes were watering.

"Dat's Coco," he choked out. "But not like I bury him."

Kaluna had cleared off enough red dirt so that we could see what was left of the carcass. As he climbed out, I peered in. The stench was unbearable. All I could discern of the animal was a mere skeleton covered by a thin hide. His once-rounded haunches and broad girth of muscle and fat and fur were gone. If there were any blood in the veins of that carcass, if there were any veins at all, I would count it a miracle. Kaluna walked slowly to the precipice overlooking Kalaupapa. He gazed silently at the distant village.

Dr. Wyllie pulled an empty syringe from her bag, then donned a surgical mask and latex gloves. She climbed down into the grave and began searching for veins. I pulled out my camera and photographed her as she checked from rump to muzzle, then shook her head and climbed out again.

"No veins we can use." The pale doctor looked relieved as she pulled down her surgical mask and began to remove her latex gloves. "Maybe a week or two ago, but not now."

Without a blood sample showing Coco had been drugged, my case was fast slipping away. I tried to think.

"Wait!" I motioned to Dr. Wyllie to keep on her gloves. "Are the mule's vital organs intact—liver and kidney and all?"

"I can't say," she replied warily. "I'd have to surgically open the carcass." Dr. Wyllie flashed that sweet frown again.

"I'm just remembering a case," I explained. "A Kaua'i man found in a pineapple field—dead for more than a month. He yielded up a liver with enough blood to show evidence of drugs."

"Well, if you want to go to that extreme, blood in the liver stores drug residues at ten times the concentration of blood in the veins."

"Perfect." Now I was hopeful again. "All we need is the mule's liver."

Dr. Wyllie was now grimacing. She didn't seem to relish the assignment, but began removing surgical instruments from her medical bag—scalpels, clamps, some other stainless tools. She snapped her surgical mask back into place, snugged her latex gloves, and again climbed into the hole. I took more photos as she cut along Coco's gut, opening a gaping cavity under the ribs. When she lifted the severed hide, the stench that emerged was beyond foul. Despite the stink, I made myself move in closer to snap more photos.

In a little while the petite vet climbed from the grave with grime and gore from her fingertips to her elbows. That nasty death smell followed her. But she had delivered the trophy. In her hands was a liver the size of a football. It looked in amazingly good shape.

Dr. Wyllie said nothing. She seemed in a somber mood.

"Are you all right?" I asked.

She nodded and removed her gory gloves, her strong voice fading. "This was my first surgery on a dead mule."

"And I bet you hope it's your last."

She gestured to the grimy organ. "To send this liver to California, you'll need a Styrofoam mailer. And an ice pack wouldn't hurt . . ." She paused. "I've got a mailer in my van, but the ice pack you'll have to find elsewhere."

"I'll pick one up in Honolulu. I'm catching the next flight out."

I stepped to where Kaluna stood, still gazing down at the distant sea. Though in a hurry to take my prize back to Honolulu, I didn't rush the mule guide. For him, opening the grave had evidently opened old wounds.

I put my arm on Kaluna's shoulder. "Coco nevah make da *wahine,* Sara, go *hala,*" I said. "Was not his fault."

"*Mahalo,* Kai." He smiled slightly. "If you nevah come hea to *nīele,* to nose around, I always wonder 'bout Coco. Now I know. He stay one good mule."

Kaluna climbed onto the backhoe and began covering his mule with red earth, while Dr. Wyllie and I hiked up the winding dirt road to the stables. She placed the oversized liver into a plastic bag fetched from her van, then put the sealed bag in a Styrofoam mailer. Next to the liver, in another of the doctor's plastic bags, I set in one of the three syringes Kaluna had found on the trail.

I had the veterinarian handwrite a statement summarizing her procedures, which I took with me on my flight back to

Honolulu. A few fellow passengers eyed curiously the box in my lap. Fortunately, the liver's unspeakable odor was trapped inside.

The Twin-Otter landed in Honolulu at four-thirty. I rushed to a drugstore to buy an ice pack, then back to the airport, barely beating FedEx's five o'clock deadline to fly my parcel overnight to San Francisco. I debated showering off the day's filth before visiting Adrienne. All things considered, it seemed unimportant. When I got to her hospital room, I found her as I had left her—pale, cool, and breathing slowly. I reassured both of us aloud that I was making progress toward vindicating her sister.

"We're going to win," I told her. "And you're going to wake up to share in the celebration."

Back at my Waikīkī apartment, two phone messages awaited: one from Niki, which, like her photo, I tried to ignore; the second was from Archibald, who now recalled that although all four mule riders had taken the Kalaupapa bus tour, the overweight physician, Dr. Goto, had asked to be dropped off early at the restroom near the tethered mules. The doctor had apparently apologized profusely, regretting that he had drunk too much water after the hot ride down.

The suspect with the least motive, Dr. Goto was, however, most likely to possess the means to sedate Coco—syringes and drugs. After dropping out of the bus tour, he could have slipped among the mules, eluded Kaluna, and injected Coco. But why?

Goto's complicity wasn't a scenario I had much envisioned. Regardless, I needed the doctor's fingerprints, and the sooner the better. If Goto's prints matched those on the three syringes, the case was nearly solved. Drug evidence linking the syringes to the mule's collapse would be the clincher. But I wasn't banking on the solution being this easy. Besides, maybe Archibald was attempting to shift suspicion from himself, if only to keep my nose out of his private life. Or maybe the paunchy Goto really had been dehydrated.

Later that night I crawled into bed with the evening *Star-Bulletin*. On the front page, a story secured one more piece of this complex puzzle—Baron Taniguchi's bloated body had been found floating in Honolulu Harbor. He had been shot, execution style, in the head.

twenty-four

Before sunrise Tuesday morning, I phoned the California lab that does my blood work. Though barely twilight in Honolulu, the laboratory technicians at Bio-Tech in Daly City had already taken their mid-morning coffee break.

The lab manager, Ernie, confirmed that the Styrofoam mailer had arrived that morning by FedEx. Elaborating on my transmittal letter, I explained that the enclosed syringe probably contained traces of the suspected drug. I suggested a sedative such as morphine.

What I needed, I added, was the drug identified in both the blood and the syringe. The job was rush. Even though blood samples sent from Hawai'i normally took a week or more to analyze, I needed results in two days.

The manager laughed. "You've got to be kidding, Kai. We have a two-week backlog. Besides, the comprehensive drug screen takes several days—even if we didn't have a backlog."

"Just test for morphine. It's a strong hunch I have."

"Then you want only the presumptive opiate test?"

"Yes—and fast."

"With luck we might complete that test in two days, if we had no backlog."

"I'll call you Wednesday afternoon for the results."

"You can call whenever you like, Kai." He laughed again. "But that doesn't guarantee . . ."

"Ernie, this is life or death."

"We've got a half dozen jobs like that!"

I took a long, deep breath. "I'm in big trouble, Ernie. You've got to help me out."

He was silent for a moment. "I'll see what I can do."

I hung up the phone. The Land Zoning Board's charade hearing to approve the Chancellor Trust resort was only three days away. By Thursday, at the latest, I needed to present my case against the *hui* to the FBI. Then a federal judge might suspend the hearing pending an investigation–that is, if I got the crucial blood evidence by Thursday. Without it, neither the FBI nor a federal judge was likely to buy a loony story about murder by mule drugging.

As the rising sun peeked above the misty Ko'olau Mountains and flooded my *lānai,* I dialed the office of Dr. Benjamin Goto. He wasn't in at this early hour, so I left a message:

"Dr. Goto, could you see me briefly today? I'd appreciate your help in identifying a suspect in the Sara Ridgely-Parke case. Please leave a message at my office as to your best time. *Mahalo."*

Whether or not the doctor responded, I wanted to be ready for him. With a fingerprint kit I keep in my flat I dusted the two remaining syringes. The Ziploc bag containing them, as I had hoped, also preserved several prints. Using pressure-wound tape, I pulled each print off the syringes and fixed it on a three-by-five card. This resulted in six cards containing reasonably good prints—whether Goto's or one of the other suspects. Perhaps by this afternoon I would know.

Before leaving for the hospital to visit Adrienne, I grabbed Niki's photo from my nightstand. I removed Sara's speech from where it was still sandwiched between the snapshot and its cardboard backing. Then with glass cleaner and paper towels, I sprayed and polished the framed photo until it shone like mirror. I slipped Niki's gleaming snapshot in a paper bag and placed the bag, along with my fingerprint kit, the syringes, and Sara's speech, in my briefcase.

By eight that morning, I was heading for the Halekōkua Medical Center. Cruising along the Ala Wai Canal, I glimpsed the smoke grey van in my rearview mirror. Trying to lose it seemed pointless, since the *hui* most likely knew where I was going. I turned right onto the McCully Street bridge, crossed the canal, then steered my Impala *mauka* toward the hospital on Punahou Street. When my destination became clear, the van dropped back and turned off on a side street.

I detoured to a one-hour photo shop at King and University streets, and dropped off the pictures I had snapped on Moloka'i of Kaluna discovering the three syringes and Dr. Wyllie extracting Coco's liver. Along with the veterinarian's written statement, these photos would document the real cause of Sara's death. All that was left for me to do was uncover its agents.

At the hospital, Adrienne slept pale and quiet in her room—an oxygen tube still assisting her breathing and an IV dripping fluids into her arm. When I touched her hand, her skin was neither cold nor warm. She seemed precariously balanced between death and life.

I left her connected to this world through only a few tubes and that gritty, determined spirit of hers that had gotten me into this.

Driving back to Maunakea Street, I kept a close eye on my rearview mirror. No van. Its absence seemed almost more ominous than if the *hui* had kept right on my tail.

Along the way I picked up my Moloka'i photos. Clear. Unmistakable. Kaluna's slithering under *kiawe* bushes to fetch the Ziploc bag and Dr. Wyllie's removal of Coco's liver were frozen in time. I could still smell the stench from that grave.

Business was slow this Tuesday morning at Fujiyama's. Just one customer picked over strands of orchids in the refrigerated display cases. In the back, Chastity and Joon were stringing *pīkake* blooms. Such a fresh fragrance arose from that *pīkake* that I asked the *lei* girls to string three intertwined strands for Adrienne. One strand of *pīkake* traditionally represents friendship; three strands, the highest degree.

I climbed the stairs to my office and listened to my phone messages:

"Eh, brah, how much you charge fo' find one missing surfboard? One dumb dodo steal mine at Hale'iwa . . ."

One drawback of calling myself the "Surfing Detective." The next message made me more alert.

"This is Dr. Goto's office," said a crisp, businesslike receptionist. "The doctor can see you this afternoon at five o'clock."

Goto had taken the bait. Though I was a little surprised at the late hour of the appointment. Since he saw patients only from ten to two, I wondered why he was waiting until five.

I picked up my briefcase and locked my office behind me. Passing back through Mrs. Fujiyama's, I grabbed Adrienne's *lei*, and paced down Maunakea toward my bank, First O'ahu Savings on King Street, where a clerk ushered me into a private booth and retrieved my safe deposit box. From my briefcase I pulled each piece of evidence I had collected and put it into the safety box, retaining copies of the fingerprints I had dusted from the syringes.

It was nearly ten-thirty when I returned to my parking garage. With six hours until the interview with Dr. Goto, I did something not every detective would understand. I drove to the North Shore and went surfing.

At exactly five o'clock I was riding a mirrored elevator to the eighteenth floor of Goto's office building. The empty waiting room looked the same as before. But today, no one sat behind the desk.

Within moments of my arrival, the doctor himself emerged from his inner office. His pale skin, hanging jowls, and rounded belly did lend credibility to Archibald's report that Goto had to drop out of the Kalaupapa bus tour to relieve himself.

"Please come into my office, Mr. Cooke." Goto greeted me with his smiling almond eyes. "It's a pleasure to see you again." His cordiality, however, failed to conceal a hint of nervousness.

As Goto slipped behind his teak desk, I noticed the photo from Caesar's Palace was gone from his wall.

"Sorry about the short notice," I said, starting my spiel. "I'm grateful for your help in solving this case."

"Anything I can do," he said graciously. "My receptionist told me you wish to speak again about the unfortunate accident on Moloka'i."

"That's correct." I opened my briefcase, pulling out the paper bag containing the framed photo of Niki. I turned the picture toward him.

"That's an attractive young woman," Goto said, staring at Niki's string bikini and sexy smile.

"I'm hoping you can identify her."

He leaned forward, studying her face. "She doesn't look like the criminal type."

"Oh, you'd be surprised, doctor, what innocent-looking people can do." I handed him the photo. "Here, take a closer look."

Goto seemed to be trembling as he grabbed hold of the clean glass.

"Did you see this woman on Moloka'i on the day of Sara Ridgely-Parke's death?"

"She looks vaguely familiar."

"Go ahead. Take your time."

The doctor squinted at Niki's smiling face. "It's funny," he finally said. "I fly quite often to medical conferences on the mainland. Denver. Chicago. Indianapolis. This woman looks like a flight attendant I've seen on several trips."

"That so?" I cringed. I hadn't thought Goto would actually recognize Niki. "You also fly to Las Vegas, don't you?" I tried to change the subject.

Dr. Goto frowned. "Not anymore." His guard, which had been perceptibly relaxing as my questions focused away from him, now went back up.

"Sorry I can't do any better with your suspect." He handed back the photo.

"Thanks for trying." I slipped it back into the paper bag, then tucked the bag in my brief case.

Dr. Goto rose, signaling that the interview had ended.

"May I ask just one more question before I leave?"

"Surely." He seemed to brace himself slightly.

"It was reported that you did not complete the Kalaupapa bus tour—that you were dropped off early to use the restroom. Is that correct?"

"I'm embarrassed to say, yes." Goto smiled self-consciously. "I was quite dehydrated after the long, hot mule ride and I drank a large quantity of water to compensate."

"How did you occupy yourself while the others completed the tour?"

"I sat down and rested, of course."

"Near the mules?" I studied his face.

He winked playfully. "I stayed upwind of the mules, if you know what I mean."

"Thank you, Doctor." I headed for the door.

"My pleasure." He made a little bow.

I saw myself out with Niki's photo, covered with Goto's prints, tucked safely in my briefcase. My hunch was that the doctor was attempting a mediocre acting job. Now with his prints all over my frame, I would finally know for sure.

In the parking lot below Goto's mirrored tower, I unlocked my Impala and set the briefcase next to Adrienne's *pīkake lei* on the front seat. I was so elated about getting the doctor's fingerprints, I didn't see the smoke grey van pull up behind me.

twenty-five

Three big mokes–huge, meaty local boys–yanked me from my Impala and tossed me into the van. Before I had stopped rolling around in the back, we were speeding down Ala Moana Boulevard toward Waikīkī.

One of the big men sat in back with me, where there were no seats, blocking the van's sliding door. He must have tipped the scales at three hundred, easy. None of the mokes spoke to me. I said nothing to them. A warm, salty-tasting liquid dripped down my face. *Blood.* I must have cut my forehead.

As the van slowed in traffic along Waikīkī Beach–where camera-toting tourists awaited another perfect sunset–then curved around Diamond Head and its lavish seaside estates, I began to doubt my hunches on this case. J. Gregory Parke I had least suspected. But now that we were headed for Kāhala– his ritzy neighborhood–I wondered. Could Parke be behind all this? And was it an ominous sign that none of my abductors took the slightest precaution to conceal our route from me?

Suddenly the van turned off Diamond Head Road short of Parke's colonial castle, headed *makai* down a palm-lined private lane, then pulled up to an imposing black wrought-iron gate with a dozen spikes shaped like the ace of spades. The gate opened automatically and the van glided over flagstones onto the grounds of a magnificent oceanfront estate.

My captors unloaded me, still without saying a word. The only sounds were the clacking of coconut palm fronds along the secluded beach and the constant splash of waves.

The mansion looked Mediterranean, with bright white walls and red tile roof that might have pleased my eyes under other circumstances. Surrounding us were expansive tropical gardens, black granite pool and spa, and clay tennis courts encircled by those whispering palms. A four-car carriage house, with only one door open, revealed a flame red Lamborghini. The exotic Italian machine displayed a personalized plate: "Manny."

Manny Lee, my cousin Alika's famous uncle, had not laid eyes on me since I was a little *keiki*. I faintly recalled him singing *"Aloha 'Oe,"* that familiar Hawaiian song of farewell, at my parents' funeral. Halfway through, his voice broke. The international star—and local tough guy—overcome by emotion.

I was taken to a marble *lānai* overlooking the sea, where he reclined on a chaise lounge, nursing a high ball. Manny was fifty-ish. His long hair black, but turning salt-and-pepper. Pixie-like face of Hawaiian and Chinese aspect, youthful considering the life it had seen. Gold chain around his neck and gold Hawaiian bracelet on one wrist emblazoned with his name.

Manny said to the biggest of the three mokes, "Bobo, t'anks, eh?"

As the trio walked away, my suspicions about the singer were instantly confirmed.

Manny Lee was a legend in and out of the islands. He was the most famous living Hawaiian pop singer, owner of multiple gold records. Tales of his exploits with women, with money, and with drink and drugs were legion. His association with underworld thugs made him feared. Messing with Manny—so it was said—led to broken bones. Of late, he had supposedly turned over the proverbial new leaf and become a leading investor in local enterprises.

He gestured to the *lānai* chair across from him. I sat. The setting sun glinted blindingly on three gold records visible in a nearby cabana and also starkly illuminated Manny's face. In the fiery orange glow he looked both saintly and devilish, a wayward spirit poised between the poles of goodness and evil. I gazed warily at this pop luminary, this aging star, this distant relation through marriage who had summoned me.

"Long time no see, Kai," said Manny in his melodious tones.

"Back when Mom and Dad died."

"I sang at their funeral," Manny recalled. "You just one *keiki* then, maybe too young to remembah."

"I remembah." I daubed a blood drop trickling down my forehead.

"Kai, family—*'ohana*—is important. You marry yet?"

I shook my head.

"Find one nice local girl. Raise some *keiki*. Living alone no good. I know." He winked.

"Thanks for the advice."

"One more piece of advice." Manny glanced toward his glinting gold disks, his eyes scouring the cabana as if searching for someone. "Kai, let da *wahine* who wen' fall from da mule on Moloka'i rest in peace."

I studied his illuminated face. "Stop my investigation?"

Manny again glanced away. "If you not one family membah, you awready be dead."

"Are you in the *hui?* With Zia and the rest?"

"Kai, I cannot make gold records forevah." He shrugged in a gesture of resignation, or maybe apology? "All entertainahs do business on da side. You be loyal and someday da *hui* cut you in, too."

I sat motionless, not wanting to believe what I was hearing.

"Take one vacation for a few days. My travel agent already book you in one oceanfront suite in Kona. First class. Meals and everyt'ing on me. Bobo give you da tickets when you leave."

"Go to Kona? What for?"

Manny peered into my eyes. "You stay in Kona until aftah Friday's zoning board hearing. You get 'um, Kai?"

"Yeah, I get 'um." At that moment I understood better than he could imagine—the arrogance of power that believes itself above the law.

"Your *'ohana* no like you die young, Kai. I doing this for dem. We all family and grow up close."

The three mokes trudged slowly into view like foraging bears. Manny rose and shook my hand. As the trio led me away in the dying sunset, Manny called in our direction.

"Kai, no forget. *'Ohana!*"

When I looked back, Manny was no longer alone. Another man, thin as a ghost and barely five feet tall in a white suit and aviator sunglasses, had emerged from the cabana and was whispering in his ear. They stood together in conspiratorial closeness, as the newcomer puffed on a brown cigarette whose raw, pungent odor I could smell from twenty feet away. Then it dawned on me: The other man was Umbro Zia.

Manny nodded to Zia in a gesture of reassurance as the two conversed in whispers. I assumed the nodding pertained to me. The *hui* had me, Manny was probably explaining to Zia. I would no longer interfere.

The mokes loaded me back into the grey van, more gently this time. The hefty driver, Bobo, handed me a packet stuffed with a first-class airline ticket, hotel voucher, and a wad of crisp green bills. Ben Franklins. Hundreds. Also inside on a handwritten slip was a Big Island phone number and a name, "Lani." Beneath that, in Manny's own hand: "Call Lani. She one *'ono* babe and she show you a good time."

I sat on the floor of the van next to a computer, monitor, and keyboard that hadn't been there before. The equipment resembled my stolen PC. As the van screeched up the flagstone driveway toward the automatic gate, I looked at the computer more closely. It *was* my PC.

The ride back to Goto's mirrored tower was uneventful. In the quiet, gathering darkness I contemplated the significance of my trip. Whatever Goto's role in the murder, whatever tangled relationships existed between Sara and Parke and McWhorter, there was no longer any doubt that the *hui* was at the center of it all.

The van pulled up to my car in the flood-lighted parking lot. As I climbed out, one of the mokes lifted the PC from the van and put it on the pavement. Before I could open my trunk, the van was gone.

My briefcase still sat miraculously on the front seat. I clicked the locks open. There was the bag with Niki's framed photo in it. The *hui* must have felt Manny's warning would be sufficient to send me packing to Kona. I loaded my computer into the trunk and drove to the hospital in a heady cloud of perfume from the *pīkake lei* I'd bought that morning for Adrienne.

By the time I reached her bedside that evening most visitors had already departed. Her stillness intensified the quiet. Drawing close to her, I explained that I knew now who had killed her sister. And I would be back soon, I said in farewell, to tell her how the rest of the business turned out. I kissed her unresponsive cheek, the same cool, pale white as the *pīkake* blossoms I placed in her open hand.

Before leaving the hospital, I called the Honolulu office of the FBI, closed for the night. I left a voice-mail message for an agent I knew named Javier. Not certain who might be listening in, I was deliberately vague:

"Bill, expect a fax from a mainland lab. I'll explain later."

Back at Mrs. Fujiyama's flower shop, I lugged my computer past the darkened display windows, around to the side door, and up the fire stairs to my office. Connecting the PC to its power and printer cables, I switched it on. All documents relating to the Ridgely-Parke case had been erased, while every other document remained. Neat job.

I shut down the computer, then turned to Niki's photo. If she only knew how much she was helping on this case. I dusted the glass and frame for fingerprints. There were several good ones. I checked them against the six cards containing prints from the syringes. They matched.

twenty-six

Until the sable hour of three the next morning, I mulled over the two options Manny had laid before me: Take an all-expenses-paid trip to Kona or get myself drilled.

I no longer doubted that the *hui* could do whatever it wanted with me. To stay on O'ahu was tantamount to suicide. Besides, I couldn't save the cliffs of Kalaupapa if I were dead.

That decided it. At 10:45 a.m. I would board the plane to Kona. *Holoholo, brah. Time fo' one pleasure trip.*

I packed a small duffel with just enough clothes for an overnight. Into my briefcase I put a microcassette tape recorder, then the cards containing Goto's fingerprints and Niki's photo covered with more of his prints. In a side pocket of the briefcase I slipped the airline tickets, hotel voucher, and Manny's cash. I also tucked in my Smith & Wesson. Something told me I might need it in the next forty-eight hours.

At seven I phoned Bio-Tech Labs. No results yet, but Ernie hoped to have a preliminary analysis by four in the afternoon, California time.

"Even if you don't hear from me again," I told him, "fax a copy of the blood work to Agent Javier, Honolulu office of the FBI."

By eight, I was heading for the Halekōkua Medical Center. Within two blocks the smoke grey van appeared behind me. Bobo and his pals must want to make sure I get to the airport on time. *How thoughtful.* They tailed me to the hospital, then pulled to the curb on Punahou Street when I turned into the garage.

I rode the elevator up to Adrienne's floor, passing the nurses' station as I walked down the hall to her room.

"Oh, Mr. Cooke!" said an animated nurse. "Good news. Ms. Ridgely opened her eyes this morning."

"Opened her eyes?" I was stoked.

"She hasn't spoken yet," the nurse said. "But Dr. Majerian is hopeful."

"Thank you." I rushed into Adrienne's room. Her eyes were closed again. She lay silent and motionless as she had for nearly a week, oxygen flowing to her through her tube. But where before her cheeks had been pale, now they showed hints of color. Her chestnut hair, too, seemed to have regained some of its luster. And her long, slender fingers curled around the *pīkake lei* I had brought last night, the fragrant white blossoms still breathing their perfume.

I sat with Adrienne for a half hour, wishing she would open her eyes—for her sake as well as mine. But that didn't happen.

Before leaving I clutched her hand, softer and warmer than before. Then a troubling thought occurred to me: What if Adrienne awoke and started talking about Kalaupapa Cliffs before Friday's hearing? How might the *hui* respond? They were watching her no doubt as closely as I was.

On my way out I explained to the on-duty nurse that for Adrienne's safety, we would need to order twenty-four hour protection—immediately. I called Island-Wide Security, who reassured me with military crispness that the first guard would arrive at the hospital within minutes.

I waited in the parking lot until the security car drove up, then pulled away from the hospital, aiming for the Mānoa Valley campus of the University of Hawai'i. The smoke grey van caught up with me after a block and tailgated me all the way there.

School was in session. Students on mopeds and in lowered Hondas that buzzed like angry bees swarmed the streets. I pulled into the law school parking lot. The van crawled by and found a nearby parking space.

From my briefcase I removed the microcassette recorder, set it to "voice activated," and slipped it into my shirt pocket. Ready, I stepped into the bunker-like complex of the law school and walked the narrow hallway to McWhorter's office, knocked, and waited. When his door finally swung open, he looked surprised. A Marlboro Light dangled from his lip.

"Well, the 'Surfing Detective.'" He stood up straight, puffing on his smoke. "To what do I owe . . ."

"So you remember me?"

"How could I forget?" He exhaled a hazy plume. "That surfer gimmick actually works."

McWhorter gestured to a chair, then slid behind his desk, silk aloha shirt framed by a leather throne. He puffed again and ran long fingers over his close-cropped hair.

"You know about Adrienne." I stated more than asked as my microcassette recorded our words.

"Terrible accident," McWhorter said in his high, thin monotone. "Can you imagine someone hitting her and just driving away?"

"It wasn't an accident," I eyed him. "No more than Sara's death was an accident. Or your student, Baron Taniguchi's."

"I wouldn't know," McWhorter coolly replied.

"No need to play games anymore. The *hui* has bought me off, too. They're sending me to Kona—all expenses paid—until after Friday's hearing on Kalaupapa Cliffs."

"Then you're easily bought off, Mr. Surfing Detective."

"What choice did I have? They would have dumped me in the harbor like Baron Taniguchi."

"I thought surfers were bold and brave."

"Surfers *are* brave, but not crazy—at least not this one. Anyway, you're the key figure in all this, not me."

He dragged on his Marlboro Light, his face as fixed as a plaster mask.

"The *hui* could never have gotten Sara or Baron Taniguchi without you. You hacked into Sara's computer and intercepted her email. That's how you discovered her Moloka'i itinerary and Baron's fishing trip to Bamboo Ridge."

McWhorter rocked back and blew more smoke. "They should have known better than to send confidential messages by email."

"You conveyed those messages straight to the Chancellor Trust." I tried to get him to echo or at least elaborate on my incriminations.

"I'm the trust's legal counsel," McWhorter said, not biting. "Had I found such vital documents—and I'm not saying I did—I couldn't very well withhold them."

"You did find some vital documents." I tried to keep him talking. "But you missed one–a crucial one."

Tiny cracks appeared in his plaster. I'd hit a nerve.

"I didn't say I found anything," McWhorter repeated. "If I had considered violating the law by going through Sara's records, it would have been merely to save her reputation. She had a private life you wouldn't imagine."

"Wasn't it your own reputation you were trying to save? Sara rejected you. She turned you away. That's why you had to get even after she married Parke. That's why you tipped off the *hui* about her trip to Moloka'i."

"Pure fiction."

"Then why did Dr. Goto just yesterday accuse you of orchestrating Sara's murder?" I had to make something up to widen those cracks in his plaster mask.

McWhorter snuffed his cigarette in the ashtray, then lit another. "It's no secret that 'quack' Goto owes the *hui* big time for his Vegas gambling debts. He would say anything to dig himself out."

"So Goto killed Sara to pay off gambling debts?"

"You can draw your own conclusions."

I looked at my watch. Nine thirty. "Maybe we can continue this conversation later. I've got a plane to catch."

I walked from his smoky office into the fresher air of the hall. While his cleverly worded responses probably wouldn't hold up as evidence against him, he had certainly provided a motive for Goto's role in Sara's murder.

twenty-seven

Keeping an eye on the van in my rearview mirror, I headed toward my bank on King Street as I replayed the taped conversation with McWhorter. His high voice came through as clearly as if he were sitting next to me. Satisfied, I popped out the cassette and deposited it in my bank box along with the other pieces of evidence.

By the time I turned back onto Nimitz Highway, both hands of the Aloha Tower clock were pointing to ten. I would just make my 10:45 flight to Kona.

I took the airport ramp, Bobo and his friends close behind. They parked a few spaces from my car in the inter-island garage, then followed me on foot to the elevator. At least they let me ride up to the terminal alone, but while checking in for my flight, I saw them lurking behind me again. *Are they going with me to Kona?*

As the ticket agent checked me in, I slipped an inter-island flight schedule into my briefcase.

"When is the last flight tonight from Hilo to Maui?" I asked in nearly a whisper.

The agent checked her computer monitor. "10:25 p.m., sir. Would you like me to hold you a seat?"

"No, thanks." I didn't want my name to appear on any reservation list. I took my ticket and briefcase, then walked toward the restrooms. The mokes split off from the passenger line without going through check-in.

Inside the men's restroom, a quick check revealed that I was alone except for one man in a toilet stall. Near the washbasins, a stainless steel trash receptacle–recently emptied by a custodian–stood against the tiled wall. It was the typical arrangement: a plastic liner set inside the stainless container. I lifted the nearly empty liner and pulled it out. At the bottom of the container lay a dozen extra liners, folded in neat little squares and stacked one upon the other. Opening my briefcase, I removed the Smith & Wesson and wrapped it in one of the liners, then placed the heavy package at the bottom of the neat stack.

My bet was that this trash bin wouldn't be emptied again for a while, and if it was, the gun probably wouldn't be noticed. I'd be returning for it soon anyway.

At 10:40, with the three mokes looking on, I ambled down the jetway onto a Boeing 737 bound for Kona. As Manny Lee had promised, my seat was in first class–a wide leather easy chair. I declined the complimentary cocktail, opting instead for guava punch. With less than forty-eight hours until the Kalaupapa Cliffs hearing, I needed a clear head.

Under the morning sun, the lush, surf-washed islands of Moloka'i, Lāna'i, and Maui shone like emeralds against the sapphire sea. The approach to Kona, by contrast, revealed a black wasteland of charred lava, the runway a thin white line etched in surrounding darkness. Though I had landed at Kona many times before, on this trip the black landscape looked especially foreboding.

The Boeing touched down smooth as silk. Inside the terminal a man in a chauffeur's uniform held an official-looking sign: Royal Kona Resort–Mr. Kai Cooke. The chauffeur retrieved my duffel from the luggage cart and escorted me to a black town car limo whose license plates said "Royal K." I climbed in.

The Royal Kona Resort was draped in coral pink bougainvillea and overlooked Keauhou Bay and its tide pools, which contained petroglyphs carved by ancient Hawaiians. Strolling the hotel's open-air lobby, I kept an eye out for signs of the *hui. Would Manny leave me alone in Kona? Doubtful.*

Once the bellboy ushered me into my suite, it was clear that Manny had forked out quite a sum for this little "vacation." My oceanfront room fronted the historic tide pools and rumbling surf. The view, as the tour books say, was breathtaking. Too bad I couldn't stick around and enjoy it.

Less than a minute after the bellboy had pocketed his tip–a five from Manny's stash–the phone rang.

"Kai," said the melodious voice, "you like da suite?"

"Manny, you really shouldn't have."

"Call Lani yet?"

"I just walked in the door."

"Lani's *'ono.*" Manny sounded like he knew firsthand just how delicious she was.

"I'll give her a call."

"Once you see Lani, brah, you nevah want to leave Kona— *nevah!*" There was a pause. "Remembah, Kai . . ." Manny suddenly turned serious. "You're your Mamma's *keiki*."

I groped for an appropriate reply. Too late. *Click.* He was gone.

I sat on my *lānai* for more than an hour watching the surf spray the tide pools and wondering how to get aboard tonight's last flight from Hilo to Maui. Once I landed on Maui, I could sack out at the airport and catch the first flight on Thursday morning to Honolulu. Making it to the Hilo airport tonight was the problem. The *hui* would be watching. And if they caught me escaping from Kona, I doubted if even Manny himself could spare my life.

Later that afternoon while walking the grounds of the resort, I kept glancing behind me. Nobody. The *hui* was playing cagey. I wandered past tennis courts, a curving *koa* bar, then the narrow ribbon of black sand between tide pools. Still seeing no one, I doubled back to a pay phone by the bar and placed a call.

"Bio-Tech Labs," said a harried-sounding receptionist.

"Kai Cooke calling for Ernie DiBello."

"One moment . . ."

I checked my watch. It was nearly two in Hawai'i. That meant almost five in California. This would be my last chance today to get results from the blood analysis on Kaluna's mule. Since tomorrow, Thursday, I needed to turn over this crucial piece of evidence to the FBI, time was running out.

"Hello, Kai," Ernie answered. "The final report isn't ready yet, but preliminary results on the mule's liver indicate Demerol."

"Demerol?"

"It's a synthetic morphine commonly used as a sedative in humans, but seldom in such high concentrations."

"What did you find in the syringe?"

"Same thing–Demerol."

"You're the best, Ernie. I owe you a Mai Tai on Waikīkī Beach."

"I'm going to show up in paradise someday, Kai, to take you up on that offer," Ernie said, laughing.

"Fax that report to the FBI by tomorrow morning and I'll throw in a dinner, too."

"The Feds will have it tomorrow." Ernie hung up.

Returning to my room I noticed someone watching me. The man stood in the shadow of a planter ablaze with red ginger. He wasn't a big local guy like Manny's three mokes. He was *haole,* pale and thin. He could have been merely a mainland visitor, but the way he watched me suggested otherwise. When I glanced back from the elevator lobby, the man was gone.

Back in my suite I picked up the phone and dialed the number Manny had given me.

"Aloha . . ." answered a breathy voice.

"Lani?"

"Who's calling?" she asked playfully, as if she already knew.

"Kai Cooke. Manny Lee suggested I call you."

"Can't wait to meet you, Kai!" She sounded almost sincere. "Manny told me all about you."

"He's told me a lot about you, too. How about dinner tonight?"

"No need to ask. I'll pick you up at quarter to six. Everything's been arranged."

"Everything?"

"Well, just the dinner." Lani giggled. "What happens afterward is up to you."

twenty-eight

With three hours until Lani arrived, I swam and sunned at the resort's beach. My shadow stayed hidden at first. Then, reclining in a lounge chair behind the *Hawaiʻi Tribune Herald,* the thin man briefly exposed his pale face. He didn't look like he was having much fun.

When I left the beach at five, the man followed me. I stopped in at the ABC Store off the hotel's lobby, bought a woman's sun hat, and carried it away in a shopping bag. The thin man watched me from outside the store, then followed me to the elevators.

Up in my room I showered and dressed for dinner in front of the TV. The local news carried a slanted report on the Kalaupapa Cliffs project. Two supposed Molokaʻi residents spoke in favor of the resort, both too slick to be believed.

The reporter mentioned Friday's Land Zoning Board hearing as the last step to approval of the development, as if approval were a foregone conclusion. No one from the coalition had been interviewed, nor was the coalition survey mentioned that showed 94 percent of Moloka'i's residents opposed the project. And, of course, no death toll was given.

At twenty minutes to six I rode the elevator to the lobby and stood outside by the valets waiting for Lani. The setting sun backlighted the tide pools in a butterscotch glow. A few minutes later she pulled up in a silver Porsche, waving through the sunroof. She screeched to the curb.

Slipping into the leather bucket on the passenger side, its soft hides reeking of newness, I offered her my hand. Lani warmed mine with both of hers and looked me square in the eyes.

"Manny didn't tell me you were so young."

"I'm thirty-four," I said, inhaling her heavy floral perfume. "I must have ten years on you."

Lani giggled. "I'll show you a good time."

She gunned the Porsche and we launched from the Royal Kona Hotel like a rocket. Suddenly I noticed on the dash the ominous word *turbo*.

"*Ono*," Manny had called her. I could see why. Luminous eyes, jet black hair, slender tanned limbs. She looked wholesome, almost innocent. Her sweet perfume magnified this impression. But the plunging neckline of her black cocktail dress and her heavy eye shadow undercut it.

Lani ripped along the waterfront toward Kona around curves at a pace that would have flipped an ordinary car. She reeved that turbocharged 911 through its countless gears.

"I *love* to go fast," she said. "But I'm just learning to drive the Porsche . . ."

No truer words could have been spoken. I braced myself around each curve as Lani talked nonstop. She must have had a drink or two before picking me up. In a short span I learned that she had met Manny once when he performed in Kona. They hit it off. Soon she found herself on the singer's payroll, "entertaining" him and his guests when they visited the Big Island. It was a strange story. And a sad story. Though Lani probably didn't think so.

On one hair-raising turn, I popped opened the Porsche's glove box. Inside were two CDs, an Almond Joy candy bar, some loose condoms, and a Big Island map. I closed it back up and glanced behind us. Nobody. Was the thin man already at the restaurant? Or did he trust Manny's girl to chaperone me?

Lani pulled up to the Windjammer, a trendy Kona seafood spot along Ali'i Drive that resembled a yacht pointed into the breakers. She emerged from her car with a large black sequined handbag that matched her cocktail dress. She was a tall, statuesque woman—quite tall for a local girl—within a few inches of my own height.

Winding our way through the bustling restaurant—appointed with the spars and beams and fixtures of a seagoing galley—we emerged onto the bow deck overlooking the twilight surf. Lani ordered a Mai Tai and I, a beer. Our drinks arrived as we scanned the long menu. I also continued to scan the restaurant for the thin man. No sign of him.

Lani wasted no time putting away her Mai Tai. When the waiter arrived, she asked for another. We ordered dinner and a bottle of Chardonnay, then chatted as Lani slugged down her second drink. She was already getting a little woozy.

By the time our entrees came Lani was well into the wine. Her cheeks blushed like ripe mangos.

"Kai . . ." Lani smiled coyly and gripped my hand. "I . . . li-like yooo."

The more she drank, the more she slurred. Despite her undeniable allure, I felt sorry for Lani. She had gotten caught in Manny Lee's web. A new Porsche, some cash, and no doubt a condo by the sea had been her payment. I wondered if ten years down the road Lani might concede she had made a mistake. Her heavy drinking made me suspect that already she had an inkling.

By the time we finished dessert, Lani was in no shape to drive. I paid the check with one of Manny's hundreds, then eased her limp body into the passenger seat. She didn't seem to mind my driving her new car. I aimed the silver rocket back to the resort, getting a feel for its breathtaking acceleration. *Da buggah fly!*

Pulling into the resort, I skipped the valets and parked the car myself in a dim corner of the lot. I slipped her keys into my pocket and helped the weaving Lani up the elevator and into my suite.

Inside she stumbled into the bedroom and fell onto the king-sized bed, sprawling there with a naughty-girl look on her face.

She giggled, kicked off her sandals, and fumbled with the zipper of her black cocktail dress.

"I shooo yooo a good time . . ."

twenty-nine

Lani made a "come hither" gesture with her little finger. I played along, helping with her zipper and slipping off my aloha shirt. I rolled back the bedspread, then the blanket and top sheet. She squirmed out of her dress, too boozed to notice my shark bite.

I wondered what the thin man, no doubt listening in through the woodwork, would expect from us. Groans and moans and banging on the wall?

"Roll over on your tummy," I said to Lani.

"Yess, yess . . ." She quickly turned over. She had a body to die for. Too bad I wasn't ready to die.

I grabbed a bed pillow, removed its case, and twisted it into a rope. I slipped the fabric into her mouth.

"Wasss going on . . ."

I tied the pillowcase behind her shimmering black hair before she could finish her muffled sentence. Then I unplugged the phone cord and bound her hands and feet behind her, snug but not painfully tight. She could sleep on her stomach comfortably enough all night until she was found the next morning.

"Ahhh!" Lani tried to scream, without much effect. The result was a muted cry such as the thin man next door no doubt expected to hear. I let out a few lusty groans myself and rocked the bed against the wall for good measure.

Next I searched Lani's black sequined handbag. Soon I found her lipstick and makeup kit, carrying them and her black cocktail dress into the bathroom.

Ten minutes later, I emerged looking like a woman—sort of. I had put on lipstick, blusher, and eye shadow and had donned Lani's bra, stuffed with toilet tissue, and her black dress. Next I put on the lady's sun hat I had bought and tied the scarves under my chin. Fortunately, I'd brought a pair of rubber slippers that would have to do with my costume. I stuffed my own clothes and my files from the case into Lani's large handbag

Before leaving the suite, I glanced again at Lani. The 'ono local beauty lay naked on the bed. Her glistening eyes looked at me with a doleful expression.

I covered her with the top sheet and blanket, then whispered in her ear: "Sorry, Lani. Your friend Manny has gotten mixed up in some nasty business. By Friday you'll know what it's all about. Sleep well."

I fluffed a pillow under her head and tiptoed from the room, locking the door behind me.

The silver Porsche opened remotely with Lani's key and I slipped into the driver's seat. The turbo motor fired with a throaty growl as I aimed toward Kona on Ali'i Drive. A mile down the road I pulled off to consult Lani's map. There is no direct route from Kona to Hilo. The high ridge between

Mauna Loa and Mauna Kea separates the two towns. The shortest route–85 miles–climbs east over the remote Saddle Road between the two volcanoes. Since at night this narrow mountain pass can be tricky, it seemed prime turf for another one of the *hui's* accidents. A longer route, the Hawai'i Belt Road, stretched north through *paniolo* country to Waimea, then turned south down the rugged Hāmākua Coast. But if the *hui* was watching the remote Saddle Road, they would likely be watching the Belt Road, too. That left the longest route to Hilo–120 miles–weaving through the coffee groves of South Kona, around the southern tip of the island, and up into Volcanoes National Park. Would the *hui* figure on my taking this long and circuitous route? I hoped not.

The Porsche's clock said 8:29, less than two hours until the last flight to Maui. Before me lay the dark two-lane Kuakini Highway curving along the Kona Coast. Stars spread like crystal dust across the sky. I revved through the Porsche's lower gears, relishing the musical notes of its turbocharged motor at red line. Almost instantly I was over the speed limit.

I checked the rearview mirrors. Empty as the night. Few cars plied the highway on this starry Wednesday. But I stayed hyperalert, checking the speedometer, whose needle on the straightaways swept to 100. Checking mirrors. Checking the fuel gauge. Adrenaline pumping.

The village of Captain Cook blinked by as the highway rose gradually through the leeward hamlets of Kainaliu and Kealakekua, into South Kona coffee country. The Porsche's powerful high beams illuminated the narrow, twisting lanes in front of me, carving through desolate lava flows. I checked the mirrors again.

A flashing blue light.

No way could I pull over tonight. I was traveling at twice the speed limit in a borrowed car, lamely disguised as a woman. The cop would stop me and lock me up. I would miss that Maui flight.

No way.

When the darkened highway swung east near the Big Island's southern tip, on a straight stretch through Hawaiian Ocean View Estates I put the pedal down. The speedometer quickly swept past 100. Then 120 . . . 140 . . . .

I was still flying when I reached the southernmost town on the island, Nā'ālehu. "35 mph" was the posted limit. I blew by at 135. I checked the mirrors. The blue light was gone.

Climbing the long grade into Volcanoes National Park in a sudden downpour, I thought about Manny and his twisted idea of 'ohana. By returning to Honolulu before the Zoning Board hearing on Friday I would be betraying him. By exposing the *hui*, if I got that far, I might tarnish his new, clean image. Or maybe put him behind bars.

Trying to save the cliffs was the right thing, the *only* thing, to do. If Manny perceived this as a violation of loyalty to family—'ohana—he was wrong. Loyalty to the land—'āina— should be higher.

The landing lights of a distant jet illuminated Hilo Bay. Hilo International Airport—the sign loomed ahead on the drenched highway and none too soon. The rain cooperatively cut back to a mist, then stopped. I pulled into the parking lot with little time to spare, locked Lani's very warm Porsche, kept the keys in case I needed them later, and hurried to the terminal.

At the ticket counter, the agent did a double take when she saw my disguise. Was I a harmless cross-dresser? Or was I dangerous? I explained that I was flying to a costume party on Maui and didn't have time to change there. She bought my story, checked my ID, and sold me a ticket.

I walked away from the counter, fast enough to catch the plane but not to call attention to my pitiful self. An airport clock said 10:15. Ten minutes to departure.

When I finally reached the gate the agent announced: "Last call for flight 946 to Kahului, Maui. All ticketed passengers should be onboard."

I scanned around the passenger lounge. No police. And no one suspicious enough to represent the *hui*.

I handed my coupon to the agent and stepped down the jetway. The Boeing 737 was less than half full. Passengers were scattered randomly among many empty seats. I commandeered a row of three all to myself, and watched as the plane pushed back from the gate. The window reflected back my disguise–smeared lipstick, frowzy eyes, blushing cheeks.

Soon the jet turbines were humming and the terminal was shrinking away from my window. With little air traffic this late, the pilot taxied directly to the runway and revved the big fans as we thundered into the darkness over Hilo Bay.

thirty

Before dawn the next morning the ripsaw whine of a Twin-Otter jolted me awake. It was Thursday. Kahului Airport, Maui. Twenty-four hours to the Kalaupapa Cliffs hearing on Oʻahu.

I uncurled from the vinyl chair that had been my bed for the night in the passenger lounge. My mouth tasted fuzzy. My back ached. My head pounded. But I had eluded the *hui*. So far.

Before going to sleep last night I had re-dressed as a tourist, complete with sunglasses purchased at an airport gift shop and a weathered L.A. Dodgers baseball cap I had bought from a genuine tourist for thirty bucks. I had heaped Lani's things and my Kalaupapa Cliffs files into a duffel, also purchased from the gift shop. Lipstick and eye shadow removed, once again I traveled as a man.

The 6:00 a.m. Twin-Otter flight I awaited offered two advantages: one, it was the first plane of the morning from Maui to Honolulu; and, two, it would arrive at the remote Island Hopper building, distant from the Inter-Island

Terminal serving the larger jets from Kona and Hilo, which was no doubt being watched by the *hui*. That my flight first stopped on Moloka'i was not my choice. Though at this point I had few choices.

The tiny airplane puttered on to the runway, throttled up, and climbed into the dawn. The plane banked over Kahului Bay, skirted the gently sloping hills of West Maui, and crossed the channel between Maui and Moloka'i.

Four passengers got off at Moloka'i and three more climbed on for the short leg to Honolulu. Soon the Twin-Otter was airborne again. The pilot swooped over the majestic Kalaupapa cliffs, aglow in the early morning light.

It had been two weeks since Adrienne hired me to investigate her sister's death. Justice for Sara is what she had wanted. A seemingly straightforward request.

But the investigation had unearthed a conspiracy at the very root of island government. To ensure approval of the Kalaupapa Cliffs project despite overwhelming opposition, the *hui* had stopped at nothing. Sara's death, the original focus of the case, now served as only one tragic example of Chancellor Trust's ruthlessness. Today they were close to victory. The Land Zoning Board was about to approve their project. Unless I could stop them.

The Twin-Otter touched down in Honolulu at 7:10 and taxied to the Island Hopper terminal. When the pilot shut down the screaming turbines, I quickly squeezed out the door. Ducking behind another passenger walking to the quiet terminal, I looked around. No one seemed to notice me.

My Smith & Wesson. It lay at the bottom of a trash receptacle in the Inter-Island Terminal, which was surely being watched. I walked there quickly. I didn't see any *hui* operatives as I slipped into the restroom.

A man with a dirty yellow beard stood at the sink brushing his teeth. I stood by the stainless waste container and turned on the faucet. Without removing my baseball cap I washed my face, shiny with sweat. My cheeks were darkened with stubble. I wished I could brush my teeth. But more than that, I wished he would finish so I could retrieve my gun.

Finally the man gathered his toilet bag and left. I reached down under the trash liner. It was there—a cold, heavy lump. I slipped the revolver into my duffel and left the restroom.

In front of me was one of Bobo's moke pals. But his dark eyes were glued to the arrival gates. *Had he spotted me?* I turned and put some distance between us, then glanced back. He was still there, still watching the gates intently.

I walked briskly from the terminal. My duffel felt heavier with the Smith & Wesson aboard. A quarter mile ahead on the corner of Aolele Street and Nimitz Highway rose the airport Holiday Inn. It was morning rush hour, seven thirty, and town-bound traffic choked Nimitz.

I crossed the street and glanced back. Still nobody.

Before 8:00 a.m. may seem an odd hour to check in to a hotel, but not in Hawai'i. I told the front desk clerk I had just flown in from Auckland on Air New Zealand, stopping over in Honolulu before returning to Los Angeles. My Dodgers cap corroborated my story.

"Very good, sir." The aloha-shirted clerk smiled blandly.

With room key in hand I stopped by the lobby gift shop and bought disposable razors, a gaudy aloha shirt displaying hula dancers and waving palms, and a straw hat who band said "Hawai'i Paradise."

By 8:30 I was showered and dressed and calling the FBI. Agent Javier's phone just rang. *Damn!* I mentally prepared a message for his voice mail. Then I heard, "Javier, FBI."

"Bill, did you receive the fax from Bio-Tech Labs in California?"

"Yeah," Javier said. "What's this about? We don't usually investigate dead mules."

Briefly I explained the Kalaupapa Cliffs conspiracy and how the Chancellor Trust *hui* had run down Adrienne and killed Sara and her student, Baron Taniguchi.

"Kalaupapa Cliffs?" Javier pondered. "I read about that in the morning paper. The Land Zoning Board hearing is tomorrow, right?"

"That hearing has to be stopped."

"Why?"

"It's rigged. I'll have the evidence at your office by noon. If I don't show, take a look at my safe deposit box at First O'ahu Savings on King Street."

"In thirty minutes I can have a car there to pick you up, Kai."

"Can't risk waiting, Bill. If you want to help, alert the U.S. Attorney's Office that you'll be requesting an injunction suspending that Zoning Board hearing tomorrow. We need to work fast."

"Where are you? Let me send a car."

"See you at the federal building." I hung up.

thirty-one

"8:41" flashed on the marquee at the airport Holiday Inn. I stood at a bus stop on Nimitz Highway gripping my duffel with both hands. Though the bus is not the fastest way to travel, I knew I couldn't call a cab. The *hui* could be monitoring the cabbies' dispatcher.

In my campy aloha shirt and wide straw hat I felt anonymous among the locals and few tourists waiting for the bus. Finally, I saw two buses in the distance slowly rolling down the street, heading for our stop. One had "Waikīkī" printed across the front, the other "Ala Moana Center."

I shifted weight from one foot to the other. I looked up at the marquee: "8:45." When I looked back at the street, I saw something I wish I hadn't. The smoke grey van was parked at the opposite curb. *Damn!*

The buses pulled between us, blocking my view. I jumped on the Ala Moana bus and held my breath as it chugged away. The Waikīkī bus followed close behind. Glancing back, I saw the van swing an illegal U-turn on Nimitz. *Had the driver seen which bus I boarded?* Before long the two buses would split off in different directions and the van would have to make a decision.

When that happened, the van followed the Waikīkī bus. I could breathe again. As the van turned away, I saw only two men through the windshield. Neither was Bobo. That meant that he was still out there somewhere looking for me.

The bus traveled along Dillingham Boulevard, then turned onto King Street in Chinatown, rumbling past sidewalks stacked high with crates of bok choy and eggplant and bean spouts. At the corner of King and Nuʻuanu I stepped off the bus. First Oʻahu Savings was just opening. The assistant manager did a double take when she saw my oversized hat and splashy aloha shirt.

"On a case today, Kai?"

I winked and asked for my safe deposit box. She led me to a private booth, where I removed all the pieces of evidence from my box—the syringes, fingerprint cards, photos, Sara's speech, and the taped conversation with McWhorter. I slipped them into my duffel.

From the bank, I walked *makai* on Fort Street, a pedestrian mall whose cliff-like towers made for a shadowy promenade. The Federal Building on Punchbowl was only a half mile away. If the van showed, those mokes would have to chase me through the maze of shops and shoppers.

At the end of dusky Fort Street, the Aloha Tower glowed in the morning sun. Around the tower, boutiques and bistros and beer gardens bustled in the marketplace. I turned onto Ala Moana Boulevard and spotted the Federal Building only a half block away.

A flame red sports car suddenly flashed in the sunlight as it raced down Punchbowl, coming toward me fast. The car was low-slung. Italian. All too familiar. The plates said "Manny."

Both doors of the red Lamborghini swung up bizarrely like opening jackknifes. Manny stepped out and onto the sidewalk. His pal Bobo joined him.

"You betray me, Kai," Manny said. "I save your life and you spit in my face . . ."

Big Bobo didn't wait for Manny's speech to end. I ran back down Ala Moana Boulevard toward the Aloha Tower, with Bobo steps behind. Bobo ran fast for a big man, like an angry bear. I hoped I could lose him in the marketplace.

I sprinted across six lanes of traffic on Ala Moana, dodging cars, the Aloha Tower firmly focused ahead of me. I raced as fast as my feet would carry me, through the parking lot, past a line of yellow cabs, and by boutiques and browsing tourists.

Bobo kept pace. Since I was lugging my duffel, the big moke was able to stay with me. I was almost at the piers now, beyond the tower, which were blocked by an iron gate. I ran up the tower steps.

Bobo climbed after me, his huge feet pounding the spiraling stairway like thunder. I glanced back and saw that he clutched something dark in his meaty right hand.

Pop! I felt a rush of air as a bullet ripped into the stairwell above me. Splinters flew.

A woman screamed as Bobo pushed her aside. *Pop!* Another shot exploded like a mousetrap being sprung.

The searing heat of a fire iron tore into my left shoulder. I grabbed the place where blood was already seeping through. I tried to squeeze away the pain.

I hunched down on a landing, my aloha shirt dripping blood. With my right hand, I fumbled with the zipper of my duffel and finally made out the cold lump of my Smith & Wesson. I shook it free of the bag and lifted it to meet Bobo's gun. He paused, pistol pointed up the stairwell, as I aimed low and squeezed off two rounds.

The big man jolted back, clutching his stomach. He buckled over and tumbled. His gun clattered down the stairs.

I lunged past him toward the foot of the tower, where a flock of tourists had crowded the entrance. Pushing through them, I ran for the first yellow cab in the line.

I hopped in, slamming the door behind me. "Federal Building," I ordered the driver

Ten minutes later, I was knocking at the door of Agent Bill Javier.

thirty-two

"Feds Probe Kalaupapa Cliffs." Friday's *Star-Bulletin* detailed a wide-ranging federal investigation into Umbro Zia and the Chancellor Trust's *hui*. It was alleged that the trust had conspired to bribe members of the Land Zoning Board and other public officials by offering financial interest in the proposed resort. *Hui* members were also being questioned in the deaths of Baron Taniguchi and Sara Ridgely-Parke, and Adrienne's hit-and-run accident in Waikīkī.

Several suspected *hui* members were named, including Zia, Dr. Goto, Rush McWhorter, and Manny Lee. Jailed *Pakalōlō* King Milton Yu was not mentioned. Nor were Emery Archibald, Heather Linborg, or J. Gregory Parke. Somehow this made the wealthy Parke seem all the more forlorn.

The article explained that a federal judge had enjoined the Land Zoning Board from meeting, pending the outcome of the investigation. An accompanying editorial noted that the Chancellor Trust's proposal to develop eighty acres of Molokaʻi conservation land–all but certain of passage yesterday–was now dead.

I reached up and touched my shoulder. Still pain. But the wound had been superficial, and was cleaned and bandaged that same afternoon. The emergency room physician had warned me to keep it out of the water for a few days. *Right.* If there was one thing I needed most in the world right now, it was surfing.

Late Friday morning, with agent Javier in tow, I visited Adrienne at the medical center. She had awakened from her long sleep and was speaking again, though faintly. To the agent, she corroborated much of what I had said about the *hui's* involvement in Sara's death.

After Javier had spoken with Adrienne a few minutes, he left us alone. Her newly regained voice began to fade.

"Save it." I took her hand. She looked so much better, I couldn't help wondering aloud if she would return to Boston immediately. Adrienne slowly shook her chestnut hair, glinting red and gold in the morning sun streaming through her hospital window. She squeezed my hand.

On my way back to my apartment that afternoon, I took a detour in Waikīkī and found myself barefoot with my board on a sun-warmed stretch of sand. Within minutes I was paddling out to Pops. My shoulder stung a little when I stroked, and even more with the first spray of salt water. Then the frothing soup from an inside set suddenly tore off my bandage. By the time I had reached the lineup, my shoulder was numb.

But I felt alive. Restored. Balanced. And ready for the next wave.

A Surfing Detective Mystery

CHIP HUGHES

SLATE RIDGE PRESS

"I'm not on the city payroll like you. If I don't have cases, I don't get paid."

"But looking for lost dogs?"

"Well, maybe I like cold noses and warm hearts."

Fernandez laughed. "Next time I'll bring my violin."

No way would I tell the homicide detective who I was working for. The dog's master, that is. Client confidentiality is a matter of principle. Even in the case of murder, and even when the finger was pointing at me.

two

Fernandez was right. I had sunk to a new low.

I had arrived there four days earlier. The June sky was the milky sapphire of a Blue Hawaiian as my '69 Impala inhaled its last fumes of no-name gasoline, pinging and belching up to the summit of Tantalus Drive—a winding mountain road with breathtaking views of Honolulu. But it wasn't the views I found tantalizing on this Monday morning, so much as the visible wealth that lined the switchback drive in the form of sprawling mansions, exotic landscaping, and luxury cars.

I was heading for one of those mansions owned by Barry Buckingham—entrepreneur, yachtsman, and charismatic radio pitchman who sold precious metals, gold mostly, over the airwaves.

I knew Mr. Buckingham had his detractors. He'd been called a fraud, charlatan, huckster, and a few other choice names. The high cost of living in Hawai'i makes islanders vulnerable to get-rich-quick schemes. And if we lose, we can always find someone to blame. Buckingham was an easy target, despite testimonials to his moneymaking wizardry. It was also common knowledge that people feared him.

Since he was my only paying client on the horizon, I gave Barry Buckingham the benefit of the doubt. Was I skeptical? Sure. But I couldn't allow skepticism to come between me and a paycheck.

Surfing all day, every day, is nice work if you can get it. Even if I could afford to surf that much, there's something about having a case that keeps me going. And ever since I found that big-wave rider in upcountry Maui who everyone thought had drowned, I've had a thing for locating missing persons. So never mind my qualms about the pitchman, I was anxious to meet him.

Mr. Buckingham's wife had vanished four months earlier in February. The papers were full of stories about the odd disappearance of Cheyenne Sin. Honolulu police hadn't come up with anything, except to suspect Mr. Buckingham himself. So when he said he needed my services, I naturally assumed he meant to search for his wife and get himself removed from the suspect list.

Since I'd never met the man, I figured he found me in the yellow pages or on the internet. My ads show a long-board rider and say SURFING DETECTIVE: CONFIDENTIAL INVESTIGATIONS—ALL ISLANDS. For the record, I'm Kai Cooke. My first name means "sea" and my last comes from an old New England family. I'm thirty-four, single, and was *hānaied,* or adopted, by Hawaiian relations after my parents died when I was eight. I have sun-bleached brown hair and stand six feet even. Well, almost. At work I wear an aloha shirt, khakis, and sandals. At play I wear board shorts. I try to keep a balance between the two. Work and play, that is.

Neither the yellow pages nor my website had generat-ed much business lately. Cases seemed as hard to catch as Waikīkī waves on a crowded Sunday afternoon. Two multi-state agencies—the PI equivalent of Walmart—had slammed their toll-free numbers and splashy ads next to mine. These agencies didn't have offices or overhead in Honolulu—just local hired guns—so they could undercut even my cheapest prices.

That's why I was climbing Tantalus to Buckingham's hill-top estate. He called it Wonderview. From up here you could see from Diamond Head all the way to Pearl Harbor—almost worth the eleven million my prospect had dropped on the place.

Standing alone outside the white privacy wall that sur-rounded the mansion, I felt even more broke than I was—like a guy down on his luck begging for a job. Not far from the truth. I wandered the wall until I found a path, blocked by a green copper gate decorated with dolphins. A few words into an intercom got me buzzed through.

Around the rambling white Mediterranean villa sprawled a tennis court, swimming pool and spa, and enough open lawn to host a *lūʻau* with several hundred guests. Whether or not Buckingham was on the up-and-up, it looked as if he could afford my services.

I climbed granite steps to a sweeping portico and stood in front of massive *koa* doors. I didn't have to knock. One swung open to a leggy teenager whose T-shirt displayed a windjam-mer at sea over the words Punahou Sailing Team. Her features were delicate, faintly Asian beneath carrot-colored hair. She did not greet me, just turned her back and shouted: "Daddy, he's here!" Then she left.

Taking this announcement for an invitation to enter, I crossed the marble threshold and waited.

The teenager returned with her father, a bigger, burlier man than I had imagined from his radio voice. It's rare to see anyone in the islands dressed like Buckingham was. I figured it was the custom down under, since he came from Australia. The gold dealer's charcoal double-breasted suit set off a cream-colored shirt and ruby tie that accentuated his ruddy complexion. Despite its elegance, his outfit looked ill-fitting on his meaty frame—shirt collar too tight, coat shoulders too broad—like of an overdressed gangster. To him, I must have looked underdressed in my aloha attire. Lucky he couldn't see my board shorts underneath.

His right hand reached out, gleaming with gold rings. One had a diamond the size of a walnut. But even the glint of that rock could not disguise the hugeness of his hand and the power of its grip—more like that of a sailor or butcher than a precious metals broker. I could see why people might be afraid of him. At the same time I could see why his smile had won over so many.

"G'day, Mr. Cooke," he announced in velvety Australian tones. "Welcome to Wonderview."

"Thank you, sir." I peered into eyes as pale blue as an empty sky. His black hair didn't match his complexion. Near his scalp I could see red roots.

"You know who *I* am, of course," he said with self-satisfaction. "And this is Lehua." The teenager nodded.

My celebrity host led me, his daughter trailing behind, into an enormous sunken living room. He gestured to the floor-to-ceiling glass where the morning sun streamed in. The ocean view took in the entire panorama of the south shore—from the cobalt green lochs of Pearl Harbor to the turquoise waves of Waikīkī. Those waves looked inviting. I hoped I could concentrate on what Mr. Buckingham was about to tell me.

I pulled my eyes away from the windows and checked out four Hawaiian quilts on the walls. They were hand-sewn in traditional patterns I recognized from living with the Kealohas, my adopted Hawaiian family. *'Ulu* or bread-fruit, *pua aloalo* or hibiscus, *hala kahiki* or pineapple, and *kukui* or candlenut tree. I was surprised how faded they were. You'd think someone who could afford such expensive pieces would take better care of them. At least keep them out of the sun. But Buckingham didn't seem to know what he had.

He pointed me to an overstuffed leather chair of white hide that must have inconvenienced one very big cow. He and his daughter took a matching sofa at a right angle to me. They sat close together. Not touching, but close. The girl glanced up into his eyes. Was she looking for reassurance? Comfort? Courage?

"Mr. Cooke, I rang you because we've had a heartbreaking loss."

"I'm so sorry about your wife, sir," I said, truly feeling for him, while secretly smug that I knew my client's needs even before he expressed them. Her disappearance had been on TV and in the papers, so it was hard to miss.

"Right. My wife, Cheyenne Sin, disappeared in February. Bloody awful! The police are looking, but have gotten nowhere. That's why I called you about this other matter. I want a proper investigation. A *discreet* investigation."

"What other matter, sir?"

"Yesterday at Kailua Beach Park where Lehua took him surfing, our beloved Kula disappeared. I believe he was pinched."

"Pinched?"

"Nicked." He gestured with his big hands. "Stolen."

"You mean kidnapped?" I asked, thinking he was telling me another family member had disappeared.

"You could say that." Buckingham pulled a starched white handkerchief from his breast pocket. "No worries, love." He dried his daughter's tears. "Mr. Cooke is going to find Kula," he told her.

"Kula is your brother?" I glanced at the teenager, who was now openly crying.

"No," she said through her tears—"my dog."

three

"Your *dog?*"

"Kula is a special dog, Mr. Cooke," Buckingham replied. "His name means 'gold' in Hawaiian, as I'm sure you know, and he's the most stunning retriever you'll ever see. A beautiful boy. Kula belonged to my wife."

Buckingham didn't strike me as the type to get sentimental about a pet—or even a wife. He did seem devoted to his daughter, though.

Lehua rose and picked up a photo album from the coffee table. She handed it to me. "This is Kula." She sighed and returned to the sofa.

I opened the book of photos. All of the dog.

Kula was not red or sandy-brown like most golden retrievers, but sunny blond. His mane and feathering were luminous. His blond lashes set off dark brown eyes. *Beautiful boy.* Even I could see that this was one stunning canine. Pedigree was written all over him. And his collar—tanned and stitched leather—was embossed in gold with his name.

"Nice-looking dog," I said. "But finding lost pets isn't my usual——"

"Kula is not just my wife's dog," Buckingham interrupted. "He's a surfing dog. And you, I understand, are the Surfing Detective?"

"Yes, but I'm not a dogcatcher."

"Take a look at this, mate." Buckingham walked to a mammoth flat-screen TV and slipped in a DVD. The screen lit up with the blond retriever careering down the face of a massive wave at Mākaha. The dog was crouched low on the nose of a longboard piloted by Lehua. The narrator from a local TV news show referred to Kula as the "famous Hawaiian surfing dog." I'd heard of dogs riding knee-high stuff, but never one who could handle a legendary big-wave venue like Mākaha. I had to admit I was impressed.

"So you can see," Buckingham said as the video ended, "why we called you."

"Yes, sir." I cleared my throat and swallowed my pride. "I'll need a retainer. One thousand up front to begin the investigation."

"You'll have the whole amount in cash before you leave."

"Thanks," I said. No surprise. Men like Buckingham carry more in their wallet than I carry in my bank account. "Now I have some questions for you." I reached for the small spiral-bound pad in the pocket of my aloha shirt and the pen clipped to it. "Do you suspect anyone of stealing your dog?"

"Our housecleaner spotted a prowler on the property not long before Kula went missing."

"What did he look like?"

"A slim, longhaired bloke. I told the police but, as usual, they came up with nothing."

"Why didn't he steal the dog here? Why go all the way across the island to Kailua Beach?" I asked.

"I don't know," Buckingham said. "Maybe he saw our security system and ran."

"Do you suspect anybody else?"

"A few of my neighbors wouldn't be above taking a dog to make a point. I heard Mrs. Gum, the old bat across the street, is going to sue me."

"What for?"

"She claims my palms block her view." Buckingham shook his head. "There's more frivolous litigation in this country . . ."

"An old lady—steal a dog?"

"She has an axe to grind, that's for sure."

"OK, I'll interview her. Anyone else?"

"Dr. Carreras, my neighbor down the hill. Used to be a psychiatrist. He's complained constantly about Kula's barking and he accuses me of damaging his bloody sports cars."

"How do you mean, damage his cars?"

"Oh, he collects vintage sports cars: Jaguar, Ferrari, Porsche. I'm a *Rolls man* myself." Buckingham winked. "Anyway, my swimming pool overflowed last winter and Carreras claimed the water leaked into his garage and harmed his precious heirlooms. I seriously doubt it, but he's a miserable bloke. Drives like the devil on these mountain roads. Going to kill somebody . . ."

"I'll talk with him too." I turned to Lehua. "Do you know of anyone who might want to take Kula? Or could he have just wandered off?"

"No way," Lehua insisted. "He always stays right with me. But after we paddled in from surfing at Flat Island that day, I turned around and he was gone. I looked everywhere."

"You didn't see anyone suspicious? No car speeding away? No prints in the sand?"

"No. He just wasn't there . . ." She wiped away a fresh tear.

Buckingham drew his daughter to his side and said to me softly, "Since her mother disappeared, Kula has been Lehua's only comfort. You can imagine how difficult this is for her."

"I understand, sir." I paused, then returned to my growing list of suspects. "And what about enemies? Anyone who might want to hurt you or your family?"

He shook his head. "I'm a public man. Thousands listen to my radio program daily. Crazy people are out there, alongside the sane ones."

"Any threats?"

"Of course, but not lately." He looked away. "Nothing that could pertain to this."

I wasn't entirely convinced. I turned again to the girl, who seemed deeply pained about the dog.

"I know Kula's disappearance must be hard for you, Lehua, but it's important that you tell me everything that happened that morning on Kailua Beach—even if it might seem unrelated to Kula."

Still tearful, she said, "I'll try."

"I'll leave you two to talk while I go fetch your retainer," said Buckingham. He left the room through two elaborately carved doors.

Standing there with the girl, who recounted in detail what she'd already told me, I still wondered why my client had hired me to search for his dog instead of his wife. I could have backed out . . . but I felt sorry for the kid. I had a dog once and lost him, so I could relate.

"Lehua, I'm going to do everything I can to find Kula."

"Thank you so much!" she said.

"I know how it feels when your dog doesn't come home one day. I know how it feels when he never comes home."

She sobbed.

"But that's not going to happen with your dog."

"I'm so sad." She leaned her tear-stained face against my chest.

"There . . . there." I patted her shoulder. "We're going to make it better. I promise."

I was about to tell her every step I would take to find Kula, when I realized I hadn't the foggiest idea where to start. I had never traced a missing pet before. And never thought I would. So I settled for . . .

"By tomorrow I'll be on Kula's trail. You can count on it."

"You'll find him," she said, looking hopeful. "I know you will."

I felt almost guilty when she said that. So now I had two reasons why I couldn't back out. The kid. And the money.

Soon the gold dealer returned with ten crisp hundreds. I took them without a second thought.

four

After leaving Wonderview I crossed Tantalus Drive to the *mauka,* or mountain, side of the street. The cream colonial sat high on an incline and appeared to command at least a partial view of my client's villa and grounds. Was this the home of the old lady who Buckingham said had an axe to grind? Had she been involved in a dog-napping I suspected Kula had just wandered off and was within a few blocks of Kailua Beach. But checking out the neighborhood would at least make it look like I was earning my fee.

I climbed the steep driveway to the colonial's door, then turned and looked back toward Buckingham's estate. Yes, his royal palms did, in fact, block what would have otherwise been a stunning ocean view. A few chinks of blue were visible through the fronds, and beneath them a piece of my client's sprawling grounds.

I knocked and the door opened immediately, as if the occupant was expecting me. A rail-thin, silver-haired Chinese lady scoured me from my sandals to my sun-bleached hair. She was either very suspicious or very curious.

"Sorry to trouble you," I said and handed her my card. "I'm investigating the disappearance of your neighbor's dog." She glanced at my card. "Well . . . I'm Mrs. Gum. Maybe you heard of Gum's?" Her eyes searched my face, as she switched to pidgin. "Was my husband's appliance store on McCully. He wen die t'ree years ago. Now I take care dis whole place all by myself."

"Yeah, I know your husband's store," I said, switching to pidgin too. "Long time ago I buy one microwave ovah dere. Good deal. Stay working fine." Gum's was a humble mom-and-pop shop, which obviously hauled in oodles of cash to underwrite a home like this one on Tantalus Drive.

Mrs. Gum's face glowed. She was proud of her late husband's business.

I proceeded with my questions about the missing retriever, but she had not seen Kula lately, though she had noticed the absence of his bark that very morning. Which reminded me of another possible suspect, Dr. Carreras. I asked if her neighbor down the hill had ever complained to her about Kula. She said she hardly knew the doctor. Nor had she seen the prowler that Buckingham believed was haunting his home.

A high-pitched car horn blasted behind us. I turned to see a ruby-colored Rolls Royce gliding down Tantalus. The sun glinted on the silver figurine perched on its long hood—the "Flying Lady." The gigantic, glitzy machine seemed to huff: "I'm rich and powerful and could squash you like a bug!"

The driver waved. *Buckingham.* I remembered him saying, "I'm a *Rolls man.*" As his mammoth car descended, I caught a glimpse of its vanity plate: GLD DLR.

Mrs. Gum's smile straightened. She nodded toward where Buckingham's car had been and whispered, "He did 'em."

"Mr. Buckingham stole his own dog?"

"No." Her whisper dropped a register. "He *make* his wife."

"Murdered his wife?" I tried to imagine it.

Mrs. Gum nodded. "Da police know. Dey jus no can prove 'em. I hear her screaming da night before she disappear. He wen kill her alright. But dey nevah going find her."

"You don't much like Mr. Buckingham," I said, beginning to think she was touched. "His palms block your view, right? That must make you mad."

She shrugged. Just then a dog barked somewhere, an octave too high for a big retriever.

"If I see da dog," she said, "I call you." With that, she shut the door.

I stood there, trying to wrap my brain around her accusation. If I didn't have my doubts about my client before, Mrs. Gum had planted the seeds. Or was she just spreading rumors about a neighbor she hated?

I began hiking down her driveway. When I glanced back, I saw the curtains part in an upstairs window and a face staring down at me. From where I stood, it was hard to tell whether it was a man or a woman. Despite what she told me, did the widow share her home with someone?

Or was I just imagining this, trying to turn the runaway dog into a real case?

five

Driving down the hill I spotted that south swell in Waikīkī I'd seen from Buckingham's living room. But I should have been watching my rear view mirror. Closing in on me from behind—too fast—was a yellow car. I could hear its motor revving. The car grew larger and larger in my mirror—on a collision course with my Impala. I stomped the accelerator, but before my V8 responded, the car—an older Porsche— swerved around me, tires squealing, and flew by.

"Maniac!" I yelled out the window as the Porsche passed at breakneck speed. All I could see of the driver was his silver hair.

I kept my foot on the pedal, trying to catch him. It would have been hopeless if the driver hadn't cut a ninety-degree turn into a side street and disappeared. When I reached the street I turned in too.

Down at the end of the short block the Porsche was parked in front of a four-car garage attached to a posh house nestled against the slope of Tantalus. In the open bays of the garage were three other vintage sports cars: a Jaguar in British racing green, a flame-red Ferrari, and a sapphire Morgan. The three were parked in perfect parallel formation, facing the open doors. Ready to roar. The Porsche's back hatch was open and the silver-haired driver walked toward it holding a wrench.

"You almost hit me back there!" I said as I got out of my car, wondering if he would hurl his wrench at me. Heat vapor rose from the back of the Porsche. The insignia on the engine hatch said 911S.

"Truly sorry," he said, placing his tool over his heart in a gesture of apology. He was a wiry man with an olive complexion and steel-gray mustache. "I just replaced the six carbs and they're giving me fits. These early air-cooled nine-elevens can be a bear to tune."

"Maybe you should save your testing for the track," I said. "Tantalus' hairpin turns aren't meant for speed."

"O'ahu's track closed," he said. "It was the only one on the island, and now it's gone. While politicians and racers argue about it, I make do. Anyway, I never drive beyond my abilities, or what conditions allow."

Having just seen him in action, I wondered.

"Max Carreras." He smiled and offered his hand. "I am sorry, honestly."

"Dr. Carreras?" I asked. "Just the man I wanted to see. I'm Kai Cooke." I handed him my card. Then I mentioned my client.

"You work for *him?*" Dr. Carreras said. "I might have to change my favorable impression of you."

"It's a long story," I said. Then I broached the subject of Buckingham's leaking swimming pool.

"Leak?" Dr. Carreras's olive complexion darkened, his gray mustache twitched. "Buckingham's pool *flooded* my garage. And the water carried a chemical that attacked the tires and wheels of my cars."

"Really?"

"See that E-Type?" He pointed to the low-slung green Jag in one of the bays. "The tires molded and the wire wheels started to pit. It took a helluva lot of work, I'll tell you, to bring them back."

"But you did, sir. They look beautiful—like brand new." I wasn't just saying that. They did look like new.

"To replace them with factory originals would have cost a small fortune. Buckingham nearly ruined all four tires and rims, and the rubber on my Porsche too." He paused. "So are you investigating the damage to my cars?"

"No, sir, I'm here about his dog. You complained to Mr. Buckingham about Kula barking?"

"Yes, I complained. And Buckingham did nothing. But since when did they start sending out PIs to deal with barking dogs?"

"The golden retriever is missing, sir, and I wondered—"

"Am I a suspect?"

"Well, I take it you don't care much for Kula?" I answered with a question of my own.

Dr. Carreras glanced at the heat vapor still rising from his Porsche. "The dog's a barker, but his master's the real problem."

"You and Mr. Buckingham don't get along?" I tried to keep him talking.

The doctor glanced up. "I've studied his type, Kai, my friend. Barry Buckingham is a phony. His business is built on empty promises and his hilltop mansion is mortgaged to the hilt. He's a fake."

"You really think so?"

"Take my advice," he said. "Collect your pay before he goes under."

"But——"

"Maybe we can continue this conversation later." The doctor bent down and began adjusting his new carburetors. "I could go on about Buckingham, but I've got to fit in another test drive before the rain comes."

"How about tomorrow?" I asked.

"Sure. But after you hear me out you won't want to work for him."

"I'll take that chance," I said. "Until tomorrow—drive safely."

"I never drive beyond my abilities," he said again. "Sorry if I gave you a scare, Kai."

"All in a day's work." I walked back to my car.

six

I pulled away from Dr. Carreras' four-bay garage with one thing on my mind—the surf. Turning onto Tantalus Drive I was surprised to see a gray cloud forming at the summit of the mountain. Was this the storm the doctor had predicted?

Leaving his stable of shining steeds behind, I couldn't help wondering about Dr. Carreras. While he appeared to take risks behind the wheel, I doubted he would be quite so reckless in other aspects of his life. A rich doctor had too much to lose if he got caught stealing a dog. Even if he was retired. Besides I found myself actually liking the man. Never mind he almost ran me off the road. I looked forward to talking to him the next day about my new client.

The doctor calling Buckingham a fake, right after Mrs. Gum's accusation of murder, shook my already shaky confidence in him. I needed time to think.

Surfing usually gives me what I need. When I'm out in the waves, my cares seem to drift away. What's back on shore can't touch me. I feel free. My head clears and I see things in a new way. That's how surfing helps me solve cases. Sherlock Holmes had his pipe—I have my surfboard.

* * *

Cunha's is a rare outside break—meaning the waves break far offshore—a few hundred yards out from the Kapahulu Avenue jetty and Prince Kūhio Beach Park in Waikīkī. The name of the surfing spot comes from an estate on the beach in the early 1900s owned by Emanuel Sylvester Cunha. Legend has it that Cunha built so close to the water that surf hitting the seawall splashed onto his *lānai*. It takes a large south swell to produce a rideable wave at Cunha's. Generally this only happens when summer storms kick up in the South Pacific. And even then, when Cunha's does break, you might wait half an hour for a ride.

But the wait is worth it. When you ride one of these sweeping rollers, you feel on top of the world. And while the long stretch between sets keeps the crowds down, it also allows plenty of time for reflective types to solve the world's problems and for a detective to sort out the details of his cases.

Cunha's surfers are patient surfers. Patience was what I needed. I, who know next to nothing about locating missing pets, had taken a case to find one. And I had taken it from a client about whom I had my doubts. I wasn't ready to buy into all the suspicions surrounding Buckingham, but I did wonder what I'd got myself into. So I paddled into the lineup and waited for a wave and an inspiration.

At Cunha's, waves form slowly and you must paddle hard to catch them. But once you're on, the tempo quickens and the curl turns sheer. I watched and waited for several minutes. Then I got lucky.

Out on the horizon a swell was coming. It looked like only a ripple in the distance, but as it approached it grew larger. Soon I could see several waves forming. I started paddling well before the first wave in the set peaked. By the time it caught up with me, I was moving as fast as it was. I dropped in. The wave suddenly jacked up and I shot down the green wall, cutting a foamy trail behind me. *Ho, brah!*

After carving my last turn, I paddled back into the lineup hooting and smiling—but still waiting for that inspiration. I took several more rides to get it.

* * *

After surfing I called Buckingham and gave him an edited version of my interviews with his two neighbors. I didn't tell him about Mrs. Gum's accusation, but I did hint at Dr. Carreras's less than flattering remarks.

"Carreras?" Buckingham groused. "For a psychiatrist, he's a bloody poor judge of character."

I hoped my client was right.

seven

That night I had dinner with my attorney friend, Tommy Woo. Tommy, thanks to Cunha's, was my inspiration.

Tommy Woo had two cats, both strays, that had wandered into his life—a tabby who he claimed liked listening to Miles Davis, and a rag doll who preferred Charlie Parker. That's what he called them: Miles and Charlie, even though the rag doll was a girl. Tommy, who lived alone after two nasty divorces, had been smitten. Then one day Miles disappeared and Tommy was beside himself. He searched for days. Finally he stopped mentioning the tabby. Had he found him? And, if so, how?

When I arrived a little before seven at the dinky chop suey house on River Street, Ah Fook was packed. I put my name in for a party of two, joined the line outside, and waited for Tommy.

Ah Fook reeked with the ambience of this notorious backwater of Chinatown, where gamblers, smugglers, pimps, murderers, and thieves once plied their trades, and where legendary HPD Detective Chang Apana—prototype for the fictional Charlie Chan—hauled them in with his whip.

The savory smells of steamed clams, dim sum and Peking duck escaped as the door opened and closed, reminding me I hadn't eaten after my session at Cunha's. Despite run-ins with the health department and liquor commission, Ah Fook could always be counted on for a good, cheap meal. And if Tommy and I had anything in common, it was this: we were both cheap.

Soon a waitress waved me in and seated me in a dim corner. I looked around. Still no Tommy. He was late again. I began to wonder if my inspiration had tricked me. Sure my *akamai*—meaning smart—attorney friend could dazzle a jury with his eloquence, wow an audience with his jazz piano, and tell off-color jokes until your face turned blue. But find a missing pet? My fingers were crossed.

As the waitress returned with two cups and a steaming teapot, the door swung open to the familiar loose-jointed, lanky figure dressed all in black—looking like a parish priest of Chinatown. He saw me from across the room, tapped his wristwatch, and mouthed: "Broken." We both knew he was lying. Attorney by day and a musician by night, Tommy Woo had a shaky relationship with time.

I poured tea, we both ordered the $8.95 dinner special, and then I got right to the point: "Tommy, what do you know about finding lost dogs?"

"Dogs?" He adjusted his tortoiseshell glasses, brushed back his gray hair, and let his first joke fly. "Did you hear the one about the three-legged Dalmatian and the sexy French poodle?"

"Many times." I lied.

Tommy looked stunned. He raised his brows and said nothing. A rare moment. The waitress came by and ladled egg drop soup into our bowls.

"I asked because a friend of mine needs help finding one." I bent the truth a little. "The dog is special. A golden retriever who rides a surfboard."

"What's his name?" Tommy sipped the hot soup.

"Kula."

"Not the dog," Tommy said. "The owner."

"Oh . . ." I paused, savoring my own soup. "Buckingham," I finally said.

"Barry Buckingham, the gold dealer?" Tommy asked, his expression returning to its usual animation. "Didn't know you knew him."

"I don't, really."

"So it's a case?" Tommy asked as our sweet-and-sour spareribs arrived. He picked up a rib and chewed on it. "Buckingham *hired* you to find his dog?"

"Right." I smothered the word in a mouthful of fried rice.

The stage was set for another of Tommy's doozies. He set down the rib, wiped the sauce from his lips, and placed his napkin back in his lap. "How can I help you?" he asked, without a hint of sarcasm. Sometimes Tommy surprised me.

"I remembered you lost that cat of yours, Miles? Did you ever find him?"

"He came home on his own," Tommy said, brushing back his hair again. "One morning I opened the door and Miles was sleeping on my doormat."

"Too bad."

"Too bad?"

"I mean that's good you found him. I was just hoping you'd tell me *how* you found him."

"I got lucky. But next time I'd call Maile."

"I knew a Maile once," I said. "What's her last name?"

"Barnes," he said. "Maile Barnes, the pet detective."

"Doesn't ring a bell. Pet detective, huh?" Was this another one of Tommy's jokes? "Like in an *Ace Ventura* movie?" I played along.

"No, she's for real. And she's the best—a former K-9 cop who finds lost animals."

The lemon chicken arrived and Tommy helped himself then passed the plate. He filled me in on Maile Barnes. Missing pet cases and now pet detectives. I was really hitting bottom.

"You should get a pet, Kai," Tommy added as he worked on his chicken. "You know, a dog or cat, so you're not alone so much."

"I don't have time for pets. Plus, the Edgewater doesn't allow them."

"Sneak one in."

"Then I'd have to feed it and walk it and pick up after it. I had a dog once, when my parents were still alive. So I know the drill."

Tommy adjusted his glasses and cocked his head. "We inhabit a lonely planet, Kai. Grab some comfort where you can."

"I do."

"You sure?"

Suddenly I felt irritated. "What makes you think I'm lonely?"

"Well . . . " He looked into my eyes. "Are you still hanging out with that Highcamp woman?"

I hesitated. "What if I am?"

Tommy kept looking at me. He said nothing.

"I gotta go." I got up and tossed a ten on the table. I didn't wait for my fortune cookie. It was bad enough that I'd been reduced to hunting missing animals; I didn't need any reminder of the dismal state of my love life.

"Phone Maile," Tommy called after me as I reached the door. I shook my head and walked out onto River Street. *What business is it of Tommy Woo who I hang out with?*

As I walked up the lamp-lit sidewalk, I cooled off a little and considered Tommy's suggestion.

eight

Tuesday morning's *Star-Advertiser* carried the following story in the "Hawai'i" section:

Fatal Crash on Tantalus

A 68-year old retired psychiatrist died yesterday as a result of injuries suffered in a one-car accident on Tantalus Drive at approximately 5 pm. The 1973 Porsche driven by Dr. Maxwell V. Carreras was traveling at a high rate of speed on upper Tantalus when it failed to negotiate a hairpin turn, slid down an embankment, and struck a tree. Rain-slick pavement from showers earlier in the day may have been a factor in the accident. Dr. Carreras was taken to Straub Clinic and Hospital in critical condition with head injuries and a collapsed lung. He was later pronounced dead at the hospital.

> There were no eyewitnesses to the fatal
> crash, but residents in the area said they
> heard the Porsche's engine, screeching tires,
> and then the collision. One resident who
> wished not to be identified said she thought
> she heard a second car also traveling at a
> high rate of speed, as if racing with Dr. Car-
> reras' car. HPD closed off upper Tantalus
> Drive for several hours on Monday evening
> while their investigation was in progress . . .

The story went on, mentioning Dr. Carreras's loved ones
left behind, his former medical practice, his hobby of collecting exotic cars, and so on. I had met him for the first time
only yesterday, talked briefly about his neighbor, my client,
and now the doctor was dead. I may have been one of the last
people to see him alive. I recalled him saying that he never
drove beyond his abilities, or what conditions allowed. He
sounded so sure of himself. But now I had to conclude that
he had been kidding himself about his abilities, or about those
sharp turns on Tantalus Drive. But I couldn't picture him racing another motorist on that narrow mountain road.

Dr. Carreras's untimely death didn't sit well with me. I
had actually liked the man. And I wondered, had the doctor survived, what more he might have told me about
Buckingham.

* * *

Later that morning I drove to Mānoa, a mist-swept valley
a few miles *mauka* of Waikīkī that lay between two ridges in

the Ko'olau Range. I liked to hike to majestic Mānoa Falls, the deepest point in the valley, and trek along the stream that meanders from the falls and down past the Chinese cemetery to the floor below. I'd been coming to Mānoa since I was a student at Punahou, before my parents died. But today my destination was a cottage perched on a wooded slope on the eastern side of the valley, in line with the cemetery and about a mile from the falls. It was the home of pet detective Maile Barnes.

When I pulled up to the cottage it looked vaguely familiar. I felt like I'd been here before. *Déjà vu.* But I couldn't recall why or when.

I knocked and the door opened to a youthful brown-haired woman in Nikes, running shorts, and a sports bra. Tiny beads of sweat dotted her flushed cheeks and tanned limbs. Suddenly I knew why the place looked familiar. The years had treated her kindly. She appeared to be barely thirty, but I knew exactly how old she was.

"Maile Ohara," I said. "It's been a while. How are you?"

"I'm fine, Kai," she said. "But it's Barnes. My name hasn't been Ohara for years. You were away on the mainland too long."

"I was," I said, "and I regret it." She was wearing a ring, so I assumed Barnes was her married name. But it was not the name I expected.

"What ever happened to Karl?" I asked. "Weren't you two engaged senior year?"

"Long story," she said. "C'mon in, Kai, and tell me what you've been up to."

"I haven't been up to much," I said as we walked into a cozy island-style living room with rattan furniture on Oriental rugs. Open jalousies admitted a balmy breeze.

"Actually Tommy had lots to say about you." Maile gave me a knowing look.

"Don't believe a word," I said, gazing into her almond-colored eyes, a shade darker than her hair. I remembered her eyes and her skin too—fragrant and tawny like the loam of the Hawaiian soil.

"Tommy told me only good things," she said. "You can fill me in on the bad."

Maile and I went way back, though we hadn't seen each other since high school. We were born the same year in the same hospital—Queens—and were classmates at the same school—Punahou. I left Punahou, and later the islands, when Maile and I were in Mrs. Fegerstrom's third grade class. During the summer before my senior year at Flintridge Prep in La Cañada, California, I returned to Oʻahu and reunited with my Punahou friends. Maile was a heartbreakingly beautiful seventeen year old then, who was dating a football star named Karl Knudson. There was still a comfortable closeness between Maile and me. I was drawn to her that summer, but Karl was never far away. She and I exchanged letters when I returned to California. We didn't write much after she became engaged.

"So what happened to Karl?" I asked.

"He played football at Stanford. He's a stockbroker in Modesto now with a wife and three kids."

"Why didn't you marry him?"

"I sent you a letter about it, but I didn't hear back from you."

"What letter? I never got it." I recalled that when I first moved to San Diego for college some of my mail got lost.

"I told you in the letter," Maile said. "My father got Parkinson's disease during my senior year. He was already in his sixties then. My mother tried to take care of him alone, but she wasn't young either. I couldn't leave them. Karl understood. We broke it off. In hindsight, it was for the best. I'm an Island girl. Can you imagine me in Modesto?"

I shook my head.

"What about you, Kai? Are you married? Do you have children?"

"No and no," I said. "I guess I've been too busy."

"Maybe you just haven't met the right person at the right time," Maile said. "Timing is everything. Karl and I—" She stopped in mid-sentence.

"But your timing must have been right later on," I said. "Who's the lucky Mr. Barnes?"

"Not so lucky, I'm afraid." Maile looked down. "Nestor was an HPD beat cop when I worked in K9. He fell in the line of duty."

"I had no idea." I was mortified. "I'm sorry."

"You had no way of knowing."

"I should have. I guess I've been out of touch."

"Stop scolding yourself and tell me about your missing dog."

I handed her Kula's photo. "I have to warn you—the last person I interviewed for this case died the same day."

Maile's eyes lit up when she saw the photo of the sunny retriever. "He's a beauty! What's his name?" She didn't ask about the dead man. A former cop, she took things in stride, I guessed.

"Kula. He's a famous surfing dog."

"I've heard of him," she said. "Wasn't he on TV?"

I nodded. She stepped to an antique roll-top desk and returned with a handful of cards.

MAILE BARNES
TRACER OF MISSING PETS
15 YEARS EXPERIENCE • K9 UNIT, H.P.D.

"Please pass them around," she said. "I always appreciate referrals."

I flipped the card over. Printed was her phone number, email address, and PO box.

"I'll be right back." She walked down the hall.

I looked around the room. Curled up on nearby rattan chairs were three contented cats. Maile soon returned in Bermudas and a tank top. She settled into a rattan loveseat opposite me and introduced her cats. "This is Coconut, a Siamese; Peppah, an Angora; and Lolo, a feral tri-color calico I'm trying to domesticate."

Judging from their looks, they had no cares in the world. The calico suddenly shot from the room when I reached for her.

"Don't mind Lolo. She's shy."

"No problem," I said. "Is she the reason you don't have a dog?"

"I used to—a German shepherd." She paused. "Rusty. He got on great with the cats, but . . ." She grew silent for a moment. "So, about your golden retriever—Kula." She uttered his name familiarly as if he were her own.

"He belongs to a Tantalus resident named Buckingham," I said. "Actually, he belongs to Mr. Buckingham's wife, Cheyenne Sin. She's missing too."

"Your client seems to be having a string of bad luck," Maile said.

"Yeah, so is his neighbor," I replied, thinking of Dr. Carreras. I shook my head. "Frankly, I don't know where to start. Then again, this is my first pet case. That's why I came to you."

Maile held Kula's photo close and studied it. "When I lost Rusty last year I searched all over O'ahu. I would have found him if he were here. But I believe he was stolen and shipped off the island. It happens—more than you'd think."

"My client is convinced his dog was stolen."

Maile put her hands together as if in prayer. Her almond eyes rested on me. "I'd like to help you, Kai, but I'm leaving tonight for a pet refuge workshop in Utah. I won't be back until Sunday. You can't wait that long. Every day Kula is missing decreases the chances he'll be found."

Not what I wanted to hear. She saw my discouraged look.

"Tell you what," Maile said, "I'll give you a crash course in pet detection. Do you have the time now?"

"I'll make the time."

"Good." She stood up and disappeared again, this time into her galley-like kitchen.

Left alone, I scanned a gallery of photos on the far wall of the room: Her late husband in uniform, a dark and handsome local man; Maile in police blues holding a rifle and a medal inscribed "Expert"; several photos of a rust and black German shepherd.

Maile returned with two tall glasses of iced tea and a plate of cookies. I sipped the mint tea and bit in to a chewy cookie whose sweet, tropical aroma reminded me of my mother. "*Mmmmmm . . .*"

"Coconut," Maile said. "For old time's sake. When Tommy said you were coming . . ." She trailed off, seeming embarrassed.

There was an uncomfortable silence.

"Your husband was a handsome man." I pointed to his photo on the wall. "And I noticed one of you with a marksmanship medal."

She glanced over at the photos. "Nestor liked to target shoot and I tagged along. I have good eyes and a steady hand. Straight shooting came easy. In fact, the department once offered to reassign me from the K-9 unit to the SWAT team. But I didn't want to leave my dogs. Anyway," she glanced down, "that's all in the past."

"I'm sorry about your husband."

Maile looked up again. "Thank you, Kai. Now let's talk about your missing retriever . . ."

nine

"When a pet disappears," Maile explained, "every minute it wanders, its life is ticking away. The chances of it being hit by a car or euthanized in an animal shelter are high. That's why you have to work fast."

"Even if Kula was stolen?" I took another sip of mint tea.

"The sooner you're on his trail, the better. A beautiful purebred like Kula, even without papers, could bring top dollar. In Hawaiʻi, dogs are stolen for various reasons: resale, breeding, hunting, fighting. Fortunately, a golden retriever is not the kind of dog people here eat."

"Let's hope not." Growing up in the islands I'd heard stories about *poi* dogs, or mixed breeds, being eaten by certain groups. But it was hard to imagine anyone making a meal of such an expensive canine as Kula. And I'd given little thought to the fact that dogs were stolen for other purposes. I'd known people are kidnapped and possessions get stolen, but I never considered that anyone might filch the family pet. Maile had my attention.

"Theft by a puppy mill," she went on, "is a definite possibility. Kula would be a gold mine as a stud dog." She paused. "I fully believe there's an organized pet theft ring in the islands—some people discount it, but there's plenty of evidence."

"So you're telling me there's enough money to be made from walking off with man's best friend to encourage organized crime?" I must not have kept the doubt out of my voice, for she sounded slightly defensive when she replied.

"Small-time, maybe," she said, "but organized all the same." From beneath the rattan coffee table she drew a scrapbook. "I started collecting these clippings after Rusty disappeared."

"We have the same hobby," I said.

She looked at me funny.

"Clippings," I said. "Mine are about big-wave wipeouts and shark attacks."

She opened her book to a random page. "Here."

KAILUA DOG THEFTS REPORTED

Kailua residents are reporting that someone is stealing expensive, purebred dogs from their homes. "Six dogs were reported stolen in the past two months," said Charlene Nogata, manager of Windward Pets in Kailua. "One dog was apparently stolen from a kennel in a front yard," she added. Police have received numerous complaints about missing dogs in Kailua, and are looking into them. Nogata became alarmed when several dog owners visited her store and asked her to watch for

> anyone selling their pets. Stolen were a pair
> of Labrador puppies, a Jack Russell terrier,
> an Airedale, and two golden retrievers, dogs
> that can fetch $500 each, without registra-
> tion papers. The store manager commented:
> "I've heard of individual owners losing their
> dogs, but never so many at once."

You'd think someone in my line of work might have taken more notice of such news. But then my business had always run more to the two-footed variety. Until now.

"Look at this." Maile turned the page to a notice in the "Pets for Sale" classifieds:

ATTN VETS & TECHNICIANS

Stolen from Pet's Haven on Beretania Street, Female King Charles Cavalier Spaniel. Microchip #500E239193. Reward for info. leading to arrest & conviction.

"Pet theft from a pet store? And a dog with an ID chip? That's bold."

"After being in law enforcement for fifteen years, Kai, I can tell you that some of the most twisted individuals I've run into are those who steal and mistreat animals. They're a sick bunch."

She turned another page.

DAD-GUM DOGNAPPERS!

Some people consider dogs fair game, just like mangoes in the yard. There's money to be made on stolen purebreds in the islands . . .

Page after page of clippings made a fairly convincing case for organized pet theft. Maile told me her role as a pet detective wasn't always an easy one. She had been cursed at, threatened, spit on, and even assaulted in her mission to rescue stolen animals. Once Maile had jumped from a window into a client's waiting pickup truck, clutching a Chihuahua after subduing the ex-husband with pepper spray. She had always had a tough side, even as a kid. But I hoped rescuing Kula wouldn't prove to be quite so dramatic.

Maile offered me some tips that would help whether he was lost or stolen: visit animal shelters, stake out and post signs where he was last seen, put ads in local newspapers, offer a substantial reward—the list went on. Before long I felt deeply in her debt.

"How can I ever thank you?" I asked.

"Could you drive me to the airport tonight? My ride fell through."

"I'd be happy to."

"And," Maile paused, "how would you feel about feeding Coconut, Peppah, and Lolo while I'm gone? Mrs. Kaneshiro, my next-door neighbor, usually does it, but she just got called to Kaua'i to care for her sick sister. I was about to make some last-minute calls, but since you stopped by today and since we're old friends with a shared passion for animals . . ."

"Well . . ." Whatever had I said or done to make her think I was an animal lover?

Maile saw the doubt on my face. "I wouldn't normally ask anyone on such short notice, but I know I can trust you, Kai. I've always felt comfortable with you. And I'm sure my cats will too. So what do you say?"

I was flattered, but her little speech made me feel completely surrounded. There was really no way out. So I said, "Your three kitties and I should get along just fine."

"This is so nice of you!" She hugged me.

Her sweet, loamy fragrance made me almost glad I'd agreed and reminded me of that summer long ago when I had yearned for her.

"I'll show you how to feed and water them tonight before we go to the airport." Maile released me. "And I'll give you my cell number in case you have questions."

"Happy to help."

My agency on the brink, my only paying gig searching for a lost dog, and now I had become the reluctant butler to three pampered cats. How low I'd sunk!

ten

Early Wednesday morning before dawn I staked out Kailua Beach. Maile had suggested I start at five. Lost and frightened animals, she explained, sometimes return early in the morning to the place where they last saw their master. I sat in my Impala sipping Kona coffee and scanning the shore.

The two-mile crescent of Kailua Beach—a white ribbon dotted with palms—was barely visible in the grayness. My eyes kept returning to the decoy I had planted on the sand by the Lanikai boat ramp, at the exact spot where Lehua had last seen Kula. It was her beach cover-up and contained her scent; though undetectable to me, it would be as strong as perfume to the sensitive nose of a retriever.

Lehua had carried her surfboard onto the beach after riding waves with the dog at Flat Island—*Popoiʻa* or "fish rot" in Hawaiian—a small coral islet and seabird sanctuary about a quarter mile off shore. When she turned around, Kula was gone.

The sky began to lighten. There was still no one on the beach. I switched on the dome light and scanned the morning's

Star-Advertiser. I flipped first to the obituaries. None yet for Dr. Carreras. I found myself thinking about him—retired psychiatrist, collector of vintage sports cars, Tantalus resident, and neighbor of my client. The doctor's death still didn't sit well with me. He had promised to tell me something about Buckingham. And now I would never know. I wondered if the doctor was putting me on. I wondered if he said what he said because he hated his neighbor. After all, Buckingham had called him a miserable bloke. The more I thought about it, the more I believed Dr. Carreras. I believed he had something to tell me—something I would find out later. The hard way.

No use fretting. I had a dog to find. I checked the "Lost & Found" section:

LOST

"Kula" golden retriever, male, 3 years,
blond coat, at Kailua Beach Park on Sunday
6/19. $1,000 reward.

The ad ended with my office phone number. The reward, suggested by Maile and approved by Buckingham, was more than the typical stolen dog could bring on the black market.

As for "Found" pets in the classifieds, there was only one:

FOUND

Small brown female dog w/short hair
and red collar in Pearl City area on 6/14.

Wrong color. Wrong size. Wrong sex. Wrong place.

The sky in the east began to glow. The beach sprang to life with early-morning walkers. Some were solitary, some in pairs, and some accompanied by canine companions that ambled alongside them or dashed into the surf after sticks and balls and floating toys. One dog looked like a spaniel, one like a black lab, another had the spots of a Dalmatian. One was a golden retriever—dark red. But no sign of Kula.

I glanced back at the *Star-Advertiser*. In the Hawai'i section, a headline and photo caught my eye:

Where Is Cheyenne Sin?
Radio Pitchman's Wife Still Missing

Cheyenne Sin had been a fashion model in her youth and still looked the part: tall and impossibly thin. Jet black hair. Skin luminescent as moonlight. In her long, shapely legs and delicate features I could see a resemblance to Lehua.

I usually have a hunch about missing-person cases. But this one wasn't sending me any strong signals. I wasn't ready to believe Mrs. Gum's theory that Buckingham murdered his wife. Nor was I ready to let him off the hook. He was a man accustomed to getting his way. But was he capable of killing anyone who might block it? Even his own wife?

To what extent Buckingham may have been involved, I could only guess. And how much the unfavorable publicity had shaken his investors' faith, I could also only guess. But I was concerned. If Buckingham went under, as the late Dr. Carreras predicted, who would pay me when my retainer ran out?

As the sun peeked above the horizon, foot traffic on the beach came to a halt. Everybody faced east like pilgrims observing a religious rite. I set down my coffee cup on the transmission hump and watched. Quite the scene. The human file glowed in the sun. Nobody moved—except the dogs. After a while I grabbed Kula's photo and walked down to get a closer look.

Before I reached the shore, the sun cleared the ocean and the rite was over. Everybody was moving again. I hailed a slim brunette in a bikini before her boxer dragged her down the beach.

"Hoku!" she commanded. "Heel!"

The boxer kept pulling.

I stepped up and flashed Kula's photo. "Have you seen this dog?"

"Looks familiar." She planted her feet in the sand as Hoku tugged at the reins. "Very familiar."

"Do you remember where you saw him last?" I was hopeful.

"Isn't he that surfing dog, the one that rides waves with the girl?"

"That's him. Have you seen him?"

"On TV."

"Right." I tried to jog her memory. "But have you seen him here on this beach?"

"Here? On Kailua Beach?"

I nodded.

"Never."

I shrugged. "Well. Thanks. If you do . . ." But Hoku had already started hauling his mistress away.

Next I tried a sandy-haired man walking a grey dog that had the gait of a racehorse.

"What kind is this?" I said to start the conversation.

"Weimaraner," he replied. "Silver, sit!" he commanded and the big dog snapped down.

"Beautiful." I handed him Kula's photo. "Ever seen this one?"

He studied Kula's image. "I saw a dog like this with a surfer on Sunday out by Flat Island."

I perked up. "What exactly did you see?"

"The golden retriever was hunched on the front of the guy's board. I saw 'em ride two or three waves. The dog never fell off. Not once. It was amazing. He just hunkered down and hung on, even in the white water."

"Could the surfer have been a girl?"

"I don't know . . . It's a long way out there." He thought for a moment. "I suppose."

"Did you see them later on the beach—either the surfer or the dog?"

"No. They were still in water when I took Silver home."

"Here's my card." I handed it to him, feeling like I'd made progress. "Please call me if you think of anything else. The golden retriever is missing. There's a reward. His owner would be very grateful for his safe return."

"OK." He took the card and Silver led him away.

Scanning the beach for my next prospect, I settled on a *tutu,* or grandmotherly type, trailing behind a fawn-colored dog that looked like a miniature hippopotamus. It had deeply wrinkled skin, a pug nose, and curling tail.

"Unusual dog," I said. "What kind is it?"

"Shar-Pei," the *tutu* said. "It's a Chinese breed."

"Are they nice dogs?"

"The best." She flashed a smile.

I handed her Kula's photo. "Ever seen this one?"

"Maybe," she said.

"Here—on Kailua Beach?" I asked.

"Not on the beach," she said, "in a car heading toward the Pali. It was on Sunday morning. Ah, two people were in the car—yeah, a man and a woman." She nodded with certainty. "The dog was in back."

"You sure it was this dog?"

"How could I miss him?" she said. "They were stopped at a red light. I stared at his pretty coat until they got the green."

"What about the two people? Was the woman a teenager with red hair?"

"No. She had black hair, I think. Definitely not red. The man was wearing a baseball cap."

"What kind of car?"

"Oh, I don't know. It was big—one of those, ah . . . SUVs. Tan or bronze." She thought for a moment. "I take it the dog shouldn't have been along for the ride?"

I nodded and handed her my card. "Please call me if you remember anything else."

"I promise," she said. Her Shar-Pei pulled her down the beach.

eleven

At eight a.m. I opened Island Insta-Print in Kailua town with my order for five hundred posters of the missing retriever. Each one listed his description and details about his disappearance—plus the $1,000 reward. The theory was that if Kula was stolen the thief might be lured by the easy money of the reward, rather than face the potential risks of reselling the dog. Even if Kula had simply wandered off, the posters would be a strong incentive to contact me.

Waiting for my order, I walked two blocks to Windward Pets and asked for the store manager, the same woman who was quoted in a story Maile had clipped. Charlene Nogata had straight black hair, brown eyes, and her ear to local gossip.

"Did you hear about that Kailua couple arrested for pet theft?" she asked.

"No," I said, "tell me."

"Spyder Silva and Reiko Infante. They're awaiting trial. The indictment says they're part of an organized pet theft ring,"

"You know them?"

"I don't know them," she said, "but I know where they live. Their address was in the paper—a front-page story a few weeks ago."

I vaguely remembered the story.

"Windward Sands apartments—about three blocks that way . . ." She pointed in the direction I had come. "Behind Aloha Auto Parts."

"Eh, thanks. I have time to kill."

"They're not the kind of people you'd want to meet in a back alley," she said.

"Understood."

"Sleazy." She pointed again towards the Windward Sands.

* * *

I hiked a few blocks and there it was. In the long shadow cast by the auto parts store stood a faded brown apartment building. It had seen better days: cracked and missing jalousies, rotting wood trim, and a parking lot that looked more like a wrecking yard. Not the sort of place you'd normally find a pedigree dog. Among a row of mailboxes on the ground floor, I found the names Silva & Infante. Apartment 1J.

It was a corner unit and I had to knock three times before someone answered. When the door finally opened there stood a man, naked from the waist up. Tattoos covered every inch of skin I could see. The largest one, on his chest, showed crossed assault rifles coiled with a cobra. Beneath that was: KILL 'EM ALL, LET GOD SORT 'EM OUT.

Sleazy. I could see what the pet store owner meant. Though I wasn't shaking in my boots. Guys like him were mostly show.

"Watchu want?" He reeked of sardines.

"Are you Spyder Silva?"

He nodded.

Behind him, a hard looking woman lounged on a sofa having a smoke. Her stained robe suggested she had just rolled out of bed. Reiko Infante?

I handed him my card, showed him Kula's photo, and hauled out my pidgin. "Evah see dis dog?"

"Who wen' send you heah?" Silva snarled.

"One neighbor ovah dere." I pointed vaguely in the direction of Windward Pets.

"Dey wrong, brah. I nevah seen dis dog." He started to close the door.

I stepped forward. "What kine car you drive?"

"Spyder!" the woman shouted. "Tell 'em to fuck off."

"Shut up, awready." The man handed me back my card. "Da black Toyota truck in da lot. Go check 'em out." The door slammed in my face.

I wandered back out to the parking lot and before long found the black pickup. It was raised high with knobby off-road tires and displayed a bumper sticker: *P.E.T.A.—People Eating Tasty Animals.* But it wasn't bronze. Or an SUV. I peeked inside. Unbelievable. On the floor in front of the passenger seat was an automatic pistol. It looked like a Beretta. Silva ought to think twice about leaving his weapon in plain view, especially when he and his playmate were under indictment. But he didn't strike me as the thinking type.

I walked away shaking my head. Though the tips I'd been getting so far added up to nothing, the two alleged pet thieves had scored a spot on my suspect list. Despite the fact that Kula didn't appear to be inside their apartment and that

Silva's truck looked nothing like a tan SUV, it was too much of a coincidence that he and Infante were awaiting trial for pet theft. And that they lived in Kailua, less than a mile from where Kula disappeared. Plus, I flat out didn't like either one of them.

* * *

Five hundred posters in hand, I made my way among the businesses of Kailua town, asking if shop owners would display them. Most were cooperative. And many offered heart-felt stories about the time their own Mele or Kaipo or Duke went missing.

My cell phone beeped. Madison Highcamp. She left a text message:

Tonight.

I didn't reply. I knew what she meant.

Then I drove to Lanikai Elementary School, on the edge of Kailua Beach. The Principal's husband, Creighton Lee, ran HPD's photo lab and was a surfing buddy. I'd never met his wife, Marianne. She looked to be in her mid-forties. She was pretty and slightly plump.

"Kai," she smiled warmly. "It's so nice to meet you. Creighton's told me so much about you."

I cringed.

"He calls you a 'soul surfer.' And to Creighton that's good."

Soul surfer meant someone who surfs for the love of riding waves—not for competition, not for glory, not to be cool, not for any other reason than pure passion.

"Creighton's too generous," I said. "He's the original soul surfer. I can't compare with him."

"So," she looked at me curiously, "what brings you to Lanikai Elementary?"

"A famous surfing dog. Maybe you've heard of him? His name is Kula."

She looked puzzled. "No, afraid I— "

Then I pleaded my case. I had a missing dog to find, time was of the essence, and her students could help by putting up posters. Not only that, I would pay.

She told me to wait outside the fifth and sixth grade rooms while, just before recess, she repeated my spiel. As the kids trotted out, three volunteered. Noe and Tiffy, two giggly girls who looked like twins, and Ronson, a cool dude in a North Shore t-shirt. The three of them were friends. After I called their parents for approval, we agreed to meet at the end of the school day.

In the meantime, I returned to my Kailua Beach stakeout. Dog-walkers were few and far between that time of day, I found out, and the dog-less folks I approached offered no help.

When school let out I picked up my student helpers. I put my surfboard on the roof racks to make room inside the Impala. They were enthusiastic. I found out each one had a pet. Ronson's family had a bichon frise, Noe's a black Lab, and Tiffy's a wayward parakeet named Blu. The two girls, it turned out, were not twins. They just looked alike. The kids chatted about their pets while I drove from one utility pole to the next. The girls' giggles went away once we got down to business. I mentioned the likelihood that Kula was stolen.

"Why would anybody steal a dog?" Noe asked.

I could have given her a list of reasons, but I just shrugged. The reasons wouldn't have answered her question anyway, which was more like, "What would possess a person to do something like that?" For that question I really had no answer.

Soon I was giving the kids directions. "Tiffy, you take the posters." I handed her about a dozen. "Noe, here's the staple gun." I gave her the heavy chrome gun.

"What do I do?" Ronson asked.

"The most important job. You watch for traffic while they put up the posters." Then I reassured him. "Don't worry. You're going to take turns with the jobs."

At each pole Tiffy popped out with a poster and Noe with the staple gun. Ronson guarded by watching and directing traffic. After a dozen poles, as promised, the kids changed roles. Between stops they entertained me with stories of pet misadventures—like the time Tiffy had to climb a mango tree to get her parakeet.

By the end of three hours, we'd covered the entire Lanikai loop, all side streets dog-walkers would use to get to the beach, and also parts of Kailua town near the water. My helpers got home before dinner and walked away with fifteen dollars each, all promising to keep an eye out for Kula.

After I dropped off the last of the three, Noe's question was still ringing in my ears: Why would anybody steal a dog?

twelve

Back at Kailua Beach Park, I removed my board from the racks, slipped off my khakis from over my board shorts, and paddled out to Flat Island. My plan was to unwind and work the case at the same time. Regulars out there might know something about Kula. And by waiting for the after-work crowd I hoped to catch some of the same surfers who were likely to be there weekends—the time that the golden retriever had disappeared.

My young helpers' happy stories about their pets got me thinking about when I had a dog. Pono was a shepherd-golden mix, a light-colored *poi* dog that looked a little like Kula. Except Pono's ears kind of half stood up like a shepherd's and half flopped over like a retriever's, in a homely, adorable way. He and I were inseparable. Until I lost him.

As I stroked toward the coral island a quarter mile off shore, its unusual shape came into view. A few acres long, the oblong island resembled a green tabletop, barely above the high tide mark. It was a bird sanctuary where you can watch pairs of seabirds nesting in *pukas,* or holes, in the coral. But most people come for the surf, rather than for the birds. On a good day, waves sweep around the south side of the island like a point break. You ride the wave to your left, steering clear of the rocks and coral heads in the shallow water near the island.

The trade winds gently drifted by as I paddled out. The water in the lee of the island was like glass and I could see the rocky bottom clearly. A half dozen surfers were having fun with a three-foot swell. I paddled into the lineup and caught a wave, riding left with my back to the curl, like any "regular foot" does. Then I paddled back and waited for another. I sat on my board, dangling my toes in the water. *Lucky you live Hawai'i,* as the saying goes.

One surf buddy of mine calls Flat Island a shark pit. But I've never seen a shark here. And I haven't heard of any- one getting bitten. But I found myself scouring the ocean for a dark shape. The semi-circle of welts on my chest always reminded me of the time I got hit at Laniākea.

It happened so fast I didn't see it coming. A tiger shark. Fortunately he didn't like the taste of me. He took one bite and swam off. There was lots of blood in the water, but noth- ing broken except my skin. I paddled in under my own power, with an escort of surfers who couldn't believe their eyes. The EMS guys gave me a ride to Kahuku Hospital. I got lucky. I didn't even stay overnight. But ever since then whenever I go surfing I say a mantra, "No Fear, No Fear," and I try to forget.

Of the dozen or so surfers at Flat Island that afternoon, I found only one who'd actually been in the water on Sun- day when Kula disappeared. A deeply-tanned Rastafarian dude named Dickie. But the dreadlocked surfer could tell me nothing new.

Dickie and I sat in the lineup together and eventually I caught a wave with him, giving him the sweetest part of the curl. After that ride he pointed toward shore, waved, and started paddling in. As he was stroking away, he cocked his head back and said, "You betta go talk wit' Moku."

"What's his numbah?"

"Doan know, brah."

I shouted mine to him across the water. "Tell Moku for call me, yeah?"

"Latahs." Dickie was soon out of earshot.

When I paddled in later, a yellow helicopter buzzed me on its way to Flat Island. On its belly was FIRE AND RESCUE. It circled the island and then hovered over the lineup, whipping whitecaps where surfers were sitting on their boards. I wondered what was up.

Once on shore I spotted two HPD cruisers, blue lights flashing. Down in the swimming area at Kailua Beach Park, no one was in the water. Guys in trunks and girls in bikinis were standing on shore, staring out to sea. Another surfer who had been at Flat Island said, "Did you see the shark?"

"What shark?"

"Tiger. Ten foot. Swimming toward Flat Island."

Shark Pit. Had my buddy been right?

I looked on the beach for Dickie. He was gone. I doubted I would ever hear from him or his friend Moku. Shouting my phone number across the water had been a long shot.

But so far, long shots were all I had.

thirteen

On the way back from Kailua, I swung by Maile's cottage to feed her cats. It should have been easy.

Peppah, the dusty black Angora, pounced on me the minute I walked in the door, meowing and clawing his way up my leg. Coconut, the Siamese, stretched casually on the sofa. The calico, Lolo, gave me one look and ripped into a bedroom.

After I fixed their food and set out three dishes—each inscribed with a name in calligraphy—Peppah and Coconut came running, but not Lolo. I went looking. I ended up in Maile's bedroom, her parents' bedroom when we were kids, finally spotting Lolo under the poster bed. *"Auwē!"* I said under my breath—the pidgin equivalent of dammit.

Once I left Maile's cottage, Peppah or Coconut or both would devour Lolo's dinner. The shy cat would go hungry. I couldn't have that on my conscience. So down on my knees I went, wondering how I'd got this gig.

"Come out, Lolo," I urged her. "Come out girl."

She retreated farther. I checked my watch. I had a dinner date at six.

Only one solution: I slipped her food dish under the bed. It went in easily for about a foot, then it hit something. I leaned down and saw an object—flat and slightly smaller than a shoebox lid. I moved it to the side and inched Lolo's food dish toward her.

When I leaned back on my heels, the object caught the light. I pulled it out. It was a picture frame holding a photo of Maile and her late husband Nestor standing arm-in-arm at the Koko Head firing range. The day was sunny and Nestor had his shirt off. He was a well-built man, his body and arms packed with muscle. Maile was all smiles. Between them was propped the same sniper rifle from the photo in her living room. *A day on the range.*

Seeing the two of them so happy together gave me a sinking feeling. First Karl, then Nester. Why did it still bother me that I wanted Maile once and couldn't have her? High school was years ago. Was I feeling something for Maile again? I nudged the photo back beneath the bed, curious why she kept it there. But not before looking at it one more time.

It must have been tough for Maile when Nestor died. And tough again when Rusty disappeared. It was all too familiar. I had Pono when my parents died. My Auntie Mae Kealoha told me that my mother and father had gone to heaven and that I mustn't worry about them because they were in a wonderful place, more wonderful than I could ever imagine. My father's rented airplane had crashed into cloud-shrouded Mauna Kea on the Big Island, the tallest mountain in the Pacific. Auntie Mae explained that I would never see him or my mother again in this life, but if I was a good boy and lived a good life I would see them in the next. My father, mother, and I would all live happily together for eternity.

That sounded good to my eight-year-old ears. But the eternal happiness didn't seem quite complete, so I asked, "What about Pono? Will he live with us in Heaven, too?"

She hardly skipped a beat. "Is Pono a good dog?"

"He's a very good dog," I said proudly.

Auntie tried to smile through her tears. "Yes, Pono will live with you forever."

I was relieved. Until I grew older and realized how long I'd have to wait for that promised bliss.

Under the poster bed, Lolo finally started to nibble on her dinner. Safe for me to go.

* * *

I drove from Maile's cottage to my studio apartment at the Waikīkī Edgewater to shower off from my session at Flat Island. "Edgewater" is kind of a stretch, since the building sits nearly half a mile from the beach. But the Edgewater does in fact flank the Ala Wai Canal. My own tiny flat on the forty-fifth floor is wedged between two penthouses and faces the airport and Pearl Harbor. It's the less glamorous view compared to the view of Diamond Head, in the opposite direction. But on a clear day I can pick out Ford Island, the Arizona Memorial, and the Mighty Mo. And beyond them, the majestic Waianae Range.

I hopped into my tiny shower, about the size of a coffin standing on its head. My bathroom and the entire apartment, for that matter, are not much bigger than a walk-in closet and resemble a discount Waikīkī hotel room, with bath and kitchenette at one end, and *lānai*, or patio, at the other. Against one wall are a double bed and nightstand with the photo of a former girlfriend. Against the other, a color TV on top of a dresser. Above that hangs a photo of my mom and dad. Next to them a surf poster. And that's it.

Before leaving for dinner I checked my messages. I was surprised to find one from Maile. She had arrived in Salt Lake City and driven to the pet refuge. She was looking forward to the four-day workshop on animal sanctuaries that began the next morning. She thanked me again for giving her a ride to the airport and feeding her cats. She even thanked me in advance for meeting her plane on Saturday.

"I'm looking forward to catching up with you, Kai . . ." She paused. "It's been too long."

It had.

Then she said, "If it turns out Kula didn't just wander off, if it turns out he was stolen, watch yourself. Pet thieves are a twisted lot. A dog is just a pawn to them. They're usually after something else—to gain advantage over someone or something. I've run into cases like that, where the dog's master owes money or has a vindictive ex. It has nothing to do with the animal and everything to do with the people. Good luck, Kai. And watch yourself."

fourteen

I had dinner that night at the posh Waikīkī Canoe Club with Madison Highcamp—Mrs. Conrad Highcamp—third wife of a wealthy hotelier whose luxury resorts dotted the globe.

Madison commanded a prime oceanfront table on the open-air *lānai*. She was puffing on a cigarette, sipping a martini, and talking nonstop on her cell phone when I arrived. Her Maltese, balled into a white puff, leaped from her lap and danced around me, yipping and making a spectacle of herself.

"Twinkie, hush!" Madison set down her phone and stood. Her dark cherry hair, pinned up in loose curls, almost tumbled down onto a beach cover-up that covered very little at all. But nobody was complaining. The former beauty queen wasn't shy about showing herself off. She mashed out her cigarette, picked up the dog, and pressed her glossy red lips on my cheek.

"Hello, darling." She smelled of Chanel, tobacco, and gin. It was a provocative, come-hither blend of odors like ripe cheddar in a mousetrap. Madison Highcamp spent her days shopping designer boutiques and sunning on the beach, and her nights hanging out in private clubs and dancing at charity balls. Her Midas-touch husband was old enough to be her father, or grandfather. She lived in a sprawling Diamond Head penthouse, while he preferred their Beverly Hills mansion, closer to his corporate headquarters in Los Angeles. They were seldom together.

I met Madison through a Canoe Club paddler who urged me to call her, saying she was lonely and enjoyed the company of surfers. "I don't date married women," I said. He persisted: "Spread some *aloha*, Kai." Against my better judgment I called her.

"Let's have a drink." She sat and planted a kiss on the Maltese's wet noise. *"Twinkie, precious!"* she whispered in the dog's ear.

"You should get a pet, Kai. You're alone too much. A nice dog like Twinkie might do wonders."

"First Tommy. Now you."

"What?" she asked.

"Never mind." The cocktail waitress came so I said: "What would you like to drink?"

"The same." She pointed to her empty martini glass.

"A martini for the lady," I told the waitress. "And a beer for me."

As the sun sunk toward the Pacific in a riot of gold, Madison waxed eloquent. "Ah, the islands," she said. "Is there anything like them?"

"Lucky you live Hawai'i," I said.

"Conrad hates it here," she said. "Can you believe that?"

"How can anyone hate Hawai'i?"

"Oh, I think he finds the islands lovely and all. But there's nothing here for him. No captains of industry on the scale he's used to. No tycoons or politicians of his stripe. No glamour of Hollywood. He prefers Beverly Hills and Palm Springs and sometimes New York."

"So he doesn't ever visit you?"

"The chances of him coming are about the same as snow falling in Waikīkī. Anyway, he knows I have friends. He's not stupid."

Our drinks came.

"Cheers," I said.

Madison's midnight eyes met mine. I studied her perfect teeth and marveled at how different we were. The fortyish perfumed debutante who never worked a day in her life and the thirty-four year old surfer and P.I. who was perpetually broke. We had almost nothing in common. But in a strange way, we did. We were both adrift on this lonely planet, as Tommy called it. Why should I question our arrangement? Maybe it was Tommy's question that was bothering me: Are you still hanging out with that Highcamp woman? He had hit a nerve. Or maybe it was seeing Maile again after all those years.

"Kai." Madison rested her chin on jeweled fingers. "Let's not go so long between rendezvous. You know how I miss you."

"I miss you too," I heard myself saying.

Her cell phone rang.

"Hello," she said cheerfully. Her expression suddenly changed. "Conrad?" She put her hand over the mouthpiece and whispered to me, *"Oh my god!"* Then she removed her hand. "Surprised to hear from you, darling . . . I'm at the Canoe Club having dinner with a friend." She reached across the table and took my hand.

"Oh, nobody you know." Madison winked at me. "Drinking . . . ? Just my usual martini before dinner." She reached for another cigarette, then frowned. "You're coming to Hawai'i?" The cigarette rested between her fingers. "Oh, anytime you like, darling. It's up to you . . . OK, love you too."

Madison's glossy lips tightened as she snapped her phone shut. I leaned forward with a lit match. "Conrad is threatening to come here again," she said. "Probably to check up on me." The flame caught the tip of her cigarette as she puffed and made it glow. "He always says he's coming, but he never does."

"Never?" I shook the match out.

"Almost never." She shrugged. "Let's eat, honey, and not talk about Conrad.

We called the waitress and ordered dinner—a warm cilantro and marinated quail salad for Madison and Canoe Club burger for me.

"Why don't you tell me all about one of your exciting cases?" Madison's eyes glittered.

"OK." I fingered the condensation dripping down my beer glass. How could I admit I'd been reduced to searching for a dog? Then I thought of Twinkie, sleeping peacefully in Madison's lap. A dog lover, maybe she would sympathize? I gave her an abridged version of the story, hinting at, but not naming my client. She figured it out. It's a small island.

"Barry Buckingham, the gold dealer?" she asked.

"You know him?"

"Slightly," she said evasively.

"How'd you meet?"

"Conrad, bless his heart, gave me a little investment money to play with—barely six figures—and I thought, why not buy some gold? After all, I love gold." She waved her rings at me. "Anyway, the other day I was driving home from Nei-man's and heard him on the radio: *'I'm certified gold expert Barry Buckingham, and you're listening to Gold Standard.'* He has such a soothing voice, you know. So British."

"Australian, I believe."

"Why he just captivated me," Madison continued, as if I hadn't spoken. "So I called him at his 'offices,' as he says on the radio, and we chatted. His voice was even more soothing than on the air. And then," she took a sip of her martini, "he invited me to dinner on his yacht tomorrow night. Can you believe that?"

I could. "Be careful," I cautioned.

"Don't worry, I'm just going to listen to what he has to say." She played with a loose curl. "Have you ever thought of investing, Kai? A nest egg for your future?"

"No." Madison had no idea how the other half lived.

"Maybe you should consider gold. Barry says it's very stable."

The waitress arrived with Madison's salad and my burger. Madison stubbed out her cigarette. We had barely taken a bite when her phone rang again.

"Hello." She made a puzzled look. *"Barry . . . ?* Oh, of course. Yes, I'm looking forward. Seven? That would be fine. See you then." She closed her phone.

"Let me guess what Barry Buckingham wanted to talk about."

"Gold . . ." she said.

Madison Highcamp—rich, idle, and beautiful—would be a prime target for smooth talkers with something glittery to sell.

"And to reconfirm dinner," she continued. "I guess he's at loose ends."

"Did you know his wife disappeared—Cheyenne Sin?"

"That was *his* wife? I didn't put two and two together."

"Four months ago," I said. "I thought Buckingham was hiring me to find her. Instead I'm looking for his dog."

"Poor man."

"Me or him?"

"Both of you."

"It's a gig." I didn't bother to tell her that HPD, and one of his neighbors, suspected Buckingham in his wife's disappearance. Madison would meet him and make up her own mind.

She fixed those eyes on me again. "Why don't you come back to my penthouse after dinner, and we can . . . talk."

"I have to get up early, Madison . . ."

She leaned forward, her breasts brushing the white linen tablecloth. "You know I'm not good with *no*'s."

"Just for a little while," I finally agreed.

"Good. You can show me your shark bite."

We both knew what that meant.

* * *

After we finished dinner, billed, against my polite objections to Conrad Highcamp's account, I walked Madison to her Diamond Head apartment, a few minutes' stroll from the Canoe Club. Her penthouse was one of only two on the entire top floor and commanded a sweeping view of Waikīkī. The view was dark at night, except for the lights of the beachfront hotels reflecting in the surf. We sat on a couch and Madison drank another martini. About half way down she got to thinking. A dangerous thing.

"Why can't I be more like you, Kai, and surf all day in the sun?"

"What's stopping you?" I said. "You've got more time and money than anybody I know." I could have told her I hadn't surfed all day since I opened my detective agency, but she wouldn't have heard me.

"Let me see your shark bite."

"Why do you want to see it again? You'll make yourself afraid of the ocean and then you'll never surf."

"I don't know," she said. "It's just so . . . wild."

"Wild? I never thought of it that way."

She pouted.

"OK. Here." I pulled up my shirt.

Madison's eyes widened and then she explored the sixteen welts with her fingertips. "You think I have everything, Kai, but you're wrong."

"You can have whatever you want."

"No I can't," she sobbed. "I'm not free." She pulled me down with her on the couch.

I don't remember much after that. Those nights we spent together in her apartment tended to blur. I've had finer moments. Madison and I both knew what we had couldn't last, but tomorrow didn't matter as long as we had tonight.

It was nearly one when I left her apartment. Wheeling my Impala through the drowsy streets of Waikīkī, I felt more alone than when the night began. And I was no closer to finding the elusive retriever. But I had learned about the gold dealer's tactics with the rich and gorgeous.

fifteen

Thursday morning's *Star-Advertiser* carried a brief story in the Hawai'i News section about Dr. Carreras. The police investigation had determined that his accident was caused by a combination of the rain-slick surface of upper Tantalus Drive and the excessive speed of the Porsche. Alcohol was not a factor.

I wondered again what Dr. Carreras was going to tell me about Buckingham.

Later that morning I pulled into my parking stall off Maunakea Street and walked to my office at the corner of Beretania above Fujiyama's Flower Leis. Parking in that part of Chinatown was murderously expensive. Thankfully Mrs. Fujiyama had three stalls reserved for her tenants. She could probably rent them for almost as much as her offices.

As I walked to the lei shop, the case started stirring up memories again of my dog, Pono.

* * *

When my parents died it was a comfort to have Pono. The Kealoha family *hānaied* me and I moved from town to their Punaluʻu home, across from the beach on Oʻahu's windward side. Pono came too. I attended school at Kahuku and had trouble adjusting. My grades tumbled. It was soon decided that I would move again, this time to the mainland to live with my Uncle Orson's family in Pasadena, California, and go to school there. My Auntie promised to take care of Pono until I got settled, then ship him to me.

After I'd been in California a few weeks, my uncle got a call from Oʻahu. He sat me down at the kitchen table, a somber expression on his face. "I have some bad news for you, Kai. Your dog was run over by a car. He didn't survive."

Pono's death, coming on the heels of my parents' accident—and without my Auntie's promises of heavenly bliss—was almost too much to bear. Later she sent me Pono's collar and license. I think I still have them somewhere in my apartment, along with her note promising I would see my dog again in Heaven with my parents. After that I couldn't imagine having another dog. And I never did. I never even gave dogs much thought—until this case.

* * *

Inside the flower shop Mrs. Fujiyama and two of her *lei* girls, Chastity and Joon, were stringing tuberose. The powerful scent raised the hair on my neck and followed me up the orange shag stairs. At the end of the hall, I stopped in front of the full-color longboard rider airbrushed on my door. Beneath were the words: SURFING DETECTIVE: CONFIDENTIAL

INVESTIGATIONS—ALL ISLANDS. Under those words I felt like scrawling: *No missing pet cases.* But it was too late.

Inside my office the red light on the answering machine was blinking. I hadn't checked for messages since yesterday. There were seven.

The first: "Can you help us find Puffy? She's a Persian cat. She wandered off two days ago. She usually comes right back. But we've looked everywhere. We live in ʻĀlewa Heights . . ."

The second: "Max is missing and I don't know what to do. He's an Airedale and he's my only companion since my husband died. Maybe you are my godsend. Please, please call me . . ."

The third: "Is this the pet detective? I found a dog . . . Uh, a black dog in Palolo . . . and I wondered if you could help me find its owner."

The fourth: "Hello, this is Mrs. Leong. I have a favor to ask. Could you help me pick a pedigree Skye Terrier puppy for my granddaughter?"

Who was referring these people? ʻĀlewa Heights? Palolo? They were nowhere near my posters in Kailua. Maybe it was my ads in the two daily papers? But no mention had been made of a pet detective. Go figure.

The fifth call came from a man who remembered seeing a leather collar embossed in gold on Kailua Beach. But he went on to say: "I came back the next day and the collar was gone." I filed that one away in my mental notebook.

The sixth call: "You want fine' one golden retrievah? Try one puppy mill in Mililani. She got all kine." He left an address that I copied down.

The last call: "I found your dog." The voice sounded old, male, Caucasian. "He's a light-colored retriever with no collar. My wife and I live near Kailua Beach. He wandered here yesterday, but I just saw your poster this morning on our walk." The man left a number and said he didn't want the reward, just for the "beautiful retriever" to be returned to his family.

I called immediately. Maybe I'd gotten lucky.

An old woman said her husband wasn't home, but that I could come claim the sunny retriever, as she described him.

"Is the dog male?" I asked.

"Yes," she replied. "He's male, and he's very pretty."

"Sounds like Kula." I was hopeful.

She gave me her address off south Kalaheo, less than two blocks from Kailua Beach Park where Kula had disappeared.

* * *

My Impala was purring over the Pali again, windward bound. The address the woman had given me was on a quiet beachside street in the residential tract of Ku'ulei. I pulled up to a ranch-style home that looked comfortably middle class. The sound of my door slamming set off a deep, authoritative barking from behind a palm hedge. The bark obviously came from a big dog.

I walked around to the front door and rang the bell. A gray-haired woman wearing a flowered *mu'umu'u* that hung on her like a sack invited me in. As she led me to her back-yard, she rambled on about the found dog.

"He's a beauty. So shiny. And his eyes . . . but you know that." She opened her screen door. "My husband doesn't care about the reward. He just wants to give the dog back to its owner."

"That's generous," I said, "but the reward is his, so long as the dog is Kula."

"It's him all right," she said. "Follow me."

We stepped onto a huge lawn so perfect it looked like a putting green. Encircling it were birds-of-paradise, red ginger, and *laua'e* ferns. I spotted the dog wandering among the plants, sniffing then lifting his leg. The moment he heard us he charged in our direction, tail wagging, almost knocking me over. This was a big, gregarious dog and his enthusiasm was over the top.

"Calm down, boy." I patted his yellow head. It wasn't Kula. "I think this is a Labrador," I said, "a yellow Labrador. He's got a shorter coat than a golden and looks a bit stockier."

"Oh," the woman said, her disappointment obvious.

"Have you called the Humane Society?" I asked.

"No. When my husband saw your poster we decided to call you first."

"Well, somebody is probably worried sick about this dog."

She nodded. "He's a beauty, all right."

I thanked her for calling me, left a poster with Kula's photo, and drove away. I don't know who was more disappointed, the old woman or me.

sixteen

I hopped onto the H-3 freeway, climbed into the Koʻolau mountains, shot through the tunnel, and headed for the leeward side. My destination was Mililani Town, where my anonymous caller had said I might find a puppy mill. Another questionable lead. But it was worth a try.

As I drove, I reviewed Buckingham's three possible suspects—two neighbors and an alleged prowler. Neither of the neighbors got me any closer to the missing dog and neither promised to be any help. Mrs. Gum's grip on reality seemed iffy, at best, and Dr. Carreras was dead. And I had found no evidence of any prowler to back Buckingham's allegation. Mostly what I had come away with were allegations against Buckingham himself—that he was a con man, fraud, potential bankrupt, and murderer.

My own fledgling efforts at pet detection had uncovered two indicted pet thieves, Spyder Silva and Reiko Infante, but neither as yet could be linked to Kula's disappearance. My dawn stakeout of Kailua beach yielded a possible sighting of Kula in an SUV leaving town, but so far I couldn't corroborate it. A surf session at Flat Island turned up a possible informant named Moku, who I had no way to contact. And he hadn't bothered to call me. My newspaper ads and posters were eliciting calls, mostly from desperate pet owners looking for their own lost Fido or Fluffy. Finally, my one promising lead to a light-colored retriever evaporated when the dog turned out to be a yellow Lab.

So here I was driving into central Oʻahu on the H-2, hoping for a breakthrough. I exited at Mililani Town, where pineapple and cane fields in the plateau between the Waiʻanae and Koʻolau ranges had been transformed into a crowded suburb of condos, townhouses, and tract homes. And also puppy mills?

The main goal of a puppy mill, Maile had told me, is to make money. Its owners don't give a rip about the health and living conditions of the puppies, or about the moms and pops that produce them. I wasn't looking forward to my visit. Criminals I run into on my everyday cases make me feel bad enough about human beings. I didn't relish the thought of meeting up with lowlifes who abuse helpless animals to fatten their wallets.

I drove along Meheula Parkway past a couple of schools, a park, and a recreation center, scouting for one particular townhouse among a sea of thousands. The address I was given by the anonymous caller was not on a street, it turned out, but a court in a secluded tract abutting the park.

The cream and baby blue townhouse had a carport with an empty mailbox—I checked—attached to one of its pillars. A grimy Jeep Cherokee wearing a Schofield Barracks sticker was parked under a portico with purple hydrangea and parched palms. A faded and torn American flag hung over the doorway.

As I approached the front door, a rotten smell crept up on me like a dead skunk. Then I heard an animal whimpering. I take that back. Not one animal—many.

I rang the bell and heard shuffling feet.

"Yeah, whadda ya want?" a woman's voice boomed through the door.

"A golden retriever," I shouted back.

The door creaked open to a fortyish dirty blonde sinking her teeth into a strawberry danish. She didn't need the danish. She had a double chin, ballooning breasts, and a sagging belly that strained her oversized T-shirt.

"How'd ya fine my place?" she asked with a full mouth. "My newspaper ads don' give no address."

"I asked around."

She swallowed her danish and let me in. Her townhouse looked fairly typical. Pale green walls, one bedroom downstairs and probably two more upstairs. A couple of baths. And a narrow kitchen with an electric range, microwave and fridge. What wasn't typical was the smell. And the mess. The place was a garbage heap. A six-pack of diet cola was perched on a rusty exercise bicycle; a case of rum sat in a laundry basket—four quarts left. The others empty. But I saw no dogs.

"What's your name?" She glanced at me with sad blue eyes.

"Tommy." I borrowed my attorney's name. "And you are?" I asked.

"Lou," she grunted. "So you' look'n for a golden retriever puppy?"

I nodded.

"Jus' a minute, Tommy." She put her plump hands on her hips. "My pups aren't ready yet, but you can look 'em over and pick one in advance."

Lou led me into a tiny half bath where a dull red bitch was nursing a half dozen scrawny pups on a bare tile floor. No bed. No blanket. The dog's tummy was so sunken I could have encircled it with my hands. And I could count her ribs. Every one stood out like a rack of lamb. Her puppies were drinking her dry.

"Check 'em out, Tommy." Lou hovered over me as I knelt down. The odor coming off the pups made my eyes water. My stomach turned, partly from the stench, partly from what I saw.

"Seventy-five dollars cash will hold a pup. It's how I pay the rent. My husband got hurt in Iraq. He's been at Tripler Hospital for months, but he ain't never gonna be the same again. Never."

"I'm sorry," I said.

"It ain't easy," she said. "We was gonna retire together, have our own kennel, and breed champions. But then . . ."

"I like this one." I pointed to one of the pups, then realized this wasn't getting me any closer to Kula. "But I'd like to see your adult dogs, too."

"Adult dogs?" She clucked her tongue. "You said you wanted a puppy!"

"I thought I did. But now that I've seen them, I don't know. Maybe one of each."

"Follow me." She trudged across a stinky carpet to a tiny bedroom. There were four crates, each containing a dark dog. Like the one in the bathroom, these adult dogs were also severely malnourished. Rib and hip bones protruding. Stomachs concave. No sign of Kula.

"These are fine," I said, "but I'd hoped for a light-colored dog. A male."

"A blond male?" she said. "I've got just the one. He's a beauty. But it'll take me a day or two to get him."

"Where is he?" I tried not to sound too excited.

"Jus' give me a call tomorrow." She recited a phone number, and walked me to the front door. "You can decide about the puppy then."

"OK, Lou," I said, forcing a smile. "Till tomorrow."

She smiled back, red jelly still between her teeth. I left feeling almost sad for Lou. But sadder for her dogs. I wondered if I was cut out for pet detection.

I knew the answer, but thought the reason was that I didn't know the ropes. But maybe I just didn't have the heart, or the stomach, to deal with animal abusers. Then I put my feelings aside and asked myself a question more pertinent to the case: Could this particular abuser deliver the famous surfing dog?

* * *

By the time I got back to my office I had two more phone messages. The first was an urgent plea to find an African grey parrot. I deleted it. The second got my attention:

"You like get da dog back, brah? Bettah geev' me one call."

It was a male voice and his phone number had a 259 prefix—Waimānalo, a good five miles from Kailua where Kula disappeared. Was it likely that a dog could have wandered that far along the heavily-trafficked Kalaniana'ole Highway that connects the two towns? Doubtful. If Kula was in Waimānalo, he had been driven there.

I dialed the number. Once I identified myself, the same male voice from the message said, "You get da t'ousand-dollah reward, brah?"

"I get da money, if you get da dog." Well, Buckingham had the money, but I could get it.

"Bring da money if you like get da dog."

"Weah I bring it?"

"I goin' tell you weah, brah."

I heard mumbling in the background, two or three more male voices in garbled pidgin. The caller came back.

"Da end of Kapu Road in Waimānalo. Know weah dat is?"

"Dono." I played dumb.

"Wen you in da valley, head *mauka*. Pass da nurseries. Den you goin' hit one dead end. Come tonight, eleven o'clock. No try bring nobody wit' you."

"What your name, brah?" I asked.

"Moku."

"Da surfah?"

"Das me."

"OK, Moku. Bring da dog or no deal."

"I bring da dog. You bring da t'ousand.

seventeen

I called Buckingham and asked if I could see him. About to begin his daily radio program, he suggested we meet later at his yacht club for a dinner sail. I agreed to meet, but declined the sail and the dinner, saying I had to follow a lead that night that might shed light on Kula's disappearance. I also wanted to avoid running into Madison, who I knew was on the guest list.

"Good on ya, mate!" Buckingham replied in his Australian lingo. "That's the best possible regret. Tell me more."

"I'll fill you in when I see you," I said. "I'd rather not discuss it on the phone."

"No worries," he said.

"Say, too bad about your neighbor," I said, referring to Dr. Carreras. "But I gather you didn't like him much."

"Dreadful news," Buckingham said. "I didn't care for the man, but I certainly didn't want him dead." My client said this in a curious way, leaving the impression that if he'd wanted the doctor dead, he would have made it happen.

On my way to the yacht club I stopped at Maile's cottage to feed her cats. An instant replay of the night before. Peppah clawed his way up my pants leg, Coconut flaked out on the sofa, and Lolo hotfooted it into Maile's bedroom.

I brought Lolo's food to the bedroom and got down on my knees.

"Come out, girl." I looked under the bed frame. Nothing. I peered into the darkness for some sign of movement. "Lolo?"

Nothing. Then I noticed Maile's closet door was ajar. I crossed the room and pushed it open further. "Come out girl. I've got places to go."

The closet was dark and smelled of mold. If Lolo was in there, I couldn't see her. Then at the edge of the closet I noticed a long, round object leaning against the doorframe. I had no business snooping in the closet of my old friend, but being nosy is an occupational hazard. I reached in and pulled it out. Maile's rifle. The Remington was a serious tactical weapon—bolt action, carbon-fiber stock, stainless steel barrel, and a scope. On impulse, I sighted through the scope. Maile's bed looked huge in its crisp crosshairs. The precision was awesome.

I knew precision when I saw it because I'd fired more weapons than the average person. After I surfed myself out of college in my freshman year, against my Uncle Orson's advice I joined the army. He paid big bucks to send me to Flintridge Prep and to Point Loma College, so he was disappointed. But even though Point Loma had three of the best surf spots in San Diego—Garbage, Ab, and New Break—I found out fast that academic life wasn't for me. So when a recruiter dangled a cushy job back home at Fort DeRussy in Waikīkī in front of me, I bit.

It didn't happen. I was never stationed in Waikīkī. I went to Fort Ord in Monterey, which closed a few years after I left, and trained for the infantry. Handguns, automatic rifles, grenade launchers, machine guns, wire-guided missiles. You name it, I shot it. I'm not a gun guy, and I think the world would be a better place without them, but circumstances have forced me to become familiar with a wide variety. Later when I became a PI, in order to register my .357 I took a course in which I shot Glocks, Sigs, Berretas, and Smith & Wessons—handguns used by law enforcement and the military. This, plus my infantry experience, is why I know more about firearms than the average person, and why I could appreciate the Remington.

I returned the weapon to Maile's closet and wondered how long it had been since she had fired it. Then I scolded myself for poking around in her things. She had trusted me, as an old friend, with her cats and her cottage, and here I was violating that trust. And getting closer to her, despite my resolve not to.

"OK, Lolo. Here's your food." I set the dish by the open closet and turned to leave. The timid cat was going to have to fend for herself.

* * *

The Ala Moana Yacht Club hugged the Diamond Head end of the beach park and Ala Wai Harbor. I wandered the posh facilities looking for Buckingham. First I tried the clubhouse that sat smack on the harbor. My client wasn't in the waterfront bar or the *koa*-paneled dining room or the lava rock swimming pool. Then I headed out to the boat slips.

Buckingham's yacht wasn't hard to find. It was taller and longer than any sailing vessel I could see. And on its stern in fancy letters was the name:

Golden Hinde
HONOLULU

I craned my neck to follow its mast up to the sky, and had to grab a handrail to steady myself. I wondered how many mom-and-pop Hawai'i investors it took to pay the gold deal-er's yacht club dues and to stock his boat with caviar and champagne.

"Kai Cooke!" Buckingham waved me onto the spotless deck, then offered his meaty right hand. I almost cut myself on his diamond ring. We sat on cushioned seats in the cockpit as two twenty-something guys in white shorts and polo shirts busily checked rigging and sails. Buckingham told me that he and his wife had sailed single-handedly from Bora Bora to Honolulu. Now with only his daughter's help, and state-of-the-art electronics and auto pilot, he claimed he could still navigate to any number of remote Pacific islands. And when the trade winds went slack, a Cummins turbo diesel kept her chugging at ten knots per hour—plus.

"Nice boat," I said to get the conversation rolling. "With a fitting name."

"The *Golden Hinde* was commanded by Sir Francis Drake," Buckingham replied, "a fearless explorer who circumnavi-gated the globe for his country and queen."

"Why do I remember Drake as a pirate?" I said, recalling AP history at Flintridge Prep. "Didn't he pillage and plunder along the way?"

"Nonsense. Your American schoolbooks gave you a distorted view of history. Drake was a great man."

I said, "Yes, sir," and let it go.

Buckingham then reminisced about the exotic South Pacific. "Now Bora Bora," he said, "that's what Hawai'i *used* to be—but is no more. Paradise."

I nodded politely and then updated him on my efforts to find Kula, mentioning the lead I was following that night. "A Waimānalo man named Moku claims to have Kula," I said. "I thought you should know, sir."

"Too right!" Buckingham hauled out his Aussie talk again and embraced his daughter who had come up from below and sat next to him. It was the first time I had seen her smile.

"I'm not sure how right, sir." I straightened in my seat. "This Moku asked me to bring the entire reward to a dead-end road in the valley at night."

"Don't trust the bloke?"

"Not sure." I gave my client the particulars of the phone call and of the plan for the meeting. Buckingham listened attentively.

"I doubt Moku will bring Kula tonight," I added. "But he may know something about his disappearance. All I can do is go see what happens."

"I'll go with you," Buckingham replied. "You could be in danger."

"That's very generous, but he insisted I come alone." I tried to reassure him. "I'm experienced enough with these kinds of meetings to not put myself at risk. If I didn't think I could walk out alive, I wouldn't walk in."

"Be careful, then." He looked genuinely concerned.

"I will, sir. As I mentioned, the man wants the thousand-dollar reward up front in cash."

"Do you want it now?" Buckingham reached for his wallet.

"Uh, no . . ." I should have known he'd have that much cash on him. "I'd rather not carry it with me tonight . . . until I check out the lead."

"No worries. Ring me on my mobile."

One of the guys in white shorts signaled Buckingham that the *Golden Hinde* was ready to go.

"Sure you won't join us for a sunset sail, Mr. Cooke?" he asked. "We're waiting on one guest and then we're off."

"No thanks. I've got my appointment tonight. I'll call you with any news."

As I stepped from the boat, I noticed a lifeguard surfboard with a red cross on it and the word RESCUE. As big as a tandem board with two pair of handles on the rails, it was mounted on the dock across from Buckingham's slip. Seeing that word made me wish I had some sort of backup that night—but not Barry Buckingham. I was wary of him as a client, let alone as a partner to cover my back.

When I pulled away from the yacht club I saw Madison's Lexus convertible whiz by in a gold blur. Her fingers were tapping the glowing ash of a cigarette into the wind. She didn't notice me. When I glanced back, her taillights were disappearing behind the club's automatic gate marked: MEMBERS ONLY.

eighteen

Waimānalo is a sleepy seaside town in windward Oʻahu, sandwiched between Kailua to the north and Makapuʻu Point to the south. Kapu Road winds deep into an isolated valley behind the town. *Kapu* means "forbidden" in Hawaiian and it's no place you'd want to meet a stranger on a dark night. Especially a stranger who expects you to be carrying a thousand bucks.

Waimānalo's tiny business district fills barely two blocks along narrow Kalanianaʻole Highway. At night there isn't much to see. Ken's In & Out Plate Lunch was closed. So were Shima's Market, Waimānalo Feed Supply, Kuni's Auto & Towing, and Glenn's Nursery. But the lights were still on at Jack in the Box and the Waimānalo 76. And in the distance the jagged ridgeline of the Koʻolau mountains, jutting a thousand feet from the valley floor, was backlit by the lights of Honolulu. In their foothills I hoped to find a clue about the missing dog.

At the one and only traffic light in Waimānalo's commercial hub, I swung a sharp right onto Kapu Road and headed into the valley. An occasional streetlamp poured a pool of light onto the black pavement. But most of the landscape was shrouded in darkness under the moonless sky. The eerie glow of city lights above the Ko'olau range only served to deepen that darkness.

I reached over and touched my surfboard, the nine-six's duckbill nose resting comfortably on the Impala's padded dash. The board, for some reason, reassured me . . . made me feel confident I would live to surf tomorrow. For safety's sake, I'd brought only one hundred and change from my client's retainer. If Moku had information to offer, he'd have to settle for that for now. And if he actually had the dog, a quick call to Buckingham could produce the full reward.

Soon the pavement ended and I started kicking up dust, driving the dirt road until it stopped at a barrier. My headlights illuminated a bullet-riddled sign: DEAD END. Beyond the sign lay a small clearing among the trees. I turned my car around facing back toward the village. When I switched off my headlights, the scene faded to black.

I checked my watch: 10:54.

The high-pitched hum of crickets added to the eerie atmosphere. Eleven came and went. I got out of my car and, with the penlight on my keychain, felt my way with my feet to the clearing. But there was nothing to see, even if I could have seen better.

Suddenly behind the DEAD END sign I heard rustling. I pulled my .357 magnum from the right front pocket of my khakis and stepped beyond the barrier. No, I don't have a license to carry a concealed weapon. But sometimes, when the situation calls for it, I do what I have to do. The sound led back into the underbrush. Probably a mongoose skittering across dry leaves. Then I heard a vehicle rattle up to the dead end and stop. Doors opened and slammed shut. Voices sounded and then I heard the shuffle of feet.

As I crept back toward my car, I saw what looked like an old Honda with its lights on, pulled up beside mine. I could barely make out the two large men who were lifting my surfboard out of my car, and a third, the largest of the three, rifling through my glove compartment. I pointed my gun at them and stepped into the headlights' glare.

"Put the board back."

The men halted then slowly began pushing the board back into my car.

"And get your hands out of that glove compartment," I said. "Which one of you is Moku?"

"Me, brah," said the biggest one.

"You nevah come alone, Moku—like you tol' me. An' I no can see da dog."

"I goin' get da dog. You get da money?"

"Firs' da dog." I kept the .357 pointed at them.

"I get 'em fo' you, brah," Moku said. "Five hundert now, five hundert wen I get 'em."

"Nah, I pay in full when you delivah. How I know you got da dog? Or dat you geev' 'em to me?"

He reached into his pants pocket and pulled out a dog collar. "Is his."

"Les see 'em."

"Five hundert, brah."

"No way. I geev' fifty, if fo' real."

"One hundert," he said. "Or no collah an' no dog."

I pulled five twenties from my wallet and pointed to an imaginary spot in front of me. "Drop 'em hea."

Moku walked up. His dark eyes studied me. Around his neck hung a shark tooth on a black cord. He got close enough that I could see an *M* etched on the tooth in scrimshaw. So *M* is for Moku? I almost said. He held out the collar. It was tanned and stitched leather and had gold-embossed letters that said *KULA*.

The real thing? I had to believe it. This crew didn't strike me as smart enough to make a fake of this quality.

"Try drop 'em." I pointed to the ground with the revolver. "Den take da money."

Moku did as I said and then walked back to his friends. He seemed used to doing business at gunpoint.

"Now you bring da dog," I said.

"Latahs." Moku kept walking. His friends followed him to their car. Not one of them looked back as the old Honda started with a plume of smoke and sped away.

nineteen

Friday morning I was looking into the accusing eyes of homicide Detective Frank Fernandez. Moku Taliaferro was dead. His shark's tooth necklace was missing. And I was suspect number one.

I had no alibi. I had pulled a gun on Moku. The case of the missing dog was turning grim.

"Whose dog is it?" Fernandez asked, impatience in his gravelly voice.

"That's confidential—you know that. Besides, what do you care? It's a dog, Frank."

He scowled.

"What about Moku's pals?" I said. "One or both of them could have killed him for the hundred bucks I handed over."

Fernandez looked incredulous. "Murder—for a hundred bucks? Anyway, they both have alibis."

"Maybe they're lying."

"Maybe." His eyes hardened. "Maybe you are, too."

"C'mon, Frank."

"Tell me your client's name."

"I can't."

"Then next time we'll be talking in my office," he said. "If I didn't know you we'd be there now."

My door had not yet closed behind Fernandez when I began to wonder why I was risking a murder rap to protect a client whose character—and wallet—was suspect. But I believed in client confidentiality. Should it disappear just because I questioned a man's integrity or his ability to pay?

My phone rang, interrupting my thoughts.

"Surfing Detective," I answered.

"If you like fine dat missing dog," whispered a female voice, "try go look in Lanikai. Address is one-o-seven Moku-lama. Da druggies dere steal any kine, even one dog. Spock fo' yo'self." She hung up.

I checked the phone—she had blocked her caller ID. I had to keep following every lead, even the questionable ones. The case wasn't just about a missing dog anymore.

Before leaving I called Lou, the Mililani puppy mill owner who had promised me a male blond golden retriever. He sounded too much like Kula to ignore. Was the dog for real? Lou's phone rang. No answer. No machine.

* * *

Soon I found myself driving over the Pali again. From Kailua Beach Park I took meandering 'A'alapapa Drive, along the backdrop of the sheer Ka'iwa Ridge, into the beachside enclave of Lanikai. Only a few days ago I had plastered five hundred posters along this drive. But today the first pole I passed was naked. Next pole, no poster. Another pole, same thing.

Instead of turning onto Mokulama Drive, I drove the entire Lanikai loop that encircles the small community, from the mountains to the sea. Every poster was gone. This was obviously not the work of kids or irritated neighbors because posters advertising lawn sales and missing property were still hanging.

So I wasn't feeling optimistic as I pulled up to 107 Mokulama. The sagging frame house stood on a narrow overgrown lot half a block from the beach—a plantation shack among glitzy McMansions. A half dozen neglected coconut palms bulged with nuts ready to drop. Beneath each tree were mounds of nuts and fronds where they had crashed. Broken windows, loose shingles, flaking paint, wild hedges, and junk cars on the brown grass screamed neglect.

I parked across the street, surprised that the old hovel looked so familiar. Then I remembered. It had been featured on the evening news—an example of a growing drug problem in the islands and the frustration of citizens trying to combat it.

The owner of the home was a destitute widower in his seventies who had invited some questionable friends to occupy his digs, rent-free, in exchange for improving the property. Most had arrest records as long as their needle-tracked arms. The improvements never happened. Soon it became clear, to his neighbors anyway, that his shack had been taken over by drug dealers, thieves, and prostitutes. So why did he let them stay? The prostitutes. He was fond of them.

His cozy arrangement went along fine until his neighbors—weary of the endless partying and brawling—dialed 911. Even after several busts, the party continued, which is possibly why I got my tip. But why would druggies steal a dog? To feed their habit?

A Doberman sleeping among the weeds darted after me when he heard my car door slam. His fangs sent me back into the cockpit. The Dobie jumped up against my driver's door, his hot breath fogging the window. His claws dug into the turquoise paint.

"Ikaika, ovah heah!" A woman of about forty with dirt-brown hair ratted up into a topknot stepped from the house.

Ikaika turned tail and retreated. The topknot woman chained him under a sagging carport. I stepped from my car and approached her. Up close, I could see a nasty scar zigzagging across her sweaty forehead and dark shadows under her eyes.

"What you want, brah?" Her voice was flat and lifeless.

"I looking for one dog." I pulled out Kula's photo—and my pidgin.

"You wen' put up da signs?" she asked.

"Yeah. You wen' take 'em down?"

"Nah. Why I like take 'em down fo'?" she asked. "You one cop?"

"Private investigatah. Dere's one reward fo' da dog. One t'ousand dollahs."

"I know who wen' take da signs." Suddenly she sounded interested.

"Who?"

"Worth somet'ing, yeah?" She held out her right hand.

"How much?" I asked.

"Hundred."

"Can replace da signs fo' less than dat."

"Fifty, den." She eyed me warily.

I opened my wallet and pulled out my last twenty. I held it up to her intense gaze.

Her eyes locked on Alexander Hamilton's chiseled face for an instant and then she grabbed the bill from my hand. "Moku."

"Moku Taliaferro?"

She nodded.

I didn't bother to poke around any longer at 107 Mokulama. If Kula was there, would she have settled so quickly for a twenty?

I also didn't bother to tell her Moku was dead.

twenty

Instead of getting back into my car, I walked down Moku-lama Drive *makai,* or toward the ocean, to a sand path lined with ironwoods. At the end of the path was Lanikai Beach. In the distance I saw the iconic Mokulua Islands—twin pyramids on the turquoise sea. Heat waves coming up from the beach made the famous islands shimmer. Postcard perfect. I planted my backside in the warm sand, pulled Maile's card from my wallet, and punched in her number on my cell.

"Kai?" She sounded concerned. "Anything wrong?"

"Your cats are fine. How's Utah?"

"The workshop is good. And your investigation?"

"Not so good. A suspect wound up dead last night. His skull was crushed."

"Oh!" The surprise in her voice traveled across the miles. "That's rare in a pet theft case. New territory for me."

"Swell."

"Do you think he was your man?"

"I think he took down every poster I put up about Kula's disappearance."

"Posters are usually taken by people who don't want the pet found, or who want the reward all to themselves. But killing somebody is, well . . . unusual." Maile was silent a moment.

"The more I dig into this case," I said, "the more I think it's not about Kula at all."

"Then who?"

"Maybe Cheyenne Sin—Buckingham's missing wife? Her disappearance has been bugging me from the start. I think Kula is just a pawn."

"A living, breathing pawn," Maile said, "with high stakes to find him."

"What I can't figure is why was Moku killed? I doubt he could be more than a bit player, hardly worth the risk . . ."

"Maybe he's the key to the whole thing," Maile replied.

"Why did I ever take this case?"

"Because you're a sucker for cold noses and warm hearts?"

That phrase again. I had used it on Fernandez. Now Maile used it on me.

"Kai?"

"Sorry, Maile. See you at the airport on Sunday," I said, ending the call. There was no point in telling her the truth— I had taken the case to save my business. No other lofty motives, let alone cold noses and warm hearts.

* * *

Back at my office later that day I played a new phone message:

"Ah foun' yur retriever, boy, an' Ah fur dam shore dezarve that-thar reward . . ." A pause. "Whut yu waitin' fur, boy?" Silence. "Boy? . . . Boy?"

The caller spoke in a drunken redneck twang, not common in the islands. He hung up without giving a number. But he did leave his caller ID.

Strange. A 775- prefix. He had called from the Big Island. Why would someone on the Big Island call about a dog lost on O'ahu?

I called him back.

"Sammy Bob," he answered, this time without the slur.

"Mr. Bob?" I picked up on his cue.

"Name's Picket—Sammy Bob Picket," he corrected me. "Whut kin ah do fer yah?"

"I'm George, and I'm looking for a dog." The name sounded plausible enough, especially on short notice.

"How're yu, George?" He perked up. "Yah dun called the rite place, boy. Whut kine ah dog yah look'n fur?"

"Not sure. What kind do you have?"

"Ah got all kine."

"Golden retrievers?" I knew I was pushing my luck, but hoped he'd forgotten his drunken call to my number.

"Got 'em."

"Are you a dog breeder?"

"Nah, but ah sells 'em, an' ah sells 'em cheap."

"Where are you?" I pushed my luck again.

"Yah doan got tah worry nun 'bout that-thar," he said evasively. "Ah deliver."

"I'd like to see your goldens before I buy one. Can I come and look?"

"Yah got five-six hundert?"

"For the right dog," I said.

"Tell yah what yah gonna do . . ."

I held my breath.

"Yah drive on up the Hāmākua Coast till yah get tah Laupāhoehoe, then yah call me. Ah'll lead yah from there."

"Where will you meet me?"

"Locals Only Café . . . " He paused. "How 'bout tomorrow afternoon?"

"Suits me." I would have agreed to anything.

"Remembah, George, yah ain't gonna get no better deal."

"See you tomorrow then."

"Muchablige." He hung up.

twenty-one

The next morning I caught a 10:50 flight to Hilo, still wondering why a guy on the Big Island would call about a dog lost on Oʻahu. His good-ol'-boy lingo and name also made me wonder.

The airplane to Hilo was packed with weekend travelers on neighbor island getaways. *Holoholo.* Looking out the window as the Hawaiian jet descended south along the Big Island's Hāmākua Coast, I saw the rustic tin roofs of Hilo town nestled along the waterfront, just as I remembered them. Over the years I've watched Hilo sink into the economic doldrums when the sugar industry tanked, and then rise again when tourism transformed the quiet hamlet into a New Age mecca of artsy shops, health food stores, and trendy restaurants. In addition to tourism, the island's recent economy depended on diversified agriculture, not the least of which included illegal cash crops like *pakalolo.*

* * *

After picking up a car at Budget, I drove to Kea'au, about ten miles south of Hilo. There the road climbs southwest into Volcanoes National Park or due south to Lava Tree State Monument. The south road continues to the former seaside village of Kalapana and its famous black sand beach, both devastated by lava flows. Kea'au, on higher ground, escaped.

Once a sugar plantation town on the slopes of the Kīlauea Volcano, Kea'au has since grown into a suburb of Hilo, boasting a Sure Save market, Ace Hardware, McDonald's, Pizza Hut, and a couple of gas stations and churches. I wasn't looking for pizza or religion in Kea'au. I came to find the Hawai'i Island Humane Society shelter, one of three on the Big Island.

The Kea'au shelter was a one-story, hollow tile, tin-roofed building with detached cathouse and dog kennels—all spotlessly clean. Its utilitarian appearance was softened by spacious green lawns, a few palms and an 'ulu, or breadfruit tree. The place had a cozy, campus-like feel.

Inside the facility I explained to a staffer named Alana, whose lava-black hair flowed down to her shoulders, that I was looking for a golden retriever lost on O'ahu. She said she'd do all she could to help.

Pet hoarders—people who gather and even steal large numbers of animals—were a problem in the area, Alana told me. They accumulated so many pets that they couldn't care for them properly and were usually prosecuted under animal cruelty statutes.

"Dis old lady bin keep mo' den one hundred cats." Alana started to "talk story" in pidgin. "Her neighbors, dey smell da stink and dey call. So we go check 'em out. Da cats bin starving. Dey living in one dump. Unsanitary, yeah? Most of 'em really sick. Some dead awready. We bring all da live cats hea. And da old lady get arrested and go to jail. Cruelty to animals."

"You know dis' guy Sammy Bob Picket?" I asked.

"Sammy who?"

"Picket," I said. "He live in Laupāhoehoe. Maybe he one dog hoarder?"

"I hear of some guy like dat. But never hear of dis Picket."

"Maybe he da same guy?"

"Maybe," she said.

Before I left, Alana told me that another animal control officer had heard rumors of a dog hoarder on the Hāmākua Coast who'd been stealing animals from shelters at Kona and Waimea. But this operator was different. He didn't just steal and hoard pets, he sold them to hunters of pig and wild boar, and to trainers of fighting dogs. The hoarder was a traumatized Gulf War veteran who drifted to Hawai'i after the war and never left. How he had ended up, years later, stealing dogs on the Big Island, no one knew.

It sounded to me like Picket might match the profile of this trafficker in stolen pets.

"I go check 'em out." I headed for the door.

Alana replied, "Maybe he *lolo.*" By which she meant crazy.

"Maybe." I waved goodbye.

"Be careful," she called after me.

* * *

I pulled away from the shelter and drove up the windward coast. A half dozen seaside villages drifted by before

I reached Laupāhoehoe. At the once-booming sugar town's most famous landmark, Laupāhoehoe Point Park, windswept ironwoods and palms clung to a craggy black point in the turbulent sea. The Point's rugged beauty wasn't speaking to me today. I was heading *mauka,* or inland, in search of a man I didn't really want to meet.

I followed Picket's directions to a fifties-style diner called Locals Only Café. Over the sweetly-sad blare of Ricky Nelson's "Poor Little Fool" on the jukebox, I asked a waitress dressed in a pink carhop outfit where I might find a man named Sammy Bob who sold dogs.

"Oh, *dat* guy." She frowned. "Why you want 'em fo'?"

"I looking for one golden retrievah."

She gave me a curious look and said she only knew general directions—up the sloping land *mauka* off the highway. She'd heard that Picket was hard to find. From the expression on her face and the way she talked about him, I could tell Picket wasn't her friend. In fact, I figured she didn't like the guy. So I wasn't worried she would tip him off that I was coming unannounced.

My plan was not to call and not to link myself with the lost dog. I would just show up as a guy wanting to buy a retriever.

I drove up a narrow blacktop called Manowai'ōpae Homestead Road. It wandered deep into the country until there was nothing but fields and woods on either side of me. The pavement ran out. I turned onto a dirt road and kept wandering, dust kicking up behind my rental car. There was nothing much out there, aside from overgrown cane fields and woods. Even if Picket didn't steal dogs, his seclusion suggested he had something to hide.

Eventually the road turned into a tire-rutted trail and then a dry creek bed. Soon I couldn't even tell if there was a road at all. The woods were thick. I was going into nowhere. I reached instinctively for my Smith & Wesson and then remembered that I hadn't packed it. The hassle of flying inter-island with a handgun.

I was cursing myself for getting lost—maybe I should have called Sammy?—when I saw a shack far off through the trees. I stopped my car in the creek bed and started walking into a jungle. The green canopy grew darker and more tangled. I began to hear dogs whining and smelled the now-familiar odor I'd whiffed at Lou's puppy mill. I hoped the breeze that brought the stink my way would also keep my scent from the dogs' keen noses.

In a clearing a rotting plantation shack stood ringed with trash. Between the shack and me were the remnants of a bonfire and what looked like charred dog collars and blackened tags and licenses. Beyond the shack was dog city. Or dog ghetto. Animals were everywhere: tied to rusted out vehicles, a cast-off refrigerator and stove, and plywood crates. There must have been three-dozen dogs in plain sight and more hidden elsewhere.

I scanned the crowd for Kula, keeping far enough away and out of sight to avoid the barking frenzy that I knew would erupt if I was sniffed or spotted. None of the dogs even remotely resembled Kula. If any were purebreds, I couldn't tell. The animals were skin and bones. Some faintly resembled breeds I'd seen before, but their emaciated bodies and mangy fur rendered them all pitifully alike.

Before that moment I couldn't have imagined animals in worse condition than those at Lou's puppy mill. But here they were, staring me in the face. I'd never been an animal rights advocate, but scenes like these might make me one. And more were coming.

Staked close to the shack were two bony pit bulls tied with leather leads. Their jaws were huge. One was white with a black spot and the other tan. Their pale yellow eyes reminded me of the tiger shark that attacked me at Laniākea. I must have gotten too close because, suddenly, their big jaws gaped, their lips curled, and out came their teeth. The leather straps tightened with a frightened snap. *Attack mode.* Pit bulls sometimes get a bad rap for being predators, but this pair seemed worthy of the reputation.

As the two dogs pulled and snarled, the shack's door flew open and a man stepped out with a double-barrel shotgun.

"Whut n' hell . . ." He pointed the shotgun at me.

I froze. He was the embodiment of the redneck voice I'd heard on the phone: stringy gray hair, greasy beard, scabby limbs scorched by the sun, cigarette dangling from his lower lip.

"Listen up. Ah gonna shoot yah ass, whoever yah are . . ." He sighted down both barrels.

twenty-two

"Don't shoot, Sammy Bob . . ." I tried to calm him. "It's me, George."

"George who?"

"I called yesterday. You said you'd show me some dogs."

"Dang-it, George." He lowered his shotgun. "Ah tol' yah to call me from the café. Doan yah remember nothin'? How n' hell did yah fine me?"

"I asked in town. Somebody said you were up here, so I just drove." I stepped into the clearing as he walked toward me. The stink coming off him was nearly as strong as the stink of his dogs.

"Alright, George." He scratched his greasy hair to help himself remember. "You was look'n for a golden retriever, right?"

I nodded.

"Ah kin give ya a better deal then them pet stores, or them fancy high-priced breeders. You jus' come with me. Ah gonna put mah gun in the house. You doan gotta worry none. Jus' come with me."

He set his shotgun inside the door and led me back toward the cobbled kennels. On the way we walked by the two pit bulls, who went ballistic. I jumped back. Their leather straps snapped so tight again I thought they'd break. I'd have preferred chains.

"Stay back! They'll take ya hand off," Picket said. "Ah otta know." He held up his left hand, whose middle finger was missing above the first knuckle. "Them dang pit bulls hate everybody, ah tell you. They'd eat me alive, if ah let 'em loose."

"Why do you keep them around?" I was curious.

"Good question, George. You'd a thunk ah'd kilt 'em awready. But ah can't. Them's worth too dang much money as fight'n dogs." He chuckled. "If they doan kill me firs'."

"So where are your retrievers?" I scanned the makeshift kennels.

"Ah doan keep my goldens out here. No way, boy. Them there dogs is fer hunt'n an' fight'n. Or fer folks that gotta hanker'n to et 'em. Nah, ya doan wan' none of them."

He turned us around and walked to the door of his shack. "Come on in, hear?" He motioned me to follow.

His shack was no larger than my Waikīkī studio apartment. Now I'm not the tidiest housekeeper, but Sammy Bob didn't bother at all. Trash was everywhere, piled up to heights that would make even Mililani Lou green with envy. But he didn't go in for rum like she did. His drink of choice was Kentucky bourbon. Empty quart bottles seemed to float like ghost ships on the sea of litter that was his floor. Maybe that's what he'd been drinking when he first called me. Anyway, his place reeked like something had crawled inside and died.

"Wanna smoke?"

I shook my head as he lit a cigarette. The shack filled with smoke; there wasn't much ventilation. I looked up and saw two tiny holes in the roof to which the smoke ascended. He then led me to an adjoining room, no more than a closet, where a half dozen animals were curled up on newspapers.

"This here's some purebreds, George. Them's nice dogs."

When I looked in, the animals cowered. A skeletal black creature that might have been a Labrador glanced up at me fearfully. Another with the brown and black markings of a Rottweiler squealed faintly. The rest hardly moved a muscle. I couldn't tell if they were drugged or traumatized or just weak from lack of food, water and fresh air. I tried to pet the black dog, but he recoiled from me.

That feeling of revulsion I had had looking at his outdoor dogs came back again. Only stronger. I wanted to turn away, but didn't.

"I don't see a golden here," I said.

"Hold on, George. Thought ya might like to see that-thar nice lab. Goldens is in the nex' room."

Picket slid open a door to a group of smaller animals. I saw what looked like a mangy Maltese, a dirty cocker spaniel with cheerless eyes, and a toy poodle with long, matted hair. Another sad sight. I tried not to show Picket what I was feeling.

"Nah, nex' room." He opened a third door to the bathroom. "Now, this here's what ya look'n fer, George. I gots two. Take yer pick for six hundert. Cash and carry, boy."

On the grungy floor curled up around a toilet and pedestal sink were two golden retrievers—thin and dull brown. Both lay unnaturally still. Compared to the photo of Kula, those famished animals looked like victims of a concentration camp—a Dachau for dogs. It made me sadder than sad. But I tried not to show it.

"These two are dark," I said. "Do you have a light-colored one?"

"Dang-it, boy!" Picket slapped his thigh. "If yah'da been here the other day. Ah got the nicest, sunniest golden retriever ya ever seed. This here dog was a beaut, ah tell you."

"That sounds like the dog I want." I tried not to appear too anxious. "Where is he?"

"Ah ain't suppose to say. Ya know how it is."

I reached for my wallet. "Sammy Bob, I know you're an honest businessman—a man of integrity." I watched his scabby face take on a proud look. "And I know you wouldn't betray your customer, but if he or she was to sell me this dog, I would cut you in. Say, two hundred?"

"Boy, trouble is, ya doan know where to look."

"Half the commission up front," I sweetened the deal. "One hundred now. One hundred when the sale goes through."

"OK, George, tell ya what ah gonna do." He stroked his beard. "Ah gonna tell ya where to go. But ah want all the money up front. All two hundert in cash."

"I haven't got it with me." I opened my wallet for him to see—four twenties, one ten, one five, and several ones.

He thought it over. "Ya gonna pay me the other hundert when ya buy that-thar dog?"

"Yes." I knew I wouldn't and he probably knew I wouldn't, but we had to go through the charade for his self-respect.

I reached into my wallet and gathered up the bills. "Here's the money." I held it in front of him.

He snatched the bills from my hand. "Georgie boy, you gotta fly Maui, then drive to Lahaina."

"Lahaina?"

"One of them big houses on the ocean. Now there's lots of condos on the beach, but there ain't that many oceanfront homes. So ya should find it easy." He walked back out to the main room.

"Do you have a name? An address?"

"Ah plum forget, George." Picket put on a sincere face. Then he casually reached over and rested his hand on his shotgun, where it leaned inside the doorway.

"Well, if you remember, call me." I gave him my home number—the answering machine there did not mention my name.

As I turned to leave his shack, I asked, "What's going to happen to those goldens? And all those dogs outside?"

"Ah gonna fine 'em good homes." He flashed a smile. "Ah does a good business."

The pit bulls snarled at me as I passed. Whines and howls of other captives followed me all the way back to the car. I was glad to get away. But I felt a tug of conscience with each step I took.

Turn him in, a voice inside me said. *Turn him in.*

But I couldn't yet, not until I found Kula. And to do that, I might have to call on Sammy Bob Picket again.

twenty-three

As my Maui-bound plane lifted off over Hilo Bay I congratulated myself that the famous surfing dog might be waiting for me in Lahaina. But why would anyone go to the trouble and expense to ship a stolen dog to several different islands? I wondered again what was really behind the case. A missing person? Murder? Even more puzzling to me was what made a hoarder like Sammy Bob Picket, or puppy mill owner like Lou, mistreat animals. It reminded me—sadly—of an episode from my small kid time in Hawai'i.

* * *

Before my parents died, my father thought it would be a good idea for my dog Pono to be obedience trained—to learn to heel, sit, and lie down on command. Since I was too young to take him to class alone, my father and I went together. The trainer was a rigid, severe woman of the old school who got very physical with the dogs. I saw her once yank a tiny terrier off its feet with a choke chain. When the terrier yelped instead of obeying, the trainer's corrections got even more physical. I covered my eyes.

One day it was Pono's turn. The trainer commanded "Down!" Pono, of course, had no idea what to do. Then she yanked him south so hard that Pono flopped onto the ground. He got back up. The trainer commanded "Down!" again. He didn't. She yanked harder. Pono flipped over and whimpered. The corrections continued.

I ran to him and covered his trembling body with mine. "Stop hurting Pono!"

My father gently peeled me off the dog. "Kai, this is how Pono will learn to obey."

"I don't care if he obeys," I cried.

I saw my father and the trainer exchanged glances.

We never came back to that class. And ever since that day, whenever I see someone abusing an animal I remember Pono and I feel like I should *do* something. So I couldn't agree more with Maile—people who harm helpless creatures are the lowest of the low. Pono's trainer was not in the same league with Sammy Bob or Lou, but in my childhood memories she was just as bad.

* * *

At Kahului Airport, I slipped into my second rental car of the day and headed for the historic whaling port of Lahaina, on West Maui's leeward coast. It was already late in the day and carloads of tourists and *kama'aina* commuters were making the slow trek west on seaside Honoapi'ilani Highway, also known as Route 30, that leads beyond Lahaina to the resorts of Kāʻanapali and Kapalua. Needless to say, the highway was jammed.

Sitting in traffic, I wondered if I'd make it to Lahaina before sundown. Otherwise, I'd have to wander around in the dark looking for an oceanfront home for which Sammy Bob had refused to give an address. I thought again about his starving animals. Well-fed and well-groomed dogs would bring more on the open market. So why keep them in such horrible shape? Was Picket a sad story like Lou's husband— wounded by war? Or was he simply depraved?

I finally reached Lahaina town just after 6:00 p.m. I pulled into a service station and checked a Maui phone directory for veterinary clinics. There was only one in Lahaina. Good news. But would the clinic be open at this hour? I hoped so. I wanted to avoid the added time and expense of spending the night in Lahaina, unless it was absolutely necessary. Plus, the sooner I made contact with Kula, the sooner I could close the case.

I dialed and waited three rings. "Lahaina Animal Clinic," a perky receptionist answered. "This is Caitlin."

"Hi, I'm a member of the Golden Retriever Club," I launched into an elaborate lie, "and I'm following up on an adoption. Has a golden retriever—male, about three years old, light in color—been brought in for a checkup in the last few days?"

"He has," she said with certainty. "What a gorgeous animal! And I assure you," she continued, "Boomer received the best medical care."

Boomer? "I'm sure he did. And so I'm wondering if you can help me. I'm on my way to visit Boomer in his new home, but I've lost the house number. I thought you might have it."

She hesitated. "Well, I do. But our policy . . ."

"I understand," I said. "It's just that I drove all the way from Upcountry and I haven't been able to reach the owner by phone. I thought I had the right number, but . . ."I paused. "It's getting so late—I hate to turn around and go all the way back."

"Well," she said, "I'm sure Mrs. Varda wouldn't mind . . ."

* * *

Armed with Mrs. Varda's address and phone number I drove north along Front Street, watching the sun sink over Lahaina town. The bars and eateries on the bustling seaside strip were hopping. But farther up the beach, where posh oceanfront homes nestled peacefully on the shore, you could hear trade winds whispering in the palms and shore break lapping the sand.

Like most seaside residences in this pricy neighborhood, Mrs. Varda's resembled a walled fortress from the street. Two identical garages with separate driveways stood at the extreme ends of her property. Their windows revealed a Jaguar convertible inside one and a pewter Mercedes inside the other. Between the garages ran a high lava rock wall and an even higher grove of areca palms. Even if Kula had become the mascot of this lavish estate, there was no seeing him, or anything, from my vantage point.

I walked down a nearby beach access to get a glimpse of the place from the water: two stories with a tile roof in china-blue. The ocean side was all glass, glowing in the setting sun. I could see no one inside the house or outside on the grounds, which included a kidney-shaped swimming pool, lounge chairs, chaises, potted palms, and a putting green. No one was swimming in the pool either. Only a yellow tennis ball floated in the water.

A mock orange hedge with a teak gate surrounded the beach side of the property, but the hedge was not so high that I couldn't peek over. Nice place. But no dog in sight.

I called his name: "Kula."

A minute passed.

I called again.

It was going to get dark soon. I was running out of time.

Then it happened. From behind a palm, where I guess he'd been napping, the golden retriever dove into the pool—*Splash!*—and swam after the tennis ball. Even half-swallowed by his own wake, his blond coat was unmistakable. He was alone, but he kept looking around, as if to see who'd called his name.

"Kula," I tried again."

He glanced my way with those vivid brown eyes. The contrast between the eyes and his almost white face was striking. The photos hadn't done him justice. He was every bit as stunning as Buckingham had said. I could see why someone might want to steal him.

Kula climbed from the pool and walked toward me. His tail flicked water every which way. His gold fur dripped on the deck. His gleaming white teeth clenched the yellow ball.

When he reached the gate he shook, drenching everything in sight, including me. His wagging tail picked up speed.

Then he barked. Not an aggressive bark. A social bark. But loud.

"Shh . . . Kula . . ."

A glass door in the house slid open and out stepped one of those wealthy middle-aged women whose bleached hair and perpetual smile look plastered in place.

I crouched behind the hedge.

"Boomer?" Mrs. Varda strolled on the pool deck. "Boomer-boy!"

The golden retriever, hearing his new name so soon after the old, looked suddenly confused. He tilted his head, peered at me, and then trotted back toward the house. He stopped before reaching Mrs. Varda and shook again. She draped a big beach towel over him and tenderly patted his damp coat.

"Does Boomer-boy like swimming in Nanah's pool?" Out came the baby talk. "Oh, yes, he does! Oh, yes he does!" She was in love.

Kula glanced back toward the hedge.

I did not approach Mrs. Varda. Whether she was unaware that the dog she purchased had been stolen or she was part of the scheme, she wasn't about to hand him over to a strange man popping up from behind her hedge. Not likely at all.

To do this job right I needed a pet recovery expert. I knew just the one. But she was in Utah at the moment. The liberation of the famous surfing dog would have to wait for another day.

twenty-four

As the setting sun silhouetted the island of Lāna'i like a humpback whale cruising across the channel, I hopped in my rental and drove back to Kahului Airport. By 8:40 I was airborne to Honolulu. By 10:00 I was in Mānoa feeding the cats. I wished Maile was there so I could tell her the good news.

Same drill as before. While Coconut and Peppah devoured their dinners in the kitchen, I catered to Lolo again on my hands and knees under Maile's bed. I felt slightly guilty about feeding the felines at such an hour, but apparently they were fine. And Maile would never know.

When I pulled away thirty minutes later I was feeling on top of the world. My first and only pet case was almost closed and I had hopes the fee would carry me until my next case—a real one with people. Not dogs and the scum that abuse them. It was too late to call Buckingham. The good news would have to wait until morning.

Then, as I drove down East Mānoa Road, I had second thoughts. Yes, I'd finally found Kula, and, yes, I could trace his disappearance back to Sammy Bob on the Big Island. But how had the retriever gotten there? Was Picket involved somehow in Moku Taliaferro's murder? And in Cheyenne Sin's disappearance?

* * *

Back at the Waikīkī Edgewater, I had two phone messages, the first from Madison: "Kai, Conrad called again from L.A." She was talking fast. "I think he suspects something."

Usually the essence of cool, Madison seldom showed concern about anything, let alone her husband. Even Twinkie was yipping frantically in the background.

"I'm sure it's only a bluff," Madison hurried on, "but Conrad says he's flying to Honolulu . . . *Twinkie, hush!*"

I skipped ahead to the second message: "Don't make me come after you, Kai," Detective Fernandez growled. "You've got two choices. Tell me who you're working for or I'm bringing you in for Moku's murder. I'll give you the weekend. I better hear from you by Monday."

* * *

Frank Fernandez's voice was still ringing in my ears when I woke up Sunday morning. I had a feeling of dread. One day left to give Fernandez an answer.

After breakfast it was still too early to call Buckingham, so I phoned Maile. It was about noon then in Utah and I imagined her workshop took Sundays off.

"Kai," she answered on the first ring, "How are you?"

"Well," I said, happy to hear her voice.

"And how are you getting on with the cats?"

"Peppah glommed on to me right away, Coconut barely blinked, and Lolo ran for cover."

"You described them to a tee."

"And how's your workshop?"

"Fantastic," she said. "I'm learning so much about animal sanctuaries, no-kill shelters, and stuff like that. Well worth the trip."

"That's good . . ." I hesitated. "Good."

"Is there something wrong, Kai?"

"Wrong? No. I just wanted to tell you the good news."

"What good news?"

"Remember Kula?"

"How could I forget that beautiful retriever?"

"Thanks to your advice, I found him."

"Brilliant, Kai! I'm so glad."

"Yes, it's a bit of a miracle, really."

"Congratulations."

"Thanks . . . uh . . . I should call my client, now that it's a decent hour here. Lehua is going to be jumping with joy."

"I'm sure she will," Maile said.

I had an inspiration. "Why don't we go out and celebrate when you get back?"

She was quiet for a moment. My knees suddenly felt weak. I found myself blurting out: "What do you say, Maile?"

"Sure, Kai, I'd like that."

"Excellent," I said. "After all, it was you who told me how to find Kula."

"I was glad to help."

"Okay, I better call Buckingham." I said. "See you soon."

"I'll look forward." she said.

When she hung up I realized that I had neglected to tell her that while I had found Kula, I hadn't actually brought him home. And that I needed her help for that. A small detail that could wait for her return.

* * *

Still glowing from Maile's congratulations, I prepared myself mentally for the barrage of thanks and attaboys I would soon receive from my client. I dialed Buckingham's Tantalus mansion.

"Good news, sir," I said. "I located your dog."

Buckingham didn't say a word.

"I'm sure your daughter will be very happy," I added.

"Why don't you pop up here, Mr. Cooke." There was a ragged edge to his velvet voice I hadn't heard before. "I have something to tell you that I'd rather not discuss on the phone."

My sense of dread returned. "I'll be right there."

* * *

Weaving up Tantalus Drive I wasn't so much wondering about Buckingham's strange tone, as I was recalling Mrs. Gum's allegation that he had killed his wife. And that shadowy face in a second floor window, ducking behind a curtain when our eyes met. Were my client's tone and the mysterious figure connected some way? Now I was really grabbing at straws.

I pulled to the curb in front of Mrs. Gum's colonial, walked across the street to Wonderview, and was buzzed through. Buckingham himself, without his daughter this time, met me at his dark *koa* doors, appearing as bleak as he had sounded on the phone. Even his three-piece suit, the same shade of charcoal he had worn at our first interview, did not soften his desperation.

"Mr. Cooke, there is something we must discuss." The edginess I had heard on the phone now sounded close to panic, the way people talk just before they lose it.

He led me into his sunken living room. I sat while he paced in front of the ocean-view glass, his dark figure a somber contrast to the sunlit sea below. Lehua still had not appeared.

"I asked you to come here, Mr. Cooke, because there is something I have to tell you that I didn't want to say on the phone."

"Is it about your golden retriever, sir?" I was still hoping for that cash reward, plus my fee. "I'll have Kula home to you shortly."

"You've done a superb job finding my daughter's pet. Superb. I wonder, though, if you have discovered *why* her dog was stolen."

"Why, sir?" I was taken aback by this unexpected question. "You hired me to find the dog, not the thief's motives."

"Right you are, Mr. Cooke. You've done your job and, I assure you, you will be rewarded." Before he got to specifics about my money, Buckingham appeared to think better of it and shifted direction. "But at present I have another problem that's more in your usual line."

"Another problem?" *What now?*

He paused and stared down at the sea. "My daughter's gone missing."

"Your daughter, sir?"

"She failed to return home from summer school Friday and I haven't seen her since," Buckingham said.

"Almost two days have gone by?" I was stunned he'd waited so long to tell me. "You must have called HPD?"

The gold dealer stopped directly in front of me, blocking the sun. "I'm a very public man, Mr. Cooke, and my reputation is essential to my business. My radio audience must have complete confidence in me or my business will wane. And as you can probably imagine, with a place like this," he gestured to his sprawling mansion, "I have to keep the money rolling in. No, I don't intend to call the police."

Not even to save his own daughter?

"I'm giving you a new case. Lehua has been kidnapped. That you found Kula so quickly makes me confident that you can also find her."

"You're sure someone has abducted her—she's not just gone AWOL like a typical teenager?" I asked. "Have you checked with her friends?"

"I can assure you, I have called all of her friends, including the few boys she has dated. She is with none of them. Her Mini was towed early Saturday morning. It had been illegally parked on Wilder Avenue."

"How do you know she was kidnapped?"

"The same man who abducted my wife and her dog has now taken my daughter."

"Do you mean the prowler, sir? Has he contacted you?"

Buckingham ran his fingers though the red roots of his black hair. "There is more I have to tell you . . ."

twenty-five

"About twenty-five years ago," began Buckingham, "down in Australia, there was a bloke named Abe Scanlon, a con man who ran a rather successful Ponzi scheme—desert land in the outback. He sold the worthless land to city dwellers who never bothered to inspect their investments. Abe promised them income each month from rent." Buckingham cleared his throat. "He got them their money—by luring in new investors. Meanwhile he was skimming off the top for himself."

"Abe Scanlon is the prowler?" I tried to make a connection to his daughter's disappearance. And maybe his wife's.

"I'll get to that." Buckingham sat across from me. He put his hands together against his chin, as if in prayer.

"He has something to do with it, then?" I pulled out my pad and pen.

"I can assure you . . ." Buckingham looked at me with his pale blue eyes. "He does."

I wrote down the name: Abe Scanlon.

"Abe wasn't much of a front man, you see," the gold dealer continued. "He had the face of a mule, thinning hair, and his voice was shrill as a bird. But then I came along. My name was Billy Brighton then."

I wrote below Scanlon's name: Billy Brighton.

"I was young then." Buckingham smiled. "Handsome, if I do say so myself. Red-headed, rough, and ready for anything. I had trained to be an actor in Sydney, then when things didn't work out in that line I took to the sea. I sailed the world. It was a tough life. I survived a few brawls in faraway ports. It was every bloke for himself. And some didn't survive. Luckily I was good with my hands . . ."

"You had to kill to survive?" I looked again at his hands and the gold rings that adorned them. Neither those rings nor the walnut-sized diamond perched on one of them could conceal the hugeness of his hands. Recalling his vice-like grip I concluded he could snap a man's or woman's neck with the ease of a nutcracker.

"I would never admit to that." Buckingham glanced at the faded quilts on the wall behind us. "Anyway, we're getting a bit off course."

"Not a problem." I looked at my pad. Two names so far: Abe Scanlon. Billy Brighton.

"Main thing, I had what Abe didn't. A voice. A handshake. A physical presence. I could inspire confidence. He saw my potential. I could make him money. Lots of money."

"So Scanlon hired you?"

"Of course. He wasn't stupid." Buckingham ran his fingers through his hair again. "With me aboard, Abe's business flourished. He paid me well enough for an apprentice, but I couldn't help seeing the torrent of cash flowing into his pockets. And I couldn't help seeing his glamorous wife—who later became my wife."

"Cheyenne Sin?"

He nodded. "She was a fashion model—far younger than Scanlon. Cheyenne was in her twenties like me and regretted marrying old Abe for his money."

"So that's how the two of you hooked up?"

"We were instantly attracted. She was a beautiful woman. Still is. But something else bonded us."

"And that was?"

"Scanlon's Ponzi scheme fell apart. The pool of gullible investors shrank. Rent payments dried up. Scanlon danced around the problem by relying on me, but investors complained. Some sued."

"Bad news."

"I saw what was coming and convinced Cheyenne to come with me to New Zealand. We took what assets we could, anything that wasn't bolted down."

"I bet Scanlon didn't like that."

"It was too late for him, mate. He got arrested."

"And you and Cheyenne took off?"

"We felt the heat, I'll tell you. So we bought a sloop and sailed to Bora Bora. We lived there unnoticed for awhile, but hardly in the style Cheyenne was accustomed to."

"So you moved again?"

"When Scanlon was convicted and thrown in prison in New South Wales, we rechristened our sloop *Golden Hinde* and sailed to Honolulu. I changed my name, for obvious reasons, from Billy Brighton to Barry Buckingham. I colored my hair. I took to wearing three-piece suits. A sort of makeover."

"Sort of." He made it sound like a small thing—changing his identity and appearance to evade the law.

"In Honolulu I went into the precious metals business, where my acting skills helped me launch my radio program, *Gold Standard.*"

"And that's how you bought this place?" I gestured to the sunken living room, one of countless rooms in his hilltop estate.

Buckingham flashed a self-satisfied smile. "It was amazing how quickly it happened."

"An overnight success?"

"You could say that. We needed lots of cash. Wonderview didn't come cheap. And then Cheyenne gave birth to our daughter, Lehua, and suddenly we were a family."

"So what about Abe Scanlon?" I asked. "Is he still in jail."

Buckingham arched his brows. "Afraid not. That's why I'm telling you this. It may sound strange to you, but . . . "

"No, sir. Continue." His story did sound strange, but I wasn't about to agree with him.

"Back in New South Wales, after serving twenty years for fraud and tax evasion, Abe got paroled. The poor man had lost everything—his fortune, his work, his wife. He'd become a bitter old man. And he blamed me, of course."

I was about to say, "I can see why." But kept it to myself.

"Once Abe was released from prison, his only thought was to find me and my wife and make us pay. In my view, he has only himself to blame. But that didn't stop him."

"So he's here? Scanlon is in Hawai'i?"

Buckingham returned to his prayerful pose. "Unfortunately yes."

"Not good." I raised my own brows.

"Abe searched the Pacific Islands for Cheyenne and me with no luck, until one day during a stopover in Honolulu he heard my voice on the radio. He dialed the number I gave on the air and threatened to turn us in to Australian authorities."

"Blackmail?"

"Exactly. He had argued in court that Cheyenne and I were equally to blame, but since we disappeared, they had only Abe to try."

"Has he made any attempt on your life?"

"Murder wouldn't have accomplished what Abe wanted: to take my life apart piece by piece."

"You're sure about that?"

"If Abe kills me, he gets nothing. He can't milk me dry unless I'm alive. Don't you see?"

It was my turn to nod.

"But Abe's demands for cash got out of hand—beyond my ability to pay. That's when Cheyenne disappeared. Then Kula. And now Lehua. So you see, Mr. Cooke, he's behind all my misfortunes."

"And you're sure he's turned from blackmailer to kidnapper?"

"No doubt." Buckingham pulled out a handwritten note:

> *Do not doubt my resolve, Billy. If you want to see your daughter alive again, put fifty thousand in cash into a briefcase and await further instructions.*
>
> *Your old partner*

"Has he given you the instructions?"

"This evening at midnight. Sand Island," Buckingham explained. "He wants me to stop at the chained gate leading to the park. I'm to come alone."

"You should definitely not go alone, sir. You don't want to jeopardize Lehua's life. . . . or yours. I'll go with you."

Buckingham sighed. "Fine," he said. "Meet me back here at eleven. Do you have a gun?"

"Yes."

"Bring it.

twenty-six

I re-crossed Tantalus Drive that Sunday morning wishing I had never set foot in Wonderview. I've had my share of sleazy clients, and the smooth-talking gold dealer was quickly rising to the top of the list. But I feared for his daughter, who had nothing to do with her father's crooked past. And I wondered why there was no ransom note for his wife—if Scanlon had in fact abducted her. And why Kula had ended up on Maui.

Walking to my Impala, I saw Mrs. Gum standing at her mailbox. Her silver hair was shining in the morning sun like the figurine on Buckingham's Rolls.

"Good morning, Mr. Cooke," said the widow.

"Ho, you have one excellent memory, Mrs. Gum! You remembah my name." I tucked in my aloha shirt which had come loose after sitting with Buckingham

"I remembah 'cause I need to tell you how he did 'em."

"How who did what?"

"How Mr. Buckingham *make* his wife."

"How did he do 'em, Mrs. Gum?" I played along, but by now was almost ready to believe her.

"He wen' strangle her an' den dump her body into da ocean from his sailboat. Das why da police no can fine her. Da sharks eat her."

"So why Mr. Buckingham want to *make* his wife?"

"To collect her life insurance. He wen' sell her Bentley car only two weeks aftah she disappear. Dat doan tell you somet'ing?"

"Maybe he need da money."

"Of course. Dey argue ovah money all da time. Das why he *make* her."

I thanked Mrs. Gum for her help and wondered about her sanity. And mine. I had agreed to meet another shady character in some deserted spot in the middle of the night. The repercussions of my last meeting were still haunting me—in the form of Detective Frank Fernandez, who seemed way too eager to put me behind bars.

* * *

Winding down Tantalus Drive, I passed the street where Dr. Carreras had lived before his vintage Porsche flew off the road into a tree. I remembered his calling Buckingham a fraud and then promising to tell me things that would make me want to drop him as a client. After the gold dealer's recital about his past, and Mrs. Gum's repeated allegations of murder, I found myself wishing, now even more, to know what Dr. Carreras might have said.

I looked down to the ocean. Off in the distance a south swell was steaming in at Ala Moana "Bowls." Later the crowds would be out. But in the morning, even on a Sunday, a persistent surfer can usually find an open wave.

That decided it. My nine-six riding beside me in the car, I aimed down the hill to Ala Moana Beach Park, slipped off my khakis down to my board shorts, and paddled out. The south swell was kicking up into a nice hollow left, the way they sometimes do in summer. The waves were shoulder high and rising. But was I wrong about the crowds! Surf city.

I didn't wait long. A set of three good ones popped up on the horizon. The first one came and was packed with riders. I let it go by. The second one was packed too. By the third wave the crowd thinned. I caught it. The green wall swept left and peaked. I stepped to the nose, crouched, and set my arms wide. I was flying, brah. *Flying.* The world suddenly contracted into that single moment. I thought of nothing but the wave . . . the ride.

Surfing has a way of easing my cares, of leaving them back on shore where they belong. But I didn't entirely forget the case. In the lull between sets I thought about Barry Buckingham (a.k.a. Billy Brighton) and his missing dog and daughter and wife. I thought about his blackmailer—Abe Scanlon. And I thought about tonight's handoff at Sand Island.

Kidnapping doesn't leave many options. The ace up the sleeve is always the hostage. The kidnapper can threaten to harm unless conditions are met. Usually a ransom. Even meeting his conditions doesn't guarantee the hostage's safe return. I hoped the smooth-talking Buckingham could talk his way through this one. But if he couldn't, I'd better have a backup plan.

* * *

Later that day I picked up Maile at the airport. It kills me how airlines announce arrival times in hours and minutes, like 12:05 and 10:13. As if the schedule is so precise you could set your watch by it. I have never known an airplane to arrive exactly on time. But so as not to stand her up, I pulled into Honolulu International well before 2:04 that Sunday afternoon. Because of the beefed-up security after 9/11, I had to wait in the windowless cellar of baggage claim. No food. No shops. No amenities except rest rooms. Just when you thought air travel couldn't get worse, it did. Mercifully, Maile's flight from Salt Lake City via San Francisco had caught a tailwind and was early.

Arriving passengers began making their way down an escalator and through sliding glass doors that led to baggage claim. I watched bedraggled adults and half as many boisterous kids stream in, keeping an eye out for Maile. Before long she stepped through the doors in denims and a peach-colored T-shirt that said "Best Friends," beneath the likeness of a doe-eyed puppy. Even at a distance I could see an aura around Maile. I found myself wondering why I'd ever lost touch with her.

"Kai!" Maile hugged me. "Thanks for coming."

Her sweet scent reminded me of Mrs. Fujiyama's *lei*. *Lei!* What an idiot! I'd forgotten one for Maile. But she didn't seem to notice. She hugged me like the old friends we were, rather than like a fellow detective. That was all right with me.

"So when do we go out and celebrate?" Maile asked.

"Well . . ." I said sheepishly. "I have a favor to ask."

"What's the favor?" Maile looked curious.

"I found Kula," I tried to explain. "Yes I did. Thanks to you . . ."

"That's fantastic, Kai," she said. "But you told me already on the phone . . . Remember?"

"Yeah, I remember. But what I forgot to tell you is . . ."

I was interrupted by an airline announcement: "Passengers on flight ninety-three from San Francisco can claim their baggage on carousel H-four. Please note that many bags look alike . . ."

"You forgot to tell me what?" Maile looked puzzled as passengers swarmed the carousel behind us. A red light flashed, a foghorn-like beeper sounded, and the carousel clattered into operation. We turned and watched the first pieces of luggage bounce down and start their slow circular journey.

"I found Kula, but . . ." I struggled on, "I didn't bring him home."

"Why not?" Her brows knit.

"Kula's on Maui. He was stolen, just as you predicted. Then sold to a woman who owns an oceanfront place in Lahaina. I went there, cased out the property, and spotted Kula. But I couldn't see how to take him without setting off alarm bells. I didn't want to botch the job, so . . ."

"So what?" She shrugged her shoulders.

"Truth is, Maile, I need a pet recovery expert. What do you say?"

Maile didn't miss a beat. "When do we go to Maui?"

"Then you'll do it?"

"No problem." She put her hands on her hips in mock gesture. "But you're still going to take me out to celebrate, right?"

"Definitely. How about tonight?" Then I remembered my date with Madison.

"Uh . . ." she hesitated. "Let's wait till we bring Kula home. Anyway, I haven't seen my cats for days. I better go spend some time with them."

I was relieved, but only said: "When will you be ready for Kula?"

"How about Tuesday?" Maile asked. "That will give us one day to prepare. We'll need a few things: A large dog carrier, plus evidence that Kula belongs to your client—AKC papers or a license. And it would help to have someone with us Kula knows well and will come to. How about the girl?"

"I'll ask Buckingham." Lehua's kidnapping and the sordid history behind it was too long to tell Maile just then.

"You know, Kai, the right way to do this would be to inform HPD that Kula was stolen. Your client could file a police report then."

"He won't."

"Okay . . . I guess. So we can get Kula home and he can deal with the legalities later."

"My client's not much for legalities."

Maile glanced at the carousel. "There's my bag!" She pointed to a plaid cloth suitcase.

I rushed to the carousel and snatched it.

"Thanks." She smiled. "We make a good team."

I should have warned her: I almost never work with a partner. I had my reasons, but kept them to myself.

twenty-seven

After dropping Maile off that afternoon, I swung by my Maunakea Street office. Inside the flower shop Mrs. Fujiyama was ringing up a customer with a white ginger *lei*. The sweet-spicy aroma followed me up the orange shag stairs to my door.

The fact that I'd already found Kula didn't stop people from calling. Only Maile, Buckingham, and I knew. I fielded five messages: Two desperate pet owners pleaded with me to find their missing Chihuahua and Airedale. A third caller asked me to train her to search for lost cats. A fourth had actually spotted a light-colored retriever, but by now I knew it couldn't be Kula. And a fifth asked if anyone had claimed the $1,000 reward.

Still no real cases. Had I been pegged as a pet detective?

* * *

When I went home to dress for dinner, another message awaited: "Georgie, now doan yah let me down, boy."

Sammy Bob Picket's twang was unmistakable.

"Remember, yah owe me another hundert when yah git that golden. Jus' put it in the mail, general delivery. Or bring it by now."

* * *

Madison sat at her usual oceanfront table when I arrived for dinner that night at the Waikīkī Canoe Club. Her cigarette, martini, and cell phone were all going—Maltese in her lap. Her cherry hair fell darkly to her shoulders. When I saw her I felt a mix of emotions. But one clear thought: we had to break it off.

Maybe Tommy was right. Maybe I *was* lonely. Or maybe loneliness was just an excuse—a smokescreen for the undeniable fact that Madison was somebody else's wife. Even if her husband was almost never around.

Then there was my old friend Maile—confident and wise enough to be just who she was: tough and independent. Yet she had a soft spot for animals and people in need. Luckily, that had always included me. I couldn't help but wonder what she was doing at that moment.

I took a chair. Twinkie leaped from Madison's lap into mine and planted her wet nose against my crotch. Madison snapped her cell phone shut.

"Twinkie! Show some restraint, girl!"

I pushed the dog's nose away.

"Did I tell you, darling," Madison flicked her cigarette ash into the tray, "that I decided to buy gold from Barry Buckingham?"

"No." I tried not to show concern. "Is that who you were on the phone with?"

"Of course not." Madison laughed. "Have you found Barry's dog yet?"

"Still working on it." I didn't want to jeopardize Kula's rescue. Not after all I'd gone through to find him. And the truth was, I wasn't really sure I could trust Madison.

"Enough about him. Conrad's still threatening to fly to Hawai'i, you know, but he doesn't say when. How can I plan my life?"

"Have you ever thought of divorce?" I asked, and then wished I hadn't.

"If I divorced Conrad, I'd get nothing. His lawyers would see to that." She took a drag from her cigarette. "Can you imagine me economizing at my age?"

"You're not even forty, Madison. And you look barely thirty." It was a politic thing to say—and true. But she wouldn't stay young long if she kept that pace of smoking and drinking.

Her face brightened. "You're a gentleman, Kai. That's why I keep you around."

The cocktail waitress approached and Madison pointed to her now-empty martini glass. "The same," she said.

* * *

After a Canoe Club burger for me and lobster bisque and scallops for Madison, she invited me to her penthouse for a nightcap. I told her I had a case to work that night.

"If you don't want to be with me," she snapped, "don't make excuses."

"It's not an excuse, Madison. I do have a case."

"Well, would you at least walk Twinkie and me home?"

We both knew what that meant. Once again, I found myself saying yes. We stood, she kissed me, and I felt a familiar rush.

* * *

When we arrived at her swanky Diamond Head apartment building, I noticed a limo leaving the garage with personalized plates that started with H. The long black Lincoln pulled away before I could read the rest of the plate. We rode the elevator to the top floor and walked the carpeted hall to her penthouse. Madison slipped in her key and turned the knob.

"That's odd," she said. "It's not locked."

"Are you sure?" I tried the key myself.

"What if somebody's in there, Kai?"

"I'll go first." I pushed open the door and stepped into the dim, sprawling apartment, Twinkie at my heels.

Someone walked toward me. Madison reached for my hand. Twinkie recoiled in fear.

A bald portly man in a satin robe and carrying a highball said: "Dear?" He spoke in a soprano that seemed at odds with his bulk.

"Conrad . . ." Madison hesitated a moment. "What a surprise. When did you get in?" She dropped my hand and put her arms around his substantial self.

"Just ten minutes ago," he said. "I had one of our resort cars drop me off. I wanted to surprise you."

That vanity plate I had spotted on the limo probably said HIGHCAMP.

"Conrad," she giggled, a little too loudly. "Oh, darling, this is a private detective." Madison pointed to me. "I didn't want to worry you, but someone has been stalking me. So I hired Kai Cooke here. I heard he's *very* good."

"Kai," he shook my hand, "the pleasure is mine."

"Mr. Highcamp," I said, "it's an honor to meet you, sir. Mrs. Highcamp has told me all about you." It was a lame thing to say, but the best I could come up with at the moment.

"That so?" He shrugged and then laughed. "Now listen, Kai, I want you to send your bill to me personally. Will you do that?"

"Yes, sir."

"Call me Conrad," he said. "Madison will give you my address in Los Angeles. She can be a little tightfisted, as I guess you know." He winked at me. "I'll expect a statement at the end of the month."

"Right, sir." I handed him one of my cards. "In case you need to get in touch with me."

He took it.

"Well, you two no doubt have a lot to catch up on," I kept talking. "Mrs. Highcamp, you probably won't be needing my services now that Mr. Highcamp is in town. But if I can assist you in the future, please give me a call."

"I'll do that, Mr. Cooke," she said with distant politeness, but I doubted her husband was buying it. I sensed that he knew what she was up to.

I turned on my heels and walked to the elevator. By the time it reached the ground floor I decided that this would be my last date with Madison Highcamp.

twenty-eight

When I met Buckingham later that night at Wonderview, he looked more like a mugger than a millionaire. No charcoal suit and ruby tie. Instead, black sweats, sneakers, and a wool cap pulled over his brows. His ruddy face looked ashen, his blue eyes eerily pale. Was this Billy Brighton, the sailor who'd stolen his partner's fortune and bride?

Buckingham led me into his living room overlooking the lights of Honolulu. He walked to a bookcase and from behind a row of gilt volumes—more for show than reading—he drew a snub-nosed pistol. He fingered it for a moment and then tucked it into a pocket in his sweats.

"Have you heard any more from Scanlon?" I asked.

"Nothing."

"Did you get the cash?"

Buckingham gestured to a leather briefcase on the Berber carpet—monogrammed in gold, B.B.—and consulted his Rolex. "It's almost eleven thirty. Shouldn't we be going?"

"Let's talk through what we're going to do first," I said.

"Yes, good idea." He seemed relieved to have me there to work out logistics.

"We'll take your car, since Scanlon is expecting you alone. I'll ride in the backseat and stay out of sight. When we reach Sand Island, we'll wait by the gate for his call. Scanlon will probably want you to carry the briefcase to a drop point. If he does, I'll shadow you. If anything goes wrong, I'll move in."

"No heroics, Mr. Cooke. This is my daughter."

"I only want to protect you and your daughter, if she's actually there."

"If she isn't, I won't leave the money," Buckingham insisted.

"Of course." I tried to calm him.

"Let's be off then." His ashen face showed a determination he might need before the night was over.

I followed Buckingham through his rambling villa to an attached three-car garage, past his daughter's mint green Mini and the empty space once occupied by his wife's Bentley, to his red Rolls. Atop its mile-long hood stood that silver figurine and beneath that his vanity plate: GLD DLR. Whoever was waiting for us could never miss this car.

I climbed into the back and sank into parchment leather. The smell of the hides was strong. Buckingham pulled away and wound down the darkened road. His briefcase rode next to me in the back seat.

As he negotiated the last few turns on lower Tantalus Drive, the gold dealer turned back to me and said out of the blue, "Like my Rolls?"

"Yes, sir, it's very nice."

"Nice?" He said in his pitchman's voice, his confidence clearly returning. "This car cost me more than your average man's home. But I'm not your average man. Am I?"

"Definitely not, sir."

It was a strange thing for him to say, dressed as he was like a hoodlum and, stranger yet, on his way to ransom his daughter. I wondered how many average men's life savings had gone to buy his Rolls. And what price his wife and only child would ultimately pay.

"I'm not being boastful, you see." He shrugged. "Just proud. I built my business from scratch. Nobody gave me anything."

Nobody but Abe Scanlon, I thought. *And as many people as you could sucker along the way.* But who was I to cast stones? I was working for the man!

When we turned onto Nimitz Highway, I wondered about the resourcefulness of our opponent. Was it likely that the old man would return Lehua for the briefcase? And what about Cheyenne? A blackmailer usually wants more. I didn't picture the old man tossing any grenades, but I didn't doubt he might enlist some muscle who would.

As Buckingham hung a left into Sand Island Access Road and crossed the bridge, a container ship slipped silently from Honolulu Harbor, its illuminated rigging resembling strands of Christmas lights. Sand Island sat in the middle of the harbor, leaving only the narrow channel for the ship to pass through. The beach park rimmed the south shore of the mile-and-a-half long island, where we were soon stopped by a chain across the entrance.

I'd been to Sand Island Beach Park in the daylight. It's a tranquil spot to grill burgers and tilt back a few beers. But at two minutes to midnight the park was black. That there was only one road in made me wonder about Scanlon's plans. I could not imagine an old man alone restraining a kidnap victim and collecting a ransom at the same time.

At midnight Buckingham's cell phone rang.

"Yes, just like you asked for . . ." He took a deep breath. "Abe, it's all there. But I have to see my daughter first." There was a long pause. "I'm on my way."

Buckingham whispered to me in the backseat. "He wants me to carry the briefcase into the park. He'll call me again near the drop point. He still hasn't told me where it is."

What was Scanlon's game? Although his criminal history had been nonviolent, as far as I knew, I was growing increasingly uncomfortable with what he might have planned for his late-night rendezvous with his former partner.

"If you don't like what you hear or see once you get there," I said to Buckingham, "tell Scanlon to wait and come back to the car. I'll meet you here."

"Right."

Buckingham stepped out of the car. I gave him a few seconds' lead and then followed behind. In the dark park he was nearly invisible in his black sweats, toting his briefcase. We walked less than twenty feet when his cell phone rang again.

He talked animatedly into his phone, but I couldn't hear what he was saying. Soon he walked to a nearby trash bin and carefully balanced the briefcase on the rim. Then he rushed back toward his car.

Already he was veering from the plan.

I ducked behind a tree as he walked by, keeping an eye on the briefcase. Buckingham's cell phone rang again. He was close enough to me this time that I could hear him clearly.

"Yes. Yes. I kept my end of it. Now you keep yours."

He put away the phone and walked back to the Rolls, opened the door, and slid into the driver's seat. I stayed out of sight, waiting for Scanlon to emerge from the darkness. Buckingham continued to sit in his car.

What was he doing?

Nearly ten minutes passed. No more phone calls. No sign of Lehua.

About to leave my post, I was stopped by a movement near the briefcase. From the shadows appeared the bent outline of an old man. I couldn't say he was running, he seemed incapable of that. But he was walking as fast as someone his age could—a halting, awkward gait.

Just as Scanlon reached the prize, Buckingham's door opened. I saw three quick flashes and heard *pop-pop-pop*. I couldn't tell if the old man was hit. He grabbed the briefcase and hobbled away.

Then in the darkness, somewhere behind where Scanlon had been, there were two more flashes and pops. Somebody was firing back!

I ran to the car. Buckingham was leaning against the open door, holding his snub-nose.

twenty-nine

"I trust I hit him," Buckingham said calmly. "I trust I hit Abe at least once."

"Get in," I said. "Let's get out of here."

Buckingham slid back into the driver's seat and closed his door. I jumped in the backseat. He turned the Rolls around and left Sand Island Beach Park behind. I looked through the back window, but saw no more flashes coming from the park.

"Who was that with the gun?" I asked. "It wasn't Scanlon. He was too busy with your briefcase."

"I don't know," Buckingham said. "I also assumed Abe had compatriots, but have never myself come face-to-face with one."

"You shouldn't have fired." I was furious. "You could have hit your daughter. Not to mention me."

"Lehua wasn't here." Buckingham slumped back into the seat. "He said she would meet me at the car if I left my brief-case on the bin. Damn him . . ."

"And now he has your daughter and your money."

"Well, not exactly, Mr. Cooke." A smile crossed his face. "I filled the briefcase with old newspapers. This was a little cat and mouse game, you see, between Abe and me. Abe had hoped to fleece me for another fifty thousand, and I had hoped to kill him. Neither one of us succeeded tonight, but there will be other nights, believe me."

"But your daughter . . . and your wife."

"Nothing means more to Abe Scanlon than money. If he harms Lehua or Cheyenne, he's lost his meal tickets."

"So you think he has your wife too?" I recalled Mrs. Gum's very different version of events.

"Of course. It's the only explanation for her disappearance."

"Then why no ransom note?"

"Abe is twisting the sword in me. He wants me to suffer. The note will come—when he's ready."

Just as I realized there was no sense in arguing with him about Scanlon's motives, Buckingham's cell phone rang again. He kept his hands on the wheel. He didn't answer.

"Abe wants to shame me," he said, "but I won't give him the satisfaction. He is not a man of honor."

Did Buckingham think of himself as honorable?

"Mr. Cooke," he cleared his throat, reclaiming his usual pompousness, "since Abe cannot be counted on, and my family's life is still at stake, I'd like to defer to your expertise at this point."

I looked in disbelief at the actor-sailor-turned-pitchman who just this morning told me his history of swindling others. Even if I didn't hate working for a crook who would throw me the sort of curveball he just had—what kind of miracle did he expect me to perform? What on earth made him think that I could find a way to get the girl from Scanlon, especially after Buckingham himself had just spooked the man with a double cross and an attempt on his life? Then I thought of Lehua and the danger she was in.

"Well," I sighed, "my fee just doubled."

"Agreed."

"First let's see if we can intercept Scanlon. We might be able to catch him on the access road, unless he's gone by boat."

I had Buckingham pull off the road after about a half mile behind a big Matson truck. He shut down the motor. In less than five minutes we saw a pair of headlights. He started his Rolls again and grabbed the wheel.

"Wait," I said. "If that's Scanlon, we need to follow him at a distance."

The headlights got bigger and soon an SUV appeared. It fit the description of the vehicle that the elderly *tutu* I'd interviewed on Kailua Beach thought she saw Kula riding in. I could see two people inside as it passed: a man hunched in the backseat, and a man wearing a baseball cap driving. Soon the SUV's taillights faded into two tiny red dots.

"Keep your headlights off," I said. "And follow him. Stay about a quarter mile back."

As we crept along in darkness Scanlon's driver turned from the isolated road onto the more heavily-trafficked Nimitz Highway. They were heading west, toward Pearl Harbor. Buckingham switched his lights back on as we entered the ramp onto the H-1.

Freeway lights revealed the SUV to be a bronze Chevy Tahoe. As the road made its sharp bend near Aloha Stadium, the Tahoe merged into the far right lane. When the H-3 Kāneʻohe exit approached, the Tahoe's right blinker came on and it took the ramp.

"Is he going back to the scene of the crime?" I wondered aloud.

Buckingham said nothing. He seemed focused on Scanlon's taillights.

The Tahoe climbed the H-3 grade to its summit and then descended through the tunnel toward Kāneʻohe and Kailua. At the Kailua ramp, they pulled off and aimed straight for Kailua town. Before long the SUV swung into a side street and then into the driveway that led past the auto parts store to the Windward Sands.

"Spyder Silva," I said. "And Reiko Infante."

Buckingham didn't react to the names.

"I've been here before," I added.

The Windward Sands looked less seedy at night than when daylight revealed its cracked windows and rotting wood. But more eerie. Flickering TVs glowed from inside through open jalousies, emitting the ghostly noise of disembodied voices. While Buckingham parked his Rolls out of sight by the auto parts store, I walked along the overgrown hedge flanking the property and positioned myself where I could see and not be seen.

The driver of the Tahoe hopped out and waited for Scanlon. Though his face was hidden by the bill of his baseball cap, I could see tattoos on Spyder Silva's arms. In his right hand was the Berretta pistol I'd seen in his truck.

"There's our shooter," I said under my breath.

Scanlon struggled from the backseat. The absence of blood on his clothes showed he hadn't been hit by Buckingham's wild firing. Then from behind the back seat another passenger got out.

Silva took the girl's bare arm with his left hand—pistol still in his right—and led her into the Windward Sands.

Lehua.

thirty

Buckingham tiptoed up to me like a two-hundred pound ballerina, wool cap pulled over his brows.

"Scanlon's inside the apartment," I said. "And Spyder Silva. And . . . Lehua."

"Lehua?" He reached into his sweats for his snub-nose.

Before I could respond we saw the blue light of a police cruiser turning into the alley. Buckingham's snub-nose disappeared back into his sweats. The cruiser pulled up, stopped, and the officer got out. He took a good long look at Buckingham. If the officer recognized him, as he could hardly help doing, he was discreet enough not to ask why Hawai'i's most famous pitchman was out at this hour dressed the way he was.

"May I see your ID, sir?" he said to Buckingham. Then he turned to me. "You too."

After we handed over identification, the officer got back into his car. His fingers danced on the keyboard of a laptop mounted above the transmission hump. He studied images on the screen. I wondered if Detective Fernandez had put out an APB on me.

The officer then got out of his car and handed our licenses back. "You have a good evening, gentlemen." He nodded and turned away. I guess I hadn't yet made HPD's most wanted list.

I waited until the blue light on the cruiser disappeared down the street before turning back to Buckingham. The situation had become too dicey for me to follow through on my first impulse. It didn't take me long to decide—as I usually do—that working without the help of law enforcement was the better choice. We would get Lehua out of there ourselves.

"Here's the plan," I said. "We'll wait for Scanlon and the others to go to sleep. I'll go in and you'll stay in the car ready to haul us out of here. Turn it around so you're facing the street. When I come out with Lehua, we'll need to hurry."

"But shouldn't I go with—"

"We have to do this right," I cut him off. "We can't risk another incident like at Sand Island. She could be in the crossfire this time."

"But—"

"Silva has a Berretta and he's already used it. He's who was firing back at you."

"Right, then." The pitchman seemed reconciled. He returned to his car and turned it around toward the street. I sat with him in the Rolls for awhile and then walked back toward the Windward Sands. Silva's corner apartment had two outside walls, with high jalousie windows. They were open wide on that warm night.

A distant streetlight cast a faint glow against the glass. I stretched to peek in. The first room was a hollow shoebox except for two single beds. One was empty. The other contained a man whose tattoo-covered arm hung over the sheet. Silva. His Berretta lay on the floor, next to the bed.

The second small room held two beds and two occupants, only their long hair visible on each of their pillows. The carrot-colored hair had to be Lehua's. And the darker, I guessed, was Reiko Infante. It didn't appear that Silva was taking turns with her watching the girl. He'd left that entirely to the one woman in the gang. Or maybe she didn't trust him with the job.

With Silva and Infante accounted for, that left Scanlon. The old man must have been in the living room—sleeping or awake, I could only guess. If I entered through a bedroom window, I could probably exit the front door without much trouble from him. I'd have to hope there were no other accomplices.

I peered through the second bedroom window again. Infante still slept soundly. I began quietly removing slats from the louvered window.

Breaking and entering. I could lose my license. But by the time we could convince HPD that Lehua had been kidnapped—even if her father would agree to that—she might be harmed or taken somewhere we couldn't track her.

After removing the last jalousie I could reach, I saw Lehua move. I couldn't understand how she could sleep after being kidnapped. Infante lay stone-still. A good time to move. I needed to climb up to the window ledge and then hoist myself in. Not easy, alone.

Scanning the dim yard, I spotted an empty planter box a few yards away. Not ideal, but it should work. I got it and flipped it over beneath the open window. Cautiously standing on its edges, I gained just enough height to lift myself up and over the ledge. Rolling down into the room, I stood still, waiting for my eyes to adjust to the dark.

I tried to approach Lehua quietly, to keep her from making a sound. But it was dark, and she couldn't see who I was. She screamed as my hand went to her mouth, muffling the sound. Infante groaned and rolled over, her back to us.

"Lehua, get up," I whispered. "It's Kai. We've got to get you out of here. Now!"

"But my mom," she whispered back in terror. "They'll kill her."

"They don't have your mom," I said. "Let's go." It was a hunch, and seemed to convince the girl.

Noises started coming from elsewhere in the apartment. Either Scanlon or Silva, or both, must have been awakened by our voices. I took Lehua by the arm and started to lead her out of the room. Somebody was coming down the dark hall. I pulled Lehua back behind the bedroom door.

Someone burst into the room. I swung the door into him and saw the old man go down on the floor. I almost felt guilty knocking over the old fellow, until I saw the hatred in his eyes and the kitchen knife in his hand. I kicked the knife across the room.

"Wake up, Spyder!" Scanlon screamed from the floor in a shrill, thin voice that hardly carried beyond the room. "You damn druggie, wake up! Your girlfriend is worthless."

Silva didn't respond. Nor did his girlfriend, though she was only steps away. I didn't bother to point my .357 at Scanlon. He wasn't getting up soon.

"She's not dead, you know." The old man looked up at me.

I glanced at Lehua, then back at Scanlon, and shook my head. "Obviously."

"Not her," he said, "her mother."

"Where is she?" I asked Scanlon, taking a shot in the dark. Then wished I hadn't. Lehua's eyes started to fill with tears.

"I bloody well don't know," the old man said. "If I did, don't you think I'd've cashed her in by now?"

He had a point. Why kidnap a former wife and then hold her for months on end without trying to gain advantage?

"You want to know where she is, mate?" Scanlon said. "Ask her father." He pointed to Lehua. "He's the one who knows."

Now the girl was crying.

"See yah later." I led her by the arm out of the room, keeping the gun on Scanlon.

Buckingham was waiting in his Rolls. The engine was running. Lehua climbed into the front seat and her father hugged her. She quickly broke free and moved as far from him as she could, huddling against the passenger door.

As Buckingham drove toward Tantalus Drive, he tried to talk to his daughter. She wasn't buying any of it.

thirty-one

It was almost 3 a.m. on Monday morning when I pulled into the Waikīkī Edgewater, rode the elevator to my studio, and fell onto my bed. I didn't undress. But beat as I was, I couldn't get the case out of my mind.

Bringing home the famous surfing dog would close my first (and definitely last) missing pet case, but it would hardly tie up all the loose ends. No way Abe Scanlon would stop blackmailing Buckingham, a.k.a. Billy Brighton. My rescuing his daughter would only make the old man gouge the gold dealer all the more. He had not seen the last of Abe Scanlon.

Then there was Buckingham's missing wife, Cheyenne Sin. According to Scanlon, she was still alive. But had the old man kidnapped her for his ultimate ransom? Or had Buckingham himself, as his neighbor Mrs. Gum alleged, done away with her? I wondered again why he hadn't hired me to find his wife, and instead sent me after his lost dog. And finally there was the crushed skull of Moku Taliaferro—a crime Detective Fernandez was still trying to pin on me.

Kula's disappearance was the tip of the iceberg. But all the rest of it beneath the surface wasn't my job. Once I brought home the golden retriever, Barry Buckingham would have to find another P.I. I was done with him. His rotten side had begun to stink. After collecting my fee, I would say goodbye to Wonderview. Forever.

* * *

My so-called sleep was interrupted by some crack-of-dawn fools drag-racing down Ala Wai Boulevard. I dozed off again until the sun flooding my apartment and the roar of morning traffic forced me out of bed. Still in my street clothes. My aloha shirt had climbed up under my armpits like a life vest. My khakis were so wrinkled I almost tossed them in the trash.

Trying to revive myself, I walked to my closet-sized kitchen and pulled down a package of old-fashioned oats. My parents had New England roots and I can still remember my mother telling me to start the day off right with a good breakfast. To her, that meant hot oatmeal. To me, it was a lot of fuss. Why dirty a pan and wait around for the oats to boil when you could pop open a box of cold cereal? I don't know why I kept oatmeal around. I never ate it. Well, almost never.

I sat a pan on one of my two burners, put in some water and a pinch of salt, and waited till it boiled. Then I put in a cup of oats. And waited some more.

"I might need my strength today," I told myself.

The kitchen steamed up. I got down a spoon and bowl and some honey. My mother used brown sugar, but I didn't have any. Once the oats were cooked, I cover the pan and let them stand, as she used to say. Then I spooned the steaming glop into my bowl.

The first spoonful reminded me how right she was. The oats warmed me all the way down.

The phone rang. I didn't recognize the number. I let the answering machine take it.

"Kai Cooke," said the quavering old Aussie voice, "don't think for a minute, mate, I'll forget or forgive. You are no better than Billy. And your fate will be no better. I know where you live."

How did Scanlon get my number? Did he have my address too? Or was he bluffing? If Buckingham was right, and Scanlon's god was money, my part in last night's adventure couldn't have endeared me to him. One more reason to watch my back.

* * *

At my office there were more phone messages concerning Kula: erroneous sightings, useless tips, and a distraught pet owner begging me to find her beagle. There was also a message from Frank Fernandez—we had reached his Monday deadline. No grizzly-bear mood this time. Teddy-bear instead, which concerned me even more.

"Reiko Infante," Feranadez said. "Remember her, Kai? You tracked her to Kailua on your lost dog case." His tone changed. "She's dead. Somebody climbed through her window last night and smothered her with her own pillow. We're checking for fingerprints, but for now we're holding her boyfriend, Silva. And guess who he says did it? *You* . . . That's two murders connected to you, Kai. Don't make me come get you."

Fingerprints? Mine would be all over Infante's windows and her bedroom. I couldn't call Fernandez right now. If he took me in, I might not come out.

I reluctantly gave Buckingham a call. His voicemail answered. I left a message that I was planning to bring Kula home on Tuesday and asked for the retriever's license and AKC papers. I also asked if Lehua could go with Maile and me. I didn't mention Reiko Infante.

Then I crossed Maunakea Street to C & K Diner and brought back a teriyaki chicken plate lunch to my office. I ate alone at my desk, picking over the chicken with a plastic fork. Until Buckingham returned my call when his radio show ended at four, I was just marking time. And trying to stay clear of Frank Fernandez.

No-brainer. I went surfing.

* * *

At Kaka'ako Waterfront Park, a few blocks from my office, I checked out the edgy break by the Kewalo Channel called Point Panic. The swell was forming into sweet green barrels that rolled about forty yards and then slammed into lava-rock boulders fronting a seawall. A half dozen bodysurfers were carving it up. They milked each wave to its last drop, pulling out a split second before crashing into the rocks. *Daredevils only.*

Point Panic got me thinking again about the case. Though I don't consider myself a daredevil, and seldom panic, I felt as if I were riding a big wave and a wall was coming fast. My gut told me that Buckingham's charcoal suits and black hair were only a surface manifestation of a darkness that lay deeper inside the man. Bad things do happen to good people. But sometimes bad things happen to bad people too. That was Buckingham.

Point Panic—despite its provocative name—was not for longboards. The sign posted by the break reads: Bodysurfing Only. Board riders there can get arrested. But a short walk *ewa,* near the channel to Honolulu Harbor, leads to a less edgy break called Flies that does welcome the rest of us. Flies produces a mushy right when the swell runs, like today, about knee-to-chest-high. Only four riders were out.

I paddled toward the lineup and hopped on the first wave of an inside set. It fizzled. I paddled farther out and waited. Had I known about Buckingham's history, not even my Impala running on fumes would have made me work for him. Kula, Lehua, and I were all pawns in the chess game he was playing with Scanlon. Not to mention Cheyenne Sin.

* * *

When I returned to my office, Buckingham had left a message. I could pick up Kula's papers at six, but he said nothing about his daughter coming with me. I called Maile and asked, a bit awkwardly, if I could spend the night on her couch. I don't know why I didn't ask Tommy Woo. Tommy lives closer than Maile and I'd sacked out in his place before.

Maile didn't hesitate. "If you don't mind sharing the couch with the cats. . ." She paused. "Well, maybe not Lolo."

"I wouldn't ask," I said, "but the bad guys found out where I live. This case is getting kind of hairy and I don't want anything to stand in the way of our trip tomorrow to Maui." I didn't mention that the good guys now seemed to regard *me* as a bad guy. And they too knew where I lived.

"Whatevah," Maile shrugged it off. "How about dinner?"

"You're sure it's no trouble?" Truth is, a home-cooked meal sounded way good.

"We'll have something simple. How about pasta?"

"Fine. What can I bring?"

"Red wine would be nice," she said.

"Red it is."

Maybe I was wrong, but it sounded like a date.

thirty-two

At a quarter to six I drove once again to the summit of Tantalus.

Buckingham buzzed me through and I climbed the granite steps to his *koa* doors. One swung open and there he stood in his charcoal suit—tie askew. His bloodshot eyes suggested he'd slept even less than I had. He handed me Kula's papers documenting his pedigree and ownership.

"And what about Lehua," I asked. "Can she come with me and my assistant to get Kula?"

"Lehua has just endured a traumatic ordeal, as I'm sure you can imagine. She best stay here . . ."

The way he said this convinced me he hadn't consulted his daughter.

"It may be more difficult without her, but I'll do my best . . ." I paused to gather my thoughts. "There is another way you could help the investigation along. I've already used the retainer you gave me to locate Kula. A second retainer, sir, would help pay for travel expenses to Maui and for Kula's safe return."

The gold dealer winced. "Rest assured, Mr. Cooke"— out came his smooth-as-silk voice—"you will be rewarded handsomely. In addition to your normal fee, I have decided to give you the reward I offered for Kula. You found him. You deserve the reward."

"That's very generous of you, sir. It's just that there will be expenses tomorrow morning that . . ."

"Mr. Cooke"—a dark shadow crossed Buckingham's face—"I have given you $1,000 in advance for Kula's safe return. That's nearly what I paid for him as a puppy. You have located him, so you tell me, but you have yet to bring him home. Now, I trust you are a man of honor, and I trust you believe I am too . . ."

"Of course, sir." I stopped myself from reminding him that I had single-handedly rescued his daughter at consider-able risk to myself. For that, he would get a separate bill.

"I will make arrangements to have your check ready when you return with Kula, including the reward." Then he said, "Cheers." The interview was over.

Something told me I would never see that check.

* * *

Driving to Maile's that night for dinner I remembered something that happened the summer I spent in Hawai'i before my senior year. Maile, her boyfriend Karl, and some other friends and I went to a movie. I can't remember what movie or where, but I do remember that Karl and I sat on either side of Maile. It was no coincidence that I sat next to her. Toward the end of the film, as if to punctuate a climatic scene, she put her hand on mine. It seemed like just a playful thing between friends, and it probably meant more to me than it did to her. What did I know? I was seventeen and had never had a girlfriend. I looked over at Karl. He was engrossed in the film. He wasn't paying attention to Maile. Her hand felt warm and seemed to bond to mine. We held hands for I don't know how long. After awhile I got scared and I guess she did too. Our hands went back into our own laps. And Karl was still watching the film.

Maile and I never talked about that time at the theatre. She left with Karl and I didn't see her much again that summer. Funny I should think of this after so many years. Maybe because it was the closet thing to a date I'd had with her before tonight?

* * *

No restaurant in Honolulu ever served a more memorable meal than she did that night in her Mānoa cottage. Homemade pasta. Sauce from scratch. Fresh-baked bread. The supermarket Chianti I brought was hardly up to her cooking, but it put me in a mellow mood. Not to mention the candlelight reflecting in Maile's eyes.

By the end of the meal—a little late—I finally got around to toasting her.

"Of your many talents, this one I like best." I hoisted my wine glass. "Here's to Maile Ohara."

"Barnes," she said.

"Sorry. It just shows you," I said, feeling the wine, "we never know how things will turn out."

She reached both hands across the table, candlelight flickering in her eyes, and took mine. "You weren't here, Kai. You were on the mainland."

"I'd rather have been here. But it's not like I had any say."

"I'm so sorry about your mom and dad. They were such good people. And I know they both adored you."

"I have my memories of them. But I've got to believe my life would have turned out different had they lived."

"How?"

"Well, maybe I'd have stayed in the islands. And maybe the guy you dated in high school would have been me."

"Maybe." She stood and abruptly began clearing the table. "Dessert?"

"If it's half as good as dinner." I followed her into the kitchen.

Maile opened the freezer, removed a stainless container covered with frost, and set it on the counter. Inside, a pale yellow ice gave off a sweet citrus fragrance that stopped me in my tracks.

"Lemon," she said. "Homemade."

That did it. I put my arms around her.

"Are you sure this is what you want?" She looked into my eyes.

"Ever since that summer," I said.

What came next started off shy and innocent, a high school kiss, and slowly grew warmer and more passionate, like the kiss of long-lost lovers.

Next thing I knew, we were in her bed and I was gazing at her naked body. She was just as gorgeous as in her younger photo with her late husband. Slipping off my shirt, I saw the expression on her face. To my surprise, it wasn't shock, but curiosity.

"How'd that happen?" She pointed to the teeth marks on my chest.

"I never told you?"

She shook her head. "I can see we have a lot to catch up on."

"Laniākea." I said. "Probably a tiger shark. But we didn't get well acquainted. He took one bite and swam away."

"Oh," she said and continued to kiss me. "I think I'll have to sample you myself."

thirty-three

Tuesday morning Maile and I flew to Maui wearing sleepy, satisfied smiles. Some passengers aboard the Hawaiian jet may have mistaken us for newlyweds on an island-hopping honeymoon. To be so lucky.

What I felt being with Maile couldn't compare with my experiences with Madison. Nights with her always ended in dark, lonely drives home. With Maile, the sun was always shining.

The airplane's cargo hold carried an extra-large portable kennel for Kula and a small duffle containing the tools of Maile's trade—leashes of various lengths, collars, pet chews and treats, a whistle and clicker, binoculars, pepper spray. I didn't figure we'd need the pepper spray, but Maile said she took it on *every* case. I had booked a return flight that would give us about three hours on the ground in Lahaina.

* * *

At Kahului Airport we rented a minivan roomy enough for the kennel and headed up the coast highway to Lahaina. As the island of Lānaʻi rose on the horizon, Maile turned to me: "Kai, I've recovered a few pets in my time. And I've resorted to some unconventional tactics. There's no predicting how a case will go. We'll just deal with what we find."

"Pet cases and people cases don't sound much different," I said.

"In pet cases, the animals aren't usually the problem. People are."

"Mrs. Varda doesn't strike me as the type," I said. "I wonder if she even knows Kula was stolen."

"Don't kid yourself," Maile replied. "She can't be that naïve. But I don't think we should confront her. It wouldn't guarantee she'd release Kula to us."

"Then why bring his papers?"

"For airport security."

* * *

We parked a few doors from the oceanfront home of Mrs. Varda, our minivan pointing toward Kahului Airport. I led Maile down the beach access to the secluded white sand beach and seaside palaces.

We hid behind some coconut palms in front of the property next to Mrs. Varda's, watching and waiting. A few beach walkers ambled by. No Mrs. Varda. No Kula.

As we sat on the sand under the palms, I noticed our conversation was different now than before last night. Not the words we spoke, but how we spoke them. We weren't the same two people anymore. We had crossed an invisible boundary together from which there was no return. And when our eyes met, they remembered. No matter how hard we tried to go on like nothing had happened.

Then Maile said something that caught me by surprise.

"Kai, I've been with only one other man since Nestor died. The relationship ended when I found out he was seeing someone else." She looked away. "Nobody will ever do that to me again. Even an old friend."

I nodded, having already decided to break it off with Madison. There was no reason Maile would find out about her. And no reason to bring her up now. I don't know much about women, but I do know that a woman expects to be number one in her man's life, with no rival. Introduce a rival, and you introduce trouble. No, I'd remain silent about Madison. Why jinx a promising relationship for one that should have never been?

* * *

By one o'clock nothing had changed at Mrs. Varda's. With barely an hour left before we had to head back, I looked again into her windows. Finally I saw Mrs. Varda herself walking to one of her glass doors. She slid it open. And from a couch, where he had apparently been napping and hidden from our view, Kula ambled behind her onto the pool deck and yawned. The golden retriever's coat lit up in the sun.

"He's *beautiful*." Maile whispered, her eyes glued to him.

The famous surfing dog circled the swimming pool, sniffing the *laua'e* ferns and red ginger on its borders. Mrs. Varda lumbered across the deck and planted her imposing figure in a patio chair.

"What do we do with her?" I asked.

"Got her phone number?"

I nodded.

"I'll call to lure her back into the house. Then we'll take Kula."

Maile flipped open her cell phone.

"Wait," I said. "Shouldn't you take Kula? You're the dog expert. Plus you've got no license to lose if you get caught."

"Kula's met you. He hasn't met me," said Maile. "All you'll need is a plan to get his attention."

"I've got one." I reached into my khakis and pulled out a spanking-new yellow tennis ball.

Maile smiled. "You're a natural, Kai. Now give me her number."

"How will you keep her talking? What if she hangs up?"

"Trust me."

That's why I don't work with a partner. Each of us had a job to do that directly affected the other's and neither of us knew for sure if the other could deliver. I had no choice but to trust Maile would.

She dialed Mrs. Varda's number and took a deep breath. Within seconds we heard the faint ringing of a telephone in the distance. The large woman rose slowly from her deck chair and stepped not into her house, but to a cordless phone on a *lānai* table a few feet away.

"*Oh, sh*——" I said. "She's not going inside. What'll we do now?"

thirty-four

Kula's new mistress picked up her phone.

"Hello, Mrs. Varda?" said Maile. "I'm calling from *Maui Home* magazine. We're planning a special photo feature on Lahaina oceanfront homes next month and we couldn't help noticing that yours is especially charming . . ."

Clever woman.

"Stick to the plan," Maile whispered to me. "This could be our only shot." She signaled to move out.

"Yes, everyone on our staff agrees that your home should be our cover story . . ." she said into her cell phone.

I stepped up to the hedge. *"Kula,"* I called in a whisper. *"Kula, come."*

The golden retriever tilted his head to one side and looked puzzled.

"Kula, come!" I called him again, louder this time.

He trotted toward the gate. Mrs. Varda meanwhile kept talking on her phone, making sweeping gestures, as if giving a grand tour of her home. When Kula reached the gate, he barked.

If his mistress couldn't hear that, she was deaf.

I opened the gate and pulled the tennis ball from my pocket. The retriever stopped barking instantly and stuck his nose so close to the yellow ball I could feel his warm breath on my hand. He eyed it intently. I faced the ocean and cocked my arm. Kula's gaze followed the ball as if he were stalking a yellow bird. He crouched low. His whole body tensed.

When Mrs. Varda looked up from the phone and saw me with her Boomer, her expression changed. She shouted: "Don't let the dog out, please!"

I pitched the ball in one swift arc over the beach, past the shore break, and into the calmer water beyond. Kula bolted across the sand and dove into the surf. He paddled furiously like a blond otter.

Mrs. Varda hung up and hurried to the gate. "Stop!"

I ran down to the water just as Kula caught up with the ball, grasping it in his teeth. Then he turned back to me with a look of pride in his eyes. His birddog genes apparently couldn't care less if it was a yellow bird or yellow ball.

"Kula, come!" I called.

He began paddling back to shore, kicking up a wake behind him. As he stepped dripping onto the sand, Maile appeared with a leather leash and looped it around Kula's neck. "Let's go for a run, boy," she coaxed him, but he'd already started off at a brisk pace.

Mrs. Varda was huffing across the sand now toward us. "Stop! I'll call the police!"

"This is a stolen dog," I shouted to her. "We're returning him to his owner."

"Stolen?" she huffed. "That can't—"

We didn't hear the rest. Maile and I ran up the beach access with Kula in the lead, tennis ball still in his teeth looking like a big goofy yellow smile. I popped open the back hatch of the van and the retriever hopped in. We were his kind of folks, I guess. I jumped behind the wheel, Maile took shotgun, and we squealed away. No Mrs. Varda in the rear-view mirror.

"She's probably dialing nine-one-one right now," I said. "We better keep Kula down and out of sight."

Maile climbed into the back and coaxed the soggy dog into the kennel. I aimed the van through Lahaina town and then onto the highway back to Kahului. After all the excitement, Kula lay down inside the crate to rest. Maile stayed with him all the way to the airport, her soothing voice reassuring the dog—and me—that we had done the right thing.

* * *

A few minutes before we pulled into Kahului Airport, my cell phone rang. I made a right turn with one hand, and with the other flipped open the phone, too preoccupied with driving to check caller ID.

"Darling, where are you? I've been calling your apartment and your office all afternoon." *Madison.*

"I'm on a case." I spoke softly. "What's the problem?"

"Conrad's gone back to L.A. I thought you'd want to know."

"So there's no problem?"

"Well, there might be," she replied. "Something strange happened to me today."

"Like what?" I glanced back at Maile. I hoped Madison would be quick.

"I sent a check to Barry Buckingham."

"Really?" Bad idea, I thought. *But it's her money.*

"Then this afternoon driving home from Gucci I tuned in Barry's show, but it wasn't on. The station was playing elevator music."

Uh-oh.

"I started to worry, since I had just sent him a check," Madison went on. "So I called the radio station. The receptionist said the show had been cancelled. She wouldn't say why."

"Hmmm." I couldn't begin to tell her the whole Barry Buckingham story. Not now.

"Then I called Barry's offices and left a message. Well, I left three messages. He hasn't returned any of them."

"When did you mail your check?"

"Saturday."

"Today's Tuesday. It may be too late."

"For what?" Madison sounded worried.

"To put a stop payment on it."

"You think it's that serious?"

"If it is, you'll lose every penny. If it's not, you can always send him another one."

"No wonder Conrad always handles the money," Madison said. "I've made a mess of this!" She hung up, without saying goodbye.

"What was that about?" Maile asked from the back of the van.

"My client's radio program has been yanked off the air. And he's not returning calls."

"What does that mean for Kula?"

"I'm not sure."

thirty-five

At Kahului Airport a skycap helped us load Kula's kennel onto a dolly. Maile stayed with the damp retriever while I returned the van. By the time I made my way to the ticket counter, the two of them were near the front of the line. Inside the kennel Kula hunkered down and glanced at me through the side grates with a bewildered look in his eyes. I felt for him. But I knew we'd have him home in no time.

* * *

It was nearly 5:30 when we claimed Kula at the inter-island terminal in Honolulu. Maile released him in baggage claim and the sunny retriever stepped stiffly from the kennel and then made a beeline for the nearest pillar and lifted his leg.

"*Kula!*" It was too late.

A yellow stream poured down the pillar and formed a puddle on the tile floor. Maile and I looked at one another. She corralled Kula and slipped on his gold-embossed collar and led him quickly out the door. We walked to the parking garage.

The surfing dog hopped into the back of my Impala where, instead of a seat, my surfboard stretched into the trunk. Kula pressed his nose against the rear window on the driver's side, smeared it, and barked. I cranked down the window. Maile sat in front with me, my board's nose resting on the seat between us. As I pulled from the garage, Kula stuck his head out the window and sniffed the breeze. Maile glanced back at him.

"We should rinse the saltwater off his coat," she said.

"We're going to Wonderview," I said. "Lehua may want to do it herself. She hasn't seen him for a week."

Soon we were climbing Tantalus. Kula grew restless when he saw the familiar winding road. He stuck his head way out the window. His mouth gaped into a big smile. As we pulled up to the white wall surrounding the mansion, Kula's energy rose to a crescendo. He barked and squirmed and tried to jump through the window.

Maile put him on leash and walked him along the white wall where he sniffed and lifted his leg in familiar places. They stopped at the copper gate. Kula barked and Maile attempted to let him in, but the gate was locked. Kula barked again. I tried the gate myself, with no luck. Then I buzzed the intercom.

Silence.

I buzzed again.

I pushed the buzzer one more time and then climbed over the wall. I hiked up the granite steps to the *koa* doors and knocked.

No answer.

I twisted the knob. It wasn't locked. I stepped inside. The entry hall lights were on.

"Hello? Mr. Buckingham? Lehua?" I said.

The only sound was the echoing of my own voice.

I wandered down the hallway. "Mr. Buckingham?"

In a bedroom plastered with surfing posters that I assumed was Lehua's, clothing was scattered on the floor. It looked like the teenager had dressed haphazardly and left in a hurry. I walked to the end of the hallway and opened a door that led to the garage. There sat Lehua's green Mini, but not her father's Rolls. It appeared they were gone.

I walked back into the house. On the opposite side of Lehua's bedroom overlooking the blue sea I found Buckingham's office and his master bedroom. The office appeared untouched—except for a wall safe. It was wide open and empty. No cash. No gold. No sign of the pitch-man's pistol.

In his mammoth bedroom I found a walk-in closet, bigger than my apartment, that looked like it had been hit by a hurricane. An antique dresser and chest were heaped with clothing and there was another pile on the white carpet. A half-full overnight bag lay next to it. It appeared that Buckingham, like his daughter, had grabbed whatever he could carry and ran.

Lying in the open top drawer was a velvet jewelry case. Empty. I slid open the next drawer: Calvin Klein boxers and undershirts. Then the next: button down Oxford shirts in pastel colors. The bottom drawer appeared to be empty. I looked more closely.

Back in a dark corner, where Buckingham had apparently forgotten it, lay a shark's tooth on a broken black cord. Not the sort of jewelry Buckingham wore. I checked out the necklace. The tooth was engraved in scrimshaw with the letter *M*.

Moku Taliaferro.

It could mean only one thing. Buckingham was involved in Moku's murder.

I stuffed the necklace into my pants pocket and called Detective Fernandez, hoping he'd believe me. I got his voicemail.

"I think I've found the man who crushed Moku's skull, Frank. Barry Buckingham. I'll deliver the evidence to you, but first I'm going after him." I paused and thought. "He probably killed Reiko Infante too. And maybe his own wife. I'm heading down to Ala Moana Yacht Club, where he keeps his boat. It's called the *Golden Hinde*."

Climbing back over the wall I found Maile still walking Kula outside the grounds. The retriever's tail was wagging. He looked happy to be almost home.

"Buckingham left," I said, "in a rush. But he forgot this." I showed her the broken necklace.

"So?"

"It belonged to the man HPD thinks I killed. They say I did it for his necklace. So this could clear me."

Maile glanced at the shark's tooth. "Homicide thinks you killed for this?"

"According to Fernandez."

"He's got to be kidding."

"He's not," I said. "And I don't find it funny."

"Can't say I blame you."

Maile put the reluctant retriever back into the car and I drove down the hill to the yacht club.

* * *

Evening was approaching and Honolulu streets were flowing freely now after rush hour. Within a few minutes we arrived at the harbor.

Kula got antsy again. His tail whacked my surfboard, making the *bop-bop-bop* like a bongo drum. Maile put him back on leash and opened the door. Kula took off like a shot toward the docks.

"Kula, heel!" Maile commanded.

The retriever pulled with purpose. He led us right to the spot where the *Golden Hinde* should have been. That rescue board still was mounted by the empty slip.

But the boat was gone.

thirty-six

Then we saw it. About forty yards from the dock, the big sloop was chugging under diesel power toward the harbor mouth. The gold dealer was at the helm.

"You forgot something, Buckingham," I shouted across the water and dangled Moku's necklace in the air. The shark's tooth glinted in the sun.

Buckingham smiled and waved and said, "Cheers," and kept going. The *Golden Hinde* was headed for the open sea.

Kula was beside himself. His master was leaving him behind. The retriever barked and pulled on his leash.

Maile grabbed the leash with both hands. "Sit!" she said.

The dog kept pulling.

Then from inside the cabin Lehua popped up and saw him on the dock. The girl screamed: *"Kula!"*

Maile tried to hold him back, but when he saw the girl Kula ripped the leash from Maile's hands and dove into the water. He swam toward the sailboat, churning up a white wake behind him. Maile and I watched him from the dock. He was a strong swimmer. And he was moving fast.

"Kula!" Lehua leaned over the sailboat's guardrail.

The dog kept swimming. But he couldn't catch up to the *Golden Hinde.*

The girl turned to her father and we heard her shout: "Daddy, please!"

But Daddy didn't stop, or even slow the boat. Lehua shouted again. Buckingham kept his hand on the throttle. Kula fell farther behind.

Suddenly the girl ran to the stern and jumped overboard.

"Oh, my God!" Maile pointed.

When Buckingham saw his daughter hit the water, he spun the wheel and turned the boat around.

We watched the dog and girl swimming toward each other, and the sloop closing in on them. When I couldn't stand it anymore, I kicked off my sandals, stripped down to my board shorts, and grabbed the rescue board.

I paddled as fast as I could to the middle of the harbor. But Buckingham's boat intercepted Lehua before I could, its starboard bow coming between me and the girl and the dog. Both were on the other side. I couldn't see the two and, luckily Buckingham, who was busy with them, couldn't see me either.

I grabbed onto a vinyl dock bumper hanging from the starboard bow of the *Golden Hinde.* The surfboard had no leash or line to tie to the boat, so I set the board free. Then I pulled myself up on the bumper and strained to see across the deck. Buckingham was bending over the port side, talking with his daughter, who apparently clung onto Kula and to another bumper.

"We'll send for him when we reach Bora Bora," Buckingham was saying.

"I won't go without him," Lehua insisted.

"Get in the boat!" he shouted.

"I don't believe you," she yelled back.

"Lehua!"

Then she said, "C'mon, Kula."

I heard splashes. Next I saw the girl and dog clear the port bow, both of them swimming for the dock. The surfboard I had set free was drifting toward them. Lehua swam for it and climbed on. Then she paddled to Kula and helped him on. The dog crawled to the nose and hung his front paws over the tip, just like I'd seen in the TV news video. The girl paddled for the slip where Maile was waiting.

"Lehua!" Buckingham shouted. "You can bring the dog."

The girl kept paddling.

"Blast you, then!" he screamed across the water. "Blast your mother too! What will you do without me, eh?"

Buckingham returned to the wheel, pushed the throttle forward, and swung the sloop back toward the harbor mouth.

I was dragged through the water as the *Golden Hinde* headed out to sea.

The boat picked up speed. I dropped down on the bumper, keeping my head below deck level. I didn't know what to do. I was unarmed and Buckingham, for sure, would have his snubnose.

The *Golden Hinde* cleared the harbor jetty and the rock pilings that surround Magic Island—the last spit of land before the open sea. He wasn't turning back. Not even for his own daughter.

Outside the jetty, a summer swell was rolling in. Bowls was ahead off the port side, and it looked six to eight feet, easy. Other breaks were going off. Lots of surfers were carving up the waves. Not me. I was hanging onto that bumper on the starboard side. And if I didn't do something soon, I would be in very deep water.

The *Golden Hinde*'s bow began to rise and fall over the swells. Buckingham shoved the throttle all the way forward and turned *ewa,* or to the west, offshore of Ala Moana Beach. He made no move to raise the sails.

Before long we were making better time than I could ever do on my board. The yacht harbor shrunk behind us in our wake. The boat passed just outside the surf spots off Ala Moana Beach Park: Tennis Courts, Concessions, Big Rights, Marineland, and finally Kewalos. Ahead was Point Panic.

I kept my eye on the gold dealer at the helm. It was time to move.

Another swell rolled under the boat. I hoisted myself up the bumper and rushed across the deck. I took Buckingham down. He went flat on his back. The wheel swung around and the sailboat yawed and started circling. I came down on top of him. He reached into his pocket and showed the snub-nose. I knocked the gun out of his hand. It slid across the deck, coming to rest against a toe rail. The boat kept circling. Going fast, but nowhere.

Buckingham rushed not for the gun, but for the helm. He righted the wheel, punched a button that must have been an autopilot, and the boat stopped going in circles. But now we were headed for Point Panic. The rocks. Full throttle.

The swells started coming at us from behind. The big sloop rode them like a seesaw. The stern rose and then the bow fell. Over and over again. I'm no sailor—I'm a surfer—but it seemed to me that this was no place for a boat to be: its tail to a summer swell and its nose heading for the rocks.

Buckingham came at me on all fours. Before I could get up, he slipped his gold fingers around my neck. Another swell picked us up and the boat rode it like an outrigger canoe. He held onto my throat, trying the strangle the life out of me. I punched him in the ribs. He groaned and loosened his grip. I pushed him off of me and he fell backwards.

Out of the corner of my eye I saw Point Panic. A body surfer was carving a big green barrel. He was milking the wave to the last drop and preparing to bail out before it hit the wall. Then I realized he was parallel to us. The *Golden Hinde* was riding the same wave right next to him! And the rocks were coming.

The wave took us. The boat swept forward in a surge. We were doomed. Buckingham hopped up on the deck and started coming for me again. He would never make it.

"Why'd you kill Moku?" I said as we were about to hit. "He was nobody."

"Hardly, mate." Buckingham kept coming. "He worked for Scan—"

Before he could finish, I heard the crack of the bow hitting the rocks and then a horrible splintering sound. The shock of our impact carried stern-ward. Buckingham, his center of gravity higher than mine, was thrown toward the rocks. The next thing I knew, he was gone and I was in the surf. The *Golden Hinde* lay on its side in splinters next to me.

The swells kept coming. I bobbed among the boat's debris. I tried to swim away from the seawall, but each successive wave washed me closer. In the distance I saw that body surfer who had just milked the same wave swimming toward me. Another wave hit, bringing something heavy and sharp from the wreck with it——more quickly than I could swim.

The lights went out.

thirty-seven

When I opened my eyes I was on a bed inside a pale green room. I felt like I was still floating. Something resembling a clothespin was attached to the tip of my right index finger. My upper left arm was encircled by a python-like band that made a *beep-beep-beep-beep* sound, echoing the beat of my heart. Numbers flashed on a monitor—48—50—52—48— counting the beeps. An IV was stuck in my left arm, connected to a tube and container above the bed. And overhead was the mother of all flood lamps blazing down on me.

I wasn't wearing my board shorts anymore. I was in something resembling a baby-blue nightshirt. Blankets covered me and I was very warm. I raised my left hand and felt my head. It was wrapped in a gauze bandage like a turban. There was a bump on the back of my head, so heavily bandaged I couldn't feel my fingers on my scalp. I lowered my arm and then heard a woman's voice.

"Detective . . ."

Two faces looked down at me. One was unfamiliar—a woman in a smock. The other, I recognized.

"How ya feeling, Kai?" said the homicide detective.

"Frank?"

"Glad you made it," he said.

"Where am I?"

"Queens Hospital. A piece of that wrecked boat smacked you in the head. You damned near drowned. A surfer pulled you out at Point Panic. You've got a pretty nasty gash, but the doc already stitched you up. You should be outta here by tomorrow."

"I don't feel anything," I said.

"You won't," the nurse spoke up, "for a while. But once the anesthetic wears off, you'll be glad for the meds Dr. Masaki prescribed for you."

"I'm not much for drugs." I've always been stubborn about this. I don't like taking anything except vitamins. My parents' New England roots again.

She shook her head, but Fernandez smiled down at me like I was his own son.

"Buckingham?" I wondered aloud about the man who had put me there.

"In surgery," Fernandez said. "Broke his leg and a couple of vertebrae. He's going to be laid up for a while."

"He killed Moku."

"Yeah, I got your message. But when I drove down to the yacht club, it was too late. You were already in the water.

"What about his daughter—

"Don't worry," Fernandez cut me off. "We'll take it from here. Buckingham's not going anywhere. He'll be held on fraud and theft charges, even if we can't hold him yet for murder."

"But what did you do with Lehua?"

"I questioned her. She didn't know much about what her father was into. Then I turned her over to Maile. She's got the dog too." Fernandez ran his fingers through his dark wavy hair. "Maile returned your car, by the way. Nice lady. The K-9 guys all liked her."

I tried to nod, but my head was going nowhere.

A little smile then turned up at the corners of Fernandez's mouth. "So you dating her, or what?"

"She's an old friend. She was helping me with the pet case."

"She hasn't dated much since Nestor died, far as I know. But when she's ready," he adjusted his belt, "yours truly is gonna be first in line."

"Lucky guy," I said.

"You should be so lucky." Fernandez winked and left the room.

* * *

The next afternoon I was released from the hospital. The lump on the back of my head was the size of a block of Sex Wax, the stuff I rub on the deck of my board. But at least I could see straight. And I could walk. I was no longer numb. But I didn't think I would need the painkillers the doc had prescribed. Remembering the nurse's warning, I picked them up at the pharmacy anyway, along with an antibiotic and ice pack.

An HPD officer was waiting for me in the lobby when I got out of the elevator. He led me to an unmarked car and we rode to the Beretania Street Station. Fernandez met me in his office and I told him the official version of the Buckingham story. I didn't mention how I bent the law along the way. Frank was supremely satisfied, even without those details.

Finally given a lift to my apartment, I fell into bed and called Maile. After four rings her answering machine kicked in. "Hi, you've reached Maile Barnes, tracer of missing pets. How can I help?"

"Maile, it's Kai . . ." I waited a few seconds, hoping she would pick up. "I just got out of the—"

"Kai," she said breathlessly, as if she'd run to the phone. "Are you okay? I would've come to the hospital to see you, but I've got Lehua and Kula with me. It's kind of a zoo around here."

"Frank Fernandez told me," I said, glad to hear her voice. "That was good of you to take them both."

"It's just temporary. But they had nowhere else to go. HPD has closed off Buckingham's house. And it's no place for Lehua to be right now anyway—after what's happened."

"How is Lehua?"

"Doing well—considering. She's a nice girl, Kai. I feel sorry for her. I don't think she had any idea what was going on."

"Not until a few days ago," I said. "I think she started to figure out then that her father wasn't the man he pretended to be. It was quite a shock for her. I was there."

"Who's going to take care of her? Her father will be doing time for the rest of his life. And her mother . . ?"

"Her mother's the wild card. If Scanlon didn't kill her or Buckingham himself."

"I hope for Lehua's sake she's alive."

"Me too. But I don't have to tell a veteran cop that after a woman's been missing for months, the odds get very long that she'll be found."

"Speaking of long odds," she said, "how did you survive that ship wreck? Frank said it was miraculous. And how's your head?"

"A surfer pulled me out of the wreckage. I guess I owe him my life.

As for my head, it's just a bump. The doc gave me a few stitches. Nothing serious. I'll be good as new in a few days. Which reminds me, how about that celebration I promised you?"

"I'd love to. When you're feeling better. And when we find out what's going to happen with Lehua and Kula."

"I'll check back." Then I remembered something. "Say, you know Frank Fernandez from Homicide?"

"Sure, everybody at HPD does. Why?"

"Oh, just curious. You know him well?"

"Nestor knew him well. They were buddies. And we used to go out together—Nestor and me, and Frank and his wife. Or should I say ex-wife?"

"I see."

"Oh, you want to know if I ever dated him?"

"Doesn't matter."

"The answer is no. I told you I dated only one person since Nestor died and that ended how I told you it ended."

"None of my business," I said.

"You better get some sleep, brah. Or you're going to have one major headache tomorrow morning."

"The doc gave me pain pills—but I won't need them. I'll be fine."

"Take them, or you'll be sorry."

"Yes, mom."

"Sometimes you may need a mom, Kai. But I'm not her. Just a friend telling you not to be a jerk. Take the pills or you won't sleep a wink."

"Later," I said. "You're the best."

"The feeling's mutual," she said.

I hung up feeling good, never mind the bump on my head.

* * *

After talking with Maile I turned on the TV and stared blankly at a rerun of *Hawaii Five-0*. I didn't feel much from the bump on my head. It didn't hurt, really. And I started thinking I was tough guy. I had survived a shipwreck and a whack on the head. I forgot the nurse's instructions to take the painkillers. Suddenly I was curious to see my wound and figured it was time to change the dressing.

I walked into the closet that passes for a bathroom in my apartment and looked in the mirror. I watched myself peel off the red-soaked gauze and looked in the mirror at the back of my head. The doc had shaved my hair just above the neckline. And there it was—a red, crusty mess, right out of a slasher movie. I was sure it would all look better later, after the swelling and purple went away. But right then it wasn't too pretty. Fresh blood seeped out between the dozen or so stitches. I put on a new bandage, glad to have that mess out of my sight.

I went back and lay in bed. A few minutes passed. Then it started. Around the wound like a mild headache. After a while it turned into a real banger. I put on an ice pack. That helped a little. But not much.

Before long my head was really throbbing. I wasn't such a tough guy after all. I gave in and popped a pain pill. I waited for it to take hold. Meanwhile I tried to fall asleep. But I just lay there, focused on the pain. It felt like somebody was drilling the back of my head. I kept wondering why the pill wasn't working. After fifteen minutes—nothing. I broke down and popped another. More time went by. Finally I started to feel some relief. The throbbing in my head turned down a notch from ten to nine. Then to eight. But by nearly an hour later, the volume was down to only seven . . . maybe.

I wanted the pain to go away. I wanted to sleep. But it wasn't happening. My two painkillers were fighting the doc's dozen stitches. My team was outgunned. So I lay there, waiting for a few more hours to pass so I could pop another pill.

Unable to sleep, I switched the TV to the late news, catching the tail end of the local broadcast.

"And, finally tonight, a mystery at the legendary Royal Hawaiian Hotel in Waikīkī. Hotel security and police are searching for an elderly Australian visitor who disappeared from the famous pink palace two days ago leaving his personal items in his room and an empty leather briefcase with the initials BB on it. Anyone with information about this man, who checked in under the name Abraham Scanlon, should contact the Honolulu Police Department . . ."

It was no mystery to me. One of two things had happened. Either Scanlon had slunk away to parts unknown without paying his hotel bill, or Buckingham got to him first.

thirty-eight

Late the next morning after I managed to drive myself—against doctor's orders—to my office, there was a knock at the door. I opened it to a statuesque Chinese woman in her late forties, in an elegant silk dress.

Next to her was Kula.

The golden retriever looked as surprised to see me as I was to see him. He bounded to my desk, barking and wagging his tail.

"*Kula,*" said the woman. "*Come.*"

"He's alright," I said and petted him. "And you are—"

But before I could even finish my sentence, I knew the answer. The exotic elegance, the faint Australian accent, she had to be Cheyenne Sin. So then I said, "You're Barry Buckingham's wife."

"Soon to be ex-wife." She glided into the office, her dress clinging to every hill and valley of her picturesque terrain. A few years earlier and she could have stepped off the pages of *Glamour.*

As she sat in my client's chair, I settled behind my desk and Kula followed me. He sat and I stroked his soft fur.

"I'm taking Lehua away from here, Mr. Cooke. I can't say where, but I'm sure you understand why." She spoke as elegantly as she dressed. "The recriminations against Barry are going to rebound on us. There will be no place safe in Hawai'i for Lehua and me. Not only that, Barry could drag me into his troubles and our daughter might end up with neither parent to care for her."

I patted the dog and nodded. "How did you find her at Maile's?"

"I called Lehua's cell phone when I heard of Barry's arrest. I picked her up—and Kula—this morning." She rolled on. "Lehua can't part with him, of course. But we leave tonight and we simply don't have time to get him the necessary inoculations and documentation. He's got to remain in Hawai'i until those things can be obtained."

"I see," I said, wondering what all this had to do with me.

"Lehua trusts you, Mr. Cooke. She trusts you so much, she's going to leave her dog with you."

"But . . ."

"Just temporarily. And if you wouldn't mind taking him surfing now and then, he'd be in seventh heaven."

My face must have registered my astonishment.

"Of course, we're going to compensate you," she quickly added. She took an envelope from her purse and dropped it on my desk. "One thousand dollars—in cash. For your trouble and for Kula's upkeep until he joins us."

"Wait a minute," I stopped her. I needed to make sense of the strange direction the case was taking—and had come from. "Have you been hiding this whole time?"

"Yes, from Barry . . . Well, from Abe too."

"Hiding from both of them?"

"Yes. I never divorced Abe. When he found me in Honolulu, he threatened to kill me. At the time, Barry was blaming me for all our money troubles." She sighed. "Our fights escalated to the point that I decided to disappear. But I couldn't be far from Lehua."

"Mrs. Gum . . ."

"Yes, Mrs. Gum was kind enough to take me in, even making up that story about Barry feeding me to the sharks. I thought he had hired you to find me."

"And you're who I saw in the upstairs window?"

Cheyenne Sin nodded. "Sometimes I snuck out at night and peeked into my daughter's bedroom window to reassure myself she was alright. I felt so terrible, watching her cry over my being gone. But I started fearing for my own life and just bolted. I tried to get a message to her, without her father knowing. I almost got caught, though. I even once set off the alarms."

"So you were the prowler your husband thought was casing his property?"

She nodded again. "When we first met in Sydney, Barry was solicitous of my every need. But as time wore on, he changed. You know what they say—all that glitters isn't gold."

I leaned farther back in my chair. Kula had found a comfortable position resting against my leg, his head in my lap. "Well, I appreciate the trust you and Lehua have put in me," I said, "and I appreciate the money, but I can't—"

"We know you'll take good care of Kula." Cheyenne Sin stood and headed for the door. "We'll be in touch."

Kula watched his mistress leave. To my surprise, he didn't move a muscle. I patted him again, but he needed no reassurance.

* * *

Within minutes I had loaded the golden retriever into my Impala and was driving to Mānoa. I didn't call first. I didn't even consider how Maile would respond to see Kula again so soon.

I knocked on the door of her cottage and she came in shorts and a t-shirt, her brown hair down. Maile looked at Kula and me standing there. Before she could get a word out, the three cats scattered.

"Coconut! Peppah! Lolo!" she shouted after their disappearing tails. "You remember Kula." Then to me: "I don't know what's wrong with them. They got on well with him before. C'mon in."

"I'm sure they'll get used to him again," I said as I walked inside, the dog leading the way. "At least I hope they will."

"So how are you, Kai?" Maile looked me up and down. "How's your head?"

"Okay."

"Let me see." She put her hand on my shoulder, looked at the bandage on the back of my head, and then kissed me.

"I feel much better now," I said, whiffing her loamy fragrance.

"And your stitches?"

"All good . . ." I said as I wondered how to approach her about Kula.

"Is there something you want to tell me?"

"Tell you?"

"Well, here you are unannounced with this beautiful animal . . . I was just wondering what's going on."

"The strangest thing happened today," I said as we sat down. "You wouldn't believe. Well, I wouldn't have believed it if it hadn't happened in my office." I paused. "You met Buckingham's wife this morning?"

"Yes, go on . . ."

So I told her about Cheyenne Sin showing up with Kula and telling me the story she did and then leaving him behind with me. I went into detail. Maile latched onto every word, as if the story involved her own best friend. I worked up slowly to the point, trying to come up with a graceful lead-in to the huge favor I was about to ask. But there was no way to soft peddle it. So I just popped the question.

"Maile, would you mind keeping Kula for a few days?" I had no idea how many, but days sounded better than weeks or months. "I'd take him myself, but I've got nowhere to keep him."

"Me? Take Kula?" Maile looked slightly bewildered. She bent down and ran her fingers through his golden fur. She didn't say anything for a while. Then softly: "No, I don't mind . . ."

"Are you sure?" I said. It wasn't like Maile to be any way but direct. She usually said what was on her mind—like when she told me not to be a jerk about taking my painkillers.

"It's fine, really." Kula's tail was waving like a victory flag. "I just haven't had a dog in the house since Rusty—"

"Thanks," I said, relieved. "Thanks a lot."

She crouched down and put her arms around the dog. I thought I saw tears in her eyes. She buried her face in his fur.

Kula had found himself a new home. At least for now.

In a minute Maile looked up. Her face was streamed with tears. I didn't know what to say. I handed her two of the hundreds Cheyenne Sin had given me. Maile shook her head, as if to say it wasn't necessary.

"There's more where that came from." I walked silently to the door and let myself out. Seemed to me, she and the dog needed to be alone.

thirty-nine

Wednesday's *Star-Advertiser* detailed the wreck of the *Golden Hinde*, with photos of the capsized boat in shallow water off Point Panic. There was also a file photo of me, and one of Buckingham in his three-piece suit. Buckingham was the prime suspect in the murders of Moku Taliaferro and Reiko Infante, not to mention multiple counts of fraud and theft and tax evasion. The story said his radio program had been cancelled. Buckingham owed Honolulu station KGHO an unspecified sum for unpaid air time. Two investors were interviewed who had purchased gold from Buckingham and received worthless certificates in return. He claimed he held the gold in his personal vaults, saving clients the expense of secure storage. But he never made good on his claim.

The story did not make a connection between Buckingham and the disappearance of Abe Scanlon from the Royal Hawaiian Hotel. Whether Buckingham had killed the old Aussie or he was wandering loose on the island, I would have liked to know. Also the whereabouts of his lieutenant, Spyder Silva. I don't take threats lightly.

* * *

In the next morning's mail I received a check from Highcamp Hotels and Resorts corporate headquarters in Los Angeles. Twenty-five hundred dollars for "services rendered to Mrs. Highcamp." There was no note. Subtracting about five hundred for unrecovered expenses from the Buckingham case, I was now two grand ahead. I didn't count the one thousand from Cheyenne Sin for Kula's care, since Maile already had two hundred of it. And I would no doubt be giving her more.

I saw Maile later that afternoon. Kula was lounging on her rattan sofa like a crown prince. He didn't even bother to bark when he saw me. He just waved his tail. An assortment of rawhide chews, three new tennis balls, and a braided tug rope were scattered about the room. Peppah and Coconut sat on nearby chairs, keeping their envious eyes on the returned prince.

"Kula isn't putting you out, is he?" I asked Maile.

"He's no bother," she said nonchalantly. "I don't mind him hanging around . . ." She paused and thought for a moment. "When do you think they'll want him back?"

"I haven't heard a word from Lehua or her mother," I said. "But Kula couldn't have found a better home."

I suddenly felt a stab of guilt. The haunting eyes and skeletal forms of Sammy Bob Picket's captives contrasted starkly to the comfort and pampering Kula was enjoying. "Remember that Big Island hoarder I told you about," I said, "the one who sold Kula to the woman on Maui?"

Maile nodded.

"We should turn him in."

"Trouble is," she said, "any seized animals that are sick or can't be adopted might be euthanized."

"Not good."

"I'm sure the Humane Society would do everything it could to place the dogs. I mean the only other way is kind of radical."

"How radical?" I asked.

"We could free the dogs ourselves and place them in a private animal sanctuary."

"We did manage to get Kula out," I said, but I wasn't sure I wanted to try again with dozens of dogs.

"I don't think there are any suitable sanctuaries on the Big Island," she said. "But I can find out."

We left it at that.

* * *

Heading back out of the Mānoa valley, I remembered puppy mill Lou, whose animal abuse was nearly as horrific as Picket's. But she was small time and here on O'ahu. Through Maile's local contacts, I didn't doubt we could take Lou down once we returned from the Big Island.

I'd barely gotten to the valley's mouth when my phone rang.

"We can go tomorrow," Maile said.

"Go where?"

"To the Big Island. I called Utah after you left and explained the situation. Turns out, some people there know of a woman who's starting up a 'no kill' shelter near Hilo. She's an ex-ALF member."

"Ex-what?"

"ALF—Animal Liberation Front. You know, the ones who wear ski masks and break into labs that experiment on animals. Their detractors call them terrorists."

"I've heard of ALF, but not around here."

"Her name is Deirdre. She's Canadian," Maile continued. "We can stop by and see her shelter tomorrow, then check out your hoarder."

"You don't mind? You don't have a case?"

"Not at the moment," she said.

"OK, but we better go to Sammy Bob's place after dark. If he knows Kula was stolen from Maui, he also knows who did it."

forty

The next afternoon, a Friday, I arrived at the Waikīkī Canoe Club for lunch with a potential client. I wore my best aloha shirt—it was Rayon but looked like silk—and my newest khakis that still had a crease in the legs. I had reserved a 3:05 p.m. flight to Hilo for Maile and me. We planned to drop by the ex-ALF's animal sanctuary, then drive up to Laupāhoehoe in the evening and case Picket's canine prison after dark.

My potential client, a pale and balding accountant named Martin Fix, was looking for someone to investigate his young second wife. Mr. Fix wanted evidence of her infidelity, photos of the Mrs. in bed with the other man. Not my favorite kind of case. But it was all I had going at the moment. And I wasn't taking any more cases involving pets, despite phone messages daily offering me work in that line.

I explained to Mr. Fix that Hawai'i is a no-fault divorce state. Photos of his wife would not be admissible in court, nor would they be necessary. He didn't care. He intended to confront her with the evidence, for whatever reason.

As the soft-spoken Mr. Fix told me his tale of woe, I couldn't help noticing the contrast between his frail arms and those of a tanned and brawny canoe club paddler sitting nearby. Mr. Fix appeared to be a nice and decent man. But apparently being nice and decent hadn't kept his wife from straying. The more I listened to him, the more I could imagine the shoals upon which his marriage had foundered. I knew this pattern all too well: Younger woman. Older man. A third party. Just fill in the blanks.

During lunch, out of the corner of my eye, I spotted Madison Highcamp at an oceanfront table with her usual martini, cigarette, and cell phone. She was alone—except for Twinkie. I hadn't talked to Madison since her frantic call about the gold dealer. It had been a few days. Not hearing from her made me wonder if she was turning over a new leaf after her husband's surprise visit.

Mr. Fix saw her and raised his brows. "If my wife's affairs were as notorious as that Highcamp woman's, I wouldn't need to hire you."

Madison noticed me just then. She made a little come hither gesture with her head.

"Excuse me," I said to Mr. Fix. "Her husband"—I pointed to Madison—"is a client of mine."

"Conrad Highcamp?" he said, sounding impressed, "The hotel tycoon?"

"Afraid so," I replied.

Madison stood when I approached and kissed my cheek. "Where have you been, darling?" She then retrieved Twinkie, who was already climbing my leg.

"I've been on a case," I said, wondering how she could have missed the news stories that would have answered her question. "Anyway, you were with your husband."

"That was days ago." She sounded miffed.

"He paid me, you know." I tried to change the subject. "I got a check in the mail."

"Conrad told me," she said. "And I stopped my check to Barry Buckingham. My money is safe."

"I'm glad." I didn't bother to tell her the gold dealer was at Queens Hospital under guard.

"I like the way you look out for me, Kai." She smiled. "Thank you, darling."

I stood there awkwardly as Mr. Fix gawked at us. "Listen, Madison, I've got a new client over there and I can't afford to keep him waiting."

"Call me, Kai. I have something to tell you. After Conrad left I thought about what you said. I've made a decision."

That worried me. I'd said a lot of foolish things when we were together, most of them forgettable.

"You know Mrs. Highcamp well?" Mr. Fix asked when I returned. "Though I guess all those wealthy society women kiss when they greet you, don't they?"

"Mrs. Highcamp is out of my league," I said casually.

"It's probably better that way," he said. "The stories I've heard . . ."

forty-one

When I picked up Maile for our flight to Hilo, she carried a duffle filled with the tools of her trade. But I wasn't prepared for the rifle case tucked under her arm.

"You're bringing your Remington?"

"Picket pointed a shotgun at you, Kai."

"Look. If it would make you feel better, I can pack my Smith & Wesson," I said. "And I'll deal with the red tape at check in."

Maile gave me stink-eye. "Kai, in fifteen years on the force I qualified with a half dozen firearms and I medaled with this one. We are going up against an armed criminal. I've seen what they can do. It's too close to home."

"OK, Maile, bring your rifle." I relented.

She walked past me to my car.

* * *

At the Honolulu Airport Maile filled out the appropriate forms and checked through her Remington, scope, and ammo. By four that afternoon we landed in Hilo and were driving north in a white van to the coastal town of Pāpaʻikou. We turned *mauka* on a narrow strip called Kaʻieʻie Homestead Road and drove for what seemed like miles. The road rose slowly into the foothills of Mauna Kea. Soon the pavement ended.

"What do we do now?" I said.

Maile glanced at her handwritten directions. "Keep going on this dirt road."

It was just a Jeep path, really, that zigzagged through hills and woods, reminding me of Picket's haunt. Finally we reached a dry creek bed and the road ran out.

"This must be it," Maile said.

"What? There's nothing here."

But I was wrong. A small cottage, that could barely be seen, stood in the distance with a rusting VW Golf parked out front. As we hiked toward the cottage, Maile explained that Deirdre was just getting started with her animal shelter. The sun was still overhead and it was hot. Very hot. After only a few steps I could feel sweat forming on my forehead.

A tall, very thin woman opened the door of the cottage and walked toward us. She was a vegan, according to Maile. I guess that accounted for her thinness. She had long silver-flecked black hair that reminded me of sixties folk singer, Joan Baez. I expected Deirdre to launch into "The Night They Drove Old Dixie Down."

"Deirdre Osteen." She reached out her hand. "And you must be Maile? And Kai?"

"Thanks for helping us on such short notice." Maile shook her hand. Then it was my turn. The hand was graceful and lean, like the rest of her. And warm.

"Anything I can do," Deirdre said. "As you can see, I'm just getting started here. I had to leave LA in kind of a hurry."

"You mentioned that on the phone," Maile said. "But Kai hasn't heard the story."

"I'll tell you about it . . ." Deirdre said "about" with the long "o" of Canadian English. "But first, come on inside and get out of the sun."

We walked with her to the cottage. The rusty Golf was parked by the door and my eye caught its bumper sticker: BIO-DIESEL: NO WARS NEEDED. Deirdre must have seen me gawking at it.

"The Golf is a TDI," she said. "It runs on one-hundred percent recycled vegetable oil. The fuel is made right here in Hawai'i."

"Your car is a vegan," I said, "just like you." I meant it to be funny, but she didn't take it that way.

"The big oil companies are almost as bad as animal abusers. They've fought saving the planet every step of the way, and they're scheming to run the bio-fuel industry out of business."

"Not if you can help it." I thought about the gas-guzzling V8 in my old Impala and wondered if I should turn over a new leaf.

Inside the place was basically one room and looked more like a camp than a home. The windows were open and a little breeze flowed through. There were a few cots and some beach chairs and a folding table. The only lamps I could see were battery powered, but not turned on at this time of day. From the personal gear piled in corners of the room, it looked like Deirdre might have a companion, but he or she wasn't around at the moment. And she didn't mention that anyone else was living there. We pulled three chairs into a small circle and sat.

"Jasmine tea?" Deirdre asked. "It's herbal. No caffeine."

Maile accepted and I passed. Deirdre went for a jar with a brownish liquid inside and several teabags. She poured glasses for Maile and herself and returned.

"It's sun tea. The electricity isn't hooked up yet," Deirdre said. "So I serve it at room temperature. I'm kind of keeping a low profile for now."

"Tell Kai what happened," Maile said and sipped her tea.

Maile had already told me that Deirdre Osteen was an animal rights activist from Ontario, Canada, who had spent the last few years in Los Angeles, heavily involved with ALF. But what Mailed didn't say, and Deirdre now did, was that she had been with a cell of ski-masked comrades that ransacked a university research lab and released dozens of caged monkeys, then spray-painted "Meat is Murder" on every available surface at four fast-food restaurants, and finally were about to hit a high-end furrier on Rodeo Drive when three of her comrades got nabbed.

"Before the day was out," Deirdre said with that long "o" again, "I was on a plane to Kona. I have some friends there and I stayed with them while I looked for land to set up a sanctuary. I decided my days with ALF were over. I'm committed to animal rights but I can't be effective if I'm in jail. So I hit on this idea. A no-kill shelter."

"How much land do you have here?" I asked.

"About twenty acres," she said. "I got a good deal on it. It's far from any town or village, as you saw, and access to the property isn't exactly, well, a super-highway."

I wondered how she could afford to buy so much land on the Big Island, but didn't ask. From her nonchalance and quiet confidence she struck me as a child of privilege.

"You're out in the middle of nowhere," Maile said.

"That's perfect for the shelter," Deirdre replied. "No one around to complain about animal smells and noises. Plus I'm starting a garden out back. By the way, do you want something to eat? I'm afraid I don't have much in the way of meat or dairy, but lots of raw vegetables and tofu."

"I'm good," I said, wishing I could sink my teeth into a cheeseburger.

Maile nodded in agreement.

"Well, about your mission," Deirdre said. "I've heard rumors about the man you're going to see."

"Sammy Bob Picket," I said. "We're not going to see him. I've done that already. Once is enough. He's got a shotgun and likes to wave it around."

"We're going to case his property," Maile said. "See his animals and how he keeps them . . . or how he abuses them."

"I've heard he's unstable and prone to violence," Deirdre added. "And like I told you, Maile, I'm willing to take his animals. I'll do the best I can with what I have so far, which isn't much."

"They'll be ten times better off," Maile replied.

"I wish I could help you rescue them," Deirdre said. "I'm sorry. My heart is with you, but I can't run this shelter from jail. I need to lie low for a while."

We declined her offer of ski masks, but listened to everything she could tell us about raiding a facility. When she walked us back to the van she spotted Maile's rifle through the window.

"ALF is a nonviolent organization," she said. "They might break the law when they liberate animals, but they don't condone firearms. I've left the organization, but I still feel that way."

"The rifle is just a precaution. We're dealing with an armed and dangerous man," Maile said. "Tonight we're just going to survey the site and figure out the best way to free his dogs. But if he pulls his shotgun, we will protect ourselves."

* * *

It was twilight by the time I drove the white van into Laupāhoehoe. In growing darkness, I turned onto the dirt road I had taken before to the shadowy undergrowth of Picket's hideout. As I parked, Maile grabbed her Remington.

"Do we really need that just to look around?"

Maile put her hands on her hips. "OK. Between you and Deirdre, I'm outnumbered. But if anything happens, it's your 'ōkole."

"My 'ōkole will be just fine," I said.

As Maile put the gun back into the van I had second thoughts. No doubt that Pickett was dangerous. And pet theft, even for a good cause, was still theft. We were already guilty on one count.

In the moments before complete darkness we hiked into the jungle that surrounded Picket's shack. It wasn't long before we heard the faint mournful moans and whiffed the stink.

Rounding a bend, we could clearly see the place. It was dark inside, but a naked bulb on a pole outside cast a harsh glare. I pointed out the fire pit in front where, on my earlier visit, I had seen charred dog collars and blackened tags and licenses. The absence of light inside suggested that either Sammy Bob wasn't at home or had turned in early. Or maybe just passed out drunk.

In the clearing beyond fire ring, at the edges of light, we glimpsed the dark shapes of dozens of dogs, still chained to rusting vehicles and cast-off appliances, or cobbed-together wood crates. Nearer to the shack his two pit bulls slept, well illuminated and secured by their thick leather leads. I hoped they slept soundly.

Gazing upon this dismal scene, Maile's expression registered something between disgust and awe.

"I've seen enough here," she said matter-of-factly. "Let's hike the perimeter and survey the site from other angles."

We kept our distance as we hiked so the dogs wouldn't see or smell us. Maile stopped every so often studying each new angle of that dog ghetto. When we returned to the fire pit, Picket's hovel was still unlit.

Maile tiptoed into the center of the ring and scanned the charred collars and tags. She looked around until she found something that interested her, then reached down and picked up a metal fragment. She held it in front of her for a long time, tilting it this way and that in the harsh light, focusing intently.

Suddenly her head bowed, as if she were praying. She shoved the blackened memento into one of her pockets and stepped abruptly away from the fire pit. She marched past me, her eyes glistening.

"What's wrong?" I asked as she headed in the direction of the van.

"I'll be right back." She disappeared into the darkness.

forty-two

I walked toward the fire ring to check it out myself, stepping over and around the charred logs scattered on its boundary. I should have known better. In the darkness my foot caught one of the logs. I went down. I hit the ground with a thud hard enough to knock the wind out of me and make the stitches in the back of my head throb. And loud enough to wake the pit bulls.

Uh-oh. They growled and pulled against their leather straps. From my position flat on my face in the dirt I looked up and saw right into their empty yellow eyes. One by one, other dogs woke up and started barking.

A light went on inside Picket's shack. The door banged open. He stumbled out bare-chested, his flabby gut hanging over a pair of jeans half tucked into hunting boots. A shotgun trembled in his hands.

"Whut 'n hell yah do'n ta mah dogs? Ah gonna shoot yo' ass!"

I was too close to him to run.

Sammy Bob Picket peered down at me with bloodshot eyes. A surprised look came over his face.

"Geeooorge?" His surprise turned to anger. "Yah sonofa-bitch! Yah stole that dog on Maui. Didn't ya? Stole 'em an' got me in trouble with the lady. An' yah nevah paid me that other hundret, either."

"You stole the dog." I caught my breath and slowly got up.

"Ah didn't steal 'em. Ah only give 'em a good home. A fellah named Spyder done brought me that dog. But Ah 'spect yah know that. Ah 'spect yah kilt his lady friend. An' now yah come tah git me." He leveled his shotgun.

"I didn't kill anybody."

"Prepare to meet yo' maker, boy."

Picket cocked his shotgun with a metallic click. There was no sense in running. I stood my ground. I had been hit only once in my life—a small-caliber pistol, that left a superficial wound. A shotgun would be different. Especially at close range. I braced.

Then I heard a second metallic click in the distance, and four loud pops.

But the blows never came.

The pit bulls were loose and sprinting toward me! I suddenly feared a death worse than by shotgun. But the dogs darted past me and went for Picket. He turned back to his shack, as his shotgun fell in front of him and landed in the red dirt.

Boom!

The load with my name on it went up into thin air. Sammy Bob swung open the door and tried frantically to pull it closed behind him. But he was too late. One pit bull clamped onto the boot of his trailing leg. The other did the same. It was a strange, savage scene as the pit bulls ripped and tore at the boot still attached to Picket's foot.

Soon Maile was standing over me with her Remington, smelling of gunpowder.

"C'mon, Kai," she said. "Help me save this scum."

"What?"

Maile pulled a small aerosol canister from her pants pocket.

"Pepper spray?" I asked.

She nodded. "Under the circumstances it's the most humane way." She handed the Remington to me and approached the two dogs. "Aim my rifle at the dogs. If one attacks me, you know what to do."

I pointed in the direction of the crazed pair.

"On my count," she said. Then "One—Two—Three!" Maile leaped in front of the dogs and sprayed the aerosol in their faces. The blasts were short, but the results were instantaneous. Both dogs began flailing about blindly, coughing and gasping for air.

"It'll wear off." Maile said as she stepped back. "I'll tie them up again before it does."

"And I'll tie up Picket."

"Take this." She handed me the pepper spay.

I took it in my left hand but kept her rifle in my right. I stepped inside the shack, where Picket was sprawled on the filthy floor, groaning. I could hear whines and barking coming from the closet-sized rooms. I glanced down at the man responsible and wondered why he wasn't dead.

"Mah leg," Sammy Bob moaned and looked up at me blurry-eyed. "Ah can't walk."

He had removed his boot and pulled up his pant leg. There was torn flesh and blood on his lower calf. He also had dark purple bruises around his ankle and foot. But he wasn't going to die.

"Yah gonna he'p me, Georgie boy?" he asked in a suddenly kind, slurred voice. He wasn't just sleepy and hurt, he was also drunk. He seemed to think I'd returned to being his buddy.

I looked around his shack for something to tie him up with. A half dozen chewed-up leashes were lying in a corner by the door. I grabbed two and rolled Picket over on his stomach. I didn't need the pepper spray. There wasn't any fight left in him. I bound his feet, wrapping a towel around his injured ankle. Then I tied his hands behind his back. I didn't bother to gag him. There was no one out there to hear him.

"Yah jus' gonna leave me like this? Ah thought yah wuz my frien'."

"I'll send for help," I said and closed the door behind me. *But I won't rush to do it,* I added to myself.

Across from the shack, Maile had finished securing the pit bulls. As I walked over, I noticed that their eyes were still dilated and their breathing hoarse.

"How'd they get loose?"

"You told me the dogs hated Picket, so I aimed for their leads. It took me four shots and some luck."

"Why didn't you just shoot him? He almost killed me."

"He needs to be held accountable for what he's done."

I handed her Remington back to her.

"You shouldn't second-guess me, Kai," she said. "Or maybe next time it *will* be your 'ōkole."

forty-three

Deirdre arrived later that night in her biodiesel Golf and, despite her earlier doubts, helped us rescue the dogs. Only afterward did we alert Big Island Police to Picket's whereabouts. We left the pit bulls and three other dogs we found dead, as evidence of his cruelty. It would be obvious to police that many more animals had been held captive there, though we felt sure Picket wouldn't admit it.

The next morning on the plane back to O'ahu, Maile took out the charred metal piece she had found in the fire pit. She held it in the sunlight streaming through the airplane's window.

It was a pet ID tag. Just a fragment, but the name was clear: *Rusty.*

Maile had spared Sammy Bob Picket—the man who had caused her so much pain—to bring him to justice. Once a good cop, always a good cop.

* * *

I spent Saturday morning in my office, catching up on paperwork and reading the *Star-Advertiser*. It had another story about Buckingham. And I also saw this:

Mililani Puppy Mill Raided

Police stormed a townhouse yesterday in Mililani and found 14 malnourished adult golden retrievers and nearly two dozen puppies. The dogs had been kept in unsanitary conditions for many months, said Hawaiian Humane Society spokesperson, Megan Watanabe. The owner of the property, Louise M. Donner, known to neighbors as "Lou," has been charged with thirty-seven counts of animal cruelty. Neighbors were alerted to problems at the townhouse by what was described as an "awful" smell coming from the home, "as if something had crawled inside and died." But it was pet detective Maile Barnes and private investigator Kai Cooke who first discovered the maltreated animals when working on another case. The rescued dogs were taken to the Hawaiian Human Society on King Street. Most have been turned over for foster care to the Golden Retriever Club of Hawai'i in private homes . . .

I wished the paper hadn't mentioned Maile or me. If Scanlon were still alive, he didn't need any help linking the two of us. We were the pair that had derailed his blackmail scheme. Before I could dwell much on that, there was a knock at my door. I set aside the paper and went for the knob.

In stepped Madison Highcamp in a low-cut leopard print dress that showed more of her than anybody on the street ought to have the right to see. Her red hair hung down to her shoulders like a sheet of fire. Gone was her usual cigarette. And her cell phone. And her Maltese. But her intoxicating scent of Chanel clung to every part of her.

"Madison, what are you doing in Chinatown?" She'd never come to my office before.

"So this is where you work, darling?" She kissed me full on the lips, and then gazed from my desk, in its normal disarray, to my only window overlooking Maunakea Street. "It's . . . *quaint*."

"Never thought of it that way." I pointed her to my client's chair. As she sat down the bounce of her barely concealed breasts hit my nerve ends like a thunderbolt.

"Kai, you didn't call me."

"I've been on a case, Madison. I got back late last night. What's up?"

"Us."

"Us?" I said. "You and me?"

She nodded. "I told you I'd been thinking about what you said. Well, I've made a decision."

"What did I say?"

"You said, 'Have you ever thought of divorce?'"

"Have you?" I was stalling.

"After Conrad left I thought about it a lot." She sat up straight. "I'm going to be brave, Kai. I'm going to file the papers."

"But you'll get nothing. You said so yourself."

"That's true. I will get nothing. I don't care. Some things are more important than money." She caressed her long hair and looked into my eyes. "Aren't they, Kai?"

"Madison, you may think you don't need money, but you've never lived without it." That might have been a cruel thing to say at that moment, but it was the truth.

"You're afraid of commitment," she shot back. "You want me when it suits you, but otherwise you never call." She fumbled nervously with her Gucci handbag, her fingers digging inside the saddle leather.

"You can't smoke here."

"Damn!" She slammed down her bag. "I'm trying to quit. But I need one right now."

"I haven't got any, Madison."

She searched my eyes.

"Hey, where's your faithful companion?" I tried to change the subject. "You don't go anywhere without Twinkie."

"She's at the doggie boutique getting groomed," Madison said, softening. "That girl's hair is more expensive than mine. Oh, that reminds me . . ." Her mood lightened. "Twinkie's groomer said one of her clients lost her Lhasa Apso. I told her you found that missing surfing dog. Her client is desperate."

"No more pet cases," I said. "But I know someone else." From my top desk drawer I pulled one of Maile's cards and handed it to her. "She can give it to her client."

Madison scanned the card. "Is she good?"

"She is," I said, "She helped me rescue Kula."

"She went with you to Maui? And the Big Island?"

I nodded.

"Just the two of you?" Madison sounded suspicious. I was starting to regret giving her Maile's card.

"It was a case, Madison." Luckily the phone rang just then. I picked up on the first ring.

"Hey, Kai, did you hear the one——"

"Hang on a minute, Tommy?" I said into the phone. I turned to Madison. "It's my attorney. This may take awhile."

She frowned and started for the door. "Call me tonight."

"OK."

forty-four

I didn't call Madison that night. And she didn't call me.

A few mornings later, and more than two weeks after Barry Buckingham had first hired me, I was sitting in my office scanning the *Star-Advertiser* when I saw this:

Gold Dealer Indicted for Murder, Fraud

Radio pitchman Barry Buckingham, recuperating at Queen's Hospital from injuries suffered when his yacht, *Golden Hinde,* ran aground at Point Panic near Kewalo Basin last Tuesday, has been indicted on two counts of murder in the first degree and multiple counts of fraud. H.P.D. Homicide Detective Frank Fernandez announced at a news conference yesterday that Buckingham has been charged in the murders of Waimanalo resident Moku Taliaferro and Reiko Infante of Kailua.

> Buckingham made a name and fortune for himself as the charismatic host of "The Gold Standard" daily radio program on KGHO, where he pitched and sold precious metals. Several former clients have filed lawsuits against him. Attorney Michael R. Holstein, who represents one of those clients, told the *Star-Advertiser:* "Barry Buckingham is a classic con man. Court records will show that he has defrauded island residents out of millions of dollars . . ."

The case of Barry Buckingham—my first and only pet case—was officially closed. The story made no mention of Abe Scanlon or his sidekick Spyder Silva. If Buckingham hadn't managed to kill both before his arrest, I hoped Scanlon and Silva would be laying low. I didn't want trouble from either of them.

* * *

A few nights later I had a date with Maile at Ah Fook in Chinatown to celebrate wrapping up the case. We planned to meet at six. I arrived fifteen minutes early. There wasn't much of a crowd at that hour, so I waited outside alone on River Street.

At 6:00, a few customers wandered up and went inside. By 6:15, she still hadn't shown. Patrons were filling the tables inside, so I left my name with the hostess. It didn't seem like Maile to be late.

When 6:30 came and went, I called her cell phone. "Hi, you've reached Maile Barnes, tracer of missing pets. How can I help?"

"Maile, it's Kai. I'm at the restaurant. Are you OK? Call me on my cell."

I called her home phone too, but she didn't answer there either. I left the same message.

I waited until 7:00, then I called both numbers again. Still no response. I was worried. I left Ah Fook without eating and drove up to Mānoa.

On the way I got a sinking feeling, pulled over, and called Madison.

"Helloooo," Madison slurred. She'd evidently had a few martinis at the club.

"Madison, it's me. Did you call Maile Barnes?"

"Yooo gave me her card, darling."

"What did you tell her?"

Silence.

"What did you say?"

"I tol' her the truth, honey, that we're talking about getting married."

I was speechless.

"Kai?"

I hung up.

By then it was dark. And I was disoriented. Instinctively I punched in Maile's number. Of course she didn't answer. I left a message:

"Maile, it's me . . ." I started rambling. "Madison lied. We're not getting married. We're not even dating. I stopped seeing her after I met you—" I could have gone on, but what was the use? Maile wasn't going to answer.

I drove to her cottage thinking I'd just blown it with the girl of my dreams. Never mind that Madison had lied. Never mind that it wasn't really my fault.

The damage had been done.

forty-five

Driving into Mānoa I recalled when I first saw Maile again after so many years. She was in her jogging togs and her face was flushed. She looked terrific. But I was too hung up on Madison at the time to really see Maile. When I told her the last man I interviewed for the case died, she didn't even ask about Dr. Carreras. But that was her way. Take things in stride—like a good cop.

When I pulled up to her cottage a few lights were on. Maile's car was parked out front, so I naturally assumed she was home. I walked to the door and knocked. No answer.

I wasn't surprised. If Maile thought I betrayed her, why would she come to the door?

I knocked again.

Then I tried the knob.

Unlocked. I walked into the familiar room—comfortable and easy-going and island-style like Maile herself. Open jalousies admitted a balmy breeze. Rattan furniture sat on Oriental rugs. But the three cozy cats that usually warmed the cushions were in hiding. Maybe Peppah and Coconut had taken after Lolo? The two gregarious cats weren't afraid of me, and by now should have been nuzzling me and climbing my pant leg. I expected a cool greeting from their mistress, but not the cold shoulder from them. And where was Kula?

"Maile?" I said.

No reply.

I looked around. Kula's water and food dishes, bearing his name in fancy gold lettering, sat on the kitchen floor. Both were full with drink and kibble. By the dishes lay a yellow tennis ball, bringing back memories of Maui. In the kitchen I saw Peppah hiding under the dining table. That wasn't like him. He made eye contact with me, but didn't dash in my direction. He didn't even move. What's going on here? The cats seemed to be sensing something was wrong.

I turned from the Angora and scanned Maile's photo collection—snapshots of her past life. Her husband Nestor in police blues, Maile herself with her rifle, and her dog Rusty—missing and never found. During the course of our investigation on the Big Island she had stumbled onto evidence of Rusty's theft. And she had spared the thief. It's a wonder she hadn't blown Sammy Bob Pickett's head off, considering what he'd done to her.

I was looking at Rusty's photo when I heard what sounded like light footsteps on the porch. Suddenly the front door pushed open and Kula walked in, dragging his leash. He was huffing and panting, his gold fur was in wild disarray. He looked like he'd been in a chase or a fight. I petted him and felt moisture. His coat was wet.

"Where have you been, boy?" I asked him. "And where's Maile?"

He barked. If only dogs could talk.

I tried to piece together what might have happened. Kula was on leash because Maile had taken him for an evening walk or run. Somehow, the two of them got separated and Kula came home alone. But why would Maile leave Kula on his own? That wasn't like her.

I decided to stay put and wait to see if she returned. It was a dark, moonless night and I didn't expect she'd stay out long. I sat in one of the rattan chairs; Kula walked to the kitchen and took a long drink from his water dish. He came back and lay down beside me, panting a little less than before. Peppah emerged from the kitchen, but kept his distance from Kula. Coconut peeked out from under a rattan chair. Lolo was nowhere in sight. At least she was acting normal.

I waited fifteen minutes. Maile didn't show. By then it was eight o'clock. I'd waited long enough.

"C'mon, Kula," I gently roused him. "Let's go find your master."

The dog got up right away like he knew exactly what I was saying. He led me to my car and jumped in the front seat beside me.

I drove through the dark narrow streets surrounding Maile's cottage. When I didn't find her there, I tried the main street into the valley, East Mānoa Road. Then its side streets. Kula looked anxiously out the passenger window. We were getting nowhere and the night was wearing on.

My cell phone rang. Caller ID said: MAILE BARNES.

"Maile, are you OK?" I asked.

"Now listen up, mate," said the quavering old Aussie voice, "if you want to see this girl again you best bring the gold dog to the Mānoa Chinese Cemetery." It was Abe Scanlon. "Come alone and bring the dog. Even exchange. The dog for the girl."

"Scanlon, you're out of your mind," I said. "The dog's worth nothing to you now that Buckingham's locked up."

"Here . . ." the old man said, "maybe she can talk some sense into you."

"Kai," Maile took the phone. "He thinks he can turn Kula into a fortune. I don't know why, but you're not going to change his mind."

I knew why. Scanlon had built his life around revenge. Now that Buckingham was beyond his reach, his old boss had become desperate and unbalanced. In better times he and Spyder Silva had dog-napped and held Kula, expecting to cash in big. But Maile and I had spoiled that. Now in Scanlon's twisted mind he had a second chance both to cash in on Kula and to strike back at Maile and me.

"Is Silva there?" I asked Maile. "Is he holding you?"

"Yes," she said.

"Does he have his Berretta?"

"Yes."

"So Silva and Scanlon intercepted you while you were out with Kula?"

"Uh-huh."

"And they wanted Kula, but somehow he got away, so they took you instead?"

"*Yes.*" She spoke hurriedly.

"They watched your cottage, waiting for his return. They saw me arrive first, then Kula."

"*Y—*" Her voice cut off.

Scanlon grabbed the phone. "Chinese cemetery at ten. Bring the dog, mate."

He hung up.

forty-six

I called my attorney friend, Tommy Woo, hoping against hope that he didn't have a gig and he'd drop everything on short notice. Thank God he answered. But before I could get a word in, Tommy said: "Hey, Kai, did you hear the one about the sushi bar on Bishop Street that caters exclusively to lawyers?"

"Can it, Tommy. I need your help and I need it fast."

"It's called Sosumi," he said.

"What?" Once he got rolling there was no stopping him.

"The sushi bar for lawyers is called Sosumi."

"Nice," I said. "Are you free tonight?"

"Yeah. What's up?"

"Can you meet me in my office in fifteen minutes?"

"Well, I'm not dressed . . . but I could throw on something."

"It's an open air gig, so dress appropriately. At the Chinese cemetery in Mānoa. We may have to hike a bit."

"Huh?"

"I'll explain later."

I could have met Tommy in Mānoa and saved the quick trip to my office, but I needed to pick up something there before I faced Silva in the cemetery.

* * *

Tommy, dressed as usual in black, was waiting for me outside the flower shop, which was closed that time of night. Kula was leading me on his leash.

"What's with the dog?" Tommy asked.

"Buckingham," I said.

"Oh, I remember . . ." He brushed back a gray lock.

I let us in through the back entrance. We climbed the stairs to the second floor and found our way to my office door: SURFING DETECTIVE: CONFIDENTIAL INVESTIGATIONS—ALL ISLANDS.

"Have a seat, Tommy," I said as I opened the door. He took my client's chair. Kula led me in and sat next to my desk. I petted him. His coat was nearly dry. His warm fur and renewed calm was reassuring. He seemed to have confidence in me, even if I didn't. I cracked my window overlooking Maunakea Street. The evening bustle of Chinatown's eateries, tourist shops and galleries was winding down. I looked across my desk at Tommy.

"Now here's what we've got," I said. "Maile Barnes is being held hostage by the scums who stole Kula. There's two of them: an old Australian named Abe Scanlon and a local pet thief named Spyder Silva. I've dealt with them before in the Buckingham case. Silva is a sleazy character and the old man is out of his head. He thinks Kula is worth a fortune and he wants to trade Maile for the dog at ten tonight at the Chinese cemetery in Mānoa.

"That's nuts," Tommy said.

"I know, but there it is," I said. "I'm going to approach them in the cemetery alone, as Scanlon specified. I won't have the dog. You will. And since Silva has his Berretta, I'll have my .357." I pulled the Smith & Wesson from the top drawer of my desk. Tommy was unimpressed.

"What do I do with the dog?" Tommy asked. "I'm a cat person, you know. I don't know much about dogs."

"Don't worry. You don't need to know much about dogs. All you need to do is keep Kula with you and keep him quiet. You two will be in my car, which I'll park a block away from the park. I'm going to tell Scanlon the dog is there with my assistant, but that Scanlon has to release Maile first before I give him the dog. He may not like it. But Scanlon, at his age, is not a physical threat. And I can handle Silva."

"What then?"

"I'm going to take Maile and bring her back to the car."

"And the dog?"

"Kula stays in the car with you. He's not going anywhere."

"You're sure you want to walk into that cemetery alone at night?" Tommy asked.

"Scanlon wants the dog badly. I'm his ticket to gold. He's not going to jeopardize his chances out of the spite he may feel for me. As for Spyder, he'll do what Scanlon tells him to."

"Shouldn't I cover you?"

"With what?"

Tommy pulled from a his black pants a Derringer pistol, bright chrome, and about the size of a cell phone. "It's only .22 calibre," he said, "but it can do the job."

"You never told me you had a firearm, Tommy. I thought it was against your principles."

Tommy adjusted his tortoiseshell glasses. "It's against my principles to get mugged. I'm out late on gigs, in the wee hours, and sometimes not in the best part of town. I'm not about to let somebody whack me on the head and walk off with my keyboard and my car. This little beauty . . ." he caressed the Derringer, "fits right into my pocket. And nobody knows. Well, except you."

"You shouldn't need it tonight. But if you hear a gunshot, you can leave Kula in the car and come running."

"Right on." Tommy grinned.

forty-seven

I closed my office window, locked the dead bolt behind us, and we descended the outside stairs and piled into my Impala—two grown men and a dog. Neither of us said much on the ride from Chinatown to Mānoa. Kula was in back with his head out the window, tail wagging and enjoying the ride. By the time we neared the Chinese cemetery it was almost ten. I parked on East Mānoa Road, a hundred yards down, left Tommy and Kula, and hiked to the cemetery. Scanlon didn't say exactly where I was supposed to meet them, but it's not a huge place and it slopes up the valley, so you can take in the whole view of the place from the lower corner, where I was headed.

But I didn't enter. I stopped and did a quick scan. The cemetery was smack in the middle of the upper Mānoa valley, which ran nearly a mile across. Two small pagodas with jade tile roofs and pillars with Chinese characters in gold stood at the lower and upper entrances. Their marquees said: MANOA CHINESE CEMETERY. The pagoda at the lower entrance, near where I stood, was flanked by royal palms and scrubs that in daylight ranged in color from bright green to flaming red. But at night they were black—like everything else. Behind the pagoda the darkened headstones and plots were carefully tended, showing the Chinese honor and respect for their dead. The cemetery happened to be the oldest and largest of its kind in Hawai'i and during its long history had been the subject of more than a few ghost stories. I couldn't allow my imagination to get started on that. Besides I didn't see any ghosts. Or any sign of Scanlon and Silva and Maile either.

I walked along one edge of the cemetery, staying out of sight and watching for Scanlon and company. The homes bordering the park were huddled close together. Mānoa wasn't Tantalus, and none of the properties resembled palaces on the hill like Wonderview. I scanned a maze of headstones, then reached into my pocket. The cold, hard surface of my Smith & Wesson felt good to the touch. I was glad it was there.

Up the street near the top of the park I spotted a bronze Chevy Tahoe–the same one used in Lehua's kidnapping. Inside were three dim profiles. That was them, all right. The Tahoe was positioned high, in view of the entire cemetery. Scanlon was watching and waiting, expecting me to make the first move. I wouldn't disappoint him.

I backtracked to the lower slope of cemetery and started walking up toward them, in plain view. I wound my way through the headstones, stepping around grave markers to avoid bad luck. I didn't need that. As the land gradually rose, I walked toward the second pagoda at the top of the cemetery. Behind its pillars and jade roof was a huge kukui or candlenut tree whose limbs stretched thirty feet in every direction.

Closing in on the pagoda I looked up again and saw the Tahoe's doors open and Spyder Silva step out wearing his baseball cap, bill pulled down low. Then the old man hobbled out. Maile came next. The two men started walking with her toward the pagoda. She was in her jogging clothes, and her hands were bound behind her. Silva had his grubby mitt on her bare shoulder. I felt like planting a slug between his eyes for that offense alone.

I walked through the pagoda to the kukui tree behind it, stopping under its outstretched limbs. The two men came toward me with Maile. I didn't fear for myself or for Maile because I assumed Scanlon wanted the dog more than he wanted either of us. But suddenly I questioned that assumption. What if wanting the dog was just a ruse? What if Scanlon's real purpose was revenge against the two people who'd ruined his revenge? Already he had Maile. And maybe he thought he'd soon have me. I wished I'd asked Tommy to keep me in sight.

But it was too late. Here came the bald and bent old man hobbling along beside the pet thief, who still had his hand, his left, on Maile. His right was in his pants pocket.

"Where's the dog, mate?" Scanlon said. "You promised to bring him. No dog, no girl."

"I've got the dog," I said. "He's with my assistant within earshot. Once you release Maile there, my assistant will bring the dog."

Scanlon scowled. He didn't like it. "That's not what we agreed on."

"It's the only way I'll do it," I said. "You want the dog—those are my terms. Release Maile first. Otherwise, what guarantee do I have that you won't take them both?"

"What guarantee do we have?" Scanlon said.

"I've got one guarantee, brah!" Hotheaded Silva reached his right hand into his pocket, pulled his Berretta. Bang! He fired it into the ground.

"Idiot," Scanlon scolded him under his breath. Then to me: "You can see that we're armed. And we mean business. You don't want the girl hurt. So you'll produce the dog like you said."

I said nothing. I was recalling my instructions to Tommy. If he heard the gunshot, he'd be on his way.

We had a standoff. Silva kept his gun out, as if he intended to use it. Scanlon whispered in his ear long enough to make me nervous. Almost a minute went by while we all stood there.

Finally, on Scanlon's command, Silva let Maile go. She walked toward me. Her face was expressionless, like a practiced professional. But not for long. Her eyes widened, her mouth gapped, and she said, "Oh, my God!"

Kula came out of the darkness on a dead run. The dog jumped on Silva and knocked him down. Kula started chewing on the pet thief. Silva shrieked and his gun went off again. The dog whelped and rolled on his side. Kula lay motionless.

Silva jumped up, "You fuckah!" he said to me. Then he fired wildly in my direction. I pulled my .357 unloaded two quick rounds into him. He went down again. This time for good.

Maile ran to Kula, who still wasn't moving. "Oh, my God!" she said again.

I subdued Scanlon. Then Tommy showed up with his Derringer pulled.

"Hold this man," I handed off Scanlon.

Tommy showed the old Aussie his Derringer and said, "Stay put."

I ran to Maile, who was standing over Kula. His coat was already bright red. He was wheezing.

"Where did Silva hit him?" I asked her as I unbound her hands.

"He's too bloody." She knelt down beside him. "I can't tell. We've got to get him to an animal hospital—fast."

"I'm on it." I ran down the hill to my car and brought it up. I climbed the curb and pulled into the cemetery, stopping under the kukui tree where Maile still knelt beside Kula.

"How's he doing?" I asked her.

"He's still breathing," Maile said. "I'm worried, Kai."

"Let's get him into the car." Maile and I gently lifted Kula and loaded him in. The upholstery quickly became a bloody mess. I gave Maile the keys, she climbed behind the wheel, and was gone.

I checked on Silva. He lay on his back in a pool of blood. From the holes and expanding stain in his t-shirt, it looked like I'd hit him with both shots in the chest. He had stopped breathing. It didn't appear there was much hope for Silva. There never had been. At the neck of his shirt I could see the border of his tattoo of the coiled cobra and the phrase: KILL 'EM ALL, LET GOD SORT 'EM OUT.

It seemed prophetic.

forty-eight

I dialed 911 and requested police and an ambulance. Silva was dead before either arrived. I was not sad. Whatever made him the way he was, I didn't know. But he had been a scum of the earth, preying on innocent people and their defenseless pets. I remembered what Maile had told me at the beginning of this case: of the many hardened criminals she'd seen during her years with HPD, none were so sick as those who abused animals.

Next I called Frank Fernanadez. The homicide detective showed up about fifteen minutes after three HPD cruisers and the ambulance arrived. Delivering Scanlon to him all neat and tidy would have seemed like a favor under other circumstances, but Silva's body lying only a few feet away with gunshot wounds from my revolver made things a bit more complicated. And I could hardly forget that not long before, Fernandez had liked me for the murders that my client Buckingham had committed.

Before we rode with Fernandez to police headquarters on Beretania Street, I asked Tommy in private: "Did you see Silva shooting at me?"

He nodded.

"Good," I said. "You're my witness. And so is Maile."

"It was self-defense," he said. "No question."

"Why did you let Kula out of the car? I suddenly found myself getting angry at Tommy. "He got shot, man! He's fighting for his life."

"I didn't mean to!" Tommy protested. "When I heard Silva's gun and opened the door to come up and cover you, the dog jumped out. He ran off before I could catch him."

"Sorry, Tommy." I had second thoughts. "It's not your fault. You did the best you could."

"He was flying. Nobody could have stopped him."

"Must be Silva's scent was strong enough for the dog to remember."

"Or maybe Kula picked up Maile's scent or yours?" Tommy shrugged. "I thought golden retrievers were mellow dogs. Yet he attacked Silva."

"Instinct," I said. "Did you hear about the golden on the mainland that fought off a mountain lion to save his human companion? The dog ended up a bloody mess, like Kula, but he survived. I hope Kula does too. Anyway, all I can figure is that he was protecting Maile."

"And you," Tommy said.

* * *

In Fernandez's office, Tommy and I had a long chat with the homicide detective. Frank was a bit torqued that we had not called him before the proposed hostage trade. But

Tommy was conveniently and fortunately not only a witness to the events, but also my lawyer. I didn't have to flip open my cell phone to call him. He was already there. And both of our weapons were duly registered in our own names. I had used mine, as Tommy and also Maile would corroborate, in self-defense. We make statements and were released shortly after midnight.

* * *

The first thing I did when I left the station was to call Maile. This time she answered.

"How's Kula?" I asked.

"I hope he's going to make it," she said. "The doc stitched him up and thinks there's a fighting chance he'll recover. He's sedated now and will be in the hospital overnight. I'll go see him first thing tomorrow morning."

"Where are you now?"

"In my cottage. I just got home."

"Ugh . . . Do you have a minute? I thought maybe we could talk—"

"I got your phone message," she said coolly.

"If you'd just let me explain . . ."

She didn't say anything for a moment, then: "OK, I'm too keyed up to sleep."

"Can we talk in person?"

"It's after midnight," she said.

"You're right. It's late . . ."

There was a long pause. Then she said, "Oh, what the heck—"

* * *

I borrowed Tommy's car and drove back to Mānoa wondering how to talk to Maile about the phone call from Madison. Nothing came to mind. It was very late.

When I pulled up the lights were still on inside her cottage. I knocked. Then I heard Maile's distant voice. "The door's open."

I stepped in. No Lolo dashing into Maile's bedroom. No Peppah and Coconut glooming onto me and climbing my leg. Maybe they were asleep?

Maile looked tired and pale. She didn't offer me anything to drink. Or eat. She didn't even say hello. She just said: "I hope Kula's going to be all right."

"Me too,'" I said.

We sat down across from each other. Maile on the rattan couch. Me in a chair. The distance between us felt greater than the few feet that separated our eyes.

She said: "You wanted to talk?"

I took a breath and swallowed hard. "Now about that phone call . . ."

ABOUT THE AUTHOR

Chip Hughes earned a Ph.D. in English at Indiana University and taught American literature, film, writing, and popular fiction for nearly three decades at the University of Hawai'i at Mānoa. His non-fiction publications include two books and numerous essays on John Steinbeck.

An active member of the Private Eye Writers of America, Chip launched the Surfing Detective mystery series with *Murder on Moloka'i* (2004) and *Wipeout!* (2007), published by Island Heritage. The series is now published exclusively by Slate Ridge Press, whose volumes include *Kula* (2011), *Murder at Volcano House* (2014), *Hanging Ten in Paris Trilogy* (2017), and reissues of the first two novels.

Chip and his wife split their time between homes in Hawai'i and upstate New York.

Made in the USA
Coppell, TX
28 February 2020

16335661R00262